MULK RAJ ANAND (1905-2004) was one of the most prominent novelists and short story writers, and with Raja Rao and R.K. Narayan, is regarded as a founding father of English fiction in India. He captured the puissance of the Punjabi and Hindi idiom to faithfully bring alive the sights, smells and sounds of the Indian landscape and its people.

Son of a coppersmith and a soldier, Mulk Raj Anand was born in Peshawar. He was educated at the Universities of Punjab, Cambridge and London. Recipient of many coveted honours, he was awarded the Sahitya Akademi Award in 1971, Padma Bhushan in 1967 and held the prestigious Tagore Chair at the Punjab University.

Across the Black Waters is widely rated as an outstanding novel and his most significant after *The Untouchable*. It is a simple story about the ultimate futility and sorrow of war. It is a journey not just from a small village in Punjab to Flanders, from farmer to soldier, field to front — but from a soul that nurtures to one that kills. Overlooking the claims of war classics like *All Quiet on the Western Front,* the British Council selected and adapted this novel into a play to mark the 80th anniversary of the end of World War I.

The book has been translated into fifteen languages.

LIBRARY OF
SOUTH ASIAN LITERATURE

Library of South Asian Literature is an ongoing endeavour to publish in English an eclectic selection of some of the finest writings from the rich diversity of South Asian Literature. It attempts to bring together books regarded as landmarks in their language, for having won literary awards or critical acclaim, or having been a major influence in their genre, creating a new narrative style or simply representing an outstanding writer's art.

Readers are invited to recommend books to make this more truly representative of the vigorous literary tradition of South Asia. These maybe sent by mail, fax or email to Publisher, Orient Paperbacks, 5A/8, Ansari Road, New Delhi-110 002. Tel: +91-11-2327 8877, email: mail@orientpaperbacks.com

ACROSS THE BLACK WATERS

MULK RAJ ANAND

Orient
Paperbacks
DELHI | MUMBAI

This book was sketched out in a rough draft in Barcelona, Madrid, during January and April 1937, and entirely rewritten in Chinnor, Oxon, between July and December, 1939.

M.R.A.

Visit www.orientpaperbacks.com to read more about all our books and to buy them. You will also find features, author interviews, offers, and you can sign up for e-newsletter so that you're always first to hear about our new releases.

www.orientpaperbacks.com

ISBN 13: 978-81-222-0258-8

New edition 2008
4th Printing 2022

Across the Black Waters

© Mulk Raj Anand, 2000, 2008

Cover design by Vision Studio

Published by
Orient Paperbacks
(A Division of Vision Books Pvt. Ltd.)
5A/8, Ansari Road, New Delhi-110 002

Printed and bound at Saurabh Printers, Noida

In the memory of
my father
Late Subedar Lal Chand Anand, M.S.M.
(2/17th Dogra)

PRAISE FOR MULK RAJ ANAND

The foremost of Indian novelists

— DAILY TELEGRAPH

His descriptions of brutality match in compassion and outrage, and perhaps also in poetic flair, those of Wilfred Owen, Siegfried Sasson, or David Jones!

— ALASTAIR NIVEN, BRITISH LITERARY CRITIC

Anand's achievement in *Across the Black Waters* is yet to be surpassed...

— MEENAKASHI MUKERJEE, CRITICAL ESSAYS IN INDIAN
WRITING IN ENGLISH

... presents us with a set of intriguing political and moral issues, the most significant of which is the justifiable reason, is any, for Indian Army's participant in a British war.... one of the greatest war novels ever written.

— PROF. K.D. VERMA, PROF. EMERITUS OF ENGLISH,
UNIVERSITY OF PITTSBURG-JOHNSTOWN

I

'MARSELS!'
'We have reached Marsels!'
'Hip Hip Hurrah!'
The sepoys were shouting excitedly on deck.
Lalu got up from where he sat watching a game of cards and went to see Marseilles.
The sun was on its downward stride on the western horizon as the convoy ships went steaming up towards the coast of France, with their cargo of the first Divisions of Indian troops who had been brought to fight in Europe, a cargo stranger than any they had carried before. The cold afternoon, stirred by a chill breeze from the stormy gulf, lay quivering on the town, which sheltered beneath a few steep rocks.
'Is the war taking place there then?' a sepoy asked.
No one answered him, as most of the sepoys did not know where the war was. In fact they had not known where they were going until it was announced in the orders of the day that a message had been intercepted through the 'telephone without wires' on the ship, that the Commander-in-Chief of the British Army, Lord Kitchener, who had once been Commander-in-Chief in Hindustan, had told the House of Lords that two Divisions of the Indian Army were on their way to France. The Lords had clapped their hands, it was said, and had sent their greetings to all brave ranks of the Indian Army. The King-Emperor, too, had sent them a message, reminding them of the personal ties which bound him and his consort, Mary, to the Indians since he had visited India for the Delhi Durbar,

congratulating them on their personal devotion to his throne, and assuring them how their one-voiced demand to be foremost in the conflict had touched his heart ... The sepoys had been excited by these messages, the edge of their curiosity sharpened by the first authentic news which they had received of their destination. And the lives of the N.C.O.s had become unbearable answering questions, 'Where is France?' 'Is that England?' 'Where is the enemy?' 'How many miles is it from here?' ... Now one of them was asking, 'Is the war there?'

Lalu felt, however, as if the naive questioner had taken the words out of his own mouth. For the rim of the sky was full of bloody contours, as if the souls of the war dead were going through the agony of being burned in their journey from hell to heaven. The battle might be raging there, though it was foolish to think so, because surely there would have been a sound of guns if the front was so near.

Lest someone should be looking at him and prying into his thoughts he began to walk away towards the prow of the ship.

'So we have come across the black waters safely,' he said to himself apprehensively, as if he really expected some calamity, the legendary fate of all those who went beyond the seas, to befall him at any moment. Truly, the black, or rather blue, water seemed uncanny, spreading for thousands of miles. It seemed as if God had spat upon the universe and the spittle had become the sea. The white flecks of the foam on the swell, where wave met wave, seemed like the froth churned out of God's angry mouth. The swish of the air as the ships tore their way across the rough sea seemed like the fury of the Almighty at the sin which the white men had committed in building their powerful engines of the Iron Age, which transported huge cities of wood and steel across vast spaces, where it was difficult to tell in which direction lay the north, the south, the east or the west.

If his father had been alive and present, he would certainly have prophesied disaster for all those who had crossed the black waters, and he would have regarded this war to which they were going as a curse laid upon the Sahibs for trying to defy nature.

'But why am I turning superstitious and thinking such thoughts?' he rebuked himself. He had always defied his father and preened himself on his schooling, and he did not realize that he had inherited many of his father's qualities, not only the enduring ones such as his short, lithe wiry frame, his love of the land, his generosity, his stubborn pride, and his humour, but also his faith and his naiveté.

A few sea-gulls were coming out to meet them, and more seemed to be seated on the hills above the bay, but on closer view these proved to be houses.

It was thrilling to be going out on this adventure, he felt, 'like the pride of the beggar who suddenly finds wealth.' The smoke from the funnels of the convoy ships before, behind, and on both sides, was talking to the sky. The sea spoke the language of his soul, restless and confused while the wind went bursting with joy in the sun. And the ship was urging him forward into the unknown. He was going to *Vilayat* after all, England, the glamorous land of his dreams, where the Sahibs came from, where people wore coats and pantaloons and led active, fashionable lives — even, so it was said, the peasants and the poor Sahibs. He wondered what was his destiny.

The rocking of the boat unsteadied his steps a little and there was a strange disturbance inside him which kept welling up and choking him as if he had eaten a frog. He had prided himself on resisting sickness, when almost all the other sepoys had rolled about in their vomit, and hoped he was not going to make a fool of himself now at the end of the journey. Perhaps he had been smoking too many cigarettes, which the Government was distributing free. Or, perhaps, it was the fear of the Unknown, now that they were getting to their destination. But he had slept badly the previous night and had dreamt a weird dream about Nandpur, in which his mother was crying over the body of his dead father, and his brother, Dayal Singh, was rebuking him for running away when they most needed him. Only to him the village seemed far from here now ...

'Oh Lalu! Son of a sea-cow! Let us go and get ready,' called young Subah, son of Subedar Major Arbel Singh, his round red face flushed as if he had got the direct commission which his father had been negotiating for him all the way, as the boy had been self-importantly telling everyone.

'You go, I am coming,' said Lalu evasively, to shake him off, and stood with the hordes of sepoys who leaned on the railings, watching the little tugs which had come out and were pushing and pulling the steamer from where it had slackened over the placid waters of the bay towards the wharves.

Lalu smelt the rich sunny smell which was in the air, and felt that the entrance of the harbour was a wonder such as only the heart could feel and remember

'Boom! Zoom!' The guns thundered from somewhere on land.

'Oh, horror! The war is there!'

'To be sure! ...'

'The *phrunt!*'

3

The sepoys burbled gravely, looking ahead of them, fascinated, in wonder and fear, intent.

But a Sikh N.C.O. said: 'Have your senses fled? These are the guns of the *Francisi* warships saluting us.'

And, indeed, the convoy ships answered back acknowledging the greetings, and the booming stopped.

Before the ship came to a standstill, a number of French officers came up on board with some British officers and shook hands with the officers of the regiment. The French Sahibs looked like the Indians with their sallow complexions, but very solemn and sad.

The sepoys looked at them and wondered. They were afraid of talking in the presence of the Sahibs and stood silent or slipped away.

The shrill crescendo of the ship's sirens shook the air with an urgent, insistent call.

Lalu was excited almost to hysteria and went down to look for Uncle Kirpu, Daddy Dhanoo or Havildar Lachman Singh, as he did not know what to do next. But the news had gone round that the sepoys would disembark here, rest for a day or two, then go by train to the front as soon as possible, for the Sarkar was anxious to avoid the disappointment which the troops might feel at not being allowed to rush and defeat the Germans at once. This relieved the tension somewhat, and soon he was hurrying to get ready to alight.

He sweated profusely as he exerted himself, and he felt a strange affection in his belly as thousands of throats on the harbour burst into an incomprehensible tumult of shouting. Then he rushed towards his bunk, losing his way going down the gangways, till he sighted Uncle Kirpu and ran up to him.

'Slowly, slowly, gentleman, Franceville is not running away,' Kirpu said, blinking his mischievous eyes, and shaking his sly, weather-beaten face in a mockery of Lalu's haste.

'Being a man of many campaigns, you feel there is nothing new,' Lalu teased.

'I don't feel peevish and shy as a virgin, as you do, son,' said Uncle Kirpu and patted Lalu on the back affectionately.

'Where is Daddy Dhanoo?' Lalu said with a pale smile.

'First on deck in full war kit! Just to set the young an example!' Kirpu said.

'Let us hurry, then, and follow his example,' Lalu said and pulled the protesting Kirpu.

As they emerged on deck, the quay seemed to be drowned in a strange and incongruous whirlpool: Pathans, Sikhs, Dogras, Gurkhas, Muhammadans in khaki, blue-jacketed French seamen and porters, and English Tommies. And there was a babble of voices, shouts, curses, salaams, and incomprehensible courtesies. He struggled into the single file which was disembarking and, before he knew where he was, stood on solid earth in the thick of the crowd, without Kirpu. The sepoys were all looking at each other embarrassedly, or talking to the *Francisis*, gesticulating and wringing their hands and turning away when they could not make themselves understood. The French carried on in their own lingo, imparting information in a tumultuous flow of words which all seemed like 'phon, phon, phon, something, something ...' to the Indians.

But they were kind and polite, these *Francisis*, bowing and smiling and moving their heads, their hands, and their bodies in broad gestures, unlike the reticent Tommies.

Lalu stamped his feet to see if the impact of the earth of France was any different from the feel of Hindustan. Curiously enough, the paved hard surface of the quay, under the shadow of gigantic ships, full of cranes and masts and steel girders, seemed different somehow, new, unlike the crumbling dust of India. He swerved, and began to tap the pavement, to jump, and caper out of sheer exuberance of spirit ...

The quick darting notes of the bugles tore the air, and the sepoys ran helter-skelter with their heavy trappings, and began to get into formation.

Lalu spotted Havildar Lachman Singh, rushing towards the wide gates which opened into a road from the high wall of the quay. He ran after the N.C.O. His company was already forming while he had been procrastinating to find out the exact orders. 'Fall in, son,' said Lachman Singh with a kind smile on that brave, keen face of the Dogra hillman which Lalu had always seen sweating, owing to the energy which the sergeant put into whatever he had in hand, whether it was plying a hockey stick, instructing at the gymnasium, taking out a fatigue party, or doing any other regimental duty.

As Lalu was rushing into line, warmed by the kindness of Lachman Singh, Subah shouted '*Oi*, Owl Singh!' and came and dragged him to his platoon.

'Then, what is the talk - how do you like the land of France?' Lalu asked, leaning over to Uncle Kirpu.

'This land,' said Kirpu with an amused smile, 'this land is like all the others, it came to be with the coming of life, and will go down with death.'

'How can the blind man know the splendour of the tulip!' Lalu said.

5

'There is one splendour in men, another in tulips,' Uncle Kirpu answered.

Lalu was too enthusiastic about the adventure to feel as Kirpu felt, but he looked at the amused unconcern in the face of the experienced soldier who accepted fate with the resignation of a mild cynic, and who smiled at everything with a gentleness born of some hurt. Then he gazed at the lined, grave, Mongoloid face of Daddy Dhanoo, who had just outlived the accidents of time, space, life, and did not speak at all, as if he had become neutral, immortal. Their behaviour was so different from Subah's blustering, and his own excited manner.

But the band struck up a tune for the route march, and the orders of the officers rang out, and the heavy tread of ammunition boots, the flashing of arms, the rustling of uniforms, transformed the air.

'*Vivonlesindu*! Something, something ...' the cry rang out, above the 'lef right lef' of the N.C.O.s, from the crowd, which stood five deep under the awnings of tall, white-shuttered houses under the shadow of the harbour walls.

Lalu felt a shiver pass down his spine, and he felt shy walking, as a man among men through a crowd of cheering spectators. But the cheering continued.

A Tommy cried back on behalf of the sepoys; 'Three cheers for the French — Hip hip hurrah!'

The sepoys repeated: 'Hip hip hurrah!' 'Hip hip hurrah!'

Lalu scanned the faces by the cafés, the dock gates, the huge sheds and warehouses with tear-dimmed eyes. An irrational impulse was persuading him to believe that the dirty, squalid outskirts of this town were a replica of the outer fringes of Karachi Harbour. The presence of trams, motors, ships, moorings and masts encouraged the illusion. And, as he peered into the narrow, filthy lanes where women and children stood crowded in the windows and on the doorsteps, under lines of dirty washing, as he saw the small, languid unkempt Frenchmen in straw hats and with flourishing moustachios, it all seemed so like the indolent, slow-moving world of an Indian city that he felt an immediate affinity with this country.

'*Vivleshindou*! *Vivongleshindu*! *Vivelesallies*! ...' the cries of the crowd became more complex as the sepoys entered a square beyond the small fort which stood on top of a hill where the warehouses ended, and where the greenish sea made an estuary, congested by hundreds of small boats painted in all the colours of the rainbow. And Lalu almost stumbled and fell out of step through the wandering of his eyes among the faces of the

6

women who shrieked and waved their hands at the pageant of the Indian Army.

'Look out, heart squanderer,' called Subah.

'Can the blind man see the splendour of the tulip?' Lalu repeated his phrase.

As the troops turned left, and marched up the hill along the Canbière, the throngs multiplied on the broad pavements outside the dainty fronts of the shops, and of the beautiful high buildings decked with flowers. They were mostly women, and children, and lo and behold, as is the custom in India, they threw flowers at the sepoys while they cried: '*Vievongleshindoos*! *Vivangleterre*! *Vievelesallies*! *Vive* ...'

Lalu could not keep his eyes off the smiling, pretty-frocked girls with breasts half showing, bright and gleaming with a happiness that he wanted to think was all for him. Such a contrast to the sedate Indian women who seemed to grow old before they were young, flabby and tired, except for a cowherd woman with breasts like pyramidal rocks! ... Why even the matrons here were dressed up and not content to remain unadorned like Indian wives, who thought that there was a greater dignity in neglecting themselves after they had had a child or two!

'*Vivonleshindou*!' a thousand throats let loose a tide that flowed down the hill from the mouths of the throngs on both sides.

'What are the rape-daughters saying?' asked Kirpu, playing on the last word affectionately to take away the sting of abuse latent in the classical curse of India.

'What knows a monkey of a mirror's beauty!' said Lalu, adapting his phrase to the current description of the hillmen as monkeys.

'You don't know either,' said Kirpu.

'They are saying something about the Hindus,' said Lalu.

'What knows a peasant of the rate at which cloves are sold; he spreads a length of cloth as though he were buying two maunds of grain,' said Subah to Lalu. 'They are saying, "Long live the Indians". I can understand, because I know *Francisi*.'

'All guesswork and no certainty,' said Kirpu sceptically.

'*Vivongleshindous*! *Vivelangleterre*! *Vivonlesallies*! ...' the cries throbbed dithyrambically.

'You don't know the meaning of that, do you?' said Lalu to Subah.

'*Ohe*, leave this talk of meanings, you learned owls,' said Kirpu. 'Any fool can see that they are greeting us with warmth and hospitality. Come give a shout after me, "Long live the *Francisis*!".'

'Long live the *Francisis*!' the boys shouted, and the calls were taken up, followed by roars of laughter.

Now the enthusiasm of the women in the crowd knew no bounds.

'*Vivonleshindous*!' they shouted and laughed.

'*Bolo Sri Ram Chander ki jai*!' one of the Hindu N.C.O.S shouted.

And the sepoys echoed the call.

'*Allah ho Akhbar*!' someone shouted, and was echoed back by the stalwarts of the Muhammadan companies.

'*Wah Guruji ka Khalsa! Wah Guruji ki Fateh*!' shouted a Sikh somewhere. And the other Sikhs took up the call while someone, more full throated than the rest, added in a shrill tenor: '*Bole so Nihal, Sat Sri Akal*!'

And as a river in flood flows unchecked when once the dams of resistance have burst, so the calls of enthusiasm flowed across the tongues of the endless legion, emphasized by the stamping of determined feet, and punctuated with snatches of talk. And the long pageant, touched by the warmth of French greetings, inflamed by the exuberance of tropical hearts marched through this air, electric with the whipped-up frenzy, past churches, monuments, past rows of shuttered houses, châteaus and grassy fields, till, tired and strained with the intoxication of glory, it reached the race-course of Parc Borely where tents had been fixed by an advance party for the troops to rest.

After a march past of various mounted English and French generals, a sudden halt was called. The general of the Lahore Division trotted his horse up to the head of the forces, adjusted a megaphone to his mouth, and shouted in a Hindustani whose broken edges gained volume from the incomprehensibility of his tone and emphasis:

'Heroes of India. After the splendid reception which you have been given by the French, and the way in which you have responded with the calls of your religions, I have no doubt that you will fulfil your duties with the bravery for which you are famous! ...'

The band struck up 'God Save the King', and all ranks presented arms. After which the various regiments marched off towards the tents allotted to them.

When they had dispersed and reached their billets, and began to take off their puttees and boots, they found that their feet, unused to walking since the voyage, were badly blistered.

8

'Wake up, lazybones, wake up, it is time for you to say prayers,' Uncle Kirpu was shouting as he crouched in bed puffing at the end of an Egyptian cigarette.

'They must be tired,' said Daddy Dhanoo affectionately, as he wrapped the blanket round himself, shivering in the dawn, and invoking various names of God, '*Om! Hari Om! Ishwar!*'

'If we don't wake early we shall not get the ticket to heaven,' said Lalu as he stretched his body taut like a lion, yawned and rose, calling: '*Ohe, Subiah.*'

'Who? What? ...' Subah burst, startled out of a fitful sleep, stared at Lalu with bleary, bloodshot eyes, and then turned on his side.

'Has the bugle gone?' Lalu asked, hurrying out of his bed as though he were frightened.

'No, I was saying that you will be late for your prayers,' said Kirpu.

'Where does one say them?' Lalu asked as he started to dress. 'And does one say them seated on English commodes or crouching like black men who relieve themselves on the ground.'

'God's name is good!' Daddy Dhanoo said before Kirpu had answered. And he yawned, his big eyes closing, while the various names, and appellations of the Almighty multiplied on his lips, his mouth opening like that of a tired Pekinese. This was his way of evading discussion on the topic because he had been the butt of all jokes since he had slipped off the polished edge of an English style commode on the ship.

'*Om! Hari Om!*' Lalu parodied him. 'May you be consigned to your own hell, and be eternally damned, Almighty Father of Fathers.' And he went out of the tent blaspheming.

Every blade of grass between the tents on the racecourse shone in the light of the rising sun, while a sharp cool breeze blew from where the blue line of the sky lost itself in the mist around the dove-coloured châteaus on the hills.

Lalu walked along, impelled by the superstition which he had practised in the village that to walk on the dew drops in the morning was good for the eyes.

He had not been out long before Subah came running after him.

A spoilt child, very conscious of his position as the son of the Indian head of the regiment, Subah wanted to go and pay his respects to his father, which usually meant that he wanted the gift of some pocket money. He persuaded Lalu to come with him by promising his friend a treat at the 'Buffet' outside the camp.

They sauntered along towards the tent of the Subedar Major, and then,

9

seeing several important looking French and British officers gathered there, stood about discussing whether Subah should go up.

With characteristic impetuosity, however, Subah ran towards his father's tent, while Lalu stood averting his eyes for fear of the officers. Lest he be seen nosing about, he began to walk away, assuming a casual expression as if he were just 'eating the air'. Even that would be considered objectionable if he were seen by a Sahib. He hurried, because the imposing cluster of bell-topped tents spread the same fear in him as the secret, hedged-in bungalows of the Sahibs in Ferozepur cantonment, where it was an intrusion even to stare through the gates.

He hurried towards the latrines.

When he came out the camp was already alive as if it were an ordinary cantonment in India. Habitual early risers, most of the sepoys were hurrying about, unpacking luggage, polishing boots, belts and brass buttons with their spittle, washing their faces, cleaning their teeth with the chewing-sticks which they had brought from home, and gargling with thunderous noises and frightening reverberations, to the tune of hymns, chants, and the names of gods, more profuse and long winded, because the cold air went creeping into their flesh.

'As if the hissing, the sighing and the remembrance of God would keep them warm!' Lalu said to himself, feeling the incongruity of their ritual with the fashionable 'air and water of France'. He showed his face to the sun and, out of sheer light heartedness, began to jump across the strings of small tents towards his own tent.

'*Ohe*, where are you going?' Uncle Kirpu shouted.

Lalu rushed in, put on his boots quickly, adjusted his turban, and walked out again.

'The boy has gone mad!' exclaimed Kirpu to Dhanoo.

But the boy was exhilarated at being in *Vilayat*, thinking of all the wonderful shops that were in the streets through which they had passed yesterday, and the general air of elegance and exaltedness that surrounded everything.

A few Sikhs of No. 4 company stood combing their long black hair. He recalled the brutality with which the fanatics of his village had blackened his face and put him on a donkey when he had had his hair cut. The humiliation had bitten deep into him. They must look odd to the Europeans, he thought. And he wondered how many of them would have their hair cut while they were abroad or after their return to India. But the Sahibs didn't like the Sikhs to have their hair shorn, as they wanted them to preserve their own customs, even though Audley Sahib had excused him when Lance-Naik Lok Nath had reported him at Ferozepur. But for Havildar Lachman Singh and Captain Owen, the Adjutant, he would have had to go to 'quarter guard', on bread and water for a week, and his record would have been spoilt. Instead of which Lok Nath's promotion had been stopped and the Corporal had been transferred to another platoon, though that was more because Subedar Major Arbel Singh wanted to get his son, Subah, rapid promotion. The boy wondered when Lok Nath would wreak his vengeance on him ...

A group of Muslim sepoys, belonging to his regiment, sat in a circle round a hookah, however, and some dark Hindu Sappers and Miners of the next regiment were jabbering in dialect as they baked *chapatees* within the ritualistic four lines of their kitchen, while a Jodhpur Lancer was gesticulating with his arms and his head as he explained something to a woman who — what was he doing?

Lalu stopped to listen.

The Sappers were using foul abuse. It seemed that the woman had walked into their kitchen.

'*Silvoup silvap...* ,' the woman said coming up to him.

Lalu just moved his head and smiled weakly.

The woman gabbled away in French.

Lalu stood dumb with humility, and was going to salute, and go away for fear an officer might see him talking to a Mem Sahib, while the Jodhpur Lancer, equally at a loss, said: 'I don't know what the sister-in-law wants.'

The French woman laughed at her own discomfiture, and then said in English 'picture', pointing at Lalu, and the Jodhpur Lancer, trying to explain with her head, her eyes, her nose, her fingers, what she wanted.

But as if the very presence of a Mem Sahib, usually so remote and unapproachable in India, had paralysed them, they stood unresponsive.

Lalu looked about furtively and scanned the cavalry horses on the right, the shouting cooks and water carriers on the left and the Baluchis and the Gurkhas who were sunning themselves ahead of him. Then he looked back towards the officers' quarters, and pointed towards them, thinking that the best thing was to send her to the Subedar Major Sahib's tent. But his gaze met Subah's, who came running along abreast of a French officer on horseback.

Lalu and the Jodhpur Lancer sprang to attention and saluted.

The officer talked in his own tongue to the woman, and then, laughing, said to Subah in English:

'The Miss wants to draw the pictures of these men.'

'Draw my picture, Mem Sahib,' Subah said coming forward.

The French woman smiled at Subah, said something to the officer, and made a gesture to the Jodhpur Lancer, Lalu and Subah, to stand together.

But Subah thrust himself forward and thumped his chest to indicate that he wanted a portrait of himself all alone.

By this time, driven by curiosity, other sepoys were gathering round.

Whereupon the French officer said in Hindustani: 'Mem Sahib would like a group.'

'Fall into the group and let all of them be in the picture,' Lalu advised Subah.

'*Han*, we also want to be in it,' said the other sepoys crowding round the woman, several rows deep, at the first touch of the pencil.

Then they all stood away, twisting their moustachios into shape and stiffening to attention as if they were going to be photographed.

The officer and the woman laughed as they talked for a moment, then the officer edged aside and the woman began to draw the picture.

'That was the interpreter sahib,' Subah said with great importance.

The French woman sketched the group. But there were any number of subjects before her now, for other sepoys from the nearby tents had gathered round. They would come and look at the woman as though she were a strange animal, because she was so homely, so informal and so unlike the white women who came to Hindustan and never condescended to greet a native. And they posed before her, proud to be sketched, their honest faces suffused with embarrassed laughter, even as they stood, stiff and motionless, their hands glued to their sides.

The woman could draw the pictures of the sitting, standing, talking, moving sepoys with a few deft strokes even before they knew they had been sketched.

And then there was much comedy, the sepoys laughing in at the caricatures of each other and exclaiming wildly as they came to life on paper, happy as children to see the sketches, and insisting on signing their name in their own language on the portraits.

When the woman had made various sketches Subah began to press for a portrait of himself. But he could not communicate his wish to her in the little French which he had learnt at school. As he came up to her with a daring familiarity, Jemadar Suchet Singh, a tall, imposing officer of No. 2 company of the 69th Rifles approached to see the confusion and said:

'Get away, don't crowd round the mem sahib! Get away!'

'Come, leave the skirt, let us go,' Subah said.

'You are getting too bumptious,' shouted Suchet Singh to Subah. 'You try to be familiar with her again, and I shall have you court-martialed. Never mind whose son you are!'

After this warning the crowd of sepoys began to slink away.

'Come on, my heart-squanderer, she is beyond your reach,' said Lalu, dragging Subah away. 'And get ready to face your father because I am sure Suchet Singh will report you! ...'

'Look out, son, I am to become a Jemadar soon,' Subah said to Lalu, as they hurried towards the main road. 'The Subedar Sahib told me today, so you behave if you value your life.'

'*Ohe, ja, ja,* don't try to impress me!' said Lalu.

'Oh, come, raper of your sister, we shall celebrate,' Subah said. 'You will be my friend, even when I am an officer.'

'Build the house before you make the door.'

'All right, wisdom, come, and run lest we be seen.'

'Where are we going?' Lalu asked. 'We have to get permission if we are going out of bounds.'

'You come with me,' said Subah, there is a stall at the end of that road. I saw it when we were marching down to camp; it seemed a wine-shop, because there were people with glasses full of red, pale and green wine before them. Come, we will walk through the camp as though we are not really going out, and then try, and evade the sentry at the end of the road, or I shall tell him that I am the son of the Subedar Major Arbel Singh. Come, we shall be happy ... You can live without fear of Lok Nath now, because now that I have got promotion he will remain where he is, in the mire ...'

'It would be strange if the lion's offspring hasn't any claws,' said Lalu. 'It seems to me that all of us will be in the mire if you become a Jemadar, not only Lok Nath!'

'You know that my father has been invited to the officers' mess tonight where the French officers, English Sahibs, Rajahs, Maharajas and some chosen Indian officers have been invited,' Subah informed him, puffed up with pride. 'And, it is said, that Sir James Willcocks, the Commander-in-Chief of the Indian Corps is to arrive here soon, accompanied by Risaldar Khwaja Muhammad Khan, who is aide-de-camp to this general, and a friend of my father. He is a Pathan from the Yussuf Zai: he was aide-de-camp to Lord Kitchener at one time ... I should like to become aide-de-camp one day ...'

'You wait, son, you will become that, and more,' said Lalu with a faint mockery in his voice.

'Really, do you think?' Subah said unconscious of his friend's irony.

13

'Then I shall make you a Jemadar.'

'The dog eats a bellyful of food if he can get it, otherwise he just licks the saucer,' said Lalu to cut short his friend.

'Oh come, why are you always stricken even when happy?' said Subah. And, catching Lalu's hand he began to caper like a horse.

Some Sikh sepoys dressed in shorts were washing their clothes while a group of French children stood around them. One of the Sikhs brought out a flute, and began to play it to amuse them. At this some French soldiers gathered round, imagining that the flute player was going to bring out a cobra. The sepoy pretended there was a snake on the ground before him, and played around its imaginary head, deliberately swelling his cheeks with his breath till they were like two rounded balls. At this the children scattered out of fear, but came back reassured when the sepoy smiled.

One of them offered the mimicking juggler a sweet which the sepoy gulped down, rolling his eyes, and twisting his face as if he were swallowing some poison. And then there was an attempt at an exchange in the language of gesture. And, what was strange, the mime worked. And soon there was complete understanding between East and West.

Lalu, who had stood to watch this scene, responded to the hilarity by accepting a cigarette from a French soldier, which the Sikhs, whose religion taboos smoking, refused. He only wished his regiment had been transferred here as from one cantonment to another, for a sojourn during peace time. But in a war? ... Now that he was in France, he felt a curious dread of the Unknown, of the things that happened in a war, even as he felt the thrill of being there.

'I am the son of Subedar Major Arbel Singh, 69th Rifles, and he has sent me to buy some cigarettes from that stall,' Subah announced to the sentry without a blush.

The sentry, a tall Baluchi, with a long crested turban, looked at him hard. 'Who is that man with you?' he asked.

'Sepoy Lal Singh, orderly to the Subedar Major Sahib Bahadur,' lied Subah.

'Go, but don't be long,' said the sentry.

The two boys passed the barrier, and made straight for the stall which stood at the crossroads.

A few French soldiers, and some Tommies were standing around drinking beer. Lalu felt embarrassed, afraid, and inferior to be going to a stall where there were only white men. With the assurance cultivated through his three years at the Bishop Cotton School, Simla, Subah dragged him to the bar.

The Frenchman who owned the stall turned to them, wiping his hands on the white skirt of his apron and said, *Mussia!*

Subah pointed to some bottles which stood on the trolley.

The Tommies at first stared at the two sepoys as if surprised that the Indians should have developed a predilection for drink. Then, contrary to their customary reticence in India, one of them said: 'Good eh, Blighty!'

'What, Blighty?' said Subah.

'He means *Vilayat*,' Lalu said laughing.

The French Sahib struck the knuckles of his finger against a bottle of white wine, and gesticulated. But before Subah could say anything, an English Sergeant-Major stalked up to the stall and snapped at the Tommies as well as the sepoys:

'Where the bloody hell do you reckon you are? Is this a cantonment or a bloody war?'

The soldiers stood with their heads hanging down.

'This is out of bounds,' the Sergeant Major rapped. And he leaned over to the Tommies and hissed at them angrily, snarling at the sepoys the while.

During the next few days the Indian corps began to be moved to Orleans, where, it was said, they were to be properly equipped with new machine guns, howitzers, mechanical transport, medical equipment and all the necessities that an army, trained to fight on the frontier and for policing the outposts of the Empire overseas, needed in operations in the West. They had handed over the rifles and ammunition which they had brought from India at Marseilles and fresh arms were issued to them. The sepoys adapted themselves to the new rifles, but they hoped that they would not be forced to have new machine guns, as that would entail more strenuous practice, when they were kept busy enough with packing and unpacking, and clothes drill, and they had also been given new warm clothes. It was said that this war to which they were going was unlike any other, fought with things called 'grenads' and 'mortas', and a rumour ran that the Germans had invented a gun which could shoot at range of seventy miles. But why hadn't the Sahibs thought of all these things in India? Of course, they had had to leave the cantonments in a hurry, and the Army Head-quarters at Simla hadn't had enough time. But the arrangements were being pushed too fast. The officers were kind, however, patting the Gurkhas on their backs and asking them to sharpen their kukhries, telling the horsemen to value their steeds more than their lives, and encouraging the others to keep fit by wrestling exercises, as they would have to face up to the 'Huns', who were 'twice as big as the Indians in size.' ... And the sepoys felt that now that they were here, they were here, and it didn't matter if they had big guns or small guns or whether they lay on mats like the beggars or slept in feather beds like the princes. Travel was good for the heart, since, contrary to the prognostications and evil forebodings of the priests, they hadn't died in crossing the black waters.

The 69th was one of the first regiments to be dispatched to Orleans.

$$\text{꙰} \quad 2 \quad \text{꙰}$$

AT ORLEANS the two Divisions camped at the Champs de Cercettes, a park about six miles out of the town. And here, almost immediately on their arrival, they were equipped with mechanical, and horse transport.

The weather, which had been indifferent except for little spells of sunshine, took a turn for the bad. At the touch of a cold wind the sparse vegetation on the outskirts of Orleans seemed to change its colour from green to gold, and dull vermilion, and a red coppery hue. A few menacing clouds gathered from the west and, wandering low over the plains, splashed the ripened earth with showers.

The sepoys who had felt cold even in the equable air of the South of France now began to shiver, and to drink more tumblerfuls of the crude mixture of tea-leaves, hot water, milk, and sugar which their cooks boiled all together in cauldrons, and called tea. They had had field service clothing on the winter scale given them in Marseilles. Most of them were fairly used to extremes of climate, but in India the torrential rains swept through the land, and left the earth pregnant, warm and swollen, while here there was a continuous drizzle, soaking the fields till they were damp and muddy.

The excitement of seeing the motor lorries, that were handed over to the corps, superior to any motor cars they had seen in India, raised their spirits somewhat. They emerged from their tents, burdened with the weight of grey skies, and gathered round the brand new vehicles with the open eyes of wonder. For the polished sheen of the trucks, the efficient air of speed that seemed to be controlled in their compact bodies, aroused

17

admiration from the men who knew the advantages and disadvantages of the bullock cart.

'How could such huge motors be driven?' Daddy Dhanoo asked, turning his bleary bulging eyes to his companions. 'My meaning is, how could they pass other vehicles on the road, for one of them would occupy the whole width of the road!'

'I would like to see the engine,' said Lalu admiring the skill of the men who had made the thing.

'How could a machine contained in such a small tin shed drag such a big body, laden with men and arms?' Uncle Kirpu said, even his cynicism vanquished by the huge buses.

'To be sure, these Sahibs can work wonders!' said Daddy Dhanoo.

'Arrest the movement of the stars on a map, eh?' said Lalu mimicking Daddy Dhanoo. 'Catch time in the hands of a watch! Harness electricity as if it were a mule!' And he went and mischievously pressed the horn, till Dhanoo, Kirpu and a few others who stood by almost ran, startled.

'And you are all donkeys who ought to be harnessed and flogged so that some sense could be driven into your heads!' said Subah, swaggering up to one of the trucks from the tent of his former mates where he had come to show off his new Jemadar's outfit. For, instead of being reprimanded for his presumption at Marseilles, he had received the direct commission of Jemadar when he was presented to the Colonel. 'Who blew that horn?' he asked angrily. Finding the men all ranged in silence against him, he sought to placate them. 'There is nothing very mysterious about trucks! They are just bigger motorcars than those which you have seen in India. The surprising thing to all of us officers, is that we have been spared any at all, because ... but I must not tell you, it is confidential ...'

'Then don't,' said Uncle Kirpu. There is *Holdar* Lachman Singh and I trust, he knows ...'

'*Ohe nahin*, fool, there are certain things which only the officers know,' said Subah eager enough to tell them. 'Well, it is rumoured that there has been a retreat at a place called Mons. The Allied Armies have paid a terrible toll. The Sarkar is being faced with difficulties in the supply of materials and transport on land and sea. You don't know what heroic efforts the General Staff and all the British officers are making. It is now known that the *Angrezi* Sarkar was completely unprepared for the war ... And if you consider that the Sarkar has to meet the demands of the front for conveyances, we should be grateful that we have been able to get this motor transport ...'

Lalu noticed the sudden exaggeration of pride and importance that had come into Subah's manner. He had always shown off, of course, but till yesterday his aggressiveness had been restrained by the humiliation of knowing he was in the ranks. But now, since he had been raised to the rank of Jemadar, he had become overbearingly masterful and all-knowing. It was extraordinary how a star on your shoulder, or a stripe on the arm, as in the case of Lok Nath, could make you talk down to everyone.

'It is all due to Lord Kitchener Sahib's solicitude for the Indian troops,' said Subah

'My father, the Subedar Major Sahib, knows Lord Kitchener ... ,' he continued and began to embellish the gossip he had heard in the officers' quarters.

'Lord Kitchener gave new barracks and new cantonments to the Indian Army, Jemadar Sahib,' said Lachman Singh seeking to direct the conversation into less confidential channels. 'He was a great officer. There were many things he did which were against the custom of the Sarkar. I remember that one of the things the Sahibs resented very much was the reduction of the number of British *paltans* in every brigade from two to one.'

'*Yus, yus,*' interrupted Subah falling into English as the ability to speak the language of the Sahibs was reputed to increase his sense of importance among the Indian ranks. My father, 'the Subedar Major Sahib, was a special orderly officer to Lord Kitchener Sahib ...'

'*Ohe,* what can you remember of that?' said Uncle Kirpu crudely demolishing the bluff that Subah was seeking to impose on them. 'You were only a kid, as big as my little finger, running about the regiment naked with your little *looli*, and the crows used to peck at your bottom ...'

Everyone laughed at this. And, as Uncle Kirpu was well known for his caustic wit and, as one of the first sepoys to join the regiment, was allowed to say anything to anyone, whether British officer, Indian officer, N.C.O. or sepoy. Subah joined in the laughter, though a pale blush of embarrassment covered his red face, and his eyes glanced furtively from side to side.

' "My father was a Sultan," the fool is said to have answered, when they asked him, "Who are you!" ' Kirpu quoted the Persian proverb with a broken accent.

'Oh, don't recall his childhood to him now,' Lalu said.

'Don't bark!' shouted Subah suddenly, his face redder than ever. 'I shall present you to the Karnel Sahib if you cut such a joke with me again.'

'If he receives the same treatment on being presented to the Karnel Sahib as you got then please to present me too,' Kirpu said slowly. 'My old shoulders could do with a star and I like the idea of a Sham Browne belt ...'

Everyone laughed again, including Subah though Lalu hung his head down and paled as he met the Jemadar's stare.

'Uncle, let go, come to your senses, and don't be a clown,' said Havildar Lachman Singh siding with the Jemnadar though he sympathized with the rest.

'Forgive me, Subah,' said Lalu, realizing his mistake.

'I am Jemadar Sahib, henceforth, remember,' said Subah with a steady glare in his eyes. 'Shun!'

Uncle Kirpu and Sepoy Lal Singh came to attention.

'Both of you report for fatigue duty every day from tomorrow,' the Jemadar ordered. And he walked away in the direction of the officer's tent, shaking a little.

The groups of sepoys who stood by Lalu and Kirpu and Lachman turned from the shining splendour of the trucks to explore each others' faces. The excitement, the exhilaration in their eyes subsided amidst the furrows of shame carved by the past humiliations inflicted on them by superior officers, and they stood baffled as though struck by an electric shock, because the bullying of an officer who was their friend a day ago seemed like a fresh wound in the changed circumstances of their lives, among all the strange things of the West. They had begun to believe that *Vilayat* was an unrelieved paradise and, encouraged by all the privileges of journeys in ships and railways through foreign lands which they had never enjoyed before, heartened by the kindness of people everywhere, they had grown to the dignity of human beings and forgotten the way in which they had always been treated as so much cattle in India. They were beginning, through contact with the ordinary white folk, and through the knowledge that even coolies here seemed to be coolies only during their work hours, and then Sahibs in their own right, who put on suits and boots and walked out with their girl friends, — to lose the fear and abjectness that their superior officers had inspired in them in the cantonments of India ... And now they had been suddenly thrown back to the realization of their real position.

The fatigue duty imposed by Jemadar Subah Singh became in fact a visit to a fair.

For as Lalu and Kirpu came out with a party of sepoys, each of whom had been condemned for similar offences, to receive the battalion's share of horse transport, they found the fields, which had been converted into marsh by the rain, bestrewn, beyond the shining steel trucks and motor lorries, with vehicles of all possible kinds and horses of all sizes and colours.

Through the discordant roar of raucous shouts and calls and the neighs and snorts which rent the air, they could see hundreds of vans, from those which could presumably be drawn by two horses and which were capable of carrying one or two tons, to small donkey carts like those which the washermen in the cantonments of India used to transport dirty linen from the lines to the river, or such as they had seen by the vegetable stalls in the side streets of Marseilles.

'Are these the wagons we have come to receive?' Uncle Kirpu asked. 'Look at the harness! This one has no collar and that other has no head or heel ropes!'

'And *wah wah* the horses!' said young Kharku, the little bugler and mascot of the 69th.

'Father of fathers!' said Lalu. 'That one seems blind of one eye!'

'You couldn't take those vehicles across a "Mal Road" to say nothing of taking them through a war even on the North Western Frontier!' said Hanumant Singh, a lemur-like veteran Dogra sepoy who was not wont to say too much.

'Well, to tell the truth, I don't know how these things are going to work,' said an N.C.O.

'They are doing their best for us, as Jemadar Subah Singh might say,' remarked Lalu. And he was going to add his quota of mockery but he saw the Jemadar coming up from behind and winced.

'Come boys, come and let us get busy,' called Jemadar Subah Singh. His round plump face was wreathed in smiles and he seemed to have relented since the quarrel, as much perhaps because he was a man of passionate temperament jumping from the extremes of gaiety to sadness, from wild anger to a childlike docility, as because he was amused by what he saw as he came to inspect the fatigue party at work.

The sepoys came to attention and saluted as soon as he came abreast of them, and he raised his cane to acknowledge their greetings.

'They are fine horses,' the Jemadar said walking smartly up and, leading the sepoys into the very thick of the fair where a snuffling, snorting, trampling herd grazed on the thin grass before them.

'Magnificent!' said the sycophant Sikh N.C.O. Chanan Singh.

'And, considering the Sarkar has been plunged into this war so suddenly,' continued the Jemadar, 'and has had to face the difficulties of fighting the Germans on one side and of making arrangements for the welfare of the troops on the other, it is a wonder that they have assembled all these things.'

'They will have to face many more difficulties repairing those vans on the field than in fighting the war,' said Kirpu the irrepressible.

'According to you, uncle, the doomsday has come,' said Subah, laughing and thumping Kirpu on the back.

'The drowning Brahmin will take his followers with him,' said Kirpu fatalistically, 'Therefore where the Sarkar goes, *Hazoor*, we have to follow like good disciples ...'

'Impudent, incorrigible uncle!' remarked Subah laughing. And he put his arm round Kirpu affectionately, as if the old man had touched some tenderness in him.

'As the Jemadar Sahib says, brother,' put in Havildar Chanan Singh to Kirpu, 'one must not be disrespectful to the Sarkar.' Lalu looked at Subah, then at Kirpu's quiet, sardonic visage and then at the faces of Chanan Singh and the other sepoys who walked respectfully behind the Jemadar Sahib and seemed to accept every word he uttered as the law of God.

'Come, *yar*, Lalu, come, why are you lagging behind?' said Subah in the friendly manner of old days. 'We shall find one of the Sahibs or an interpreter and ask him where our horses are.'

Lalu followed a little quicker after this overture of kindliness, and leapt across the shafts of miniature carts, more fragile than the bullock carts in his village and general make-up, past carriages which, though they were improvements on the *yekka* of Gughi's father and more like the phaetons in Manabad and the big cities, were rusty with years of damp on their springs.

As he came abreast of Uncle Kirpu and the other sepoys he saw them pull up and salute Major Peacock Sahib of the regiment who stood ahead of them. He clicked his heels and took his hand to his head though he was not noticed. For the Major Sahib, a short, quick-tempered, agile man was speaking peevishly in a twisted Hindustani to Jemadar Subah Singh.

'*Francisi log acha bandobast nahin!*' And he spoke in English. 'They know nothing about horses! Look, all the animals running loose. Muddle! No one knows which horses are whose!'

And he puckered his brow and frowned, closing his eyes and looking round.

'We shall wait for orders, then, *Huzoor*,' said Jemadar Subah Singh.

'Some of the horses have strayed towards the river there,' Major

Peacock said, pointing with his stick to a line of gleaming silver that flowed through long stalks of waving grass.

'Get the sepoys to catch them and bring them here for inspection.'

'*Huzoor*,' said Subah clicking his heels and saluting with such alacrity that his head and torso bent forward. And he turned to the men:

'Come boys, I shall give you leave to go to town after we have finished our work. And what's more I shall treat you to some sherbet.'

'Come boys, if the Sahib speaks so plainly about the mismanagement of the *Francisis*,' called Kirpu, 'you be sure he will tell us a thing or two in his own language if we don't look sharp.'

Apart from such fatigue duties as were imposed by cussed superiors, the sepoys had plenty of leisure to go sightseeing.

Daddy Dhanoo, squeezed into himself with the cold. Uncle Kirpu was not too fond of pleasure. Lalu took permission from Havildar Lachman Singh to go to town.

The boy would not go alone, however, and he hung about Kirpu like a child persuading an elder to accompany him.

'Oh come *Chacha*, come,' he begged.

'You go along, son, you will meet other sepoys from the regiment. You will go prancing along.'

'But horses go in herds, *Chacha*, come, don't be a donkey.'

'I know you will not cease pestering me,' said Kirpu at last. 'Tell that cook, Santu, to give Dhanoo some more tea and I shall get ready.'

Lalu jumped up, pranced like a horse and shouted to Santu to give Dhanoo a tumblerful of tea. And, covering the old man with all the available blankets, they walked away from the camp through the weak sunshine of a cold autumnal afternoon.

Lalu was full of excitement to be going along to this city. The march through Marseilles had been merely a fleeting expedition, and he was obsessed with something which struggled to burst through all the restraints and the embarrassment of the unfamiliar, to break through the fear of the exalted life that the Europeans lived, the rare high life of which he, like all the sepoys, had only had distant glimpses from the holes and the crevices in the thick hedges outside the Sahibs' bungalows in India.

And, as he walked under the shadows of mansions with shuttered windows like those on the houses of Marseilles, reading the names of shops on the boards, as he walked past vineyards dappled by the pale sun, past stretches of grassy land which seemed, from the droves of sheep clustered on it, to be pasturages, his tongue played with the name of this city, Orleans, and there was an echo in his mind, from the memory of something which had happened here, something which he could not remember.

'A quieter city than Marsels,' Uncle Kirpu said.

Indeed, in spite of the smoke of factory chimneys that trailed across the sky, in spite of the modern lettering on shop fronts, the delicate grassy lawns, the small detached houses, and old doors of buildings, there was something fascinating about the place and different from Marseilles.

'Oh! water, oh there is a stream!' shouted the sepoys whose impetuosity knew no bounds.

Lalu rushed up and saw the stream on the right, flowing slowly, gently, and shouted: 'River!'

'Everything is small in these parts,' Kirpu said. 'Look at their rivers — not bigger than our small *nullahs*. Their whole land can be crossed in a night's journey, when it takes two nights and days from the frontier to my village in the district of Kangra. Their rain is like the pissing of a child. And their storms are a mere breeze in the tall grass ...'

'To be sure, they are small, the streams,' confirmed a Punjabi Muhammadan. 'The width of seven of these won't make the bed of the Jhelum at its narrowest.'

'It is about the same size as the Jhelum at Srinagar,' said a Dogra from Jammu and Kashmir. 'Why, it is just like Srinagar, this city, built on two sides of a river. Look, there are boats on it, too, like the houseboats at Srinagar.' And he pointed towards the river.

'*Ils ... Looa ... Looa!*' a burly Frenchman in a straw hat said, smiling as he stopped to look at the sepoys watching the river flow.

The sepoys shook their hands to signify that they couldn't understand and, as the Frenchman pointed again to the accompaniment of a copious commentary, they nodded out of politeness.

'What does he say!' asked one of the sepoys.

'Something in *Francisi*, Allah knows what,' answered another.

At that the Frenchman bowed very politely, smiled and went his way.

'Salaam *Huzoor*,' said the sepoys saluting and almost coming to attention in the face of the white man. For all white men, military or civil, were to them superior like the English Sahibs in India who surrounded themselves with thick hedges.

24

'Look, look, there are two sweepers drinking wine by two Tommies, and also a woman!' said a sepoy naively. 'They have little religion or shame!'

'There are no untouchables in this country,' said Kirpu firmly. 'And there is no consideration of pollution.'

'And if you compare that café to our cook-house, you know what cleanliness means,' said Lalu enthusiastic and surprised at the change that had come into Uncle Kirpu's outlook.

'Son, that is a question of rupees,' said Kirpu. 'Some are rich here and run shops, some are poor and do the work of sweepers.

Our cook-shop keepers have little money to spend on decorations. They are illiterate. And they have to sell food cheap. But oh! the bread baked in the oven! I wonder when we shall have some of that bread with clarified butter on it and a good pot of mustard spinach!

Lalu agreed weakly. He had aspired to this Europe as to some heaven, and sought to justify everything in Blighty. He was inclined to forget the good things at home. 'There seems more equality in this land,' he added.

'The Sahibs travel first class,' commented Kirpu with an air of finality. 'The Indian officers second class, Tommies, Havildars, Naiks and sepoys in the third class — remember this and don't be led astray.'

'Look, look, a bridge!' a group of sepoys called to those behind them as they began to run, their heavy boots clattering on the stone pavements, and the few French men and women scattered away at their onrush.

'Ohe, wild men, stop, go slowly!' called Kirpu after them.

But Lalu turned and saw that it was a quaint enough structure, this bridge, with its nine arches.

'It is curious,' he said reflecting more to himself than to Kirpu, 'that most cities of the world were originally built near rivers, lakes or springs.' And without waiting for an answer, he contemplated the tower of a Church which probed the sky, at the opposite end of the river, from the base of an intricate mesh of ancient architecture, decorated with statues, steeples, minarets and crevices in which pigeons fluttered as in the mono-lithic temples of India. So absorbed was he that he barred the way of a fat French woman who came across the bridge with a basket in her hand. And, as she was a veritable elephant, she in turn barred the way of a stream of men and women behind her.

'Ohe, look, ohe look, get aside,' called Kirpu.

And Lalu jumped away with a start, the fat woman burbled something, then bowed, and the young woman behind her laughed a laugh which was so contagious that they caught the sepoys, and Lalu. But just then a motor came rushing across the narrow road of the bridge and sent him scurrying up to the pavement till he nearly fell.

'Come to your senses, son,' admonished Kirpu.

Smiling at his own discomfiture, keeping to the edge of the pavement to make room for the French women, Lalu caught up with Kirpu. And they both began to carve their way through a wide web of streets, crammed with little shops. All of these had transparent glass windows, like the shops in Marseilles. Some displayed wax effigies of men and women dressed in silken dresses, strange shaped hats and coats, uncannily like real men and women, some showed shining silver utensils, watches and golden rings. And, wonder of wonders, even the great big carcasses of cows and goats hanging down from hooks in butchers' shops were kept behind windows, while in a grocer's shop legs of pig, covered with gauze, hung down, their flesh brown and green with what seemed like rot.

'Let us go to the other side!' Uncle Kirpu exclaimed on seeing these. And, with his handkerchief to his nose to ward off the imaginary smell, he darted across the street, saying, 'I don't know how men can eat these!'

So absorbed was Lalu that while Kirpu crossed the street, he continued on his way, fascinated by the chocolates, cakes and sweets arrayed in the window of an adjacent shop, and then by the tables and chairs, arrayed as if in a room, and by the neckties, shirts and collars, all the richest things he had ever seen and which he would never be able to buy, but among which he felt happy to be moving at leisure. He had not felt free at Marseilles, because he had been too humble then to stare at this superior life, immediately after his arrival.

The shadow of the Church which he had seen from a distance now inclined in a great hulk across a street; its hoary sculptures seemed to be like some time-infused memorials to the strange incarnate spirits of the past, dressed in robes which had no connection with the straight cut styles of the French of today, saints whose heads and bodies were covered with the droppings of pigeons and who seemed like crumbling images of a forlorn age in the midst of a new world.

Lalu's gaze was staggered by the impact of this immense, ancient structure and groped among the dusky lengths of its florid pillars for some meaning.

He suddenly found himself in a square at the end of which was inscribed the name Place du Martin.

A number of sepoys stood here with elementary stares, round a statue in the middle of an empty space, while some Frenchmen waved with their hands quick and impatient gestures, and repeated, 'Something ... something ... Jindac ...' in their soft but unintelligible lingo. Some of the soldiers walked away with clumsy steps, and awkward movements as if they were bored. But Lalu rushed up, and craned his neck to see the figure of a young girl with a sword in her hand, her head thrust heroically forward, and her whole body speaking of some brave deed which she had performed. *'Jean d'Arc'* the inscription at the foot of the statue said. In a flash the last clue to Orleans returned to his memory from the story of *Joan of Arc* in the *Highroads of History* which he had read at the Church Mission School at Sherkot.

'Who is it supposed to be?' one sepoy was asking.

'What a gigantic statue!' another exclaimed.

'Who is it, anyhow?' queried Uncle Kirpu walking up with an abounding curiosity.

And the whole place seemed to be in a ferment, the bulging eyes of the sepoys bewildered by the figure, while the French were bewildered by them in turn.

Lalu explored among the aisles of his memory for details and, supplementing the incomprehensible explanations of the natives, volunteered the information to the sepoys, in his own tongue.

'In the fourteenth century there was a hundred years' war in which the English were fighting the French ...'

'Then, do you mean to say, that the Angrez Sahib and the *Francisis* were enemies at one time?' one of the sepoys asked rather shocked.

'*Han,*' Lalu answered, and continued his narrative while a whole group of sepoys clustered round him.

The sepoys who had kept turning to the statue of the girl even as they heard Lalu's story now contemplated the dark image with a naive sense of awe and wonder.

'Is this really true?' one said.

'Could such things be?' put in a second.

'A girl *Jarnel* who drove out *Angrezi* army!' commented a third.

And the maid seemed to become a heroine like the Rani of Jhansi. Lalu felt the blood coursing in his veins with the ambition to follow her on the path of glory.

'Come, come let us go to a café!' came Subah's voice suddenly, 'you have become a very learned man, come!' And the Jemadar strode up from behind the statue with a swagger and thumped Lalu on the back with the old heartiness of an equal.

'Come, come, my hero!' said Kirpu, noticing that Lalu was being carried away. 'Come, us folk have different work, we are sepoys of the Sarkar and let us not forget that when we talk brave words ...'

Lalu's eyes fell upon a couple of French girls. He was fascinated by the profile of one of them, a stately girl of about twenty and he stared hard at her. She smiled coquettishly and then turned her blue eyes away.

'Come,' said Jemadar Subah Singh and dragged him away.

Lalu followed, but took the opportunity of turning round and caressing in his eyes the shapely contours of the girl's breasts, her hips and her legs with a hunger that spread the panic of abandon in his body.

'You will be court-martialed if you don't behave!' warned Kirpu and pulled him away. Lalu strode forward excited, exultant, yet sad and alone and frustrated in some curious way.

Sitting in a comfortable basket-chair by a table like a Sahib, under the awnings outside a café by a busy boulevard, watching the crowd of casual, courteous, laughing Frenchmen and gaily painted, pretty women, sitting in the half dark of the evening, was the utterest happiness for Lalu.

The difficulty was that they did not know the name of any drink when the waiter Sahib came to get their order, a brisk little man as big as a thumb, dressed in a crisp white shirt and black coat — a veritable juggler, the way he balanced a tray full of glasses and bottles on the palm of his left hand. Subah tried hard to remember what he had drunk at Marseilles and looked among the hundreds of bottles arrayed in the café to recognize the wine, in vain, till Lalu suddenly recalled the word 'Graves' and the Jemadar shouted, 'Han, Han, "Graves".' The waiter and the customers in the café seemed amused. But the French were indulgent and kindly. The only wine Uncle Kirpu had ever drunk was 'Rum', and, since Lalu had felt warmer after a ration of this, these two said 'Rum', a word which the waiter Sahib could not understand, till a Tommy, who sat in a group near by, got up and, trying to interpret the word, pointed his finger to a bottle of Martell Cognac in the window, as he could not see any Rum.

'Cognac Cognac!' the waiter repeated, and ran with the agility of a clown towards the bar inside the café, studded with tall mirrors and huge chandeliers and decorated with plush sofas on which sat well-dressed superior Sahibs, eating with silver forks and knives, off tables covered with immaculate white cloths.

'So even the Tommies don't know the language of the *Francisis!*' Uncle Kirpu said.

'What is more, they are not allowed to sit with the big Sahibs and officers inside there!' said Subah.

'You are an officer — why don't you go and sit inside there?' Lalu wanted to say. But he restrained himself and only cast a furtive glance at the rich atmosphere inside, and felt ashamed and inferior and afraid lest the intrusion of his stare be interpreted as rudeness by the Sahibs there. For it was said in the cantonment that the Sahibs did not like the idea of being stared at while they were eating in the officers' mess or even drinking by the hockey pitch after a match.

'Compared to them, we folk from Punjab are truly like oxen,' Uncle Kirpu said moving his head as if he were very impressed with the splendour of the place.

'*Ohe*, this is nothing compared to what I shall show you if you come with me,' said Subah thumping Kirpu on the thigh. 'You wait till the Indian merchant, whose friendship I made this afternoon, comes.'

'In every land, even in our own country, it could be like this,' said Lalu. 'But our elders say, "It is not the custom to do this, it is not the custom to do that." Fools! If you are seen drinking a pot of wine you are automatically declared a drunkard, and if you look at a woman you at once become notorious as a rogue, a pimp and a whoremonger and your parents tell you that you have cut their nose in the brotherhood and no one will give you his daughter in marriage. Burnt up people! Owls!'

'Oh! Grave! Grave! Grave!' Subah shouted to recognize the bottle of white wine which he had drunk at Marseilles on the waiter's tray, and he interrupted Lalu's diatribe.

The waiter Sahib came smiling, brushed the marble top of the table, put his tray on it, opened a bottle and poured their drinks into glasses. He bowed and was retreating when the Jemadar lifted his glass and gulped down the liquid and, recalling the word for waiter, shouted, *Garcon*. The waiter came back, smiled, bowed and poured some more 'Graves' into his glass. Subah gulped that too. At this the waiter laughed and the Sahibs sitting by stared at the Jemadar. Subah's face was flushed and, for a moment, it seemed he would be angry and resentful at becoming the object of a joke. But some sepoys of the 69th, a Baluchi and two Sikhs, came over to the Jemadar's table, and, in order to ingratiate themselves with the officer, called flatteringly, '*Wah*! *Wah*! Jemadar Sahib.'

'Come brave men and sit down with me,' Subah shouted and, turning to the Baluchi, began to recite a Persian verse,

'O *Saki*, bring the cup …'

Lalu sat away, detached, as he was too frightened after the curt manner in which Subah had, in the pride of his advancement to a direct commission, condemned him and Kirpu, his old cronies, to fatigue duty the other day. He was happy. Sipping a cognac, sipping it gently without the spitting, spattering, spluttering noises with which he himself want to drink milk, or tea in India, and without gulping it like Subah. Sipping a cognac had warmed his senses to an indulgent tenderness. And he merely watched the flashing of fine forms clad in superior silks and serges, the flowering of the spirit in the accents of *Francisi*, as polished and gentle to the ear as well-spoken Hindustani, and the gorgeous interplay of colour and movement and speech, which seemed to him the very essence of life here.

'All men in all countries are perhaps the same', Uncle Kirpu reflected. 'At least, all are equal in the grave. And in life all must have duties and responsibilities: these people must have families: they are probably fathers, mothers, sons, daughters and sisters.'

'Only their customs are different.' Lalu said with a trace of bitterness in his voice at Kirpu's reference to the family.

'Life wouldn't be worth living, my son, without the spirit of service which is in members of a family,' said Uncle Kirpu vaguely.

'But the spirit of service ought not to become a way of extracting pain out of people in the guise of duties,' said Lalu raising his voice a little so that he sounded priggish in his denunciation. 'You must always put on a miserable expression and remain quiet in the presence of your elders, that is respect. And, of course, you must never commit the crime of being happy! Always follow custom!'

'*Ohe*! leave such talk, come drink up and let us have some more, and let us go and be happy,' said Subah boisterously thumping the table before him. And he began to sing.

'*Wah! Wah!* Jemadar Sahib!' said the Baluchi sepoy.

'Son of a lion!' flattered the Sikh, impressed to see the Subedar Major's son drinking as only a peasant.

The waiter Sahib who, incredible as it seemed to the sepoys, was their servant for the while, mistook, Subah's thump for a gesture demanding his services and came smiling up to the table with a polite: '*Vee Musia!*'

'*Hancore!*' Subah said pointing to his glass and then, thinking that brandy was the drink of those lower orders of the human species, sepoys and the like, raised four fingers above the glasses of cognac with an exaggerated flourish of his hand, so that the neighbours who, apart from an occasional stare, had taken the Indians for granted, laughed affectionately.

Then the Jemadar's eyes fell upon a young girl who had joined in the laughter. He breathed a deep sigh as if his heart had been suddenly punctured, and then burst in the highest-pitched Punjabi: '*Hai*! May I die for you! May I become a sacrifice for your laughter! *Hai*! May I take you in my arms!'

'*Ohe, ohe*, son, have some shame, have some respect for yourself before these sepoys and before everyone else!' said Uncle Kirpu.

'Don't you care for the limp lord!' said Subah, loudly. 'We are now in the fair land of France, and in this land, as Lalu says, there is complete liberty. Look at that man kissing a girl in the corner.'

'But some British officer may see you and report us,' said Kirpu.

'I don't care, I don't care,' sang Subah in a boisterous singsong, his face flushed.

Kirpu sat aside frightened and anxious.

Lalu felt that if Kirpu persisted in his admonitions, Subah might lose his head altogether, and, anyhow, as he looked into himself he felt very much like Subah himself and thought that he was only restrained from confessing to his admiration for the French girls by his inferior status as a sepoy: he wished he could again see that girl with the bronzed oval face who had fascinated him near the statue ... And he lent himself to the subtle, indefinable air which bubbled like the froth on open bottles, which trailed along the talk, along thin wisps of curling smoke, and drifted among the shadows, and which mingled with waves from the quickened heart beats of all the men and women, the strivings of their wills in the irregular, irrelevant movements of their gestures. Life had become action. He was no longer half dead as at home in the village.

The waiter Sahib brought the drinks and Subah put a bundle of notes on the table from which the *garcon* chose one, saying something like 'Fron fron'.

'Come then, brothers, gulp it down,' said Subah. 'And then let us go and meet the Hindustani merchant. He said he would be near the statue and he knows all about the secret life here ...'

Before they had gulped down their drinks, however, the Indian merchant arrived. With the effusive heartiness that marked him out as a Punjabi, though he could otherwise have passed for a Frenchman, with his little pointed beard, and his affectation of the outer bearing of the natives of his

31

country, he embraced Subah, shouting the while: 'Ah, Jemadar Sahib, so you can see that I never break a promise.'

'Come, come, what will you have to drink?' Subah said, glowing with enthusiasm.

'Now listen,' the merchant said, raising his finger, 'I don't meet a countryman of mine for days, sometimes for months and years, so you are to be my guests ...'

'No, take this,' said Subah and began to pour some of his 'Graves' into his own glass for his friend.

'What is this? — Oh! no, thank you very much, but I would like you to order some absinthe for me if you really must insist on treating me.' And he called the *garcon*, who happened to be standing by, and said something to him in French.

'We are very happy to meet you, in this foreign land,' said Kirpu with characteristic Indian informality. 'What is your respected name, and what kind of business do you do here?'

'They call your servant Diwan Amar Nath,' the merchant replied with a calculated politeness which twisted his padded, pockmarked face, with the thick lips and beady eyes, into a patently clear expression of feigned humility. And he continued with an exalted air: 'I do all kinds of things. I have sold diamonds and jewels in my time. And I have supplied carpets and rugs to the princes of Europe ... I have done many things... I know some of the richest men in this country and, to be sure, they are in every way above the rabble, for they honour us and our ancient country ...'

The sepoys gaped at Diwan Amar Nath admiringly, as if he were no less a person than the Aga Khan who, they had heard, also lived in these parts and was friendly with kings and queens and noblemen, and who had recently offered himself as the first recruit to the Sarkar.

'It is very gracious of you to deign to sit with us,' said Kirpu faintly ironical.

The waiter brought a drink and put it before the Diwan.

'Oh, you are my countrymen, of course, and you come on my head and I go to your feet,' the Diwan began apologetically after a sip. Then he continued in a voice which made every word strike like the note of a gong. 'But these Europeans — I know them inside out. I have had several personal friends here, among the Barons and Baronesses, Counts and Countesses, who are about the same status as our Rajahs and Ranis, in India. Some of the most aristocratic ladies have offered me their daughters, while one invited me to tea and begged me to marry her. But, brothers, I have my own dignity to keep and these people respect you if you are stern with them. Only last year a princess fell in love with me. She came to my shop in Paris and asked me to accept her home, her jewels and her servants as my own. But I said to her, "Madam, I am a Hindu and an honourable man! You have got your husband and though he is an old man and is incapable, he is nice to you because he has given you all his wealth ... I am a Hindu and a respectable man ...!" And she wept and cried and implored me to accept her, but as one of the greatest of our sages, Kabir, has said, "If a businessman builds his home in a woman's eyes his business will be ruined ..."

'Oh you should have yielded!' said Subah, warming to the Diwan's lasciviousness.

'Brother, sin in the soul is like fire in the chaff,' said Kirpu pretending to take the Diwan's point of view.

'To be sure, you do the right talk,' said the Diwan, inclined to win the shrewd Uncle Kirpu over. 'One has to be pure as unsmoked sugar.'

Lalu couldn't reconcile the bombast of his previous manner with the saintly views which the Diwan was now expressing. And if he was a rich man why was he going about from place to place? From the assumed smile on his face there seemed to be something crooked about him. It was curious how Subah had picked him up.

'Now, you are not going to talk of "unsmoked sugar?" Subah said to the Diwan, 'I have been telling these lusty swines that you will take us to some place ...'

'Come, come, for the sake of you, brothers, I could go to hell, not to say a whorehouse,' said the Diwan.

'Come then, we are ready,' Subah said thumping his shoulder. 'I can hardly hold him down ...'

The sepoys laughed at the Jemadar's words with such abrupt boisterousness that they became the centre of attention of the whole café, their shining faces glowing an exultant, intoxicated brown, curiously beautiful yet menacing through the tresses of smoke which drifted up from their cigarettes into the quickening shadows of the street outside.

'Have you any money?' the Diwan asked Subah in a whisper, leaning over to the Jemadar's chair. 'I have forgotten my wallet at home.'

'Don't you care for the limp lord,' the Jemadar said and, taking a wad of notes from his pocket, held them before his friend.

'That won't be enough,' said the Diwan with a grimace which made his padded face contract somewhat. 'You had better give that to me and I shall negotiate the business for you.'

'With great happiness,' said Subah. 'Now, let us go.' And, thrusting the money into the Diwan's hand, he threw up his arms like a child.

The Diwan got up with casual self-assurance and walked ahead, while Subah and the sepoys followed blushing as they saluted the smiling people in the café.

As they emerged into big street, Uncle Kirpu stopped short and said: 'I will be going back to camp, boys.' And then, turning to the merchant, he continued: 'Diwan Sahib, it was good to meet you.'

'I shall come with you, Uncle,' said Lalu out of mere fellow-feeling, though he was really full of curiosity about the secret life they were going to see.

'Oh come, Uncle, come, don't be such a killjoy,' begged Subah. 'I didn't refuse to come through the prostitutes' bazaar in the cantonment with you when you used to fetch me back from school. Come Lalu, come and see the fun.'

'Someone may report us,' said Uncle Kirpu. 'You youngsters are all right, but it will bring shame on my grey hairs.'

'Oh come, I shall see that not a hair of your head is touched,' said Subah, and then, pulling himself to his full height, thumped his chest with his hand and declared, 'I am not a Jemadar for nothing.'

'No,' Uncle Kirpu said emphatically and turned away.

Subah put his arms round Lalu and proceeded to catch up the Diwan who had already walked ahead with the Baluchi and Sikhs.

Stumbling, blundering, nervous and eager, the group of heart-squanderers walked through a side street, past a few shops, displaying strings of dirty brown sausages and other cooked meats in their windows, up a dark lane off the main square in the shadow of the church.

'That meat is a funny shape,' said Subah and giggled lewdly.

'About the same size too,' said the Diwan.

'I am a North-Indian,' said the Baluchi.

'You can't compete with us Sikhs,' said one of the Sikhs.

'You are a pack of shameless fools,' said Lalu, though he was on edge with expectancy and could hear his eardrums thrumming.

Not a soul was in sight in the thickening shadows, and it seemed uncanny that a few yards away from the glittering street there should be the stillness of a gloom in which he could hear the echo of each heartbeat. Only the tall houses, shuttered with wooden windows, stood solemnly against the cold that permeated through the thin mist spreading from the corners of the church.

'There's a house up there,' said the Diwan in a hoarse, half-suppressed tone, as he looked this side and that, 'where a woman runs what she calls a "Massage Hindu".' And he laughed and repeated, 'Hindu Massage.'

'What does that mean?' inquired Subah tense with emotion now, so that his drunken, hot breath came and went in short, sharp gasps.

'She says that a Rajah once visited her and taught her that,' the Diwan said, 'You come and see.'

'Let us go and see this "Massage Hindu"!' Subah said dragging the Diwan ahead and encouraging the others with his enthusiasm.

'But there is one thing,' the Diwan said. 'She will want more money than you gave me.'

'There is no talk of that,' said Subah. 'We will give you all we have.' And he turned to the sepoys even as he plunged his hand into his own pockets: 'How much have you got, brothers? Let us give Diwan Amar Nath all that she may want ... This is the happiest day of our lives. We are having the real pleasures of *Vilayat*.'

The sepoys dug into their pockets and handed over the little money they had. The Baluchi handed over a fifty franc note, saying: 'In my religion it is legal to go with a Christian girl! Prophet himself said so.'

Lalu wished he had had more money to give, for he felt quite reckless now. He wanted to go and see things once in his life. He had cheated himself of this experience in Sherkot and Manabad all this time for fear he might bring disgrace on his family if he were seen going anywhere near the forbidden quarters. And he had heard that the women in the Ferozepur cantonment were diseased and gave you either a gold medal or a silver medal for your money. And yet, passing through any big town in India, he had seen prostitutes sitting in their windows and he had often felt like breaking the limits of his modesty, though the difficulty was how to run up the stairs without being seen by some acquaintance or other. And, then he had pretended that he was disgusted by the loads of imitation jewellery these prostitutes wore and the tinselly splendour of the clothes with which they decked themselves ... But the truth was that he had never had the courage ... This time he would go. He was bent on it. This man, the Diwan, seemed to know, though there was something odd about him. And it was uncanny how the air of twisting and turning made this desolate street look like a bad Indian gulley. It was funny also how the Diwan said, 'Hindu Massage!' And that a Rajah had been here.

'What is this "Hindu Massage", Diwan Sahib?' a Sikh sepoy asked, snatching the question almost out of Lalu's mouth.

'You have to ...' the Diwan halted and whispered, 'you have to take your clothes off. And then the girl you choose comes and washes your horse and her mare, and ...'

'Oh come along, hurry,' — Subah called.

The Diwan beckoned, looked around to see if there were any strangers. And, then, walking up to a huge door, he pulled a knob out of the wall and let it go.

A tense second passed during which everyone's breath seemed to be suspended. Another second during which Subah came stamping back. A third, and the group explored each other's faces, smiling and embarrassed when their eyes met. And then they suddenly suppressed their nervousness and breathed deeply from their huge chests. Nothing seemed to happen. The Diwan turned politely round and pulled the knob again, two or three times, and looked up.

Just then, however, the huge door opened, and a heavy woman's voice shouted something in French

The Diwan said something like, 'Noosoonce.'

Then, through the cavernous? beyond the door, a small window opened in another door and the heavy red face of a middle aged woman stared out into the blackness. She whispered. And she nodded without relaxing the frown which was visible on her face under the shadow of the lamp hanging behind her.

Diwan Amar Nath motioned to his friends to enter.

As they pushed forward on their heavy boots, almost falling over each other in the dark, the door closed behind them of its own accord and the inner door opened.

'Come on,' Subah urged.

But the sepoys were all too shy to push through the crowd at the door, through the quarrelous air of a hiccuping music, into the boisterous atmosphere where a crowd of unblushing men and women were swaying about in swift pushing movements, like those which the sepoys had heard the Sahibs in India performed with Mems at dances in clubs. Subah rushed up with characteristic bravado, craned his neck over the shoulders of the crowd and clapped with his hands to the rhythm of the music. But the sepoys were relieved that the crowd did not turn round and stare at them and laugh, for they knew that with their turbans and uniforms they looked strange enough.

Then the Diwan came, led by the elephantine woman who had opened the door and whose face now revealed a fearsome moustachio and a beard like that of a witch.

As if the crowd at the door had sensed the approach of Majesty it made way for the procession.

'Oh, where have we got entangled?' said Lalu with an embarrassed laugh as he followed with bent head and nervous mien.

'Walk along now,' Subah urged as he dragged Lalu, brushing past the wall precariously near the happy, hoarse, hilarious dancing couples through a corridor into a room where there were a few tables and chairs, as in a café. It was only about ten steps from the hall, but the red-hot waves of shame which swirled through his forehead, behind his eyes, eager to look at the dancers and yet bent in shyness, made these steps a perspiring ordeal.

He drew his handkerchief from the pocket of his breeches and, sinking sideways into a chair by his companions, began to mop the sweat off his face and neck, affecting a deliberate casualness as he glanced open-eyed around the bare walls, seeking to understand the meaning of it all.

'What will you have?' the Diwan said turning away from Madame, the she-elephant, who stood hulking by the table with an enigmatic smile on her face. 'You must have something to drink here. It will be a little dearer per bottle, but it is the custom to buy some from her if you want to get girls later.'

The sepoys remained silent as the price of pleasure seemed to be increasing beyond the limits of their purses.

'Get anything you like!' Subah said with a nervous smile.

'You have got some money, haven't you?' the Diwan asked. 'I have only five francs left after paying the entrance fee.'

'Money is dirt,' said Subah jerking his head and waving his arms. 'Let us have some fun.' And he emptied the contents of his second pocket into the Diwan's hands.

The Diwan spoke to the woman, who frowned a little as she edged away.

Lalu and Subah looked at each other for a moment, and smiled shyly as if seeking to recognize each other. For in this pursuit of happiness they seemed to have become disconnected, detached, as if they had lost contact with the familiar persons in each other, the darkness of night covered Lalu's soul. The daylight seemed to disappear. His heart throbbed.

At that instant a French boy came in a stampede across the corridor behind a shrieking, heavy-bodied girl and, inspirited by her laughter and shrieks, caught her from the waist, swung her round in a wild abandon and then bent the whole weight of his torso on her bosom and kissed her.

'*Wah*! *Wah*! son of your father, kiss her again!' shouted the Baluchi and smacked his lips.

'*Shabash*!' the Sikhs roared.

'May I die for you! The fun has begun!' said Subah.

'This is nothing, yon wait and see,' said Diwan.

'They kiss on the mouth then here?' asked Lalu blushing with a modesty that had received a shock and a thrill at the same time.

The other sepoys also turned to each other as they realized that they had seen a mouth kiss, because they had always kissed their wives on the cheeks and foreheads in India. They were eager to taste this new sensation, but even as they waxed enthusiastic they were restrained by the humility of their position as sepoys who had never dared to look at a white woman with the eyes of desire. And the sense of the poverty of their pockets threatened to put all these pleasures beyond their reach.

Another boy and girl came in and, embracing each other, sat down in a corner and began to kiss.

The Indians were watching the couple with their rudimentary stares when the Diwan suddenly touched Lalu's shoulder with his hand and said: 'Look there in the corridor!'

As they lifted their eyes to the corridor they saw a series of girls followed by boys passing into the inner recesses of the house with clean new towels, and chunks of soap in their hands.

'Shall we remain dry, then?' said Subah to the Diwan fidgeting in his chair. 'Go and bring some girls!'

'Costs some money,' said the Diwan with a mock-serious expression on his face.

'There is no shortage of money,' said Subah. 'I can hardly hold it down …'

'Let the Madame come,' answered Diwan.

There was no sign of Madame, but a bovine young woman with a treble chin, fashioned in the image of Madame, came, a bottle in her hand. And, lifting her skirt wantonly to show her naked thigh, and, holding up the bottle, moved her head as if to ask which will you have.

Subah jumped up and, catching hold of her, tried to emulate the boy who had kissed a girl full on the mouth in the doorway.

'*Non, non*,' the girl shrieked challengingly. And, finding it difficult to secure her release from Subah's hard embrace, slapped him full on the face.

Subah let her go and tried to laugh away his chagrin though the pallor on his excited face betrayed his hurt pride.

Putting the bottle on the table she laughed and, inclining her head in blandishment, said something to the Diwan in French.

'She says it costs money to do that,' said the Diwan.

'Oh, she can have as much of that as she wants,' said Subah. And, plunging his hand into his pocket, he emptied all the change on the table before him.

'That will pay only for the wine,' said the Diwan counting the coins.

Seeing the injured expression on Subah's face, the girl laughed an artificial, wooden laugh and, with pouting lips, came to sit in the Jemadar's lap.

Subah's face was saved and the sepoys laughed at this.

Whereupon the girl lifted the edge of her skirt to show the naked flesh between her legs and then, with a deliberate 'Ooh' dropped it again.

The sepoys began to talk to her, the Diwan interpreting, while Subah explored her form impatiently for its content.

Instead of laughing or smiling as the others did, Lalu found himself contracting into his own skin, till he felt himself reduced to an emptiness from the centre of which his two eyes seemed to see this world as an enormous enclosure, crowded by hordes of hard, gigantic shapes which were oppressing him. In order not to sit aside, apart from his companions, he tried to persuade himself that he was happy, as happy as Subah and the Baluchi. And he tried to put on a smile and thought of saying something. But his eyes met Subah's and the deliberate smile on his face broke up into the edges of a nervous laugh which suddenly stopped short and gave place to a grim, set expression.

At that instant another girl came into the room and, seeing Subah's flushed face and a colleague on his knee, purred with the stimulation of pleasure and rubbed her form felinely against him and brushed his cheeks with her hand.

Subah put his arms around her and began to hold a conversation with her in the few French phrases he knew.

'There is no talk,' said the Baluchi, 'so long as they are kind to one of us.'

Lalu looked at the scene now quite detachedly as if he was a creature of some other world who, however, understood the meaning of this. The girls seemed to be laughing at all of them in spite of all the blandishments which they were practising. Their wanton obscenity was so much in excess of the coyness they affected to titillate the men into passion, that they looked like spoiled and grimy dolls oozing the smell of their stuffing.

They were originally perhaps merely ignorant, poor girls who fell a prey to the advice of someone who told them of a way to earn easy money, and were lured by the life of the senses, till they were fouled and used and couldn't get back to ordinary life. But, as in India, perhaps prostitutes were meant to show the young the various ways of lovemaking. The barrier of language prevented any real contact between these girls and the sepoys. He felt sad for Subah because the attempt at conversation had broken down and the Jemadar seemed at a loss.

But just as Lalu was exciting his will on Subah's behalf he saw him catch a third girl who was coming towards the group and it seemed he was quite capable of dealing with the lot of them.

'Come Diwan, arrange it for me,' Subah said as another girl came up to him. 'With this fair one who is tall and is stroking my cheeks.'

'They like the Jemadar Sahib,' the Baluchi said, respectfully submitting to the monopoly of the girls by the superior officer. 'But *Huzoor*, let us have a turn after you.'

The tall girl who had come last said something to the Diwan and, extricating herself from Subah's grasp suddenly came and sat on Lalu's knee, stroking his chin to the accompaniment of short, pitying sounds, while the boy looked at her thickly painted, small, irregular face and blushed. Lalu lifted his eyes to her and he contemplated for a moment the loneliness behind the mockery of outraged innocence in her eyes, lustreless and dull with cynicism as if they had seen too much, known too much, and were now empty and didn't know anything at all. And yet he felt happy to be near her.

The two other girls also got up and came round Lalu, talking among each other the while, even as they brushed the crumpled shiny satin dresses which they wore.

'What are these sisters-in-law saying to each other in their own tongue?' said Subah insistent and angry. 'And why don't you arrange one for me?'

'How much money have you got?' asked the Diwan, 'for the first money you gave me is finished.'

Subah fumbled in the pockets of his trousers whereupon the fat girl, who was hewn in the image of Madame, jumped on to, his lap affecting an air of raped modesty, crying, 'Oooi ... Oooi ... la ... la ...'

'There is no question of money because I can give you some tomorrow,' said Subah finding his pockets empty.

'I am afraid you can't have anything in this place for less than fifty francs,' said the Diwan in a bored, impersonal voice.

Subah glared at him for a moment from the liquid of his bleary eyes. Then he shot two sun arrows of hard glances at him and, kicking him on the shins furiously, shouted:

'Son of a pimp! Thief! Dog! Illegally begotten! Where is the money I have given you already! Thieving son of a dog, fleecing me with your tales and soft words!'

And he got up and struck the Diwan right and left, slaps, fisticuffs, kicks, and with the ferocity of a madman.

The girls ran shrieking, crying, shouting with the most piercing voices.

The Baluchi separated Subah from the Diwan, counselling him the while: 'Cool down! Be calm! Jemadar Sahib! Leave the rogue! Leave the rascal!'

But the Madame came rushing, shouting and flinging her arms in the air, uttering a flood of invective which sounded doubly powerful in her hoarse, querulous voice.

Before the sepoys knew where they were, they and the Jemadar were being collared, pushed, dragged and pulled, and kicked and driven out of the brothel into the abyss of the night.

The corps practised route-marching during the next few days, first in full service order with all transports, then on a small scale, the companies of the various regiments in the Division being taken out under their respective company commanders.

And then there was a constant drilling which broke the sepoys up, as the conditions for hard training in the camp at Orleans were far from satisfactory. This rigorous work left very little time for pleasure. Indeed, apart from the fact that parades kept them warm in the fast gathering cold, the intensive routine seemed to the sepoys the harbinger of arduous times to come. For, it was rumoured that the Germans had made a big attack and driven the allied armies back, inflicting great losses on the Sarkar, and that the Commander of the Indian Corps had been summoned to the General Headquarters as soon as he landed at Marseilles and that he had been told by Sir John French, that the British Army was to be transferred to Flanders, and the Indian corps was to hurry, and join it.

They waited anxiously, therefore, stealing as much rest from their duties as they could, making occasional expeditions to the cafés near the camp as they were beginning now to acquire the taste of 'Cafeolé', and 'Vane' and French cigarettes.

But, after days of this, they began to grow more and more tense and expectant for the orders which were soon to come.

At length on the evening of October 17th orders came for the Lahore Division to entrain the next day, while the Meerut Division, with the Secunderabad Cavalry Brigade and the Jodhpur Lancers, were to stay behind, and follow at short intervals later.

There were fevered preparations for the departure. Lal Singh was harnessed to fatigue duty since, after the scene at the brothel, Jemadar Subah Singh seemed displeased and, what was remarkable after their previous uncordiality, very much 'You whisper in my ear and I whisper in yours' with Lance-Naik Lok Nath. The only consolation was that every other man in the regiment seemed to be on fatigue duty of one kind or another on the day of departure, packing his kitbag and giving a comrade a hand if not doing any heavier work. And the camp was busy as an anthill: here a sepoy sitting by a line of unpacked luggage, wondering how to fit all the things into his kitbag while a pair of boots lay outside besides a pan and a water-bottle; there some of the men sat on ammunition boxes, shouting for an N.C.O. to ask what to do with themselves; next horses of the artillery neighing and coughing and stamping nervously while their riders polished the skin of their flanks; and there were orders, shouts, cries and laughter and the babble of an army speaking a hundred different tongues.

Uncle Kirpu and Daddy Dhanoo had been sent to pack the kit on general service wagons. These were to be placed loaded on the train.

Lalu had been with a party set to rolling tents which were to be handed over to the Ordnance department and he was just finishing this job.

As he tightened the ropes round the poles and strained to pull the fabric into shape, he sweated and sat back, contemplating the empty ground from which the tents had been removed, as if he were sad to leave the place where he had first begun to feel the pulse of the land, and where he had begun to taste the life of France. He lingered for a moment as if he were preoccupied by a superstition and looked at the bare space, cleaned of everything except the camp smell, a mixture of wood-smoke, chapatees, leather, oil and horse-dung, which seemed to hang in thick layers over the chill air before the jaundiced eye of the autumn sun.

An N.C.O. from No. 4 company put him in charge of a party carrying two days' cooked rations which were to be taken for the men in supply wagons in the train. And, as the cooks raced against time serving the meals and preparing extra food for the journey, Lalu gave them a helping hand.

Seeing that he himself and the other sepoys were going freely about the kitchens with their boots of cowhide skins and their leather belts, and handling food without washing their hands, he thought that if Dhanoo and Kirpu needed any more proof of the spoilation of their religion they could see it here. But everyone went about casually, and he marvelled at the ease with which the men were forgetting their customs. Perhaps it was a concession to the difficulties of cooking Indian food in a strange country, but he hoped that it was the 'air and water' on 'Franceville'.

There was not much time for idle reflection, however, as the mule carts were almost ready, loaded with the cooked food, and the contingent with which Lalu was going to the station was ready. After the long and wearisome activities of the whole morning the boy was happy to be off, though he would have to come back and do another round.

The sun was shining a transparent white as Lalu rode away by the side of a dark South Indian Sapper, and there was a melancholy breeze in the copper-coloured branches of the trees which had shed a profusion of pink leaves on the wayside and excited the mules in the long caravan. He felt strange riding past civilians who stood to stare and smile.

Where was the war? How was it being fought and what would the sepoys be asked to do? The questions flashed through his eager mind. But there was no answer. And as there was a dread about the future he sought to drown this train of thoughts in a melody ... The thought seemed to return, however. If only there was not this discreet veil of silence drawn over the movements of the troops by the Sarkar which left everything to rumours and legends!

As they got to the station the scene was one of complete turmoil. Some of the sepoys on fatigue duty were hauling things into the supply wagons, shouting and swearing as they strained to lift the weights, and being shouted and sworn at by the N.C.O.s. Some stood by sacks and rifles and others sat on collections of kitbags, apparently waiting for orders. Everywhere there was the wild confusion of loud talk and furious gesticulation, the rustling of clothes, the movement of forms. But there was a glow of warmth among the sepoys, a strange sense of fellowship, as if they felt that they ought to hang together because they were going farther into the Unknown. He felt he was nothing without them.

The N.C.O. in charge of the foodstuffs came with a group of sepoys who were to unload the carts before these returned to camp for the second contingent.

And now he suddenly felt isolated from his cronies. So he took advantage of the temporary respite to slink off in search of Kirpu and

Dhanoo. He made his way through the helter-skelter of the crowd pretending to be doing something very important. They had originally been put on duty at helping to remove the luggage in the officers' mess. But it seemed hopeless to find them among the uniformly dressed sepoys of even his own regiment, while here the men were mixed up anyhow.

He went back and helped to unload the wagons, to share the labour.

He was tired and did not want to go back to the camp with the carts for the next round. But he felt guilty like a criminal, hovering around aimlessly, thinking of an excuse to avoid the return journey. As he was procrastinating he caught sight of Babu Khushi Ram, the small, beady-eyed, button-nosed head clerk of the regiment, supervising the loading of the office chests into a wagon. He ran to greet him. But the Babu was too preoccupied and flurried to accept or reject courtesies.

'Come and help with those boxes, don't stand staring at me, son,' he said to Lalu.

The boy felt guilty about not belonging and went to the aid of an orderly who was heaving a boxful of documents up to the men standing in the wagon.

'Oh falling, falling, oh save, someone, help Dhanoo!'

Kirpu stood shouting at the door of the wagon.

'Don't you worry,' said Lalu, as he took the weight off the head of old Dhanoo and pushed it to Uncle Kirpu's feet.

Daddy Dhanoo stood back, his face uplifted to Lalu like that of a bullock who had been relieved of the weight of a plough on his neck.

'Where are you? What?' asked Kirpu tensely, in a panic of pleasure at seeing the boy.

'Where are you?' Lalu asked, 'I am lost.'

'We have already occupied places in the train there,' Dhanoo said with the air of a child, pointing towards the outlying platforms. We have kept a place secure for you ...!

'Ohe, you can talk later, get on with the job in hand,' said Babu Khushi Ram impatiently. 'Lift those three last boxes and then you can renounce this world.'

Lalu hurried and helped Dhanoo. He guessed that the Babu had given them this easy job to save them from more arduous fatigue. And, since Khushi Ram had ordered him to give a hand here, he craftily thought that he had a good excuse to evade his other duty. If Lok Nath came to know, Lalu would have hell to pay, but the boy looked round, became busy and drowned all thoughts of the future in the fatigue routine.

'Good!' Daddy Dhanoo was saying as Lalu lifted the next box on to his back while the old man just held the rope by the side.

And, after Lalu had thrown it at Kirpu's feet, he stood back and saw Dhanoo staring at him with admiration in his big eyes.

'You are a hero, son!' the old man exclaimed.

Lalu thumped Dhanoo's back and smiled at him. He was radiant with happiness at being with his comrades again, almost like an orphan who had found the parents he had lost.

They waited in the oppressive dark of the unlit cattle truck. which was their compartment, for the train to start, some dozing, some half asleep, some shaking or shuffling uncomfortably. They had gone off to the outer fringes of the town after dark, walked round and bought cigarettes and drunk coffee mixed with brandy to warm themselves, and they had been waiting for the hour of eleven-thirty when the train was due to start. And now the hundreds of lights which illuminated the city had been extinguished and they stared with sleepy eyes at the red and green lamps of the signals and the silver sheen of the rails, as if these could tell them when the train would move. For the most part the doors of the compartments were closed and they were stewing in the sweat of their bodies, packed almost on top of each other, so that there was no room to move an inch without treading on someone's feet. The smoke of endless cigarettes had made the atmosphere dense and hot and suffocating.

'The raper of its sister, this train, it is worse than the train from Amritsar to Pathankot during Diwali fair,' said Uncle Kirpu coughing after several vigorous puffs at his cigarette.

'You have never been to the Kumbh fair at Hardwar,' Daddy Dhanoo 'burrburred' from where he lay mindless of the heat. He seemed to be able to doze off anywhere.

'You should be happy at your good fortune,' said Lalu with a certain impatience which gained intensity from the heat of the truck. 'Some regiments on the other sidings are loaded in open cattle trucks.'

'I'd rather be in the open trucks,' said Uncle Kirpu peevishly, fanning himself with a rag.

The bitterness in Kirpu's remark seemed to express the general mood. And, for a moment, everything was still. Then hoarse chatter could be heard from the platform and the confused whispers of the sepoys sunk in the apathy of all-pervading gloom.

45

Lalu reclined in a corner. He could hear his heart beating as a kind of undertone to the brooding layers of heat that streamed out from the tense, tight-stretched senses of men, in invisible, intangible masses of clouds which hovered before the heavy-lidded eyes of the cooped up sepoys, thundery and electric.

'A strange fair,' the boy muttered.

'Havildar Lachman Singh!' interrupted an authoritative voice, the stern ring of which was one of Lalu's earliest memories of the army.

'He has already gone to the fair,' Lalu whispered.

'Of course, it is a fair we are going to,' said Lok Nath, the tall, lanky tyrant lance-corporal, entering the truck. 'Some of us eat the salt of the Sarkar and are not even prepared to do a little fatigue for it. Who is this — whining?' And he craned to look so that the prominent Adam's apple of his long neck moved up and down.

'No one, no one, Havildar Lachman Singh is not here,' Kirpu intervened to avert the unpleasantness which he anticipated.

Lalu felt the imperceptible shudder of a warm horror arise from the back of his head. He knew that Lok Nath had been waiting for days for an opportunity to get at him. Having been transferred to another platoon by the Subedar Major Sahib's orders, because Arbel Singh wanted his own son to get a direct commission and supersede all other claimants in the Dogra Company, the lance-naik had no direct contact with his old platoon, which was under Lachman Singh. Lalu who had once been the object of Lok Nath's spite, felt that the corporal was insinuating all that about betraying salt for his benefit. He hoped that the bit about fatigue duty was not a reference to his default today when he had suddenly left the food wagons and helped to get office chests into the train.

'Would you like a pull at my *cigrut, Holdara*?' Kirpu said in a tone which sought to disguise the inexpressible mockery of his manner in exaggerated courtesy.

'*Ohe*, stop smoking,' said Babu Khushi Ram peevishly. 'It will create more smoke in the stagnant air ...'

'There is no talk of that,' said Kirpu, 'let us entertain the lance-naik. He is, after all, our officer and comes so seldom to our platoon.'

'No, I will not have a *cigrut*,' Lok Nath said, 'but Kirpu is right. Officers and men belong to one family. In the English regiments they play their games together, work together and share all the discomforts together ... The difficulty with our Hindustani regiments is that the ranks lose all sense of respect for their superiors as soon as the officers begin to mix with them ... I learnt drill instruction from a Sergeant-Major Sahib in a Gora regiment, and the thing which impressed me was the devoted and fatherly care which every English officer, from the second lieutenant to the *Karnel* Sahib, had for all the men under his charge. Just father-mother. And, from the fact that they are all equally white, eat the same food in the same way with forks and knives, you might think that the Tommies do not respect their officers. But, this was a revelation for me for which I was hardly prepared. They did. They always recognized the status of an officer ... They may look small and insignificant, but they know how to observe discipline: they click their heels and salute as if they were machines. Our sepoys are lazy and inefficient and disrespectful ...'

'The French soldiers seem like us,' young Kharku said from somewhere in the dark.

'That's why I have been hard on you at times when you were recruits,' said Lok Nath. 'I learnt a good deal from that Sergeant Major, Hudson Sahib his name was. And I don't mind telling you that he sometimes slapped my face. Of course, I did not get angry like our recruits because I knew it was for my good, I have always respected a strong-headed man who will make a man of you and teach you how to fight ...'

At that stage, Havildar Lachman Singh came up, shouting: '*Ohe* where are you, *ohe* Kirpu, *ohe* Bapu, *ohe* Lal Singha?'

'Here we are,' the men shouted in a chorus. 'Here *Holdara* ...'

'Subedar Major Sahib wants to see you,' said Lok Nath, standing up as Lachman Singh came in.

' have been to see him,' Lachman said.

'God, what is the time, Lachman? We are dying of this congestion!' exclaimed Babu Khushi Ram puffing and blowing to express his anger at Lok Nath's blusterings.

'I can't understand this *Sansar*! Where is the war!' murmured Daddy Dhanoo. 'When does this train start?'

'What is the time, *Holdara*?' asked Lalu.

'Now I can't answer you all,' Lachman said. 'Make room for me. I can hardly see you.' And he stumbled a little.

Upon this Lok Nath said: 'I shall be going.' And he began to carve his way out.

'It is getting on for two o'clock in the morning,' said Lachman. 'And the train is about to start.' And he struggled to sit down, rather surprised that the corporal should have been among men whom he despised. When he felt that Lok Nath was out of audible distance he said in a whisper: 'Wants my recommendation to get promotion now!'

'Oh, is that what the matter is with him?' said Kirpu.

'I wondered why he was so nice to us sitting here.'

'I think he is frightened of the war,' said Babu Khushi Ram, 'and he may have felt lonely.'

'But he seemed to give the impression that he won all the wars for the Sarkar,' said Lalu.

'Oh, he puts on airs, the illegally begotten!' said Kirpu. 'I understand him, but what I can't understand is why this train won't move.'

Just then, however, the engine spat a lot of steam into the night, made a noise like the protracted neighing of a hundred horses, whistled a heart-rending, agonized shriek, as if it were unwilling to carry its load of orphans to the jaws of death, but at last began to move.

'Ram! Ram! thanks be to you!' explained Daddy Dhanoo. 'Lok Nath is gone, is he? God is on our side.'

'Forget that bastard, there is no one of his name here,' Kharku said.

The sepoys laughed at this ambiguous reference.

'The Karnel Sahib was very worried,' Havildar Lachman said leaning over to Babu Khushi Ram.

Lalu knew that Havildar Lachman Singh's 'worried' meant a little more than mere anxiety. Was there any special reason why the train was so late in moving? What was happening? Apart from Havildar Lachman Singh, no one who had a stripe or a star would tell them anything. Not even where they were going ...

A soft breeze was coming in like the breath of heaven itself and the names of God multiplied on the lips of the sepoys.

Lalu shuffled himself into a restful position and slept fitfully.

॥ 3 ॥

THE BREATH of heaven which the sepoys had wished for before the train
left Orleans station had soon become a cold draught, rushing through the
doors of the trucks, stealing through the slits and creeping into the flesh,
till no one envied the lot of the regiments which were travelling in open
trucks.

Lalu had slept fitfully through the night and morning, the combative
roar of the train dinning into his ears and breaking the irrelevant, disconnected thoughts in his head into absurder irrelevancies

And then the mature morning itself pressed the full weight of its light
on his eyes. He sat up and shook his clothes and rubbed his face with his
hands to warm himself. His mouth was parched and dry with the stale
and acrid taste of the endless cigarettes he had smoked, his nostrils closed
with the touch of a cold and his eyes were still glued. He yawned, twisted
his limbs and looked out of the door. A long stretch of corn-growing plains
lay interspersed by the pale vegetation of small forests.

'In December the pot boils in this country, then?' Kirpu was saying to a
young French soldier who sat by him.

The soldier could not understand this and said something in broken
English.

'Monsieur says,' Babu Khushi Ram interpreted as he crouched a
blanket round him, 'in December it is very cold.'

'Who in the name of saints is he?' asked Lalu opening his eyes wide.

'He is the orderly of the French staff officer who is travelling with us,'
said Khushi Ram.

'Then, we shall die of cold,' said Daddy Dhanoo. 'If it is colder than this where we are going.'

'Your days are numbered anyhow, Bapu,' said Uncle Kirpu.

'Look at uncle assuming the airs of a prophet!' said Lalu as he turned towards the Frenchman.

He wanted to talk to him. But, as a preliminary to opening negotiations, he got up, opened the door of the carriage to get a breath of fresh air, poked his head out and suddenly withdrew it, for a gust of cold breeze caught him full in the face.

'What is the name of this man, anyhow?' Lalu ventured.

'Francois St. Denis,' the soldier answered, smiling in a very homely manner and bowing even as he rubbed the two days' growth of unshaven beard on his face.

'Fron, fron, fron,' mimicked Kirpu, deliberately clumsy.

'What has he been telling you, then, uncle, this man?' Lalu asked in a whisper.

'What do you mean, "what has he been telling you, uncle?" Fool! He speaks *Angrezi*, why don't you ask him?' said Kirpu. 'Of course he talks like a man, not like the grinning, young scoundrel of an ape that you are, except that he asked me how many wives I had ...'

'And how many wives have you?' asked Lalu loudly. The whole compartment exploded at the question.

'He has got five that I know of,' said Havildar Lachman Singh, waking from where he had dozed in a crouching position.

'Five,' Lalu said. And then showing his five fingers to the Frenchman he said in English, 'Uncle Kirpu — he has five wives.'

'Yes,' the soldier said, quite credulous in spite of the laughter in the compartment. And, smacking his lips, he leaned over Uncle Kirpu and said, 'Good, eh?'

'*Nahin*,' Uncle Kirpu said, waving his head and his hands to signify that it was not so.

But the Frenchman seemed the more convinced by Kirpu's protestations that he really had a harem.

'Every Rajah has ... four wives. Haa?' he asked.

'Rajah, Rajah, me no Rajah,' protested Kirpu, histrionically affecting to speak English.

'It is different with the Rajahs,' Babu Khushi Ram explained. 'They can afford a hundred wives, but the poor people only have one wife — the same in India as in your country.'

'You have no polygamy?' said the Frenchman. 'Then I no like your country.' And he laughed and the sepoys laughed with him, the more when Lalu explained the meaning of what the Frenchman had said.

'Ask him what his father does, what profession,' said Kirpu.

'Ask him where he comes from,' called tubby Dhayan Singh from the corner where he lay sprawled, panting but not uncomfortable with a grin on his cherubic face.

'*Han*, ask him what is his father's name,' insisted Rikhi Ram with a surly indifference, his lean face wrinkled from under his artful eyes to his beaked nose.

'In this country every one has a family name like his name St. Denis, and then a first Christian name added to it, as his name Francois,' said Lalu.

'All right, all wise, we know that you are very learned,' said Kirpu, 'but ask him what his family does for a living.'

Lalu interpreted Kirpu's question.

And the Frenchman began to tell the story of his life with gusto, using his head and his hands profusely. The sepoys listened though they couldn't follow a word and abused him affectionately the while, calling him a jackanapes, a white monkey, a doll, a raper of his daughter, as they were pleased with the extraordinary informality with which he had joined their company. Afterwards Lalu interpreted:

'His father was a peasant and he was a field worker. Then he ran away from home and worked in a shop. At the age of eighteen he was called for military service. Then he became apprenticed to an artist and later took a job painting wax figures in England. And then the war came and be returned and is now in the army. He comes from Rambouillet, where the President of France lives, near Paris, capital of France...'

'*Ohe*, you are an owl indeed,' said Kirpu. 'Did you ask whether he owned land, whether they plough the land, like us, with oxen? Whether they use a plough to break the soil, and the scythe and sickle to cut the crop, and flail? And how they thresh? That is what we want to know, and what is their religion? Do they wonder about this existence? And believe in Karma!'

'Don't bother him any more,' said Babu Khushi Ram. 'You people don't see that these *Goras* don't like to be pestered.'

'You mean the officers don't like to be pestered,' said Kirpu. 'I know you urinate in your pyjamas when you hear the Karnel Sahib's footsteps. But both the Tommies and *Francisi* soldiers are different; the *Francewallas* like to talk and are friendly. At Orleans they offered us cigarettes. In Hong Kong I got on well with the American sailors ...'

'I want to know whether his father owned the land he cultivated,' Daddy Dhanoo asked with redoubtable common sense.

'He says that his father was a field worker,' said Khushi Ram, 'a mere labourer and owned no land though I can't understand why the peasants in this country should be so poor. After the revolution, the land was divided up and the peasants who were slaves were given small holdings.'

'The people who give you small holdings take them back,' said Kirpu sardonically. 'It is the same in the Kangra district as in Franceville and in China. In the reign of Raja Sansar Chand ...'

'You have told us of that before, uncle,' said Kharku, the mischievous mascot.

'What religion, you?' the French soldier suddenly asked Lalu. And he pointed to Kirpu and Dhanoo and Havildar Lachman Singh.

'Hindu, all Hindus,' Lalu said. 'Rajputs.'

'Ah, Rajapoot, Rajah, eh?' the soldier seemed to brighten up at anything in the remotest way connected with Rajahs about whom he had read strange things in the papers.

'No — fighting caste,' Lalu explained.

'Of course, their ancestors were once Rajahs,' said Khushi Ram tracing the etymology of the word 'rajput'.

'Ah ... *oui, oui* ...' the French soldier waved his head courteously, very impressed.

'Oh, leave the raper of his daughter alone,' said Daddy Dhanoo shrinking into his own shell, cold and apparently incapable of adapting himself to this land or its people. They have no religion. No law. 'They drink wine and make eyes at women. They believe in this life only. Eat, drink, shit!'

'And that is all you know,' exclaimed Lalu taking up cudgels on behalf of Europe. 'But Owen Sahib told us on the route march that the peasant here is laborious, independent, and a strong fighter ... To be sure, they have a religion like ours and their women work hard and are honourable, except a few; and here wine is drunk like water and no one is seen with his face in the drain as at home ... Yessuh Messih is their God!'

'But, son, they may be Sahibs or anything, but they eat cows and pigs and don't seem to practise much religion,' Daddy Dhanoo complained with the stubborn finality of age and orthodoxy.

'We are all "bledy fools", said Lalu. 'Hypocrites!'

'Now this is the result of becoming fashionable that you call everyone a "bledy fool" as the Tommies do, even people who are old enough to be your father,' said Kirpu. 'You have no respect for age ... And you have forgotten Guru Nanak.'

'In this Iron age ...' said Babu Khushi Ram indulgently but did not finish his moralization.

'He talks of their skill!' said Kirpu deliberately teasing the boy. 'Why this soldier doesn't even know how a Hindu is different from a Muhammadan and both of them from a Christian. Certainly, the Hindustani bullocks have more sense than to ask such absurd questions, as if every Indian is a Raja!'

Lalu was about to laugh at this when suddenly at that moment he sneezed.

'Die, die!' mocked Kirpu. 'God will punish you for your ways. Why don't you button your coat? Is that a new fashion? Now fetch that haversack of mine and I shall give you a medicine ...'

'Medicine!' the boy said. 'Not above drinking yourself, are you?' And he plunged his hand into the haversack for the bottle.

'I forgot I have it here in my coat,' called Kirpu with a mischievous glint in his eyes.

'*Acha*!' exclaimed Lalu. 'So you have been regaling yourself all night.'

'I bought it for illnesses like yours, swine!' explained Kirpu.

But Lalu had already snatched the half bottle of brandy from his hand and was going to apply it to his mouth.

'Give some to our guest first, you good for nothing fool!' growled Kirpu.

'Oh, forgive,' said Lalu and turned to Francois and offered him the bottle.

'*Merci! Merci!*' Francois whispered and smiling, bowed gratefully and put his mouth to the bottle!

Francois handed the bottle back to Lalu and the boy offered it to Dhanoo.

'Ram! Hari! Om! I won't spoil my religion! Are you going to apply your mouth to it after he has been drinking?' Daddy Dhanoo hissed and whispered, taking his hands to his ears.

'Oh, pure ones!' said Lalu and applied it to his mouth.

'*Ohe*, come, give me some,' said Babu Khushi Ram. And. making a wry mouth, as if he were overcoming all the scruples of the good Hindu, he began to gulp it down.

'Give me a little too,' said Dhanoo, stretching out a small cup of beaten silver which he always kept in his overcoat pocket with all his other odds and ends.

'Don't forget Havildar Lachman Singh and me in your greed now, brothers,' Kirpu said.

'The spiteful microbe of influenza is on its hind legs,' began Babu Khushi Ram, to cover his embarrassment at eagerly snatching the bottle after he had previously deplored the evils of the Iron age. 'We must all see the doctor when we get to our destination.'

Lalu laughed as he felt the lassitude of an unwashed, unkempt, soot-covered body mingle with a curious heaviness in his limbs in spite of the draughts of brandy which he had drunk. He stretched his arms and legs and then looked out of the door again.

A weak light shone on the bare trunks of trees and over the black mounds of freshly ploughed fields which stretched like the Punjab plains without any conspicuous ups and downs, except towards the depression of a ravine beyond which the steeples of a city were rising, overtopped by the tall spire of a church through haze which enveloped the whole landscape.

'Getting towards noon by the looks of it,' said Kirpu.

'To be precise like everyone in the Western world,' said Babu Khushi Ram looking at his wrist watch: 'Twelve twenty-five.

'I feel hungry,' Lalu said, and then thought to himself, I must get a watch, a wrist watch like that of Babu Khushi Ram.

'First wait till you can go to the latrine,' said Kirpu. 'Or have you become such a *pukka* sahib that you must eat and drink before your bowels move?'

'The station is coming near,' Lalu said, smiling, looking out again. 'I wonder if the train will stop here.'

The depression which had seemed to be a ravine became a winding river, looping away with the swollen waters of some recent rains and washing past a city which began beyond some bridges in a cluster of enormous old buildings browned and dirtied by time resplendent, antiquated monuments which seemed older even than the buildings of Orleans and Marseilles; a huge, solid city, a little frightening in its profusion and ageoldness.

'Rouen.' Lalu read the boards on the outskirts of the station.

'Where Joan of Arc was burnt,' informed Babu Khushi Ram.

'*Oui, oui, si, si,*' Francois nodded.

'Yes, I remember,' Lalu confirmed.

'Are they going to serve our food here?' asked Daddy Dhanoo to whom it was all the same where Joan of Arc was born or burnt, so wrapped up was he with the Eternal and His manifestations.

The song of soot and fire which the train had been singing subsided. The sepoys prepared to alight and straighten their legs, heaving their aching bones to the accompaniment of prayers, shouts, abuses, curses, and mimickings of French greetings.

They had hardly opened the doors of the carriages, however, when some N.C.O.S came with their faces screwed as if they all had toothache and, lifting their fingers to their mouths, pointing to trains with red crosses on them, counselled silence.

Before the N.C.O.s had explained anything the sepoys knew from the smell of medicines that spread from the trains on the adjoining platforms that they were full of wounded soldiers.

And there was a grim silence, only broken here and there by the loud oaths of a sepoy who had suddenly awakened and had not yet become aware of the necessity for calm, till almost the whole train-load of sepoys was spellbound. The men stared as if fascinated by a chimera that had been conjured up in their heads by the smell of blood and drugs.

'Where do they come from?' one whispered to another.'

From the war, of course,' the other whispered back.

But no one asked where the war was or why it was being fought and how it happened that they were going there. For there had been no answers to such queries in the past, and now they took it for granted. They only stared at the trains, probing the corners and crevices of the curtained windows for a sight of the wounded, smacking their tongues and waving their heads in sympathy, screwing their faces and spitting the while, because the smell of iodine and disinfectants spread thicker than in the wards of any hospital in the cantonment where they had been sent during bouts of malaria or for medical inspection or inoculation.

Lalu who had been one of the first and most impetuous to go to the door stood with his head protruding out of the truck, while Babu Khushi Ram edged him aside to lean out and see if he could get some information. But Havildar Lachman Singh was nowhere to be seen and Khushi Ram was waiting in the hope of being able to talk to one of the Indian or British officers who stood at the head of the platform by a canteen.

At length, after much shuffling. Khushi Ram decided to get out and go and talk to Owen Sahib, the adjutant. The peevish, little Babu had tended to be more and more unhappy with the fact that he was consigned to a sepoys' compartment. If not by the rights of his rank, which was Colour Havildar, then on account of his extraordinary position as the head clerk of the regiment, he thought he ought to be travelling with Indian officers in the second class.

Lalu stared in front of him and, wondering where the train of the wounded was going, he craned his neck and strained to scan the whole length of it — the engine was pointing in the direction opposite to their own train. Apparently it had come from the front.

A sudden tremor of dread spread like panic in his brain above the vague cloud on which hovered the confusion of silence. Would these soldiers ultimately die or recover from their wounds? ... The question seemed to come rushing up with the pressure of blood in his veins and become the subtle ache of trepidation. He stared vacantly at the Station Master, who was talking to some British officers even as he kept pushing his peak cap back ... Where was the war going on, north, west, east or south? ... It couldn't be far, otherwise the wounded wouldn't be here. But perhaps they were taking them away from the danger zone, though it wasn't much use for the poor men now to be saved. He himself would prefer to die rather than lose the use of a limb ... He wished he had a map of France. He had wanted to buy one at the shops in Marseilles and Orleans but he didn't know the French word for map ... Havildar Lachman Singh and even Babu Khushi Ram didn't seem to know where they were bound for either. Nobody knew ... nobody knew anything ...

The smell of the hospital train seemed to overpower him now. He shook his head and tried to extricate himself from the position in which he stood, but Kirpu was next to him and he had let another sepoy push his head into the door. He waited so as not to disturb them. But he felt the stench creeping into his nostrils while his veins swelled. He was faint. The bile of sickness was gathering saliva in his mouth. He kept rigidly where he was, hoping that the waves of nausea would pass. And he tried to breathe deeply as he felt the atmosphere getting rarer. Before he could move and recover, however, the dark of weakness descended on him and his head hung limply on one side.

'*Ohe*, he has swooned,' shouted Kirpu. And he exhorted: 'Get away, get away, give him air ...!'

And he bore the boy to the floor and shouted to the sepoy who held Lalu's feet: 'Give him air ... Get that bottle from my pocket ...' And he fanned him, and caressed him with soothing words: 'Come, my son, it was the thought of the wounded, eh? And that sister-in-law medicine, it is so strong! Come, my lion ... wake up ...' And he applied the bottle of brandy to Lalu's mouth, even as he ordered the men who gathered round: 'Get away, this is no fun, the boy has fainted because of you ...'

As Lalu awakened, his eyes fell on the swaying edges of equipment, and luggage in the truck, and he could feel the train jolting again. He smiled weakly and looked up at Kirpu on whose thigh his head lay pillowed.

'We are almost there, son!' Kirpu said.

'Where are we going?'

'To some siding, where we can eat, away from that stench.'

'Why doesn't this rape-daughter train stop?' said Daddy Dhanoo. 'The boy must be hungry.'

Lalu felt angry and ashamed for his weakness. And he raised his head to get up.

'Stay where you are, son, or you will faint again,' admonished Kirpu.

'Yes, you keep lying and rest,' said Lachman Singh.

'Give him some more of that stuff,' said Dhanoo.

The boy was dumb in the face of all this kindness.

It seemed unending, this tortuous journey into the unknown. And, when one's body was cramped from lying down at night and sitting up all day, when all the talk was done and all the sights seen, the fields and the foliage of the trees, the tapering crests of mountains and the deep navels of the valleys, the small wayside stations by which the train flashed like a cyclone, and big stations where it stopped to spread rumours about the strange characters of the *Arabian Nights* enclosed in it, when the food which the cooks had given at wayside station became stale and sickened, when all the restful postures of the body which one could adopt had been adopted and readopted, till every movement was a back-aching abomination, when all the thoughts that one could think had been thought, there was nothing to do but to endure it.

Lalu had dozed through the day lain and had therefore in a half sleep all night. He lay knotted now where he had sat hunched in a corner with his legs on Daddy Dhanoo's shoulders and his head on Uncle Kirpu's rumps, while both Dhanoo and Kirpu rested precariously on Lachman's trunk. His eyes were closed but he was awake and restless.

'Look, look, we have reached the sea!' said sepoy Rikhi Ram who was accustomed to rise early at dawn.

'The sea! The sea!' Dhayan Singh repeated enthusiastically.

'Oh, why don't you sleep?' muttered Uncle Kirpu.

Someone sneezed farther down the carriage, violently, once, twice, three times, and another muttered foul abuse and oaths as he still clung to his half-sleep, while others sat up dozing meditatively or eager to look at the sea.

'How could we be near the sea?' said one of them. 'Surely we are not going back across the black waters already.'

'There is a sea round France,' said Lalu rubbing his eyes.

'We are reaching Calais, perhaps,' said Havildar Lachman Singh coming to and arranging himself in readiness for duty. 'Sahibs say the ships go to *Englistan* from there ...'

'It is not an earthquake or a flood which is threatening you,' said Kirpu. 'Sleep!'

'If only you could see yourself at rest, with one leg in the sky and another in the netherworld,' said Lalu. And he looked out towards the horizon: a line of sea swayed mournfully under a colourless sky, while above the watery clouds — what was it? — a couple of seagulls wheeled over the rocks by the dull blue water. All was sombre and silent in the dawn, and cold.

The sepoys shivered in the early morning as they dozed or sat up and sought the semblance of warmth, donning their turbans and collecting their coats round their bodies and reciting whole chapters of holy verses, even as they lit cigarettes and sat serious and glum without talking to each other, looking out to see how near their destination they were.

Someone spat the morning breath out of his mouth.

Lalu got up to escape from the stale, acrid atmosphere, and went and stood by the door, balancing himself uneasily in the smallest space above the bodies of the sepoys, who sprawled on the floor, and he stared into the half light.

Above the boulders of high white rocks ahead of the train the contours of little white houses were beginning to define themselves. Although the châteaus edged on to the sea there seemed no beach and the tide seemed to cut right into the land to the shoulder of a great cliff on which clustered a group of houses.

Lalu wished that he knew the name of the place and where it was situated.

This seemed a big town. For as the train was skirting round a rock past rows of buildings he could see wide boulevards bordered by trees with kiosks and domed lavatories.

His senses tingled with eagerness as he imagined that they might stop near this town where there would be pleasures of sightseeing and drinking.

'Have we reached there, then?' the sepoys were asking. And, without waiting for an answer, they were beginning to get ready to alight.

'Fools, we are not going to get down here,' informed Havildar Lachman Singh. 'Tea will be served in the train. And then the train will start again, but we are nearing the front. So be vigilant...'

The engine shrieked as if demanding the all clear signal, as it slowed down by the outskirts of the town. A strong smell of fish came on the nimble autumn air from the quayside which was full of ropes and masts and the funnels of small ships and sailing boats.

He wished he could get a view of England from here.

'There are no diamonds studded to that harbour,' said Kirpu pricking the boy's sentiments. 'Nor is *Vilayat* studded with rubies.'

'I hope I shall see *Vilayat* before I go back home,' he said. He felt that he would not be able to tell a complete story of his adventures to Gughi, Ghulam and Churanji if he had not been to England.

This eagerness for *Vilayat* became a riotous panic as the train reached Calais station congested with uniforms.

But there came noise of raucous shouting above the din of the slow engine. They could see hordes of European soldiers standing by cattle-truck trains, who lifted their hands and cheered the sepoys: '*Viveles Hindus!*'

The sepoys rushed to the doors and cheered back in the only English greeting they knew; 'Hip hip hurrah!'

The echo filled Lalu's heart with a sympathetic exhilaration. He wanted to rush out and shake hands with them.

But as the train came to a standstill, Havildar Lachman Singh was giving out the orders: ... 'All ranks ...'

The cheering had died down almost as suddenly as it bad begun and there was a confused babble of voices. In spite of Havildar Lachman Singh's clear orders the sepoys were asking how long they were to stop here and how far the front was. And they were venturing vague guesses and all kinds of explanations. As Lachman Singh had gone out towards the officers' compartment, they were in suspense.

In the undarkening morning Lalu could see a few civilians, mostly women and children, presumably relatives of the soldiers, sitting peaceably on numerous and diverse packages, even as he had often seen people in India sit down anyhow on odd bundles on the platforms of railway stations. And, as before, during his journey through France, so now, he felt how like the Indians the French were. The frail, sombre French women, patiently waiting there, looked so like the Indian women. Even the black clothes they wore were the colour preferred by the matrons in India. Of course, the styles of clothes were more uniform here. The women's dresses were more fashionable and showed their bodies. And, somehow, these women were more desirable.

He looked intently among the group seated on the platform, so that perhaps he could discover a pretty face to linger on. But they seemed sad and forlorn as they sat there, their noses red with crying ... And he felt embarrassed and irreverent to be looking at them with desire and he lifted his gaze and scanned the platform.

Throngs of French soldiers stood by awaiting trains, lounging against the doorways. With their shuffling gait, some in red trousers and blue coats, but mostly in khaki, they were not models of soldierly bearing, according to the definitions he had learnt through the kicks of Corporal Lok Nath. He couldn't make anything of their quick voices, shouting greetings and speaking subtle inflexions of their queer lingo. But they seemed lithe and active and hearty though they were small, even smaller than the Tommies.

'Are we going to get some tea or coffee in this place?' asked Kirpu as he still lay huddled without betraying much curiosity in the world of Calais station.

'Havildar Lachman Singh has gone to see, Impatience!' said Lalu.

Suddenly hoarse shouts came down the adjacent platform and eased the strain of waiting.

The soldiers who had crowded the platform by the train began to take leave of their aged mothers, fathers, wives and sisters and then hurry into the train.

'They even embrace before parting like us Hindustanis,' Lalu said. 'They are even like us in affection.'

'Rape-daughters! The men kiss each other on the cheeks,' said Kirpu.

Some of the women were crying even as his mother had cried when he had left home after the holiday. He was sad, because they were sad. His blood seemed to be congealed. And yet, there was an insidious fascination about their suffering, for he had never seen the Sahibs behave like this. Somehow the English in India always concealed their emotions. He himself had been shy in saying farewell to his own people. But he had done so from the mistaken belief that it was against fashion.

A woman on the platform was sobbing hysterically, a poor frail thing, as she clung to her husband while he was whispering something as he stroked her and soothed her.

Lalu waved his head as if he were drunk with a sudden tenderness now and he felt as if there was happiness in that embrace as well as pain ... He felt he could have taken Maya into his arms and soothed her like that ...

But the guard came shouting for the men to enter.

'Oh no, oh no, let the train not go. Let it not break their hearts,' Lalu said to himself agitatedly.

The guard was calling persistently, however, '*Envoiture! Envoiture!*'

The soldier who had been embracing his wife separated from her and went towards his heedless son who had been straying.

'Oh, go and be kissed by your father,' Lalu almost wanted to shout to the child.

But the soldier caught the lad, picked him up, threw him aloft as if he were a doll, and smothered him with kisses.

The train whistled.

One hurried flourish of his hand towards his wife who now stood sobbing and the soldier went into the carriage. The train began to move. The man was now blowing kisses to his loved ones. All the soldiers were blowing kisses to their friends, waving their hands, and shouting to their relations, while those left on the platform were waving little white hand-kerchiefs. The wife of the soldier was sobbing more hysterically as she held her child. She sobbed and sobbed and was going to wheel round like a sea-gull and sink when a porter held her and led her away.

Lalu sank back exhausted by the strain of the scene he had witnessed. He sensed that their parting might be forever.

On the other side of the station a cattle-truck train was coming in and most of the sepoys went stampeding to the windows to look and cheer.

At that moment, Havildar Lachman Singh came in and said: 'Belgian infantry there, coming back from the front. They have seen service and are returning to rest and to be re-equipped.'

'Where is the tea, *Havildara*? That's what we want to know,' asked Kirpu.

'The pot is boiling,' said Lachman.

Lalu got up to look at the regiment which had just returned from the war. He gaped at them. Outwardly they didn't look any the worse for having been in action, though their uniforms didn't look smart, but then the uniforms of the continental troops were loose and dirty anyway. And they had come through the valley of death.

'Tea!' Santu the cook shouted.

And the sepoys stampeded down to take their places in line.

The train shrieked and groaned out of Calais followed by the cheers of the Belgian infantry, who sprawled about on the adjacent platform.

Now they were really off to the front, he had been told, and they would soon get there. Soon he would see the real thing, the war, the final reality, and then he could reckon whether he would live or die — because people had been known to die in wars, though Uncle Kirpu seemed to have come unscathed through his various campaigns!

The countryside through which the train was moving at tortoise speed was flat after the grassy green of the hills and valleys, beyond Orleans. The cornfields nestling under the ragged, dirty dark were all stubble, except here and there were crops, which seemed like clover and beetroot or potatoes, still stood uncut by small farmhouses. And yet everything seemed as usual and there was nothing to show that there was a war on in this land.

Perhaps the train would land them right behind the front and they would have to get out at once and begin to fight the enemy. The train seemed to be dribbling along, slower than ever. He wondered naively if the engine driver was afraid.

And, somehow, he seemed to be contracting into himself, and felt alone, alone in the grey morning of this vast alien earth, beyond which was a vaster earth or a vaster sea, beyond which again was the vaster sky where every one faded away.

A dim star stood on the rim of the horizon.

Someone had said at school that the earth was only a chunk chipped off the moon when this planet had grazed with another in its rotation round the sun, and that it was only about as big as a small star. How much bigger must the other planets be then, how much bigger than the distances he had travelled? — And that was not the largest distance on earth, there being much longer distances which ships and trains and motors had spanned, distances which he would never be able to cover himself. And there were the snowy regions of the North Pole and the South Pole that no one had yet crossed.

He felt small in comparison with this gigantic world, a poor insignificant fool of a peasant boy who had had to run away from the village and join the army and who had now come to fight, a joke among these grown-up men for his new-fangled notions, a ridiculous fool in spite of the grave, wise airs he gave himself, small and feeble and half-afraid, among other frightened folk.

'What is the talk son, then?' Kirpu asked him.

'Until he comes under the mountain, brother, the camel says there is no greater than I,' said Lalu with a feigned humility.

'Your meaning in that the camel always sobs at loading time?'

At that instant the train creaked and pulled up somewhat like an overloaded camel. And everyone laughed. After a minute of suspense broken by whispers it jerked along again, like a branch line train in India, almost at the pace at which one could have walked or at least run along.

Lalu recalled how the peasants in Central Punjab often turned thieves and dacoits during famine time and boarded the slow trains, looted the passengers' property and disappeared into the forests. From their docile, harmless looks there was no chance of the peasants doing that here. And, anyhow, they wouldn't get anything from a troop train. But the enemy could suddenly attack the train and kill them all, loot their rifles and the few machine guns and the big guns that were being carried on some of the open trucks. Perhaps it was because of this fear that the train was going slowly: the engine driver was being cautious. They were certainly in a mysterious zone, and every move was being negotiated carefully ... There, the train was slowing down. 'What was happening?' Slower, slower ... it had stopped again ... for fear of Yama, God of death?

The air was filled with a deafening roar like the booming of the big gun at Brigade Headquarters at the hour of twelve. He looked out to see what it was. He felt tense and excited. But there seemed nothing unusual ahead of the train or on its sides. Only a farmhouse nestled under a few trees in the flat country which was wet and soggy. There was a nip in the air and it seemed that it had rained here overnight, though it had been quite clear the way they had come.

'The hour of twelve has struck,' Uncle Kirpu said.

At that moment, wonder of all wonders, Captain Owen came up to their compartment like a fashionable young yokel jumping to the footboard of a train.

'*Acha hai*, sepoy *log*?... Not far now – the destination!'

'God may sweeten your mouth for saying so, *Huzoor*,' said Kirpu. 'Come in and grace us with your company.'

Captain Owen smiled his gracious, shy smile, but did not enter.

All the sepoys turned to him with respect, arranging themselves the while.

'Don't move, as you were,' said Owen Sahib.

'This is like going to a war on the frontier, *Huzoor*,' said Havildar Lachman Singh, referring to the comradeship that was reflected in the

Sahib's visit, for he recalled how the British officers of the 69th had once shared the same lorries with the sepoys in Waziristan.

The Adjutant moved his head, then flushed and, shading his mouth shouted:

'Yes. *Jung!*' And he made a gesture of despair.

But his words were being smothered by the shrieking of the brakes, and, for a moment, he closed his eyes, and contracted his face. Then he said: 'Too much traffic near the front.'

'Come inside, *Huzoor,*' Kirpu said.

'*Sab acha?*' said the Sahib and, jumping down, walked towards his compartment.

'He is a good man,' Havildar Lachman Singh said as he left.

'Strange thing, the Sahib coming to talk to us,' said young Kharku.

'They want to give you heart,' said Kirpu who had himself been surprised.

'He is gentle,' said Lalu.

'I hear that the *Angrezi* Badshah is a gentleman,' said Dhanoo. 'But German Kaiser is bad tempered.'

'They are cousins, though, Daddy,' Lalu informed Dhanoo.

'He speaks well in our tongue,' said Rikhi Ram.

'It is not good for Sahibs to be so familiar with sepoys,' said Daddy Dhanoo. 'Some men will misunderstand ...'

Lalu moved his eyes away, caressed the silence, sat back and closed his eyes. What was the meaning of existence? he asked himself.

The next thing he knew was Kirpu shaking him and shouting at him: 'Wake up, lazy bones, we are there!'

Lalu opened his eyes, yawned and stretched his arms to relieve the fatigue of his body.

'Stretch your hand to your pack and do something useful, son, come hurry,' admonished Kirpu impatiently.

For orders were ringing through as the train pulled up by a small station, deserted except for a few straggling soldiers.

'Come, sons, hurry,' said Havildar Lachman Singh. 'This is the station where we are to alight.'

Lalu stretched his hand to his pack even as he looked out and explored the surroundings, as if he expected to see some novelty on the platforms of this railhead which was the destination of the long journey across thousands of miles of land and sea, as if he had expected to see a marvellous station with towers and cupolas. But there was nothing new about the drab sidings in the wilderness, except that presently he could see a few more soldiers. A contingent of transport wagons stood farther up and there were motor-car ambulances on the road beyond, with red crosses on them, also field batteries, rolls of barbed wire and ammunition boxes.

'Come along, come along, boys, hurry and form up on the platform for the roll call,' said Lachman Singh. 'The camp is a few miles march from here.'

'69TH RIFLES! Company commanders forward! Right turn!' Colonel Green's voice rose sharply above the babble. Then it fell to a conversational aside, 'Pass the word back.'

The company commanders passed the orders, and hundreds of forms shuffled and swung round, with an efficiency that had to be repaired by angry whispers and hard looks from the Indian officers and N.C.O.s: 'You have slackened through the journey.'

'Quick march!' Colonel Green shouted. 'Pass the word back!' The regiment began to move.

'Lef-right, lef-right, lef ...' the company commanders breathed the words like an incantation to put vigour into the sepoys' feet.

And soon the regiment was tramping along with the hard military tread which had become second nature with them, relieved to be easing their joints, which were stiff and cramped from two days of inactivity.

There was nothing much to see during the first half a mile except the monotonous stretch of the flat country, with a solitary French, or English sentry at a level-crossing who saluted the Colonel. But as they went across a little bridge by a few hamlets, a motor cyclist shot by on the narrow road, smiling and curious. And, about half a mile ahead a French gardener came walking ahead of his cart, which was loaded with vegetables. The old man did not stare at them as most of the natives seemed to, but he just stood and held the reins of his pony to wait till the sepoys had passed, impassive, with his head slightly bent.

The slow rumble of a gun rose from somewhere in the direction in which they were proceeding, and disturbed Lalu's thoughts as well as his steps. But before he had time to move an eyelid there followed a huge detonation ... So they were getting nearer the real thing. And, suddenly, he wondered if he would ever march back the way he was going to the front ...

'Gird your loins, now, boys,' said Uncle Kirpu. 'We are in it ...'

'We are in it up to the tuft knot — with that thunder!' agreed Daddy Dhanoo awakening to the realities beyond the world of snuff and sleep. 'But how far would you say is this artillery, Kirpu?'

'If the war be in Landi Kotal, then you are in Landi Khana and the cantonment of Peshawar has been left miles behind — that is about the distance,' answered Kirpu.

At that instant there was a distant roar and the men in the ranks seemed to scatter like horses in a cavalry, shying at the sound of danger.

'No big words when the camel is swept away,' said Uncle Kirpu shaking a little. 'Like the ant I say, "I must find shelter".'

'Oh, you will seek safety and leave us behind.' said Lalu.

'Come, come, son, have a heart,' said Dhanoo. 'Uncle is only joking. We shall be together wherever we go ...'

They were nearing a cluster of houses, thicker than most of the farm-house Lalu had seen during the railway journey and thinner than a village, outside which some women and children and a few old men were collecting something in baskets from the fields.

'There are so few people here — the land seems deserted,' said Kirpu.

'To be sure it is deserted,' said Lalu. 'There is a war on, and most of the men are away fighting. The young men are at war and you can see from the slow gait of the bent figures who are picking potatoes that they are past their prime ...'

A group of bedraggled French soldiers who were busy cleaning the putrid black mud out of the ditches, full of autumn leaves and weeds, looked up for a moment at this strangest of armies and then resumed work unconcernedly.

Lalu's eyes were attracted by the shadow of the roofless church whose steeples lay broken by deeply rusted walls, beyond the square lined with vehicles of all sorts and sizes, by houses which were mere debris.

'That is war,' he almost muttered to himself as if to convince himself that a war was on. For, farther ahead, on a bridge which spanned a stream some villagers sat fishing completely unconcernedly.

The columns ahead were coming to a standstill at the shouting of orders by N.C.O.s, and it seemed they were going to rest here a while before going on.

Some food tins, jam jars, cigarette boxes and torn envelopes lay strewn about, from which it seemed that soldiers had rested here on their way to, or back from the front. But such rubbish could be seen anywhere by the canteen of an English regiment in a cantonment in peace time, and was no proof of war.

The element of sanity in Lalu persisted in the face of guns and in the face of the insanity which had blown off the towers of the churches, and he could not believe that ordinary men and women of good sense, and the Governments of France, England and Germany, which were saner and wiser than the ordinary people over whom they ruled, could be engaged in a war in which men were being killed and wounded and houses shattered.

As the regiment moved out of the village again after an hour's rest and refreshments, they met a platoon of stalwart black troops who wore white turbans and white tunics with red sashes, long, baggy trousers and scarlet stockings.

'*Habshis*,' said someone in an undertone half-suppressed by the clatter of marching feet, and there were other inquisitive whispers.

'They are sepoys like us of the *Francisi* Army,' said Havildar Lachman Singh. 'Watch your step, boys, watch your step! ...'

'But they have got curly hair and are jet black and not brown as we are,' young Kharku protested, his belief in the superior brown skin of his inheritance shocked by the comparison which Lachman had put them to.

Lalu stared at the swarthy faces of the black troops aglow with white teeth and was greeted with smiles. His face paled with embarrassment, however, and he withdrew his eyes. Assuming a natural air, he tried to think what nationality they could be. They were black like the Africans, but, unlike the thick-lipped Negroes, their features were ordinary.

'Moors,' the word came down from Havildar Lachman Singh who had asked the company commander.

Lalu felt guilty at having averted his eyes from them. At Marseilles he had seen a few African soldiers talking openly to girls in the cafés and the French Sahibs did not mind, though he himself had been rather surprised, for the English did not like even the brown-skinned Indians to look at white women. He wondered how the English liked the French being so free and easy. And if the French liked the blacks, why shouldn't he like them? Why had he thought himself superior? He felt ashamed. But he and the other boys at school used to mock at the black sons of the Madrasi Babu in the Deputy Commissioner's office.

'Why are you excited like a cobra?' Kirpu asked.

'Because we are owls,' said Lalu in self-reproach.

'To be sure, you are,' teased Kirpu.

'*Ohe*, fool, Uncle, we didn't return the salaams of those Moorish sepoys,' Lalu said impatiently.

'They are surely savages, are they not?' ventured Dhanoo.

'They are not the same as Hindus, or Muslims, or Sikhs, who have a religion!'

'Don't talk like a Brahmin dog,' whispered Kirpu. 'They have some religion. The Chinese in Hong Kong are followers of the *Budh Mat*, and surely every people has its own religion and God is one, and whether they be black or yellow or pink they all have eyes, legs, arms, heads: "Naked we came into the world and naked we will go" ...'

'You have a head, a pin also has a head,' Lalu mocked at Kirpu, so that Kirpu laughed.

'So they too have some religion,' Daddy Dhanoo muttered lamely.

But Kirpu dropped the subject, and they walked on seeing only the calves of the men ahead of them.

It was dark when they halted by a collection of farmhouses which they were told was the village of Arques. Half the troops were ordered to rest here while the other half were dispatched to a village whose name sounded like Bunderpur.

The 69th Rifles was to rest in Arques.

The sepoys who were to stay felt relieved after the wearing march through the dismal plain, dotted here and there with farmhouses and clumps of trees whose amber and copper hues were blackened by a thickening mist.

As they waited about in the grey afternoon on the crossroads by the old low houses of the village, groups of women and children gaped at them.

'Come children,' Uncle Kirpu said, affectionately to the boys and girls who had left their game and rushed excitedly to join their playmates who already stood staring at the sepoys. Then he beckoned to a little girl who clung to an elder sister.

The child, finger dubiously in her mouth, stood shyly hesitant.

'Come *Mooni*, come here,' Uncle Kirpu called her endearingly in his dialect.

The elder sister of the child encouraged her to talk but the little girl stood peering at the strange phenomena of turbaned, brown men, with her untrusting hazel eyes.

'Come, daughter, come,' Daddy Dhanoo coaxed.

But she still stood shy and enigmatic.

Whereupon Uncle Kirpu lunged forward and picked her up in his arms and caressed her in the best fatherly tradition of India. Just then Major Peacock Sahib, the regimental second-in-command came that way. Kirpu did not know what to do. He was half-afraid to be seen holding a child, because in the Indian cantonment the sepoys were asked to refrain from touching the English children who were to be seen playing with their ayahs by the Sahibs' bungalows. Also, the N.C.O.s had dropped hints that the Sahibs did not like the growing familiarity between the sepoys and the inhabitants of this country. But the Major Sahib, hard in ordinary times, smiled to see the pale, flustered Kirpu, changed his course and left the doting sepoys to amuse themselves.

At this Daddy Dhanoo got courage and, fumbling into his pocket, brought out a copper pice and gave it to her.

'What is the use of that Hindustani coin to her?' Kharku said.

Dhanoo fished into his pocket and brought out a nickel anna which he pressed into the hands of the elder girl.

'Since you can't find anything more suitable than that,' Lalu said, and he got some centimes out of his breeches pocket and threw them into the air.

The children ran for the loot, shoving, pushing and snarling.

'They are like little monkeys,' said Kirpu affectionately. And he set the child in his arms down.

Hardly had he put her down when she cut and ran towards the loot.

'There are swarms of them,' Dhanoo said genially.

'I suppose in a cold country like this the love game is the only pleasure of the poor,' Kirpu said.

'Oh Uncle!' exclaimed Kharku. 'Same is in Hindustan.'

'Uncle is no trouble,' said Kirpu. 'Uncle is in love with the saints. Uncle is a saint. But even saints can lose patience with the way we have to wait about in this campaign...' And catching sight of Havildar Lachman Singh, he shouted:

'*Holdara*! Where are we? Shall we ever move? ...'

'Men are tested when set to work, brothers,' said Lachman as he came sweating and intent. 'By the oath of God, the Sarkar is marvellous in its organization. Come, we are to rest in that lane there.'

There was no afterglow in the twilight of France, and they had to be wary as they groped along in the darkness and the mist, trying to keep clear of enemies. For their idea of the war was still of the campaigns on the frontier, where hungry tribesmen often came into villages dressed as goats, sheep or crows, looted rifles and ammunition and made off into the hills. The Germans might surprise them like the Afridis: from the loud detonations of guns, the village seemed to be very near the front.

As they reached a house off the main street which they were told was to be the quarters of No. 1 platoon, 2 company, some of them were detailed off to help the cooks to prepare the food and the rest lay down as if they had collapsed.

Lalu lay where he had drooped without wanting to move, only staring emptily through the gloom at the low ceiling of the small dark room, littered with straw.

There was a sound of heavy guns outside, however, and the sepoys were shouting: '*Ohe*! Undone! *Ohe*! Someone's time has come!'

Now Lalu ran out with the greatest alacrity.

Rockets came flying very low over the village, in the evening sky, like coconut grenades in the fireworks display on Diwali night at home.

Instead of running for shelter the sepoys rushed out into the streets to watch the wonder.

Lalu found himself stumbling over a rough mound, soft underfoot and smelly.

An N.C.O.s hurricane lamp illuminated the hillock for a moment; it was a mound of farm rubbish with the feathers of a hen scattered over it.

'Don't be frightened, my lion,' said a Sikh sepoy who stood by a sentry with a glistening bayonet.

But pop-pop, pop-pop, came another and sharper sound.

As they stood searching each other's faces there was a 'Bang-Thawack,' and the stuttering of machine guns.

They listened speechlessly.

And then there was the prolonged, unceasing rattle of musketry.

'The Sahib says that there is an offensive on not very far from here,' the Sikh sepoy volunteered the information.

'How far?' Lalu asked exploring the face of the sentry whom he guessed from the Sikh's words to be a Tommy.

'Only a few miles,' the sentry said, rather surprised to hear a sepoy speaking English as he had been conducting conversation with the Sikh with gestures and exclamations before Lalu arrived. 'It's only our boys getting at it,' he continued in a quick, incomprehensible accent which left Lalu vaguely guessing at his meaning.

'Never heard a gun before?' Tommy resumed the conversation after a while.

And then, as Lalu, unable to understand his words, remained silent, the sentry said 'Hope the Boche will get it!'

Lalu stood for a moment or two, embarrassed at not being able to catch the Tommy's words. Then he said 'Salaam Sahib' to the sentry and retraced his steps towards the billets.

For a moment he was not sure that he had taken the right way back. But the flame of his platoon's kitchen fire glowed and his eyes were used to the dark now. As he came towards the house he heard the men shouting, cursing and abusing; it was almost like meal times after parade in the barracks at Ferozepur when the sepoys rushed to the kitchens. He hoped the potatoes had boiled by now and been garnished.

On entering the outhouse where the cooks were, he found some of the sepoys already eating as they sat by the kitchen fire in the courtyard, while others quarrelled with the cook saying that the lentils were not tender and not of the right consistency. He hurried to get his aluminium plate from his pack.

'Where have you been, *Mishtar*?' mocked Kirpu as he sat in the light of two lamps. 'I have got food for you here; it is getting cold.'

'Oh — in one half of the village the feast of lanterns, in another half of the village the spilling of blood!' Lalu said, startled by the bright and cheerful atmosphere which prevailed in the billets. And he sat down to his meal.

Before he had swallowed a mouthful, however, Havildar Lachman Singh came in dangling a hurricane lamp and shouting across the street.

'We go into trenches tomorrow, boys. All ranks assemble for parade in the village square at 7.30. All ranks ...'

Lalu listened to the orders and felt a voracious hunger in his belly. He tore larger chunks of chapatee, dipped them in lentil gravy and filled his mouth with morsel after morsel. He felt curiously calm except for this voracity and ate as if he would never be able to eat again.

'I should turn in early, boys, if I were you,' said Kirpu, 'as it will be difficult to get up in the cold morning.'

But the boys didn't need much encouragement that night: they were tired and dozed off soon with the last belching after the meal, sleeping the sleep which follows a good day's march.

Daddy Dhanoo prayed late into the night.

The dead leaves of amber trees which lay on the sodden earth stuck to the sepoys' boots as they stood round to fall into line before marching forward to the area around Wallon Cappel, or 'Cappel Wallah' as they called it.

It had rained during the night, and thick clouds rolled across the sky gathering moisture from the fields, and concentrated in an ominous blackness in the east.

The cold fresh of the morning was bracing, especially as there was some delay in starting, though the mule carts stood ready loaded in the market square of the village, and all the other arrangements seemed to be complete.

'Squad-shun!' Lance-Naik Lok Nath's voice rang out. Apparently Havildar Lachman Singh was busy and Lok Nath, though transferred to No. 4 platoon, was still the second senior N.C.O. in No. 2 company.

Lal Singh hurried and fell into his place.

'Squad-shun!' Lok Nath snapped to hasten the men and growled, 'You have forgotten even to form a straight line since you have been in this country. Squad-shuns *Phormphor!*'

The odd numbers stood fast, the even numbers took a sharp pace to the rear and another to the right, all rather loosely.

'All ranks, pull yourself together, donkeys!' Lok Nath ground the words between his jaws, half injunction, half challenge. 'This is serious. We are on active service now. And each man will have to acquit himself so as to win honour for himself and his regiment!'

The boom of a gun cut Lok Nath's homily and shook the earth. The first dangerous sound to be heard that morning made the sepoys jump as they formed up in squads on the uneven cobblestones of the village.

As the corps got under way, leaving behind the group of squat square farmhouses with their barns, pigsties, stables and rubbish heaps, topped by a church, the men were ordered to sling their rifles across their shoulders and they turned their serious, sombre faces blandly towards the opposite sky, breathing fast and muttering a few good-humoured curses as they shifted under their trappings and felt easier.

The road emerged through the thick haze of the morning mist, across a bridge, under the shadow of a tall and elegant white château which stood superior, and remote on an incline like the bungalows of the Sahibs in India.

'The Sahibs slept there last night,' someone ventured the information:

This hardly needed confirmation, because just at that moment they saw the Colonel with the adjutant, and some other officers at the foot of the drive, and the voices of the N.C.O.s rang out: 'Eyes right!'

'There is our Lachman, too, with Owen Sahib,' said Kirpu.

'Where?' queried Daddy Dhanoo, eager as at the sight of royalty.

Lalu looked across the bare branches of the trees and the undergrowth, probing into the mysteries of the big house. It seemed like the residence of the landlord of the village. So here too they had landlords.

'A bit scratched!' he said as he saw the debris on a flank where a shell seemed to have caught it.

'The lord who owns it and who is said to be like our Rajahs in prestige is in a city called Paris,' Uncle Kirpu offered the information. 'His son is an officer and his Mem Sahib and Miss Sahib are working as nurses in a hospital.'

Everyone turned to him inquiringly, amazed at his comprehensive knowledge.

'How do you know all this?' Lalu challenged.

'Don't worry about how I know,' said Kirpu. 'There is only one consolation, these rape-daughters, the Sahibs, had as bad a night as we had. Some of them slept on the floor.'

'I suppose *Holdar* Lachman Singh told you,' said Lalu.

'Those frogs shouting all night made my sleep illegal,' said Dhanoo, straining beneath the weight of his pack, though his wiry frame seemed, in all its angularity, to be equal to these endless journeyings.

'There is no talk of frogs,' said Kharku. 'A rat almost nibbled the toes off my feet ...'

'You are not the only one, brother,' said Kirpu, always going one better. 'Last night there was such fun as you have never seen. Officers and men were all brought to bay by the pest ... But no one had the courage which I had in going to sleep out in the open. And no one saw what I saw: a huge balloon rise from the enemy's side over a lurid sky which was brought down by bullets from our side ...'

'You shot an arrow and pricked it, Uncle, didn't you?' mocked Lalu.

The sepoys sniggered behind him.

At that instant, however, a gun bellowed somewhere across the rain-soaked fields under the sky-line and a terrible stillness spread down the moving columns ... It was followed by another detonation, and another, and another at regular intervals.

'We are going to have some fun by the sound of it,' Lalu said after a second.

'Not yet, my son,' said Kirpu imperturbably, 'though I have heard a flying rumour that we will all embrace Goddess tonight! ...'

After a few miles march they began to see a town looming up beneath the roar of constant shell-fire which seemed to come more from the sky overhead than from any particular direction.

'Is it Lund or Kake Wallah?' Kirpu asked.

And the answer came back from somewhere up the platoon: 'Wallah Cap.'

On entering the town they were called to attention, and Havildar Lachman Singh read out further orders.

'Listen boys, listen: First Battalion Connaught Rangers, Ferozepur Brigade, will go by motor transport at once to Wulvergham to join Cavalry Corps under General Allenby. On the return of the motors, the 69th Rifles under the command of Karnel Green Sahib will move up to Wulvergham and join the 2nd Cavalry Division under General Gough Sahib Bahadur.'

'But what about the rest of the Brigade?' asked tubby Dhayan Singh.

'Aren't we all going into action together since we have come together?' queried Rikhi Ram.

'Shall we be separated even from our Brigade?' asked Kharku.

The sepoys seemed to be panic-stricken at the announcement.

'Our regiment will be together,' said Havildar Lachman Singh to console them. 'So we will be all right.'

But the sepoys edged away, their faces tinged with the regret that from now on there would be partings after which each man would probably have to go by himself. From the congregational life of their past and, more particularly, through the long journeys with thousands of sepoys, they had come to accept their togetherness as a law of nature and they had naively expected that they would all be put to fight side by side with each other.

'Where is Wulvaga?' a sepoy was asking.

'Where is the place, *Holdara*?' another repeated the inquiry. 'When are we going?'

'Why is it that only the *Gora* regiment and our regiment is going, Uncle?' Kharku turned to Kirpu. 'What is the meaning of all this?'

'The Sarkar is like a bitch, son,' said Kirpu. 'It barks its orders and does not explain. What I am concerned about is where are we going to stay.

Can't stay in the cold out here ... I hardly slept a wink last night: These Sahibs are ...'

'Illegally begotten!' added Kharku.

'*Holdara*!' Lalu shouted to Lachman Singh and went towards some of the sepoys who had caught the N.C.O.

'Now, boys, don't get excited,' assured Lachman. 'Be patient! Just a little patience and we are going to rest ...'

But the sepoys were inconsolable. They fell away murmuring and protesting weakly.

'Brothers, this is not the right talk!' complained one. 'They ought to tell us where we are going.'

'And why we are going,' added Lalu, so that the first sepoy did not know whether his colleague was joking.

A shell roared overhead.

But the sepoys did not stop their bickerings. 'Is this any talk?' 'What do they think, making us hang round here?' 'Rape-daughters!' They were now more concerned about personal inconveniences of life in an unknown land.

'This is only the beginning, my children,' said Kirpu the hardened campaigner.

And the sepoys turned to him, warmly, like a brood of chicks round the mother hen.

But a woman, with a dirty apron covering her black frock up to the waist, was grumbling at a bearded soldier, who stood playing with the children who were gaping at the sepoys by the water pump, smiles of wonder and apprehension on their faces. The profusion of her eloquence rose above the babble of the sepoys so shrilly that they dropped their complaints and became engrossed in the domestic war that seemed imminent as the woman came with upraised hands to beat the goat beard.

The sepoys laughed and stood about unconcernedly.

Soon Havildar Lachman Singh came and beckoned the men of No. 2 company to follow him.

They moved up desultorily to the crossroads at the entrance of the town where Colonel Green was talking to some officers.

A member of the billeting party came up and saluted Owen Sahib and Jemadar Subah Singh. The Jemadar turned to the men and ordered:

'The men will disperse and get their meals, after which the general orders are that the men will remain off duty till tomorrow morning.'

'God be thanked for granting us this rest,' Dhayan Singh sighed, exhausted by the endless journeying towards he knew not where.

'Now we shall be able to sleep our full sleep out,' said Rikhi Ram.
'Soon, you will sleep forever!' someone said.

As if to remind them that they were not being spared for ever if they were being allowed to rest now, Jemadar Subah Singh said: 'Until tomorrow at dawn, remember!'

'Oh God! Oh heavens! Cold in the mornings!' howls of impatience went up.

For once Havildar Lachman Singh found himself in agreement with Lok Nath and Jemadar Subah Singh as he rebuked them.

'They never slept on straw, but they now dream of beds.'

On the afternoon of the next day the 69th was ordered to move to Wulvergham near Ypres by motor buses which returned after conveying the Connaught Rangers to the trenches.

There was a chilly wind blowing across the road on which the motors stood lined and a thin blue haze gathered over the hedges like the whispered grief of naked fields supplicating to a hard grey sky.

The sepoys walked up shivering from the cold, but silent as if they had arisen from some melancholy sleep.

'Bay horses in all their eight joints, these motors,' said Kirpu as he surveyed the buses.

'Look at your heel, lest you drop while it flies away,' mocked Lalu as Kirpu was stepping up.

'My heel has no wings: it isn't like your imagination,' retorted Kirpu.

'But these motors have wings,' said Lalu.

And, naive as they were, there was a rush of men behind Kirpu eager to see if the motor really had wings. But they found only hard wooden seats. They scurried inside for fear of the cold on top. They had hardly settled down when the engines started and began shaking the great hulks of the buses.

Some of the sepoys looked wistfully at the members of other regiments who had gathered round to see the 69th depart, while others smiled embarrassedly or laughed artificially over a joke. And, as the buses began to move, there were half-hearted attempts at calls of battle in their own tongue.

They passed through the main streets of the town into a winding road, dotted here and there by chalets, which looked ruggedly unimpressive behind the undergrowth of vegetation, like deserted ruins.

A slow crawl across the wooden bridge over a stream and the buses began to ascend a hill crowned by a white château.

But the road soon declined to the surface of flat, low fields deeply rutted by the footprints of peasants, who had recently traversed them.

The cold wind swept across their faces. Uncle Kirpu sat grimly silent and Daddy Dhanoo was shrinking into his huge uniform, while Lalu sought warmth in the smoke of endless cigarettes, ruminating on the curse that the machines seemed now to him who had thought of them as wonders of the new age. Was there a *Satyug* which his mother often talked about?

The sound of rifle fire could now be heard distinctly and they felt excited at the immediacy of the front.

A gun belched in the folds, of some distant fields, in which direction no one could tell, and there was an echo, and then another gun belched or the same gun belched again ... But neither the earth, nor the sky, nor the air seemed to be any different after the thunder had died down, as if just because the guns were not visible they had no relation with the universe, as if they were just booming in some unknown world, far away.

Lalu stared wide-eyed into the distances beyond the open stretch of desolate fields, beyond the wooded hills into the danger zone, to see where they were going, but his gaze returned empty of content and turned inwards, baffled by the experience he was going through, this strange enterprise to which his destiny had goaded him as if according to a prearranged plan, considering how he had run away from the village suddenly and joined the army just a year before he was pushed into active service in Europe where, after the felicity of a day's sojourn and constant journeyings, he had now to face up to the threat of a consummation which he had never wished for nor dreamt in his wildest dreams.

The bus gathered speed in the effort to catch up with the Motors ahead, bumping its way on the rutted road, charging into the unknown ...

———

'The 69th there! The 69th!' Someone greeted them from the shadow of a wood which skirted round the bluff of a hill at the foot of which they had alighted.

They could now hear the spasmodic bursting of rifle and machine-gun fire like the barking of dogs on the outskirts of the village.

Lalu stood away with some of the Sepoys on a patch of ground by the roadside where a big gun stood hidden under dry leaves and twigs almost in the lap of some Tommies who were busy securing an aim at something beyond the uprise.

The orderly who had come calling from the 69th clicked his heels and saluted the Colonel.

For a moment everything was still and, from the whispering and the undertones, the situation seemed very serious.

The orderly officer who had greeted the colonel stood quite casually up the road as if he did not hear the firing at all.

Lalu brushed the back of his tunic and pulled it into shape. That done, he brushed his sides with his left hand and looked furtively about, eager to get a move on.

The colonel was talking to the adjutant. Then he ran to talk to the orderly Sahib in a manner in which he had seldom been known to run in the cantonment, and made quick gestures as he talked. The whole atmosphere seemed to become informal and disorderly as at a Boy Scout meet in Nandpur, especially as now the colonel turned and addressed them in broken Hindustani:

'All ranks! Attention! Half the battalion will be attached to the 4th Cavalry Brigade under General Bingham. The other half will be attached to 5th Cavalry Brigade under General Chetwoode! Both parts of the regiment will be near each other in the trenches. First six companies forward!'

No one understood the orders, as the colonel had spoken quickly.

'Number 1 company forward! By sections!' Major Peacock, commander of 1 company ordered in Sahib's Hindustani and there was a noise of heavy feet moving forward.

'Number 2 company forward! Owen Sahib ordered.

And Lalu found himself stepping forward.

'Right wheel. No crowding!'

'March!'

'Single file!'

As each platoon advanced the orderly officer who had met them ordered a runner from his party to attach himself to it to lead the men through the fields and show them the way.

The sepoys dived into a ditch and emerged on to a muddy track, slipping in the pits in the ground. The machine gun fire became incessant and they scattered to dodge the bullets.

A bright light rose near the crest of the hill on the road behind and, lifting their heads to see this phenomena and watching their steps at the same time, many of them took false ones ...

'There is no danger, boys, no danger, come along, my sons!' Havildar Lachman Singh whispered to reassure the sepoys.

The sepoys struggled ahead, swinging their shoulders, and heaving their rumps across the desolation.

A Tommy sat relieving himself by a dug-out covered with dry leaves and mud, and his white buttocks glistened.

'So we are not the only people who relieve ourselves on the ground,' said Uncle Kirpu significantly to Daddy Dhanoo.

The whole platoon burst with laughter.

They had hardly passed the dug-out when the bullets came whistling over their heads. All of them instantaneously lay down and ducked their heads as they had been told to do during practice. They were to wait till the bullets subsided.

'It is not the singing bullets which are so dangerous,' Jemadar Subah Singh passed the word of the runner, 'but the silent ones.'

'Come on, sons, come on,' Lachman called. 'Beware of the telephone wires and don't fall.'

They went forward hesitatingly, some laughing nervous chuckles, some abusing the bullets, others pale and grim.

By now half of No. 1 company had entered the communication trenches and was out of sight and the first platoon of 2 company was lowering into ditches. The men strove eagerly forward, almost tripping over each other's heels, in order to get out of the range of the bullets which came steadily over their heads with a weird half-fascinating song. The machine guns were snapping more frequently and the N.C.O.s ordered the sepoys to keep their heads down.

Now each moment seemed to Lalu to be his last, for the bullets came whizzing fast, invisible and deadly, from the sound of them ... But suddenly he jerked himself forward; for, on his right, by the opening of the communication trench some forms lay sprawled on the ground, their faces covered with their caps, their uniforms bespattered with blood, hard and inert, their putteed legs straight as logs of wood.

The runner of the platoon lifted the cap of one with a smile and made a gesture as much as to say 'finished'. The dead man's face was a curious coppery green, and elongated, as if in an angry snarl, his teeth showing the yellow decay, his glazed eyes staring hard.

The runner pointed to the boots of a corpse and made a sign as much as to say that he wished he had them. But then he smiled and waved his head to signify that he must not.

Lalu stared at the corpses and counted them. There were eight in number, eight dead men, hard and inert ... The man from whose face the runner had taken the cap seemed to have been about thirty. 'Finished,' Lalu muttered the word to himself stupidly. 'Dead and finished!' He wanted to lift the coverings from the faces of the others and look at them, but he was frightened to think that they would all be ugly and deformed. 'Finished,' he muttered again. 'After having prepared themselves for life all these years. Dead and finished ...'

A HAIL of lead greeted them as they advanced.

The sepoys tried to keep their backs bent and their heads lifted, according to the orders. Groups of Tommies stood in the trenches behind sandbags firing an occasional shot with their rifles, or clustered round a rare machine gun nest.

The trenches, or more properly ditches, since they were so shallow and narrow, were slippery, as the passage of many feet had kneaded the mud into fine dough.

'Keep your heads down,' Havildar Lachman Singh looked back and whispered cautiously all the way down the length of the column.

The trenches were certainly too small for these Indian stalwarts.

Lalu struggled eagerly through the ditches, keeping as close to Havildar Lachman Singh as possible. His gaze explored the indistinguishably similar faces of the Tommies, the belts of cartridges that lay like garlands round the necks of the machine gunners. Curiously, he felt thrilled to be among them, for, in spite of their haggard faces, the Tommies had not lost that look of exalted Sahibhood, respect for which was so deeply ingrained in these colonial troops.

But why were these trenches so shapeless and irregular? They were so different from the regular trenches built for mimic warfare in the parade grounds at Ferozepur. Perhaps these had been improvised.

'How far is the enemy from here, *Holdara*?' he ventured to ask Lachman Singh.

'Come on, son, walk along. We must follow the runner,' the Havildar replied, kindly but impatient.

Lalu lurched along listening to the ominous silence which was soon broken by a storm of bullets and the continuous barking of the machine guns. He would have liked to have been able to look over the sandbags.

'*Salaam*,' a Tommy who had apparently been to India greeted Havildar Lachman Singh from where he sat on the edge of the firing step, and then he smiled and nodded to Lalu and asked, '*Ache hai?*'

'*Salaam Sahib*,' replied Lachman. And he stopped to shake hands with him.

The Tommy had not quite expected such warmth, and his face was flushed though he gave his hand cordially, while some of the others smiled and mumbled greetings.

Lalu looked surreptitiously at the other Tommies as he went by, looked eagerly to see how life was being lived in the trenches. Some of them were sitting casually around, smoking, while, curiously enough, other Sahibs lay asleep in small dugouts and holes in the walls of the trenches as if they had 'sold their grains' and were enjoying a well-earned rest in the dirt.

'Asleep, very tired,' said a Tommy who stood by his rifle, pointing to a companion in the dugout. And he put his hand to his cheek to indicate a babe asleep even as he mimicked a mother singing a lullaby. And he offered a cigarette to Havildar Lachman Singh and Lalu. The Havildar smiled and declined, but Lalu took the cigarette and bent over the flicker of flame which the soldier held shaded under his cap.

'Leave these rape daughters alone, they are settled and we have yet to find our billets,' urged Kirpu from behind.

Lalu felt proud to be smoking this cigarette, and he wondered why these soldiers, who were so remote in India, had suddenly become so hospitable. Perhaps, they were always respectful to N.C.O.s, even in India, and he was only basking in the glory of Havildar Lachman Singh, the real recipient of the salaams.

His feet slipped into a puddle which he had sought to avoid and he lifted his hand to one side in an attempt to steady himself. Immediately a full tornado of shots fell on the sandbags.

'Steady! Steady!' the runner called angrily. 'Keep your heads down ...'

Lalu paled and shambled and felt a fool for thinking stray thoughts and not looking at his feet. And he rushed forward involuntarily, his heart beating and his body taut, watching every step.

But now the number of soldiers who manned the trenches was thinning and the runner at the head was beckoning Havildar Lachman Singh even as he indicated to the sepoys to sit down.

Lalu moved up through the empty trench a yard or two behind Lachman Singh. And while the Havildar ran to talk to the runner and Jemadar Subah Singh, where platoons of an English regiment were being relieved by No. 3 company of the 69th, he sat down by a cave and contemplated the sandbags which lay upon the parapet and the sodden earth at his feet.

So this was where they were to fight. He mopped the sweat off his brow, puffed deeply at his cigarette and looked for a hold in the sandbags to survey the enemy and get into position.

With his rifle adjusted into a hole in the sandbags, with Havildar Lachman Singh, Uncle Kirpu and Daddy Dhanoo at intervals of a few yards from him, and each other, with his neck craned over the butt end of his rifle as his feet rested against the back wall, Lalu stood in the dark, waiting for something to happen. The firing had stopped for a moment and he had not yet taken the first shot, both because he had been told only to fire occasionally in reply to the enemy's bullets, just to remind the enemy that 'we' were there and vigilant, and because it was a crucial act for him to fire the first shot, torn as he was between the excitement of shooting at a real enemy in a real war and the fear of killing the person he aimed at. The last feeling arose not out of any humanitarian considerations so much as from the feeling that if he did not shoot the enemy, the enemy would not be a gentleman and not make him a target.

He applied his eyes again to the hole in the sandbags, where he had fixed the muzzle of his rifle, to see what they were doing. But, apart from the contours of the sandbags on the opposite trenches, nothing was visible. And yet the inexorable pressure of his curiosity strained his eyes to explore the darkness, to look, to see and recognize the form of the enemy.

There was a burst of fire from a nest manned by the men of the machine gun company who had been put in charge of Havildar Lachman Singh. It was the first belt which they had probably fired to test their weapon since putting it together, and perhaps for the same reasons for which he himself was itching to have a go at his rifle. The enemy answered back.

'*Ohe*, keep your heads down, fools, if you value your lives,' Havildar Lachman Singh shouted, impatient and angry.

'Where are we, *Havildara*?' Lalu shouted lamely.

'Never mind where you are, son. Fire a round at them and give them the proper answer,' Lachman shouted back.

'The fool!' exclaimed Kirpu. 'Shoot for heaven's sake, shoot and keep at it. All armies have lived amidst the unknown ... You are not the only man who is left alone for a while ...'

Embarrassed and flustered and without taking aim, he pressed the trigger. The bullet fell somewhere in no-man's-land.

There was a lull in the air.

'That is the spirit,' encouraged Lachman. 'You see you have already stopped their barking!'

Lalu felt foolish and incompetent. He braced himself to take a precise aim and, closing his left eye, and tried to fix his target in order to shoot straight. He couldn't see anyone in the enemy line and waited impatiently for a while. After a few minutes he despaired of seeing the Germans and looked about for something else to shoot at. Again there was nothing in sight but sandbags ... At last he spotted a tin a hundred yards away in direct range. He pulled the trigger. No luck. But he was determined to get it. He began to practise his marksmanship.

The tension increased with the night. The rifle fire was continuous, and now and then the machine-guns barked as if each side was reminding the other that they hadn't gone to sleep.

Lalu lay in uneasy sleep in one of those little holes that had been dug by the previous occupant of the trench, clothes line and rifle rack all complete. The bunk in the dugout was cold, damp and suffocating.

He shifted about under the blanket and curled himself up into a tighter knot and listened to an enemy machine-gun which was more persistent than any other ... He pressed his hands between his knees, as if by so doing he would be warmer and tried to forget everything in sleep. The cold made him shiver, however, and his brain was in a whirl ... 'What are the enemy's intentions?' The question recurred in him as if he were a general, or a colonel planning a campaign. He felt he could do wonders if he were allowed to direct the battle. He would devise some kind of machine with which he could transport his armies across the enemy's fire on selected points of the front and take the Germans in the rear; or he would take over hundreds and thousands of soldiers in those airships they talked about; or he would — but the whole thing seemed absurd. He would try to sleep.

'*Ohe*! It is raining as at harvest time in the unluckiest year!' came Uncle Kirpu's voice from where he still stood by the parapet.

Lalu heard the pit-a-pat of the slow rain falling and, for a moment, felt selfishly secure in the clay cavity. But soon he felt conscience stricken for Kirpu, and Dhanoo, and Havildar Lachman Singh who had been so considerate as to urge him to sleep because they had seen him pale and tired. He felt he should go and join them, for there was no comfort lying here. He would rather that one of them came into this cold, dark, sodden hole and tried to sleep in it. He felt impatient and tried to think of something cheerful. He was trying to track incident after incident in his memory to pick on the most profitable train of thought when — he felt a veritable stream of water trickling down his face and neck.

'Oh, rape-sister, this rain!' he muttered.

But thinking that the water had flowed across the roof from the mouth of the dugout, he withdrew his head a little more snugly into his chest, squeezing himself farther down the hole as tightly as he could.

Immediately as he did so he felt his wet clothes hanging on to his side like icy rags. He lifted himself on his elbow and, stretching his hand to his waist, found his jacket soaking wet and mud-bespattered. He heaved himself and crawled out.

'Flooded!' he said emerging from the cave, for he had not even the energy to feel angry with the elements. And he passed his hand down to separate his uniform from where it was sticking to his flesh.

'Don't come riding on at us as a September cloud, all mud and dirt!' Uncle Kirpu said phlegmatically as he himself sat squeezing the rain water out of his knee breeches, while his rifle rested in an honoured place under a hood.

' "The peasant left his plough and met an accident," ' said Dhanoo philosophically.

Not finding a very warm reception from his cronies Lalu went up to the machine gun nest. A rivulet of water was flowing down by Havildar Lachman Singh's head, and the other sepoys sat in heaps like beggars in the monsoon.

'*Holdara*! *Holdara*!' someone called. 'Ajitan Sahib ...'

Before any of them could get up to salute as ceremoniously as trench conditions allowed, Owen Sahib and Subah had come steering through the mud and water.

'Lachman Singh,' Owen Sahib said in the anxious hurried accent of his broken Hindustani. 'Enemy is going to attack on the left flank where we entered the trenches. Hold yourself in readiness to cover the retreat of the men if necessary.'

Kirpu and Dhanoo adjusted themselves to the alertness of defence even before Lachman had transmitted the order.

Lalu went to his place, taut in every limb, mumbling stupidly, 'sleep or wake at your own pleasure.'

The rain fell persistently, raising a dense smoke over those parts of the trenches where the gun fire was deafening.

'How are we situated, *Huzoor* — to the enemy, where he is attacking?' Lachman Singh asked the adjutant.

A swift bullet went over the parapet as if in answer to the Havildar's inquiry.

'How are we situated?' asked the adjutant with a smile ... And then in a casual manner which was unlike the authoritarian attitude of other Sahibs, he began seriously to explain the position:

'We folk, the Dogra Company, are situated between Wystchaete and Messines. The Afridi Company is in trenches near a place called Oost Taverne farther away! Other companies are scattered over the intervening space. The enemy is beginning an offensive all along the line, which is situated on a ridge about eleven miles long. We hold the key to the town of Ypres. For several days there have been gains and losses on each side ...'

Punctuated by the resounding hail of fire on the left and by difficult incomprehensible names, the Sahib's words were difficult to catch, except to Kirpu who must have understood enough to raise a laugh when he commented:

'So, Sahib, we brave lions have come just in time to stop the enemy ...'

Owen 'Sahib laughed. The reputation of Uncle Kirpu as a humorist made the very sound of his voice infectious with light heartedness.

'*Huzoor!*' Jemadar Subah Singh called from where he had been talking to Kharku and Hanumant Singh. 'An orderly has come from Karnel Sahib ...'

Captain Owen shrugged his shoulders where he stood, smiled, salaamed and retreated, his long face longer than ever.

The sepoys followed his retreating figure in the dark wondering what the Colonel wanted.

For a while they stood in suspense, awaiting the attack.

Then the cannonading thunders seemed to abate on the right flank somewhat, though the rifle fire still continued like a rapid dysentery of lead.

A sepoy came up to Havildar Lachman Singh and said: 'Ajitan Sahib's orders. The enemy seems to have abandoned the attack, but all ranks must remain vigilant.'

The eyes of the night opened to the day, red-streaked and sore, and heavy lidded with fatigue.

Legs athwart, legs sprawled over the length of the trench, legs propped up to adjacent walls, legs bent and squeezed into knots, legs, legs, legs, a conglomeration of legs was all that was visible of the sepoys as they sat about in the trenches, gathering their coats and blankets about them in the cold, while a few stood at their post behind their rifles in the slime. Above their heads, the snipers' bullets could be heard continuously.

Lalu crouched as he alternately dozed and contemplated the layers of mud sticking to his boots. They would take a long time to polish, and oceans of spittle to brighten them. And inside the boots, his feet seemed frozen ... But that was nothing: under the damp puttees his shins seemed to have become wooden with cramp, while his right leg was sleeping as if it were paralysed. And he felt hungry — though he would rather he had a little fire to warm himself than food to eat.

He began to unroll the puttees and to rub himself to warmth. The thick woollen lengths sagged in his hands, sodden and thick with the mud

'Can't we light a fire of some sort?' he said.

'We can, but there is only one objection, and that is that there is an enmity between fire and water,' said Kirpu dryly. And then he yawned and the words '*Ishwar!*' issued out of his mouth.

'You are awake then, boys,' came the muffled voice of Daddy Dhanoo from the dugout where Lalu had first taken shelter and, following the voice, the old man himself appeared, weighted by his blanket which he had wrapped round himself so that he looked like a great big black Himalayan bear. And, without waiting for an answer, he went stumbling over Kirpu's legs, splashing the water in a puddle towards where Havildar Lachman Singh should have been but was not. Apparently he had taken shelter in the dugout and slept soundly, and was still half asleep as he walked.

'Jackal of an elephant of a fool! *Jungli!*' Uncle Kirpu growled.

Daddy Dhanoo stopped suddenly and, poking his flat-nosed, slit-eyed, swarthy face at him said: 'Where is Lachman?'

For a moment no one answered him. And he stood bent, a ridiculous sight in spite of the strained, solemn look in his wizened face.

Then Lalu, who was massaging his feet, asked: 'What do you want the Havildar for?'

'I want to know where to go and relieve myself,' answered Dhanoo arranging his sacred thread round his ears in readiness for the ritual. 'What shall I do?'

'Eat it,' said Kirpu.

Daddy Dhanoo was always punctilious in the ritual of answering the call of nature, and lent himself to fooling without fail. The sepoys laughed at him.

'The *Holdar* has gone to look at the things further down the line — I think,' Lalu said.

At this Dhanoo fairly ran down the line to look for Havildar Lachman Singh, while Kharku and Hanumant Singh, Rikhi Ram, and Dhayan Singh, who stood by their rifles swore at the old man who went stumbling over their legs.

'He must have felt the urge badly, otherwise I can't see him moving out of that hole,' said Kirpu.

'But how could he sleep there?' said Lalu. 'It was water-logged last night; that is why I came out of it.'

'The bastard emptied the water out with the palms of his hands,' said Uncle Kirpu. "Until man has been wet he will not build a hut, nor learn to stoop until his head has been bumped." And now I have learnt my lesson. I have a good mind to clear myself a sleeping hole too somewhere. It is the only thing to do if we are to last out ...

'There is Lachman Singh,' said Lalu eagerly.

'What are the orders?' Uncle Kirpu mocked.

'You can sleep, boys. The attack was repulsed last night, farther up the line,' Lachman informed them. 'And now we shall be safe to dig in and sleep.'

'Sleep where? On the water?' said Lalu.

'Now that we have the day before us we can make arrangements for the night,' said Lachman. 'We must dig some more holes. Farther up the line they are already busy making dugouts. 3 platoon was lucky. They discovered a covered passage in a ditch in front of a communication trench in an emergency exit, a row of ramshackle hovels. And they scooped out caves out of the clay walls and rested there in turns at night. You should dig some too. For you must sleep your full sleep out today. There may be another attack soon. And we are not going to be outdone by the Pathan company.'

'What have they done?' asked Uncle Kirpu

'Bravery,' said Lachman: 'What bravery! Sepoy Usman Khan was hit by rifle fire. He was hit a second time, but he stood like a Bahadur. A large piece of flesh was blown away from both his legs by a splinter and he had to be carried back. Karnel Sahib has recommended him for a medal ...'

'He can hang it on his — ,' said Kirpu, 'now that he has no body left to decorate.'

'What is this, *Holdara*?' asked Lalu.

'A periscope, son,' said Lachman. 'You can see everything around by lifting it up in the air and looking at the base.'

Lalu left his boots, and puttees, and socks, and scrambled for it like a child attracted by a toy.

'You will die of cold,' warned Kirpu.

But Lalu took the periscope and, lifting it in his hands, applied his eyes to the base. After a little effort at adjustment he concentrated his glance for a movement and then burst out laughing.

'Have you gone mad?' Uncle Kirpu said.

But Lalu giggled like a child with glee.

'*Ohe*, what is the matter?' Kirpu insisted and got up to wrest the periscope out of the boy's hands.

'Look at Daddy Dhanoo,' he said, 'pale with fear and murmuring prayers to God as he sits relieving himself.'

'Fool! Idiot! Call out to him, and don't show your teeth like a monkey,' said Kirpu. 'Call him to come, for he might die as he sits there if a bullet hits his bottom.' And he took the periscope from Lalu's hand and sought to apply it to see for himself.

Lalu came back and, scraping the mud from his feet, put on his coat and sat down to look for a fresh pair of socks from his bag.

'Now look after the boys, Uncle,' Havildar Lachman Singh said. 'I must go and see about the rations.' And he sloshed away through the mud of the ditch, pieces of straw sticking to his boots.

Lalu felt childishly happy that the Havildar had not taken the periscope away. And, as Lachman disappeared beyond Kharku, he rushed up to Kirpu and took the instrument from him. Kirpu gave up the periscope without any fuss, as if he were not at all curious to see the world in front of him. Instead he reverted to his seat by the machine gun nest.

Lalu adjusted the toy to his gaze and tried to explore the surroundings.

From behind the trenches in the depression, where the twisted contours of some ruined cottages were barely visible, under a grey, muddy sky, stretched a large expanse of fields in the sombre light, torn with shell holes, filled with water, dented here and there with the ruts of a tree that had been uprooted, and strewn with outworn belts, cartridge boxes, paper, twigs, torn sandbags and rolls of barbed wire.

He raised his neck a little and lifted the periscope to see farther afield.

Not a soul seemed to be in sight anywhere beyond, only vistas of dark, wet fields with the boulders of other broken houses and shell holes. There was a sudden, shrieking whistle overhead and, even as he ducked his head, he saw behind the wooded slopes of the ridge, a white château glistening in the fire of the enemy's artillery.

He looked uneasily around lest a superior officer should be near and then turned to a projection from where he could get a good view of the field ahead to confirm his vision of the previous night. He found that their own front line was a zigzag which often stood not two hundred but about four hundred yards away from the German trenches, being at other places only about twenty yards across a 'no-man's-land', defined by barbed wire covered with rags and torn strips of cloth which stretched loosely in a continuous line.

At that instant he espied a German helmet lying on top of a hedge. And he felt it would be a good trophy to capture, but hardly had the thought crossed his mind when he saw an inert corpse sprawled headlong by it ... He listed himself on his toes, strained himself to look more closely. To be sure it was a dead body ... And — there were two others stretched in no-man's-land.

'*Ohe*, sit down, fool!' said Kirpu.

'Look at those poor wretches,' Daddy Dhanoo said coming down the ditch, 'Twelve Muslims of number four company gone to the celestial heavens.'

'They will get fairies there if their Prophet was right,' said Kirpu as he sat placidly.

Lalu splashed past Dhanoo and craned his neck to look. Unable to satisfy his curiosity he strained to get a better view. But a volley of musketry from rifle or machine-gun flew over his head.

'*Ohe*, sit down. I tell you, you will be the death of us all!' said Kirpu.

Lalu withdrew, pale and much sobered.

The rifle and machine-gun fire quickened.

'Now you have disturbed the hive of wasps,' Kirpu said, 'just when I wanted to go and relieve myself ...'

'Half the day has gone and there is no sign of cook Santu,' complained Kirpu. 'And whatever has happened to Lachman?'

'He went for the rations a long time ago,' said Lalu, his voice strained to breaking-point as he stood behind his rifle.

'He is an officer and is allowed to drink eight bowls of milk and to eat sixteen loaves of bread,' mocked Kirpu. 'There would be no grief at his death, for hunger would flee.'

'Don't cut such inauspicious jokes,' said Dhayan Singh from farther up.

'When he dies, then the end for us,' said Lalu throwing a half-smoked French cigarette away.

'Only I wish he would hurry up. I am feeling sick!' said Kharku.

'Half a cigarette is better than a hungry belly,' said Dhanoo picking up the cigarette end from the mud and puffing at it in order to keep it alight.

'If you consider that we haven't eaten since midday yesterday,' said Rikhi Ram surlily. 'What can they be thinking of? That son of the Subedar Major is the most incompetent young fool we could have for an officer. He must be well fed in his father's dugout while we starve.'

' "For two days and a half the water-carrier was king," ' said Kirpu.

'It is nothing to me who is king and who is queen,' said fatty Dhayan Singh. 'What I want to know is why the food is so late in coming. What are all these officers doing?'

'The ration party may have been shelled on their way here,' said Lalu. 'It can't be an easy job to get here. For that road behind the trenches must be within range of enemy fire.'

'Oh, you don't say so?' said Daddy Dhanoo concernedly.

'If they prevent our ration party from getting across we could prevent their food from reaching them,' said Kirpu. 'And both the armies couldn't go on fighting on empty stomachs ...'

'They ought to make Uncle Kirpu an officer,' Lalu mocked. 'Then he will be the same as all the other officers,' said Dhanoo. 'He will keep us waiting for our food.'

'I shall murder that cook of ours, Santu!' burst Kirpu, 'as soon as I see him. The other day he asked me if he would get a medal for coming here. I shall give him a medal when I meet him!'

Just then the cook and two men on fatigue duty showed up behind

Havildar Lachman Singh, puffing and blowing as they brought two tins full of lentils and a basket of chapatees between them. And they sat down and wiped their sweating faces and necks on the sleeves of their jackets. The men of the platoon came crowding round them.

'So you have come,' said one sepoy lurching back from his observation post in the communication trench.

'What have you brought to eat?' asked another.

'Lentils...' said Santu the cook, a Brahmin boy with the features of a god.

'Lentils as usual! Lentils!' shouted Kharku rushing to have a look.

'It is difficult to light a fire, Maharaj!' said the cook. 'And it is our first day here. We couldn't make a proper oven ... And all the provisions have not been unpacked ...'

'It is like when the regiment was transferred from Peshawar to Ferozepur,' explained one of the sepoys of the ration party. 'There at least the previous regiment had left the kitchens intact and we were only inconvenienced for two days ...'

'*Huzoor*, there are no kitchens anywhere,' apologized Santu. 'We have been in trains and on the road, *Huzoor*, and I have been marching with you, and then I have had to cook for the whole company after reaching the destination. Have pity on me and forgive me this time. Do justice, Sarkar.'

'There is no talk, Santu, there is no talk,' consoled Havildar Lachman Singh.

'Truly, Maharaj, my life is not worth living,' continued Santu weeping tears at this sympathy. 'I'd rather be in uniform and fighting here in the trenches, *Huzoor*...'

'And win the Victoria Cross, eh, bastard?' said Kirpu.

'Of course everything is the talk, *Holdara*,' said Kharku.

' "Forgive me, have pity on me" — that is his tune always,' said Rikhi Ram.

'Look at the lentil curry!' said Kirpu.

'And as for the chapatees,' said Dhayan Singh, 'they are half done. We will have a bellyache for the next three years ...'

'You have a bellyache now that you are talking like that,' said Lalu.

'Come, boys, eat,' said Lachman in a kind, fatherly voice.

'Come and serve them the food, Santu, son. They are hungry. I shall get you a reward.'

The cook began to dole out portions, whining and complaining about his difficulties as the sepoys teased him, snatching the ladle out of his hands and helping themselves.

93

And then as they walked away or stood or sat, they ate large mouthfuls like ravenous, voracious beasts, growling at each other and laughing at the cook who trembled to hear the snipers' bullets going overhead, their mouths full, their jaws opening and closing in loud bawdy talk even as their tongues smacked the taste of the coarse chapatees and the coarser lentils.

Some of the men tried to sleep off the previous night's sleeplessness after the meal. Others sought to revive themselves by squandering endless matches on the damp cigarettes which they had retrieved from their dugouts. Others still had to go on duty as sentries in the communication trenches or stand to in their places.

The rifle fire was continuous and the shells came over intermittently; tearing the grey skies.

As Lalu stood on guard a nameless apprehension spread in his flesh like a stupor. Afraid of the invisible doom he turned with a half-suppressed whisper, 'I am not afraid', to a naked determination and stamped his feet on the mud as if to assert his conquest of cowardice.

' "A dog is a lion in his own street," ' Uncle Kirpu said opening his eyes to hear Lalu's whispered words from where he reclined by his rifle, while Daddy Dhanoo who had twisted the end of his turban round his face for warmth still slept the sleep of the carefree in spite of the discomfort of his position as he lay belted with protruding cartridge boxes.

'Where is a dog who doesn't bark and whine?' said Lalu.

'Look, look, beware you watchdog of the Sarkar,' shouted Kirpu suddenly pointing to the sky.

But before the words were out of Uncle's mouth the sentries in the observation posts let loose a salvo upwards at heaven, and the men who curled or crouched with their hands in their armpits or in the sleeves of their coats awoke, shouting with lifted hands:

'Oh havoc!'

Lalu too fired instinctively.

But the aeroplane was flying very high and was not hit.

The awakened platoon stood full length watching the steel bird being attacked by the bursts of anti-aircraft guns which were being aimed at it from somewhere behind the lines. For most of the sepoys it was the first clear glimpse of an aeroplane. But they couldn't look long as they soon

94

began to draw fire from German trenches, and there were warning shouts and cries from the N.C.O.s to the men to duck their heads.

'It is truly a wonder thing,' said Daddy Dhanoo who had awakened but stayed where he was. 'Truly a wonder object. The Badshah of the enemy, the Kaiser, must be an incarnation of God to have made these flying steel birds even as the Divine Ram who discovered the Garuda bird on which he rode to Lanka.'

'Then our Badshah, George *Panjam*, is also an incarnation of God,' said Lalu, 'for he too has invented such flying birds.'

'My wooden owls, look at that!' said Kirpu.

And as they looked they saw the aeroplane turn, twist quickly many times, swing and fall, nose downwards, some miles away. Apparently it had been hit by an anti-aircraft battery. Then there was a burst of cheering among the Connaught Rangers on the left flank. Hearing this the sepoys raised cries of their religions, mixed with curses and abuse.

'The Kaiser's bird is wounded in the wings,' said Lalu to Dhanoo.

Daddy Dhanoo didn't answer for a moment. Then as if to cover his faith and, also because he felt compassionate, he said, 'Son, think of the poor men in it who are their mothers' sons.'

Indeed what a horrible death it must have been for the men in the aeroplane. And yet the pilot had thrown bombs and killed people. And perhaps it was, as Daddy Dhanoo would say, the just retribution which God meted out to people, the fate of all who fought in war. And as Lalu thought this he looked at the grey sky which frowned on the earth as if it were the face of God looking at the world, sullen and angry though sad at the travail of men warring in this soggy wet earth, torn by shells and bullets in the haze of an ever-thickening mist.

'Get ready to do a spot of work, boys,' came Havildar Lachman Singh's voice. 'Let us try and dig these trenches deeper so that you don't get your heads shot off every time you look up to the sky. There is an attack expected: the enemy has the range clear and the fire is speaking death. And we have got to make some traverses to lessen the effect of shrapnel, and listening posts so that we can plant sentries there to give us information of a possible night attack.'

'What are traverses, *Holdara*?' Kharku asked.

'Come, I will show you,' Lachman said as he humorously pulled him away by the ear.

The threatened offensive did not come that night.

Nor did it come the next day and night, nor the next few days and nights.

The brief German attack on the evening of their arrival was said to have been so bravely repulsed that the enemy seemed to have abandoned the attempt to break through the line.

So the sepoys settled down grimly to routine.

The day's work began in the night. Advantage was taken of the darkness for the men to steal out beyond the parapet into no-man's-land and repair the barbed wire which had been broken by the shrapnel, to cut the grass and bushes wherever they had grown to inconvenient heights, to clear the masses of mud that had risen above shell holes and craters like little hills with the broken tangles of saplings and wire sticking out of them, and to repair the parapet itself, which was being shattered by the enemy, so that it exposed the trenches and opened them to enfilading fire, specially as the trenches, concave in shape had, through the attempts to dig them deeper, been turned into nullahs, with tributary rivulets flowing down into them from the communication trenches and the trickles from the pools and puddles made by footsteps. Apart from the fascination of danger and the adventure of fear in crawling out on one's belly, and the similarity of this operation with that which was employed on the frontier, it was cold work, being particularly shivery in the beginning. But by the time the positions and emplacements were improved, communication trenches widened and made more secure, sentry posts constructed, they only felt warm pins and needles in the flesh and the tickling of congealed blood in the frosty numbness of the night or the nip of the early morning. Hardly had they sat down with their hands interlaced in the muffs of their overcoats or dug into the warm shelter of their armpits, when they were drafted to fetch rations, and water, and ammunition, where it waited, half a mile away, behind the ruins of the shelled village, or to bear away the wounded who had been lying in the dressing station in the reserve trench to the field ambulance farther down the road. The darkness was difficult to work in, because of the ruts and the shell holes in the waterlogged earth, the puddles, pools, the mud, the slime, the slippery craters, and the stakes. And one counted the heart-beats if the enemy sent up a hail of shells, or saw someone crawling, and turned on a searchlight to make sure that he was indeed crawling, and then fired a few shots, if only to make assurance doubly sure ... But strange as it seemed it was really quite safe, because there was a kind of informal truce between both parties founded, Uncle Kirpu said, on the Indian notion of chivalry, that "the wood of the lathe gets cut in the cutting", which Lalu interpreted as the simple principle of live and let live. For both parties had to attend to the elemental necessities and it would have been easy for either of the parties to wipe out the other or to shell the roads behind the trenches where the supply wagons stood. Still occasionally the enemies ignored the Indian notion of chivalry if a member of a fatigue party strayed too near, for then a machine gun yelped like a lean house dog at the thief of the night, though generally these moments of the night were comparatively silent.

Only moments, however.

———————

The enemy's big guns, rifles and machine guns began to hurry the sepoys back from the barbed wire entanglements and the empty ration wagons, or the fatigue parties, issuing at first a gentle reminder, then a clear challenge, then a well-aimed shot, accompanied by curses and imprecations uttered through rifles, then the angry stutter of a machine gun, an impatient insistent threat which became the ferocious growling of a hundred fire-tongued lions, of a thousand flaming tigers, of a million roaring elephants, bursting upon the world from the jungle. And since there were always a few slow-moving stragglers, or the masses of darkness clustering like men to the hallucinated vision of the tired, crazed brains on duty in the trenches, the thunderous reverberations of the storm-tempered beasts filled the air, night and morning, morning and night. But as primitive men learned to live, and prowl about in the midst of the jungle, to brave the dangers of the dark, and to breathe its precarious air, as if it were the free air of an inhabited world, so the sepoys settled down. They would return tired out, after three or four hours of intense work in the starless, dirty, drizzling night, and then they burrowed like rats into the damp, clayey, odorous dugouts, pulled their turbans or strips of mufflers or torn rags round their faces and ears, their overcoats and blankets round their crumpled, shapeless mounds of bodies and tried to forget everything in sleep, muttering to themselves the eternal curses and the names of the Eternal as if Sri Krishna would keep them warm in the icy nights ...

'Stand to arms!' a harsh whisper went down the trenches about dawn and they awakened with a start, for that was the signal of daybreak, but relapsed back to sleep, moaning, and hissing, and shivering, their heads cracking with the sudden impact of the morning hate that whirred through the air ...

'Awake! Awake!' called the sentries.

But these calls were like the sharp edges of the cold draught and everyone had protected himself against them, specially round the ears.

'Awake! Dead ones!' shouted the N.C.O.s while the sentries impatiently prodded the depths of the dugouts with the butts of their rifles.

And then some conscientious sepoy awoke with a start and invoked the name of God, another swore, and kicked and relapsed into sleep, a third smacked his lips and snuggled deeper into his own arms muttering incomprehensible, dribbling monosyllables in the language of night.

Lance-Naik Lok Nath came waking the whole length of the company with characteristic high-handedness:

'Rape-sisters! Wake up! The enemy's guns may open fire at any moment or they may cross over two hundred yards in a body and descend upon us, swine! And then where will you be? Awake, or you will be facing a firing squad!'

In a few moments the parapet was lined with the yawning, dirty, mud-besmeared hulking forms of sepoys, rubbing their glued heavy eyes and scratching their ritualistic tuft knots under their turbans, baring their cheeks over-grown with bristling moustaches from under the wraps, even as they puffed and blew the stale smoke of their breath and spat on their hands to warm them before adjusting the cold steel of their rifles into position.

'Please to come out of the dugout, Daddy Dhanoo, but bring something.' Lalu called, hinting at the baksheesh of a cigarette.

'*Ohe*, why talk of gifts in this trench,' said Daddy Dhanoo, his wrinkled face tied in a knot. And he came and settled down to a few more pinches of snuff.

'To cry before the blind is to spoil one's eyesight,' said Uncle Kirpu turning to Lalu. 'Come, son, give me a match to light the end of this cigarette. It will brighten life in the dark a little. I wonder what time it is …'

'In a dark city all cats are grey as also the hours in this "Franceville",' said Lalu, handing over a packet.

The reference to the atmosphere was depressing so that they were again possessed by their doom and sat silent and glum. For indeed, if the cats were all of the same colour in a dark city, the days were the colours of the nights, or only a shade lighter, and the murky, greenish grey sky was the exact colour of the roof of hell which the sages in India spoke about, where the souls of the sinners were subjected to ordeals, first of trailing through the mud of marshes, full of slimy, ravenous rats and blood-sucking leeches, then through a forest of tangled bushes and thickets of thorns, then to wait in misery, naked and cold and hungry, for the coming of the rain which was to wash them clean of their sins, for the ordeal of fire which was to purge them, and for the final judgment before the throne of Brahma seated in all his glory on a mighty throne surrounded by hosts of angels and fairies. They had already come through the long and weary trail and were now in the stage of waiting in this vast, timeless universe for their fate to fulfil itself as if they had been suddenly transplanted into the world of their ancestors where men struggled against the elements, the Gods and Destiny. What a world! What a country! What a war!

Then the first shrapnel could be heard bursting on the reserve trenches and the enemy explored the wood on the right flank for something, opened machine-gun batteries on the traverses of the second line where some cooks were boiling tea in a tin on a smoky fire, and dropped some shells on the ruins of the village behind the lines. After this everything was silent again, till the snipers' bullets started and there was a rickety-tickety stuttering of machine guns and the recurrence of the full barrage of artillery and shell-fire ... like the beating of the drums in the marriage procession of a washerman going to meet his bride in the adjacent regimental lines.

The response of the sepoys seemed to show as if they had resigned themselves to their *kismet*. Covered by their army blankets, like hooded, bell-topped tents, snuggling in the folds of blankets, wrapped in their greatcoats, strapped and bandaged with an assortment of woollen rags on their legs, their backs, and their faces, they huddled together as they crouched over the warmth of a cigarette tip or the end of a candle, or stood by their rifles, elephantine mounds of flesh, placid and immobile and dumb, who would have to be drugged with liquor into warmth and madness before they could charge the enemy. For, although they had been in the trenches only a few days, one hour had begun to seem to them like the other and each day like the last and the dreary sameness of life in this unknown had begun to assert itself. A passionate people, prone to sudden exaltations and depressions, more faithful than any other if they believed, they were neutral in this war, because this was not a war for any of the religions of their inheritance, nor for any ideal which could fire their blood and make their hair stand on end. Ordered about by the Sarkar, they were as ready to thrust their bayonets into the bellies of the Germans as they had been to disembowel the frontier tribesmen, or their own countrymen, for the pound a month which the Sahibs paid them. But they were like conscripts, brutalized and willing to fight like trained bulls, but without a will of their own, soulless automations in the execution of the army code, though in the strange dark deeps of their natures, unschooled by the Sarkar, there lay the sensitiveness of their own humanity, their hopes, their fears and their doubts. And as if convinced by centuries of faith that the sentinels of Yama, the God of Death, alone would be able to awaken them from their bored somnolence in the corridors of their journey to the nether-worlds, they would begin to move, however slowly, when an N.C.O. came and shunted them off into fatigue parties.

'Come boys,' the N.C.O. urgently shouted, 'the wounded couldn't be carried on the stretchers the other night as the trenches are not yet deep enough.'

And they began digging to facilitate easy passage for the dead, the souls of the dead, the wounded and the half-dead, through the trenches, the communication trenches, the traverses; they began digging at the projection of the ditches, digging furiously as if there was no time to lose, digging round the corners, shovelling ,ud and throwing frozen water with their hands across the open until their limbs were heavy and numb, and life seemed a more intolerable burden on their backs than the fear of death.

But exercise of this kind conduced to warmth: it also made them vora-ciously hungry and the love of life asserted itself once again. And then the cooks of hell came in for all the abuse that these doomed desperados had nurtured in the store-house of the Indian national memory for generations, as if specially for use in 'Franceville.'

'That one-eyed son of a gun mixed huge stones with the lentils yester-day,' said young Kharku. 'And, of course, stones won't boil so easily ...'

'Don't abuse them,' said the gentle Hanumant Singh.

'The lop-eared sons of whores! They are a pack of curs!' said Rikhi Ram.

'They do themselves well, the illegally-begotten!' said Dhayan Singh smacking his lips.

'Oh, it is not them so much as that Lok Nath who is on fatigue duty with the cooks today,' said Kirpu. ' "The dog asks the bitch not to feed the pups while he is eating".'

'Hey *Ishwar*! *Ishwar*! Thanks be to you!' prayed Dhanoo. 'From of old you are the worker of great miracles ...' And then he turned to his friends, 'Patience, brothers, patience. "Contentment is a great gain!" ...

'Patience! Contentment! While the rats are eating our bellies away,' said Lalu.

But the cooks had learnt from all the bullying and the abuse they had received on the previous occasion to be in time with the meal and, apart from the usual chapatees and dal, biscuits, jam and tinned fruit had become available, all through the courtesy, as the N.C.O.s and Indian, officers were never tired of telling the sepoys, of "Sahibs and Mem Sahibs who admired their loyal Sikhs and Gurkhas."

'Where do the Dogras come into this picture of loyalty?' Kirpu asked. 'Among us it is said: "Whose friend is starter he — eats and goes".'

But after their hunger and thirst had been quenched, they had cigarettes, any number of cigarettes, and comment died down. And then there was the tense wait, broken by bouts of sleep and the sudden sharp shrieking and screaming of the hounds of Yama in the lowest depths of the netherworld.

$$\approx \quad 6 \quad \approx$$

ON THE MORNING of October 26 rumours of an impending attack became current.

It had rained all night and the day broke misty and grey. The trenches were deep in mud and water. And the sepoys sat in the bottomless pits of their misery after trying to drain the ditches, scooping out water in handfuls and with the few utensils they had.

'It is not only the urine of God, but the earth has been emptying its bladder too,' Uncle Kirpu said as he came puffing and panting from a communication trench.

'*Ohe*, talk plainly and don't always be uttering conundrums,' protested Kharku impatiently.

'*Ohe*, massage your brain a little, and open your eyes to see,' replied Kirpu. 'Why does a night's drizzle fill these ditches knee deep with water? Because when you try to dig them deeper you find more water.'

'Which means,' said Lalu ponderously, 'that in the low-lying ground the water level is high.'

'As my learned Babu wishes,' said Uncle Kirpu. 'Touch the tuft knot with the right hand or with the left, that is about the place where your head is located.'

'It is not a question of the head, brothers, it is a question of the heart,' said Daddy Dhanoo. 'Take the name of *Bhagwan* and be patient! Remember Ram...'

'Ram, Ram, forget Ram,' said Lalu. 'What I want to know is: what are the orders?'

'Don't worry about orders son, the cat in the house knows as little as the rats in the trench,' said Kirpu.

Lalu dug his feet on a raised pitch which he had constructed for himself and sought to secure himself against the damp by scratching mounds of earth from the front wall of the trench to fill up the puddles. The trench face yielded: the soil was soft and liquid ... This seemed curious to Lalu who somehow naively expected everything here to be hard. But the earth didn't seem to be a part of this war, from the way it let itself be torn up.

'*Chacha*, when will be this attack which you were talking about and against whom?' he asked.

'*Holdar* Lachman Singh whispered to me that we should be in readiness as he went out with some Indian officer to the Karnel Sahib's dugout where they have been summoned,' informed Kirpu.

'But are we going to attack or is an attack expected from the enemy?' Lalu asked.

'Well, son, God only knows — and the Sarkar,' said Kirpu.

' "And soldier's duty is to obey",' Lalu repeated Kirpu's phrase.

'That is the first maxim of the army,' continued *Chacha* Kirpu. 'But there is another law of army life. No doubts and fears, or such-like thoughts, shall be allowed to stand between a sepoy and his Destiny. And if you should ask what is that Destiny then the Sarkar will tell you it is ...'

' "Obey the orders of the Sarkar and of God who made us servants of the Sarkar for our past misdeeds",' interrupted Lal Singh.

'If you ask what is that Destiny you will be told it is a medal won for bravery in battle. Mention in despatches,' continued Kirpu. 'And death. This is so all the world over, the same in China, in Japan, on the frontier and in *Vilayat*.'

'We have eaten the salt,' said Daddy Dhanoo gobbling his words in a unique eloquence. 'It is a question of gratitude.'

'Gratitude and honour,' mocked Uncle Kirpu. 'Ask me: I am a man of many campaigns, though I have left my medals behind!'

'One can't refuse to obey orders,' said Dhanoo.

'I won't refuse to go to my destruction, but I say this, that if one who slays one is a murderer then he who slays a thousand is not a hero,' said Lalu.

'All Jarnels say: "Whosoever has the staff has the buffalo",' put in Dhanoo.

'How are we situated now?' asked Lalu eagerly. 'Are we strong or weak?'

'Don't get dysentery before the battle,' replied Kirpu. 'How do I know what is happening?' ... And for a moment he kept silent. Then, as if he was not living up to his reputation for all knowingness he chattered on: 'The melon gets colour from seeing other melons.' There are Tommies farther up the line who have been in the fighting since the beginning. When I went out behind the lines the other day I got talking to one of them who said that he had come with the regiment from a place called Ain, farther to the east of the front. He told me that the fighting all along the line for some months has been of the hammer and tongs kind. Sometimes the enemy won ground and the Sarkar lost; sometimes the Sarkar gained the upper hand and the enemy retreated. But there have been many attacks. First the enemy attacks and then we attack; the enemy attacks again and then we attack ... Like me the Gora was a man of more than one campaign. He said that he was grateful the sepoys had come from Hindustan. '*Pucca*,' he said. '*Chapatee*.' And he fired off all the Hindustani he had learnt in India. So I spoke in *Angrezi* to him - git mit, git mit ... thank you.'

' "The melon takes colour from the melon" indeed,' mocked Lalu. 'The melon falls on the knife: the melon suffers. The knife falls on the melon: the melon suffers!'

They had hardly quietened down, however, when the thunder of the artillery increased to deafening roar. They were surprised at the unexpected intensity of the shell-fire at that time of the day, for it seemed to be about midday tiffin time.

But Havildar Lachman Singh came down the trench looking as if he were trying to put on a brave and smiling face.

'Well, boys,' he said.

'You sit down *Holdara*,' said Kirpu solicitous of his welfare.

'I have been with the Owen Sahib,' Lachman said, panting. 'I have great news for you, "Men are tested when set to work".'

'But what is the work, *Holdara*?' asked Kharku.

'The enemy has been attacking farther up the line. And the *Angrezi* and the *Francisi* corps have been on the defensive. The position is critical. The Germans, not knowing of our arrival, believe that the British Army is without support. And they are beginning to press forward in the hope of breaking through the line. If we are true to the salt of the Sarkar we can win glory and honour and save the day. We must advance. So, boys, get ready, for we are about to attack ... 'He paused for breath, then continued!'

'Our artillery will pound the enemy on the right flank and we are to help with machine-gun and rifle fire. The Connaught *Goras* and our companies of the 69th Rifles will attack the enemy from centre, while others of our corps will attack from the left. We must be brave and rush to enemy front line trenches, then their second and third lines. If you see any Germans about, charge them with your bayonets, or capture them. Get as many prisoners as you can. Push wherever they leave gaps and don't let them look at their heels. From the Commander-in-Chief to every man there is complete confidence in success. Now, brothers, you hold the prestige of your forefathers in your hands ...'

With his eyes averted from the men, Lachman sat still for a moment.

The Sepoys looked at him intently as if they expected him to say something more. Then they began slowly to rise.

'Lie down for a while and rest, *Holdara*,' Kirpu said importunately.

'I must go and pass the orders to other men in the company, brother,' said Lachman coming suddenly from where he sat, his kind, keen face tired, haggard and unshaven, his puttees and boots plastered with mud as he had apparently been running round in the squelchy bog.

The attack was to commence about three o'clock.

The sepoys were ready a little earlier. Some stood by their rifles, others sat on their haunches. Their packs were beside them. They didn't know what to do with their time. There were not even the proverbial flies to kill. And their heads hung down with the weight of slow, heavy moments. Now and then terrific detonations of guns enveloped the air. It seemed as if the attack had begun and they stretched their hands towards their packs ready to go. But there was no sign of Havildar Lachman Singh. And they waited again in suspense, relieved only by the uncanny sight of Daddy Dhanoo dozing where he had sat mumbling the name of God to the rosary of his heart.

'Woe to the enemy if they see such warriors as Dhanoo,' said Lalu.

'He came to this world to worship, but he has been set to ginning,' said Uncle Kirpu, likening the noise of gun fire to that in a primitive cotton factory.

'*Oon, hain* ...' Daddy Dhanoo said, opening his heavy-lidded eyes and smiling apologetically,

'Nothing, nothing, there is no talk,' Kirpu assured him. 'You go to sleep; only don't snore, or you will frighten the enemy.'

Daddy Dhanoo needed no encouragement, however. The food he had eaten at midday, the snuff he had snuffed and his general sense of fatality drugged him into a stupor which made him impervious to everything except orders. Though he had hoped on the outbreak of the war that he would be disqualified from service abroad, and sent on pension, he had had no objections to the idea of going to fight and die in foreign lands. 'It is the orders of the Sarkar,' he had said. And when Uncle Kirpu had waxed ironically eloquent about 'Duty', Daddy Dhanoo had just sat stupefied and uncomprehending in his innocence, asking Lalu, 'Tell me, son, you are learned, what is the war all about?' For to him, 'Obedience' and 'Duty' were with 'God' not only the ultimate laws of the Universe, but interchangeable. If loyalty to the spirit which creates the Universe was only possible through worship and the remembrance of the Almighty, then the 'obedience' to the Sarkar, whose salt one had eaten, was the highest 'Dharma'. And his pantheism was activist; it demanded the utmost sacrifice of which he was capable. He heard badly, but his ears seemed surprisingly sensitive to the words of officers; his eyes were bleary and weak and often remained closed in sleep, but they opened, red-streaked and big, and nearly popped out of their sockets, if he saw a superior coming; his rough, shapeless body was awkward in the ordinary way but he could keep his step in a route march when everyone else flagged; his head which could only grasp the elemental life was capable of infinite shades of subtlety if it came to the interpretation of what was right and what was wrong according to the unwritten code of military law summed-up in 'Duty'; and everything else was reduced to the test of the heart, the ultimate arbiter. This all-pervading sense of 'Dharma' spread like an invisible cancer through his system, the cancer which had eaten him, till there was not much vitality left in the resources of his hardy hillman's will and he had to nourish his resignation on snuff and more snuff.

The gunfire died down for a moment.

There was still no sign of Lachman, but Jemadar Subah Singh and Lance-Naik Lok Nath came with hasty flourishes of their arms.

'Be in readiness and alert! Get your packs,' said Jemadar Subah Singh in emphatic whispers, assuming a surreptitious manner as if he were preparing to play a game.

'Has Lachman told you what to do?' Lok Nath asked, affecting a stern cordiality as he lengthened the shadow of his presence over the men.

And before they had answered, he began to explain to them: 'Between this trench and the enemy there is a space of level ground which ends in a jungle on the right flank. The Gora regiments on our right may be pressed hard and may be forced to fall back. So we ...'

'We know that but what are we waiting for?' asked Kharku.

'When you get up there,' continued Lok Nath ignoring the interruption, 'you must remember to take advantage of the unexpectedness of our attack. The Germans, the Sahibs say, fear us. They think we are all Gurkhas with kukhries in our mouths, savages who will creep up to them, take them by surprise and kill them. And the Sarkar is treating you as the shock troops for that reason. Now you show them some of your savagery. All brave men like hand-to-hand fighting. And I have always tried to instil in you the fact that as brave sepoys, you must charge the enemy without fear, with your bayonets, wherever you find him! Hit him in vital spot. Aim at the heart, remember, the belly or the testicles of the enemy! If he has the advantage in attack, swiftly fell him with a blow from the butt end of your rifle and trample upon him and drive the bayonet deep into the body, and draw it out so that he bleeds and dies ... Understand? ... *Acha*?' And he warmed a curious red as he finished his lecture.

'We must go and give the final instructions to the other platoons,' said Jemadar Subah Singh.

'Come of your own accord, go with your own desire,' said Kirpu confronting them both bluntly.

But neither of the two toughs was in the mood to notice Kirpu's banter or rudeness, so puffed-up were they in the glory and might of the role assigned to them to save the day for the Sarkar by dint of their savagery.

After Lok Nath's enumeration of the tender spots as the heart, the belly and the testicles, curiosity, which had turned to fear in Lalu became horror of several bayonet points sticking into his own belly. It was strange that they were aimed at no other point but the belly, as if there was no other vulnerable part of his body. But he could see his entrails with the dark liver hanging to them like the inside of the diseased oxen which the village cobbler butchered by the swamps in Nandpur. He would have to kill if he didn't get killed first, the thought suddenly came to him. Anyhow whether he killed or did not kill he would have to go there where the enemy was.

Involuntarily he trembled. Then he tried to remember the tactics of bayonet fighting, like a schoolboy recalling his lesson before the examination. And, like the frightened schoolboy, he felt he had forgotten, and the dread loomed before his eyes, occupying the hollow of his body which shook against his will.

He tried to steady himself so that he could become neutral, like his companions, who sat patient and tranquil though rather pale and silent, as if they were reflecting on their doom and yet seeking to control their flesh from giving any sign of weakness, each to his own, as if everyone were alone in this ordeal.

The artillery barrage was increasing. Lachman Singh came rushing like an angry bull, slipping in the sluggish mud, falling, tottering and furious. With his hand on his heart he stopped for the barest second to take breath. Then he said: 'The Connaughts are ahead of us. Get your packs. Up we go. Keep them in sight.' And then, as if he had regained the lightness of the old gymnast he was, he leapt up to the parapet.

Spurred on by Lachman, the whole platoon was climbing. Lalu took the parapet in a jump, dragging his rifle butt first, unafraid now, but feeling as if by handling the musket upside down he had begun badly.

The suddenness with which Lachman Singh uprooted them made them unsteady. And they were surprised after days of bending in the trenches, to find themselves stretched almost to their full heights, rushing along towards the enemy. Some of the Connaughts on their right had already advanced about a hundred to a hundred and fifty yards, and the Baluchis of the 129th were out on the left.

The gun fire seemed to rend the air with a deafening roar. The clusters of mist which hung down from the sky were melting in a slow drizzle. The ground was difficult with stakes, roots and deep declivities, rising unevenly like low hills and then sloping suddenly to fall away beyond the end of the Connaughts' line.

Lalu ran with his head bent forward, as if by so doing he expected to avert any bullets that might come his way. The particles of rain seemed to freeze on his flesh. He shivered a little and ran with a gurgling noise in his throat.

A hail of bullets scattered the men and Lachman Singh shouted to them to lie down and crawl.

A thick ragged blanket of darkness seemed to cover them as they inclined to the earth. The smoke of the guns had mixed with the curtain of rain.

As he dragged himself forward he could only see the rumps, the packs, the swinging hands and heavy feet of the men.

Some of the Connaught *Goras* seemed to have run about five hundred yards ahead. Kirpu and Dhanoo were several yards behind him, following like ghostly shadows with their eyelashes, eyebrows, their turbans and the serge of their coats greyed by the mist, while Lachman, Kharku and Hanumant were ahead of him. The foreknowledge of death swished past him with the tempestuous music of the bullets. And now the mist reeked of a sulphurous powder as it clung clammy and wet like venom on the skin.

Lachman Singh turned and shouted; 'Get abreast of the Connaughts.'

Taken aback by the order, they hesitated, then hurtled forward, falling over each other.

Lalu got abreast of Kharku and shaded his eyes to look for the Tommies. They seemed invisible, except perhaps as the gestures of falling men in the distance.

He stopped to take breath, for a withering rifle fire rent the air. There was a swamp with the stubble of a bush half buried in it, at his feet. He jumped across it panting. The detonations seemed to throw up great clods of earth and limbs and smoke along the line. He did not know what to do, where to go, whether to advance or retreat, for Lachman Singh had swerved towards the left and run to the end of the company, while Kharku had doubled-up with a shell fragment and fallen.

He was convulsed by the volleys of machine-gun fire which came in the train of explosions on the left where the heavies seemed to be bursting.

He lay down and began to crawl. For a moment he was cut off from everyone. And he felt as he had felt once when as a child he had gone with his parents to a cattle fair and had got lost and had run in a panic, weeping salty tears, looking for someone he could recognize. Another crash and a whirlwind of earth and smoke flew up from an explosion near him, while rifle and machine-gun fire poured down like a rainstorm.

'Oh pity! *Wah Guru!*' he shrieked as the swish of steel and gusts of smoke and mounds of earth and iron blew past him.

'Turn back!' the voices of officers came.

To be sure no one could go forward in the face of that fire. But having come so far Lalu felt he would have gone farther. And strangely enough he had forgotten to be afraid.

He turned round, running in short capers with bent back, then lay flat, crawled on his hands and knees, stopped and ran again. He stumbled upon a pit and fell, deafened, his heart crying with anger.

'Oh God!' he mumbled even as he wondered how he would reach the trenches alive and who would be left behind dead, besides Kharku. A great many Tommies had fallen. Kirpu, Dhanoo — were they safe he wondered. And Lachman Singh?

He felt all over his stomach as he crawled in the shell hole where he found himself, to see if there was any blood on his body. Only the damp of rain and mud came up with his hand. He halted to breathe and coughed to ease his throat: a queer growling noise came out of his lungs, half sob, half moan, a broken, hoarse grief that receded into the silence of his larynx even as the detonations of the artillery barrage smothered everything ahead of him. Fear gripped his throat.

'Come on, son,' he heard Lachman Singh whispering to him. And he espied the form of N.C.O. dragging Kharku's body in the mud.

'Which is dearest, work or your hide, asked the iron tongue?' Lalu heard Kirpu's voice behind him.

'What did you answer?' the boy queried.

'Hide of course, the hide,' said Kirpu sweating and breathless. And he came abreast of Lalu, stopped for a moment, and covered his face with his hands as if to prevent himself from coughing or moaning.

The boy was moved by some instinctive weakness to creep up to him and shouted to him:

'I hope nothing has happened to you.'

'I am all right, son...' Kirpu said, but he was hoarse with fatigue and could not finish the answer.

'Where is Dhanoo?' Lalu asked, his loud voice crumbling among the bursting fragments of the shells.

Uncle Kirpu looked back and, not finding Dhanoo waved his head to signify that he did not know.

Suspense was wearing him down.

But just then he saw part of the company on his left retreating.

'Come on boys,' Lachman called.

Lalu craned his neck, lifted himself and followed Lachman. In a moment he was helping to drag Kharku, who had lain by the Havildar. The dead face was twisted into an ugly grimace, his mouth stretched open apparently through the writhing of some deep pain he had suffered before he died. Lalu's legs were shaking involuntarily, but he helped Lachman to heave the dead body and they retreated, their feet slipping in the mud, their torsos strained forward .... They were almost running now, losing consciousness of yards, losing touch with others ...

The cyclone of bullets was still rushing overhead.

He ducked his back and sat on his knees for a moment as if he were a Muhammadan who had suddenly stopped to say prayers before the gates of hell. He swept the right flank with a glance as he struggled to lie down. Lachman also dropped Kharku's body and rested.

A sepoy doubled up with an agonized groan and another caught his head and, throwing his rifle away, set to wiping mud on a wound on his leg; while, farther away in a clearing, the sepoys were crawling back or lay huddled for safety.

The lead whined and whimpered while the shells crashed after curious gurgle under darkening sky.

And not an inch of the ground seemed immune from the metal, not even the parapet of their trenches, now only six or seven yards away. They had apparently advanced three hundred yards before meeting the hurricane of fire.

'Come, push along and don't bar the way,' Kirpu called.

Lalu dragged Kharku's flagging body till he got to the parapet. Then he let himself drop into the trench through sheer exhaustion, pulling the body after him.

———

When they got back it all seemed to have happened in a flash, the whole violent, furious, breathless rush towards the enemy, the protracted, unending shocks of fire and the retreat.

'*Bale! Oh, Bale! Bale!*' Kirpu belched after he had poured a draught of water down his throat.

'Why did we have to attack if we had to retreat?' Lalu said in order to drown the shattering ache of confusion at the back of his head, as if a post-mortem would help.

'We were exposed from the front and the flanks, son,' said Lachman Singh. 'We were badly exposed. The enemy artillery built up a barrage against us. And we lost touch with the Connaughts ...'

'It was that fog, the rape of its mother,' said Kirpu.

'*Han*, mist was a nuisance,' admitted Lachman with a strained smile.

'Where were our guns?' Lalu ventured tentatively. 'I thought they would cover our advance.'

'I don't know what happened to our guns,' Lachman said palely.

'Where are our guns? Where are our guns? — We haven't got any guns!' burst Kirpu with a red hot anger. 'The big guns, the big guns, we haven't got any big guns, otherwise they could have saved the *Goras* on the right from destruction Support of big guns ... I tell you, if we had had big guns and more big guns, we could have silenced the opposite tornado of shrapnel and bullets. But this bitch of a Sarkar hasn't got as many big guns as the Germans ...'

'How do you know?' Lachman Singh asked, assuming a sternness which Lalu had never seen in him

'One of the Tommies there told me,' said Kirpu as he flung himself down with a shake of his head and began to light a cigarette.

For a moment everything was still and the three of them crouched, lay or leaned back. Havildar Lachman Singh's face was hard, drawn and piti-less as if he were choking with resentment. He seemed to know that it was wrong for him for the Sarkar not to tell the soldiers the truth. And yet the instinct of the disciplined soldier, who had earned his position by dint of the qualities of courage and persistence, quarrelled with the kindliness he had always brought to the treatment of the men. He seemed to say to himself: 'What has all that about the guns got to do with the men? I myself don't know how strong the Sarkar is. From the talk of the Sahibs we seem to have come in time to save a very bad situation. But what has that got to do with us? ... I hate to have to order you to your death. What can I do? This is our Destiny, since we took the oath of service to Sarkar!'

Lalu looked at him from the aura of his own indifference and tiredness: there was a hurt tenderness in Lachman's embarrassed smile and tears in the Havildar's eyes.

He tried to break the mask of his own resignation, twitched with a curious agitation and sought to ask himself what the Havildar felt. But the apathy of his fatigue congealed his blood, and he could only say: 'Don't mind Kirpu clown, *Holdara*.'

At that instant a runner came shouting in the dark as if he were drunk, '*Holdar* Lachman Singh!'

'Coming.' Lachman answered.

'The *Karnel* Sahib was hit in the shoulder, and you are to report to the Ajitan Sahib,' the runner said, surveying Lalu and Kirpu as if with the eyes of another world.

'What happened, do you know?' Lachman asked him, referring to the attack.

'The *Goras* are said to have rushed the enemy trenches and captured an officer and two men,' the runner blustered. 'They lost touch with the 69th in the dark ... But the Sahibs think that the behaviour of our troops was good considering it was our first action, and they have asked the Indian officers to tell the men that the British officers appreciate disappointment of the sepoys at being asked to retire before coming to grips with enemy.'

Lachman nodded as if he were listening and yet not listening.

'There were eleven casualties in the regiment,' the runner said freshly. And then he asked: 'Any in this platoon?'

'Yes,' said Lachman. 'Sepoy Kharku was killed.'

'*Ohe*, and where is Dhanoo?' Kirpu asked Lalu.

Lalu sat up, looked around himself and said: 'Where is he? He was behind you.'

Uncle Kirpu got up and scurried up to the parapet like a madman, surveying the ground.

'No, he is not up there,' said Lachman. 'I surveyed the ground thoroughly for the dead and wounded before I returned.'

'Come, *Holdara*,' the runner urged.

As the two men walked away Kirpu beat his forehead with his right hand and fell back in a stupor of exhaustion, while Lalu explored the cold dark with his brooding, enigmatic face. The rain was still drizzling and the water trickled down the clouded ditches.

That night Lalu was crazed by dark thoughts which crumbled like agitated phantoms in his head and swirled before his sleep-weighted eyes.

He lay knotted in the dugout twisting his shoulders into his armpits to ward off the chill that came creeping into his flesh through the mounds of damp earth. But the rain dripped outside and the rumbling echoes of fire abused his sleep.

He tried to assimilate his quaking limbs. The vague weight of sadness for the missing Dhanoc, however, lingered like a ghost in the vacuum.

Afraid but tired he sought to lull himself into a half sleep. As he lay thus in foetal sleep he remembered how he had snuggled in the barn where bulls Thiba and Rondu, and cow Suchi slept, in the severe winters at home, the winters during which his mother used to give him a sweet semolina plum with a tumbler of hot milk before he went to bed, the winters during which he used to eat hot maize bread cakes and the spinach of mustard ... As the ration party had failed to come back this evening his mouth watered at the memory of these delicacies.

He drew the blanket on to his face and tried not to think. He hugged himself in the cold. The mournful refrain of a cowherd's song came to his throat and soon he was drifting on the track of another dream memory: He was a child and his mother was singing him to sleep on a cot in the court-yard at the end of the day, even though she was tired. She seemed to have an amazing inexhaustible energy as she went from one job to another, tire-lessly, day and night. On his last visit to Nandpur, he recalled that her hair seemed to have turned all grey and her face was wrinkled, yet she had not lost the shapeliness of her features. And there was a living vitality in her that filled the home.

He felt that he was suffocating as he lay hooded in the blanket, and uncovered his face. There was the thud, thud of an ache behind his head and he wished he could drown it in sleep.

Applying the famous formula of counting sheep as they passed through the gate of a fold, he dozed. But behind the sheep came cows and goats and bulls and elephants hurtling in quick succession into his brain, till he felt stupid to have to resort to such tricks in order to make himself rest.

And lo, the roaming, restless images of the past receded into the vacuum, and he fell asleep.

Towards dawn, as he still lay glue eyed, the panic of a nightmare shook the roots of his being.

From the mud-walled cottages in the midst of a sea, which stank with a stagnant cream of green scum, appeared a woman with a naked coal black body, with eyes that glistened like burning stars and with a tongue that scattered sparks of fire, a sword in one of her ten hands and rifles in the others. And she stalked ruthlessly across the scrap heap, strewn with the butchered heads of goats, frightening fowls which ruffled and ran with shrill squawks, dropping myriads of feathers into the ashes and dust.

At first she seemed to Lalu like the scarecrow he had put up once in order to frighten the droves of parrots, rooks, blackbirds and sparrows which descended on the corn of his father's field, but then he stole a glance at her frightening glamour and knew it was the Goddess Kali.

Hardly had she emerged when she began to blow fireworks out of her mouth like a juggler on the cross roads of Manabad, haranguing the crowd of sepoys and animals and Sahibs, who all seemed to have gathered round. When the concourse of people who came to watch the spectacle had increased sufficiently, she suddenly blew a bugle and struck her foot on the earth.

There was a fissure in the field and out of it emerged rampaging hordes of demons, headed by Yama, the God of Death, with fencing stick and a shield in his hands, fighting mock battles with his followers ... The black woman gnashed her teeth, rolled her eyes, and then cut off her tongue with the sword, so that the blood dripped in a brook which coloured the earth a deep crimson. And then she shook the bells on her feet so that a great music of annihilation began, loud blares of trumpets, the banging of gongs, the drumming of drums. And the mud houses began to fall, the towers of huge buildings collapsed, the earth cracked and only a window remained through which a green land came to view.

The Goddess blew a hot breath and the whole verdure was on fire, and all that Lalu could hear was the crackling of the insects which had desecrated the harvest. Ghostly Owen Sahib said it was a mutiny started by the sepoys while Havildar Lachman Singh was persuading him that it was the battle hymn of Hindustan and he need not be frightened.

The village was festering with the dirty water which had been let loose by the demons to smother the fire, but in the foreground a great battle was raging between the hosts of Kali and the sepoys. And a multitude of dead was piling up, with contorted legs, blue nails, folded arms, bulging eyes and frothing angry mouths, men whose pain-racked faces spread a trembling dread and sorrow. Lalu could hear the fury of the war drums and, terror stricken, he wanted to moan, to cry out, to whimper, but he couldn't even open his mouth to speak.

'Come, son, I will show you something, come,' Uncle Kirpu was saying as he shook him by the shoulders to awaken him.

'Why, what is it? What has happened?' Lalu asked, startled.

Usually Uncle Kirpu was indulgent to him and let him sleep, even spreading his own blanket over him in the morning. But today he jerked him rudely and said in a peremptory voice:

'*Ohe*, wake up and come and see.'

Lalu sat up on his elbow, almost hitting his head against the low ceiling of the dugout, and crawled out without any of the yawning and stretching with which he used lazily to warm himself to action. The silhouettes of the nightmare cracked in his head as he sought to widen his eyes to see what Kirpu wanted to show him. But there was nothing extraordinary outside the dugout, only the puddles of water and mud which Lachman Singh was busy clearing. Uncle Kirpu walked ahead silently, past the N.C.O., towards the communication trench where the ration party used to come.

Lalu followed.

'You are up early today,' called Lachman Singh.

'Not earlier than when you set to work, *Holdaro*,' said Lalu apologetically.

'Oh, son, the work when done is soon forgotten,' answered Lachman. 'But what is the matter with Uncle this morning?'

The question had really been aimed at Kirpu, but the old man had already taken the turning into the communication trench.

Lalu paced up behind the old man, shouting the while:

'*Ohe*! Where are you leading me?'

Kirpu showed his face to his friend like a naughty boy in a game of hide and seek, and beckoned him with his head to follow.

Lalu hurried and soon came up to the old man.

They faced not a puddle nor a pool, but a reservoir into which the surface water of the surrounding country had, after the rain overnight, drained itself, so that the dams in the zigzags of the traverses had broken and become water-logged with a squelchy mud.

'Was it to show me this that you woke me up?' said Lalu indignantly.

'Come, I will show you where Daddy Dhanoo is,' Kirpu replied solemnly.

And he headed for an emergency exit which some sepoys had made, by scooping out the clay walls, to make a short cut to the fields

Lalu wondered why Daddy Dhanoo had gone to rest so far away from the dugout he had previously occupied. But perhaps Lok Nath had put him on sentry-go, or consigned him to a dugout away from his friends. He sloshed into the narrow passage, rubbing his sides against the sodden clay.

After they had gone a few yards they came to some sandbags which stood in a graduated series as a sort of ladder to enable the men to climb up to the top.

'Climb up there and look on your left into the communication trench,' Uncle Kirpu said. 'Careful.'

Lalu looked at him and hesitated for a moment; then he began to ascend the slippery sandbags according to Uncle Kirpu's behests. Up on the flat he felt exhilarated to find himself breathing the open air of the ten-acre field, cold and wet and mud-besmirched but free. He was torn between looking at the fields and the contours of the ramshackle, broken houses at the left flank of the line, and the officers' dugouts with sandbags and leaves about them, and greeting Dhanoo. Perhaps if Dhanoo was well-placed he would be able to come here often and get glimpses of the Sahibs in their huts ... He leaned on his belly towards the communication trench where Daddy Dhanoo was supposed to be.

There was only more squelchy mud and water under the shadow of frosted foliage and the clouds of mist in the ditch, and no sentry could have stood guard there.

'I can't see him there, Uncle,' Lalu said, and then called: '*Bapu* Dhanoo! *Ohe*, Dhanoo!'

There was no answer from the flooded ditch or the caves and cavities beyond it, but Kirpu shouted:

'Look in the water.'

Lalu explored the reservoir under his nose.

Almost two yards away from him he could see the swollen dead face of Daddy Dhanoo floating in the water, while the rest of his body was submerged with the weight of his equipment. There was a ghastly purplish pallor on the skin which did not improve the shrunken ugliness of Daddy Dhanoo's visage, while his big bulging eyes looked up with the widened stare of a horrible and lonely death. Already Dhanoo looked like the ghost of himself as it would visit the dreams of his friends, distorted and frightening, yet pathetic.

Lalu looked on without blinking, as if to assure himself that he was not afraid and to see how Dhanoo came to die. From the half-open mouth of the old man it seemed that he had screamed or shouted for help before his voice was strangled by Death. But how had he died? The leprous white black of Dhanoo's fingers showed above the water, stained by crimson-yellow clots of blood and there were some scratches by his chin, gruesome and frightening. Had he been wounded then? The boy looked for the wreckage of Dhanoo's body. But it was invisible under the muddy water. Only the grey face stared at him, senseless, grimly ludicrous and horribly empty.

Shells were beginning to travel overhead and there was a steady rifle fire. And the desolation and the loneliness of these back trenches filled him with a curious dread. Perhaps there were other bodies which lay drowned farther ahead and it would be more difficult than ever to sleep a dreamless night near these open graves of the dead.

Lalu hurried lest the rigid mouth of the dead Dhanoo should begin to mumble one of his interested prayers. A bullet came and fell sizzling into the water. He was breathless and panting from a sense of escape.

'How did it happen?' he asked, staring Kirpu in the face.

'However it happened it has happened,' said Kirpu. 'He was a little behind me in the retreat, and he must have gone into the communication trench in the dark and lost his way.'

'What is the matter, boys?' came the voice of Havildar Lachman Singh. Apparently his curiosity had been aroused by the solemn manner in which Kirpu had brushed past him in the attempt to conceal the trouble in his eyes.

Neither Kirpu, nor Lalu answered for a moment.

Then Lalu said:

'Dhanoo was drowned, *Holdara*.'

'*Hein!*' Lachman growled half stunned. And he came rushing to see.

Lalu waited in the cemetery silence of the improvised passageway till Lachman had seen Daddy Dhanoo. He pressed his lips tight, and ground his teeth lest he should lose his grip on himself, lest he should be seized by the grotesque terrors of the night in broad daylight, lest his imagination should burst into the demented murmurs of mad despair.

༄ 7 ༅

DURING THE NEXT three days it seemed that the enemy was preparing to revenge himself. The Germans kept up a heavy bombardment to which the English guns, inferior in strength, as Kirpu had guessed, replied now and then. The village of Messines behind the trenches was shelled day and night till, it seemed to the sepoys, that nothing could have been left of even the foundations of the houses. And the Germans made minor attacks here and there by way of feelers, as if they were testing their strength before launching a big offensive.

The pall of Dhanoo's death enveloped the universe of the sector occupied by the Dogra company, almost as if he had mingled with the elements and become the chief spirit behind all the malignant ghosts and ghouls which would not rise from the earth. The old man had seemed so much like a ghost as he had gone about, silent and non-attached in life, that his transformation into a spirit seemed an inevitable and a foregone conclusion. Not only so. He had always insisted on the performance of the last rites on his dead body, and his dread of the impossibility of this in a foreign land had been his only objection to the orders of the Sarkar to cross the black waters. So that the circumstances of his death inclined his friends to believe that his unhoused ghost was still going round the trenches demanding the ceremonial rites. No one knew very much about his past, except Lalu whom he had told a few facts of his life as a cowherd, as an evicted, tenant turned labourer and then sepoy, which however, had still left him very much of a shadow. And, ever since the campaign began, apart from jokes about his unadaptability to the contingencies of European life, he had been deliberately unobtrusive, involved very much in his own world of misery, seeking continually to alleviate it by bouts of prayer, or pinches of snuff, living and moving in a dark furtive underground life of his own, in a state of somnambulistic confabulation which was perhaps his only defence against the strangely complex behaviour of men in civilization and the avalanche of horrors that the Sahibs hurled on each others' heads.

Besides the ghost of Dhanoo, and the other ghosts wandering in the rain and mist and cold, there were the ghosts of their own presence, all leading a sleepless, restless, furtive subterranean life in the darkness, unhoused ghosts, the spectres of their own broodings, apparitions of their shivering sleep, essentially unknown to each other, and only knit together by occasional shouted orders in this world of quaking earth, of shells, and bullets and torn, lacerated limbs.

Isolated and apart they sat thus, these ghosts from another, warmer world, transplanted into this creeping wet, cold autumnal underworld of 'Franceville', they who had never suffered heavy shell fire, who had no experience of high explosives, who had never seen steel birds fly in the air, who had never been taught anything but the bayonet charge which had been so useful for generations on the frontier, who had only two machine guns to each regiment, and behind whom, Uncle Kirpu believed, were no big guns, facing, what the experience of their repulsed attack and the enemy's expenditure of ammunition proved, to be the work of that 'incarnation of the Devil, the Kaiser'. They had hardly reached *Vilayat* and begun to see the wonder of its sights when they had been hurried into action. And, almost from the beginning, things had gone wrong ...

Lalu sat coiled up on the slimy damp straw in the clay cave, scraping the mud off his boots and clothes. If he had been told even a fortnight ago that in *Vilayat*, the land of his dreams, where he had been so happy and eager to come as on an adventure, the Sahibs, whom he admired so much, were wilfully destroying each other, ruining their villages and their cities, he would not have believed it. Sometimes he felt that the whole of this fighting and devastation was accidental, the fault of some General who had given the wrong orders, that if only the General's superiors knew they would call off the war. But he recalled some of the things be had read in the *Fauji Akhbar* in Havildar Lachman Singh's room in the barracks at Ferozepur, after the outbreak of the war. And he vaguely knew that, somehow, it was predetermined, that the first spark was kindled by the murder of a prince in Serbia, that this fire and carnage had something to do with the 'fiendish will to power' of the Kaiser, as the drum beater of Havildar

Lehna Singh, the recruiting Sergeant had declared. But the gap of thousands of miles of sea and the rich experience of wonder cities had come between those words and the present reality. And, since he had really been eager to come to see *Vilayat*, and not because of the loud speeches of Feroz Shah Mehta, Pandit Madan Mohan Malaviya, and His Highness the Aga Khan, he somehow felt he had nothing to do with it. But now he was in it, he was in it. And he reproached himself for his predilection for the fashionable life.

So ashamed was he of thinking of the enthusiasm which he had felt as he started out on this journey, particularly because he had received the news of his father's death by wire just at the moment he boarded the steamer, that he smothered his thoughts by a shake of the head, hacked at the mud on his boots with his trench-digging tools and tried to think of something different. But deep and resonant, the shell bursts filled the air, and he waited tensely, as if he were listening to the demons behind the explosions.

Then he fell emptily to scraping the mud off his boots and clothes again, hacking at himself with his bayonet, fidgety and irritable.

When he was tired of doing that, he got up to take a little exercise in the trench, and seeing it desolate and deserted, except for the ghost of Daddy Dhanoo, which seemed to be lurking in every corner, he returned with more mud on his puttees and boots and fell to scraping it once again.

All the joy of eating seemed to have gone out of life, and he did not care now whether the Ration party had come back with the food or not. All the joy of talking seemed to have fled, because Uncle Kirpu seemed to resent the sight of other human beings. The only joy was in lying about in army blankets, shivering, and paralysed and dozing in a half sleep, perforated by the sound of firing, broken by an occasional order, smashed to smithereens by the horrors of dreams.

If Lalu's sleep was murdered in the night, as often happened, then he sat waiting for the morning, listening to the slow drizzle of the perpetual rain, or, if the rain had stopped for a while, to the seeping of the water in the mud, till the guns announced sunrise, and the staccato of a machine gun indicated the arrival of *chota hazri*. If, however, the bombardment had increased in violence, then it seemed that an attack was going on in some sector.

And now everyone in the company rushed to the parapet, and they stared accusingly at each other, as much as to say, 'I am not afraid, are you?' And, as if to confirm this belief in his own courage, each sepoy let off a round of shots to supplement the inadequate replies which those on night duty had been giving. And, from behind their own trenches, some shells went leaping up, till the enemy's rifle fire ceased somewhat, and the surprise element having disappeared, they knew it was just bluff on both sides, or as Uncle Kirpu put it more aptly, 'The dogs must bark early in the morning to show their masters that they have been keeping watch all night.'

A searing shell went overhead and a few snipers' bullets followed.

'They seem to be well treated, these German hounds! They show mettle,' said Kirpu. 'What about our food?'

'If food comes, well; if not, no matter,' said Lalu. And he resigned himself to the compensation of a cigarette.

'To be sure, men like us cannot walk back to their homes,' said Kirpu.

Lalu was contemplating the dirty smudges of clouds on the tormented sky of such a morning, the second day after the attack, when Havildar Lachman Singh came and said tiredly with a trace of anger in his voice:

'More orders, boys, and truly strange ones! Half the 69th will stay here and half will go with the 4th Cavalry Brigade ...'

'What! What, *Holdara*, is it true?' Dhayan Singh came rushing to hear the orders.

'What is more, two companies of the regiment will be transferred to the First Cavalry Division to relieve the Connaught *Goras*, who go farther south ...'

'Really, truly?' asked Rikhi Ram.

'The master asks the dogs to go hunting when they are dying and they must go,' said Kirpu with the finality of exasperation.

It was 4 a.m. by Havildar Lachman Singh's heavy pocket watch in the light of a guttering candle in the dugout when they started. They did not know where they were going, where Messines was and who composed the 4th Cavalry Brigade to which they had been suddenly assigned. But they emerged out of the alluvial depths of their trenches into the foggy morning and proceeded. Now grumbling, now cursing, now silent, they stumbled up into the sodden field beyond the communication trenches and tripped grimly along.

Lalu tried to open his sleepy eyes and explore the heavy mist which enveloped the land, but he could not see more than two yards ahead. And now the dugouts in the waterlogged trenches he had left seemed like a comfortable home in view of the uncertainty of the future. He had made no friends among the Sikh company, because of his self-consciousness at being known to be a Sikh who was registered as a Dogra as he had had his hair cut, and he had not come very much into contact with the Punjabi Muhammadan company except once or twice when be had eaten the minced meat kababs which were a speciality of Muslim cooks. But now he felt lonely at the thought that those two companies had been separated from his own. Why was the regiment being split up into fragments?

Exploring the ground for shell holes and craters to make sure of his steps, he splashed across the soggy field behind Uncle Kirpu. The old man kept looking back as if he wanted to make sure that he didn't lose him as he had lost Daddy Dhanoo.

The company seemed to be going in single file at an angle of forty-five to the trenches.

Lalu looked round to see if the Ajitan Sahib was with them. For, some-how, since the kindly Captain Owen had saved him from the clutches of the law which the landlord of the village had set on him, the boy had warmed to him. Owen Sahib's kindness was a byword in the regiment, but the particular kindness which he had shown to Lalu in Ferozepur had been noted by the sepoys and he had been singled out as the favourite of the Sahib. The adjutant's friendship for Havildar Lachman Singh had probably encouraged the Sahib's regard for Lachman's friends, but he never missed an occasion to have a word with Lalu at any time and seemed very concerned for his welfare. Naturally, the boy hero-worshipped him.

As he peered through the fog, however, he couldn't see the Sahib, and he was afraid that Captain Owen might have been sent with some other company. Since the colonel was wounded on the 26th there might have been some reshuffling of officers.

He scrambled across an uprise on the edge of an officers dugout and slid past the broken flanks of a door heaped with sandbags towards some stunted trees which stood eerily still with cloaks of mist around them, like the ghosts of the dead in battle. And he recalled how frightened he had felt in that trench for fear of Dhanoo's spirit. Perhaps it was as well that they were leaving that particular sector and going somewhere else.

A difficult hundred yards and they slid from the field onto a road.

Owen Sahib was standing there, watching the soldiers file past him, smiling even as his blue eyes vigilantly examined each man and acknowl-edged the silent salutes which the sepoys flung at him to cover up their inability to offer a more efficient military greeting.

'Salaam, *Huzoor*,' Lalu offered a specially informal address.'

Ah, Lal Singh, *acha hai*?' the Sahib said, patting him.'

'*Huzoor!*' returned Lalu.

'Where are the other companies gone, *Huzoor*?' a sepoy taking advantage of the adjutant's informal exchange with Lalu to put a query which was really a grievance.

'*Bohat mushkil hai*,' said Captain Owen, 'without putting on any of the airs and graces of authority in Hindustani. Then he spoke to Lalu in English, 'The regiment has to face difficult conditions ... But the officers of each company will remain with us ...'

At that instant Subedar Major Arbel Singh came back to where the company had collected on the cross roads. Agile and determined, his sartorial dignity unruffled by the privations of dugouts, he turned with his lean wolf's face to the Adjutant and said: 'Sahib, Brigade Headquarters do not understand anything of us. For Indian troops are not like other troops. They do not speak *Angrezi* or *Francisi*. And I hope the various platoons in this regiment will be kept together if the Brigade is dispersed...' But he realized that he was speaking in a tone loud enough to be heard by the sepoys. So he led Captain Owen away.

'Where's Havildar Lachman Singh?' the Sahib asked, turning to Lalu, as if apologizing for the way their conversation had been cut short.

'*Huzoor*,' came the voice of Havildar Lachman Singh promptly from where the men were falling in.

Lalu hurried and joined the ranks.

They were numbered off, '*phorm-phored*,' 'two deep' and 'staneteased,' the orders being less raucous and noisily stern than usual.

And then they waited.

Again they were called to attention. And Owen Sahib passed along the ranks, inspecting them.

Lalu looked at him intently. Even now there was the same flicker on the corners of his lips, an enigmatic smile which combined kindness and a certain cheerfulness of temper with severity of determination, inscrutable and incomprehensible, but nevertheless very reassuring from the dignity it reflected.

After the inspection the voice of Lieutenant Audley, the company commander, rang out above the noise of sepoys' heavy feet and the rustling of their clothes as they swung about and became whited ghosts in the mist.

For some time the 'lef-right lef-right' filled Lalu's mind. Then the rhythmic trampling feet seemed to give place to a slurred movement as if they were wrestling with the earth again ... Soon he himself had waded into a marshy field where the water drained away after every foot-fall and the boots became heavier and heavier with the mud.

With mumbled curses and sighs of resignation they slowed their pace, striding along as best they could, while the few outhouses and trees on the flanks of the road slid by ...

'Steady! Steady! The trenches are not far,' encouraged Owen Sahib, and epithets died down.

The dawn was scattering heavy mist as they got into new trenches and, here and there, the fog was discoloured a pale thin white which improved visibility.

The sepoys began to scramble about and have a good look at their new abode, but it was not very different from their habitation of the past few days, except for the greater profusion of empty tins and damp cigarette packets, which indicated that this part of the line had been occupied by English regiment. Some of the men retired to the dugouts to sleep off the fatigue, while others set about to make themselves at home.

Always anxious to size up the situation, Lalu lifted his head above the parapet, only to discover the same kind of vast shell-pitted turnip field, full of stakes and roots, as had stretched out before the trenches which they had left. Only there were the isolated remnants of a house in no-man's-land on the right, just where the trenches were lost in a wooded rise. Perhaps that cottage was part of the shattered village which was visible behind their trenches. The mist was still dense in places and obscured the view. Not a soul was to be seen, however, beyond no-man's land. But a shrieking whistle went overhead, followed by a zoom which compelled silence.

He retreated from the parapet and stood looking about him. There was a momentary pause in the fire. But hardly had he turned to look for Uncle Kirpu when a series of shrieking whistles filled the hollows of the earth.

Havildar Lachman Singh, who had just lain down to rest, came out adjusting his turban, startled by the suddenness with which this avalanche had begun. For a moment he stood to listen and then ran up to the left flank of the company.

'What is the matter?' Kirpu asked emerging from his lair. 'Rape-daughters, they won't give us any rest! ...'

'The Germans are shelling our lines,' Lalu said.

'To which our guns, being non-existent, cannot reply,' said Kirpu bitterly. 'To be sure the enemy will be attacking us this morning.'

Lalu cowered instinctively under the shrill crescendo of a shell which burst somewhere in the communication trenches.

As if ashamed at being nervous, he tried to look Uncle Kirpu straight in the face.

'*Acha*, son, we will be all right,' Kirpu said. And, fetching out a bucket stuffed with straw, he continued: 'I am sure the *Goras* lit fire in this. We will warm some tea which I kept in my water-bottle...'

Lalu came to the bucket as to a newly-found toy and began to help Uncle Kirpu to make a fire.

'Go and get the brass jug from my pack,' Kirpu said.

Spurred on by picnicky feeling the boy hurried. As he came back with jug he met the tall Hanumant Singh who came groping along and said: 'The Ajitan Sahib has passed word that the enemy is attacking all along the line and we must be in readiness.'

'*Aloo* right,' said Uncle Kirpu with imperturbable calm. 'Don't make such a noise. Come and have some tea.'

'Where is the tea?' said fatty Dhayan Singh rushing up like a big guy for office.

'Come along, boys,' Kirpu called. 'Don't stand there looking at the stars to foretell your fate — that is known to you ...'

Lalu came over and sat quietly while Uncle Kirpu emptied the contents of the water bottle into the brass jug and warmed it and his hands on the crackling straw in the bucket. The boys admired Kirpu's thoughtfulness in always putting things by for use on a rainy day, but neither of them said anything. It was curious how they had become quieter since they had been in action. They did not even complain about the inconvenience of changing trenches and this red-hot reception they were getting from the enemy, as if after the hardships of the first attack they were now prepared to accept anything. Perhaps, as Uncle Kirpu said, 'they knew their fate.' Or perhaps they were seeking to know it and had therefore withdrawn themselves from others and turned inwards so as to fight out all the doubts and fears and the terrors of their minds in order the more effectively to relinquish themselves to vague feelings, the only certainty in this world of ruin and carnage. And, since this battle was going on at the same time as the war within them, they were involved in protracted deliberations and then in long periods of silence.

A piece of shrapnel fell right into the dugout, sizzling like a chunk of butter.

'Drink up your tea, boys, and get to your positions,' Kirpu said. 'The God of Death is looking for someone ...'

Hanumant retreated without waiting for the tea, while Dhayan Singh began to make himself comfortable.

Lalu took half the jugful in his ration plate and gulped it at a draught it was lukewarm, but it moistened the stale taste in his mouth and filled the gap in his belly.

Then he took his rifle and went to his post.

The morning light was breaking across the sky, but damp mist still hung on the land, closing its cold grip on everything, greying eyelashes, eyebrows and small hair on their faces, as if they had suddenly become hundreds of years old in a night, from rottenness in the earth as well as the sulphurous smell of the fireworks.

Lalu naively wondered whether the Germans had spotted them as they took over the new lines. The enemy seemed to be prodigal of lead, for German artillery fired relentlessly, hard and without a break.

He withdrew his rifle from the spyhole to look at the ground before him. Behind the mist he imagined he could see the helmeted shapes of Germans advancing. And he thought he could hear the sound of the mud sucking at their heavy boots. Here and there the smoke mingled with the mist and rose, and it seemed to him that the Germans were running and crawling.

'Here, take this,' Uncle Kirpu said, handing him a packet of cigarettes and matches.

Lalu took them, stole a glance at his friend, as if he were afraid of Kirpu's vigilance.

He puffed at the cigarette, several short, brisk puffs, and then inhaled a large quantity of smoke which tickled his throat, so that he was caught in the paroxysms of a black cough. His eyes were full of tears when he recovered. He smiled nervously and felt relieved.

The enemy artillery fire became heavier and heavier through the morning and forenoon.

And yet the Dogra company waited for orders, keeping up a steady, rapid fire towards the German lines to keep themselves safe. There was the contagion of madness in the riot. Lalu kept firing round after round, persistent and hard, as if he had been drugged into a passion of violence.

Kirpu was doing the same.

Suddenly there was a confused uproar on the right flank: the tom-tom of Death's door-keeper seemed to be announcing the entry of some of the sepoys into the gates of hell, while the reluctant spirits yelled and screamed and shouted, and refused to go in at the bidding of Yama's army, whose steel mouths issued the orders with enfilading machine-gun fire.

'They are on us, boys' Havildar Lachman Singh raved.

'Has the attack begun?' asked Dhayan Singh.

Lachman nodded, as he stood sweating and eager. Then he took his own rifle.

Lalu withdrew his rifle from the sandbags where it rested and faced right. As far as he could see there was no one in the traverses for about fifty yards, but beyond that the men were at grips with each other: it suddenly dawned on him that the defensive line consisted of a thin scroll of detached posts. And the tragedy was that the Germans had taken a section of the line, from where they were enfilading post after post.

There they were, masses of heavy-coated men, steel-helmeted and large, shouting in guttural accents, rushing, leaping and jumping on the traverses and falling, mown down by the fire of the Indian platoon.

Hurrah!' the sepoys were shouting as they ran excitedly to the right.

'Fire! fire!' the orders rang out behind him.

And, as Lalu looked round, Owen Sahib, Audley Sahib, Subedar Suchet Singh, Jemadar Subah Singh and Lance Naik Lok Nath came rushing through the trench with men, some of whom were leaping over the traverses, lying down taking cover and then running again.

'Let them have it!' Lachman shouted. And himself he jumped over the parapet, like an accomplished hunter, and ran into the traverses beyond the officers.

'*Bol Kali mai ki jai!*' shouted the sepoys and rushed after him.

Then the earth seemed to crack and they seemed to go down the fissures. Some ran and met the enemy half way with bared bayonets, others fell, fantastic contortions, wounded and torn by the vigorous rifle and machine-gun fire which the energy discharged at them.

Lalu could feel his rifle red hot in his hand but he persevered, keeping close to Kirpu, shooting continuously from the broken wall of a house in the traverse into which he had leapt. Havildar Lachman Singh was dangerously near the enfiladers farther ahead.

'*Holdara!*' Lalu shouted to warn him of the danger.

'There is no talk, son,' said Kirpu. 'Shoot and keep faith ...'

Everyone was in the whirlpool, and it was of no avail to be afraid for oneself, or for anyone else. The only thing was to guard against exhaustion, to be grim and right in, naked and vulnerable.

'Charge with bayonets!' Lieutenant Audley cried, as, grabbing the rifle of a fallen sepoy, he ran on the parapet.

But hardly had he leapt up when he was mown down and fell, head first. Beyond him the advance guard was facing up to a furious onslaught.

And then the enemy came hurling down from where they had taken cover, thrusting their bayonets home into the sepoys, advancing in spite of the continuous rifle fire, like a wall of steel, pressing home their advantage with a relentless fury.

'Keep up the fire,' shouted Owen Sahib to Jemadar Subah Singh. 'Can't stay here any longer. But cover your retreat.'

'Retire!' shouted Subedar Suchet Singh.

Staggering like drunken men, plastered with mud, streaming with sweat with no hope for the comrades they were leaving behind, they retreated step by step, firing the while.

They kept up the fire but it was no use,, for now they had taken the corner into a traverse. They hurried back across the mouldering earth of the communication trench.

'Rape-mother!' said Hanumant Singh, who had never been known to swear.

As Lalu scrambled back through the maze of the trenches, the enemy's barrage grew more ferocious, while the platoon's rifles seemed to have been silenced. He was fascinated by the horror that would be raging there and could not help thinking of Havildar Lachman Singh who had been left behind. But ahead of him there seemed nothing to oppose the remnants of the company in the field except the occasional splinters that flew hither and thither and the noise of pounding guns.

He did not know how long it had all lasted, but he crept out of the trench and followed the men who were making a detour behind the ruined walls of the farmhouse, exhausted, unable to think or feel, resurrected from the very jaws of monster Death.

8

DARKNESS WAS FALLING over the ruins of Messines as the smoke of battle clouded the grey sky. Now and then a shell illumined the wreckage through which the men were treading their way, or the flash of a gun flickered on someone's face. But the firing. was incessant. They seemed to be reaching the trenches rather than receding away from them.

Lalu explored the ground carefully before each step and tripped over a boulder into a shell hole, turning a complete somersault.

'Oh, what's the matter with me!'

But anxious not to lose touch with the men, he wiped his muddy hands on his coat and was getting ready to emerge from the hole when the boulder across which he had stumbled fell across him. As he looked round he saw a corpse ...

With a half-suppressed moan, he ran hitting his knees his rifle, unmindful of everything except escape from the horror which he felt was pursuing him ... The half-distant shapes of the sepoys were disappearing behind the broken wall of the farmhouse on the road where they had assembled before going to their trenches at dawn. He did not want to run in case he should fall again; and yet the ghost of the corpse, became the spirit of Dhanoo, was pursuing him, for to his crazed brain it seemed as if the old man was following him about, chastising him, the adopted son, to offer the last rites on his body.

He hurried, only stopping when he saw Kirpu waiting for him impatiently at the foot of the road. The grotesque horrors in his mind seemed to have been left behind, and he followed his friends to where the men were assembling behind the ruined farmhouse.

'Fall in! Fall in!' Lance-Naik Lok Nath was shouting as though he were intoxicated by the smoke of war.

'There is no need to dress ranks,' Subedar Suchet Singh said. And, as though not certain, he turned first to Jemadar Subah Singh and then to Owen Sahib who stood with Major Peacock. The officers seemed to go about automatically.

Captain Owen came over, dishevelled, mud bespattered, surveyed the men who had half formed up, and then jerked his head, whispering something to Subedar Suchet Singh, something which sounded like 'Dismiss.'

'Come on, boys, we rest awhile in the Sahibs' dugout,' said Subedar Suchet Singh.

The men began to creep through the haze of night mist into a cellar across the road.

Uncle Kirpu walked up to Subedar Suchet Singh for some reason and stood talking to him anxiously, so Lalu went ahead.

'Are we to go to billets or where?' he asked Hanumant Singh. who looked more like a lemur as he walked along, his face begrimed and black and stamped with an animal ferocity.

'Each one for himself, brother,' Hanumant replied.

They entered the cellar.

Some of the sepoys crouched on the stone floor, others sat down and sprawled all over the place, while still others were collecting themselves around a bucketful of smouldering ashes, almost as if they were assembling at a meeting of the brotherhood to perform the last rites on the sacrificial fire for the dead.

No one spoke for long moments.

They all sat about, their brooding, serious faces lined and twisted by fatigue, empty, and downcast with the indefinable misery of battle.

Lalu had lain in a half sleep in the cellar, when he awakened with a sudden jerk and found his body convulsed with the tremors of a nightmare. He opened his eyes for the barest moment to assure himself that he was safe and Kirpu near him. The old man was sitting up smoking a cigarette, while most of the other sepoys lay in heaps on every side, shuddering, snoring or twitching. The guns were still roaring with endless violence. He shivered and collected his limbs together against the cold, and in order to avoid touching Hanumant who lay next to him. And he tried to recollect the details of the bad dream which had disturbed him. But the threads seemed to have slipped. In the festering restlessness of his brain, however, he recalled his mother's description of the various hells through which sinners had to go: the hell where beings are cut, wounded and bruised by Yama and his hosts; the hell where, reborn, beings are struck down with blazing weapons, severed into pieces and left to rot in the mud and the slime; the hot and cold hells; the hell where the sinners are crushed like sesame seeds; and the hell where they have to swim through oceanic expanses of dirty drains.

He turned over to avoid the thought and sought to sleep again. But his active agitated mind was filled with the vision of Daddy Dhanoo's dead face, wooden and hard. And as he shook himself to forget Dhanoo, his mind filled with the memory of those who had fallen in the defence against the German enfilading fire, as they jumped with chests thrown open to bullets.

Before he could be disturbed again he tried to gather the sinews of his face in sleep. But his mind (cocooned in the brain) was weaving another web in which putteed legs tangled and untangled themselves. He shook himself, opened his eyes bravely and sat wide awake for a while. The noise outside unnerved him and he looked towards Kirpu like a frightened puppy towards an older dog.

'Do you hear the bombs?' he asked for a moment.

'What?' Kirpu answered startled. Then, moistening his lips on his tongue and clearing his throat with a cough which was like a moan, he continued: 'They are crying at the bottom of the well.'

'Who are crying?'

Uncle Kirpu looked at the boy furtively in the dark and then closed his eyes without answering. But then he heaved himself against the wall to rest his back, and said in a doleful and sighing voice:

'Hemp has fallen in the well and they are weeping tears of blood.'

What was the matter with him? Was the old man also dreaming? He had been sitting there smoking silently, with wide-awake eyes only a little while ago. Perhaps, he had caught the contagion of restlessness that spread from the bodies of the whispering, moaning men about them.

'Do you understand something?' mocked Lalu impatiently, 'I also understand something.'

'*Ohe, Ooloo!*' exclaimed Uncle Kirpu in a shriek. 'Havildar Lachman Singh is dead ...' And saying this he deliberately bumped his head against the wall, beat his forehead with his hands and burst out crying.

Lalu was stunned. Then he spoke:

'Was he killed in that rush then? ... Who told you? ... Are you sure? ... Did he die at once?'

'*Ohe*, he was a lion,' Uncle Kirpu sobbed without attempting to answer the boy's questions. 'He was a wonder, son — Havildar Lachman Singh! The lion has gone and now the jackals will reign. *Hai*! ... What has happened? ... Why did God have to do this? ... But he died a hero, son, a hero. Neither his hand, nor his heart was defiled by cowardice. Suchet Singh says that when the enemy burst in upon him in the traverse, he fought single-handed and killed five Germans before his bayonet failed. And then, as if the lion was not to be daunted, be picked up a broken bayonet and continued an unequal combat against three of the enemy until he collapsed.' Kirpu paused with a lump in his throat and then wailed in a mournful sing song inside him: 'Oh my lion! You have blessed the womb that bore you and gave you birth, my Lachman ...'

Lalu contemplated the face of his comrade, a brave, lively, mischievous face at the worst of times, now old with wrinkles of grief. The boy had never imagined that the wise, cynical Uncle Kirpu would break down in the face of anything. He stared at him embarrassed and full of tenderness. He could not bear to see the old man crying like a child when he himself felt curiously detached. And he put his arm around him.

'Uncle Kirpu, patience now, brother, we must have patience'.

Uncle Kirpu bit his lips and the ends of his moustache to control himself.

'Come,' Lalu said, stretching his hand to Kirpu's shoulder. 'We are still together, we shall stick together, shan't we?'

'All right, son, I am a silly old man, forgive me,' said Kirpu. 'Of course, we shall stick together.'

And he leaned back and coughed out the choking breath in his throat.

'Wake up! Awake!' came Subedar Suchet Singh's husky voice.

'Get up, you gum-eyed bastards!' came Jemadar Subah Singh's orders.

'Stand to! Drink this tea and get ready to move! Wake up!' Lance-Naik Lok Nath bullied even as he ran amok and kicked a huddled up sepoy here and pulled the arm of another there.

Kirpu shook Lalu who lay with his eyes closed.

This drew the attention of Lance-Naik Lok Nath. 'Get up you cock-eyed son of a Sahib!' Lok Nath shouted as he charged upon Lalu. 'Get up! There is no Havildar Lachman Singh to put you to sleep and cover you with blankets now! Get up!'

And then, turning to Uncle Kirpu, he shook him by the arm and snarled, showing his long teeth under the thin lips.

The sepoys heaved their bodies and rubbed their faces with their palms. Some of them just hung down their heads and belched, others stared stonily at the officers. Lok Nath raced to the corners and shook the bodies of those who were sound asleep with impatient shouts, abuses and kicks.

'*Ohe*, wake them but give them time!' Subedar Suchet Singh shouted from the passage way to restrain Lok Nath. 'We shall go and find out what is happening. Come, Jemadar Subah Singh.'

Lalu had sat up wondering what it was all about. It was dead of night and long past meal time. Outside, the bombardment was still going on.

'Get ready!' Lok Nath bawled as he walked with lifted chest towards the passageway. 'Take your "biscoots" and tea.'

'*Wah, ohe* Mishtar Lok Nath!' Lalu mumbled at the Lance-Naik's anglicism. '*Wah*!'

'Keep quiet,' Uncle Kirpu laid a significant finger on his mouth.

'What's happened?' Lalu asked, embarrassed to have been seen being kicked.

Kirpu raised his head towards the bucket of steaming tea a ration party were bringing in.

'What are we waiting for now, Uncle?' Lalu said, seeing the ration party men standing still while Lok Nath went upstairs.

'For orders, from the orders from above on high,' said Uncle Kirpu, seeking to suppress the rage and hatred in his heart. 'We are always waiting for orders, son. We have been waiting for orders for months, for years, son. Always waiting — for orders! From above ... And a sepoy's duty is — to obey, son, to obey. And as that snake told you now ... Havildar Lachman Singh is dead!'

'Come then, pour that tea, now that you have awakened us,' Dhayan Singh shouted to the cook.

'Come, that tea! Yes, what are we waiting for?' shouted Rikhi Ram.

'Judgment Day,' muttered Lalu to himself.

'We are going to warm you up with rum, boys,' said a member of the ration party. 'Tea and rum — before action.'

'*Hein*?'

'Really?'

'Is that the truth?'

Inquiring voices arose.

'So we go back to the trenches!' Lalu said. 'But the Ajitan Sahib dismissed us after that roll call. Why didn't he tell us then?'

'The Ajitan Sahib is not the Jarnel Sahib,' said Kirpu mildly. 'And he would have had to yield his sword and belt to be imprisoned in the "quarter-guard" had he given such orders on his own initiative. We are in the army, not peeling carrots at home. In Chin it was different; even a corporal or a soldier could keep his two eyes open to the possibility of a situation. And the Afridis on the border are the same. But the Angrez Jarnel is like God, who doesn't hasten, and is said never to make a mistake!

Lok Nath came back, his tall body stiff as a threat.

'Here, pour a little of this into everyone's tea,' the Lance Naik said handing a bottle of rum to the ration party.

'All ranks come up on top after you have finished!'. Lok Nath snapped, every word a bullet.

For a moment they sat there as if they had listened to the sentence of death.

'Come on, boys,' said the ration party men, and began to dole out tea and rum.

The sepoys fumbled for their utensils even as they assembled their packs.

Lalu got up and went with outstretched vessel to the cooks.

'That will make you feel better, *Huzoor*,' Santu said abjectly even as he shivered.

Lalu gulped the hot liquid and brushed himself, trying to get a grip on himself.

Outside it was a clear night, with stars hanging down like lanterns as on the Red Sea, incredibly many stars for a land where the sepoys imagined that stars had ceased to exist. Three-fourths of a moon stood high, silly and pale and seemingly frightened by the bombardment which was going on.

He gazed at Mars, the star of war, which he had come to recognize on the voyage from its redness, but apart from its brilliance there seemed no meaning in it. The village priest and astrologer who had always unfolded his calendar to fix propitious dates for births and marriages, had talked of the influence of the planets on people. The ancient holy men, he said, had measured the universe exactly ... Lalu wondered, if the stars really moulded the destiny of men, or if they were inhabited.

'Shun!' the order went forth and ended his speculations.

As he fell into position he felt relieved to be doing something.

They were told by Subedar Suchet Singh simply, that orders had come for the company to counter-attack. And he asked all ranks to show their bravery and follow their officers.

Although they expected some such orders, they were sullen because an attack meant hurling themselves at the enemy with bayonets, and being mown down by machine-gun fire.

Suddenly there was a commotion farther up the line.

'Get up, get up!' Subedar Suchet Singh was shouting.

'Oh Subedarji, forgive me, leave me here, I have got fever, forgive me! the soft voice of the tall lemur-like Hanumant Singh could be heard. 'I can't fight! I will not fight for this dirty Sarkar.'

'Stand up! Coward!'

'Up!'

'Son of a swine!'

The voices of officers multiplied.

But Hanumant simply lay down, resisting like a child, and stubbornly rolled on the ground, refusing to get up.

'Stand up!' roared Lok Nath.

'*Ohe*, illegally begotten!' shouted Subah.

'I shall deal with him,' said Suchet Singh, taking out his revolver. 'If you don't get up while I count three ... one, two ... three ...' And he shot at Hanumant so that the sepoy shrieked and doubled over with a '*Hai, hai*, oh my ...'

'Subedar Sahib!' Lok Nath cried horror-struck.

'Go ahead boys! Get along!' Subedar Suchet Singh ordered, panting for breath. 'Leave him!'

The sepoys began to move away, dazed and wooden.

And they advanced slowly, ponderously.

'If we did not die other deaths we shall survive this one,' Dhayan Singh said hopefully.

'You will not die even if stoned to death!' Rikhi Ram answered him.

'He has one leg in the sky, another in the netherworlds,' said Lalu mocking at his comrade, but really describing himself.

They had now entered a field on the right of the trench, and were within the range of enemy fire.

A couple of German guns near 'Plug Street Wood' explored them relentlessly through the smoke, and Lalu felt the shrapnel splinter and scatter around him.

He muttered a curse to steady himself.

Some Tommies from a company which was converging in the direction to which they were going, were struck by a shell and their legs, hands, heads, clothes and bayonets all shot up and fell into the pit where the metal buried itself.

Lalu's legs were shaking, but he kept calm and, for a moment he could see everything clearly in vivid flashes. The Tommies seemed pale in the light as they advanced clumsily, but determinedly.

He paused to see if there were any wounded whom he could help. But every one was edging away from the shell hole and proceeding towards the communication trenches ahead.

He hurried to catch up Kirpu.

There was the smell of burning flesh and scorched greenery.

The detonation of another bomb rent the sky, leaving a trail of fire, which smothered the smoke.

They rushed forward into a trench, hurtling after each other and almost choking the narrow passageway, because Owen Sahib and the other officers wouldn't move. The men behind shouted and raved, and the blast and concussion of exploding shells created panic. Someone pushed Lalu from behind, and he felt trapped, confused and angry.

When the advance guard began to move Lalu pushed and shoved. Somehow, in a moment, he had become chock-full of anger and impatience, and the fear in him was smothered. He felt like a monster who would annihilate everything on his way.

As they threaded their way through the maze of communication trenches the path was comparatively clear, except that they could hear fire farther ahead.

In spite of the resurgence of fear, Lalu was master of himself now. He remembered that he had felt this sureness in himself during the days when he used to lead mock battles for the castle. like mound on the top of the hill near the brick ovens at Nandpur. The resourcefulness and ingenuity of his youth seemed to return to him. His feet trod the ground with the lightness of a conqueror. But, as if to sustain himself at the pitch of excitement, or because the fear in him was only quiescent, he mumbled like Padre Anandale, as he proceeded bent at an angle of forty-five: 'The sun, the moon and the stars were darkening ...'

Before he knew where he was, the advance line met some Germans in a trench which had been widened by a shell crater. Uncle Kirpu had jumped right in.

Lalu looked round for the barest moment, and then leaped in too. A German from a nest beyond the parapet had fixed his aim on him, but hesitated and only pulled the trigger a little after Lalu decided to go into the crater.

With instantaneous resolution, the boy stooped low like a lion on the prowl and charged him with his bayonet, fixing him with such force that the butt of his rifle resounded back on his chest. The man gnashed his teeth and groaned as he fell. Lalu groped for his victim, to finish him, murmuring: '*Jahanam*! hell...'

He had not suspected such cruelty in himself, but before his fear or pity could restrain him, a shell soared in the sky and illuminated the shadows and the glass of a wrist-watch on his victim's wrist. He swooped upon the prize, slightly afraid that the man's ghost might strike him or possess him. He had longed for a wrist-watch. He undid the leather strap and, trembling, took the watch and let the hand drop, still warm, on the German's side ...

'Go ahead, *ohe*, hurry,' the shouts followed him.

And he raced behind the advance guard which was clearing the front line of Germans with hand-to-hand bayonet fighting.

The men behind him had overflowed the shell hole. Then, maddened and desperate like beasts, they had raced up the parapet, climbed it and were running towards the front line, against a withering machine-gun fire.

The trenches here were so narrow that the littered up bodies of the dead almost choked the passage.

Lalu swerved round and made his way to the front line by a tortuous route through another pit by which Kirpu was heaving himself along.

'Why *Chacha*?' he shouted.

'*Aloo* right!' he said imitating Kirpu.

As they crawled up the front line trench from a strip of open ground, wave after wave of Dogras and Tommies were rushing at the few Germans left in that part of the trench.

'Lie still and low,' Kirpu warned the boy.

The Dogras who had filled the crater were spreading through the recaptured front line now, a small strip of trench which was all they had gained for the loss of those choking bodies which lay heaped farther up.

'Come on, son,' Kirpu said.

Lalu was glad to be on the move as he had had to hold his breath every time a stray shell burst and he felt exposed to enemy fire.

Owen Sahib was bending over someone's body, with his own left arm held to his chest.

Lalu went up towards him hoping it was not Jemadar Subah Singh, for in spite of the boy's arrogance his old comrades were concerned about him. No, it was the Subedar...

'Suchet Singh is gone,' he said returning to Kirpu. 'Suppose God has revenged Hanumant on the dog.

'Who? What?' the men in the trenches queried as they stood or sat now with bent heads, looking at themselves spitting, coughing or leaning back exhausted.

Lance-Naik Lok Nath came down and shot the bullets of his glance at Kirpu and Lalu.

'Where were you two, asses?'

'Obeying orders,' Kirpu answered.

'*Ohe*, protecting your skins! ...'

As if there was still some pain in the bodies of the dead and the half dead left to extract, the hosts of Death were extracting it till the dawn. A rain of shells fell on every side of their strip of trench. And there was a hail of machine gun fire from the right where the Germans still seemed to occupy long stretches of the allied front line ... The sepoys just had to stand there and receive the punishment, without retaliating for fear of drawing more fire on themselves. There were only a handful of the original company left.

Cold and numb and tottering with sleep, Lalu was surprised to discover in the early morning that he could still see, hear, smell, feel, that he was still in existence, that be had, indeed, advanced the short distance from the ruined farm-house and survived overwhelming odds which Destiny had put on his way.

He was more surprised still to find the other sepoys moving about, people whom he knew slightly or merely by name. They were slow and mechanical in their movement, or seemed so from the sameness of their khaki, because really they sat or lay about in the most extraordinary contortions, embroiled in their own doom and seeking to possess in the same manner.

And, perhaps, because they had shared a common suffering and were now trying to recover their balance, they left each other alone, saying little, except the words necessary to borrow a match or a cigarette, as if they knew each other instinctively and were bound in a curious distant sympathy.

They would have lain there brooding, reflecting on the past to recapture their faith, or lent themselves to their broken dreams and reveries. But Major Peacock, who had become the head of the regiment since Colonel Green was wounded some days ago, arrived with a few men from the Punjabi Muslim company and orders were given for the troops to spread themselves to the left where, it was said, a hundred men of the Sikh company were still holding out under Major Dunlop Sahib. These orders evoked the inevitable response, smothering the smoke of that hall-incandescent despair which had agitated their bodies with involuntary shudderings, mutterings, and silent torment.

'Where's *Holdar* Lachman Singh?' Lance-Naik Aslam Khan of the Punjabi Muslim company asked Kirpu after they had rearranged themselves over the line.

'He — he has become a resident of the Celestial Heavens!' said Kirpu with a tremor on his lower lip. And though Aslam Khan had not asked him about anyone else, he proceeded: 'Also Dhanoo — he was drowned, the poor bastard, and his ghost is still unhoused. And Hanumant who refused to fight for "the dirty Sarkar", as he called it, was shot at close range by Subedar Suchet Singh, who was himself blown to bits there.' And he shook his head towards the scene of the last night's counterattack, a frown on his face that was sad and pitiless. 'And now I suppose you will ask me about my torn uniform?'

Aslam Khan respected his friend's bitterness and kept quiet.

And, for a moment, the scorn and hatred of Uncle Kirpu's voice filled the air.

'What happened to you?' Kirpu asked, curt and indifferent even as he tried to be human.

'Our Subedar withdrew us to half a mile behind the village after we had made a bayonet charge,' said Aslam Khan. 'And we became separated in the fields. We found our way back to the streets, but there were only sister-raper *Goras* there, and not a sepoy to be seen. I asked several Tommies the way but they do not understand anything of us. Then I met a Sahib who spoke Hindustani and he led us to where Peacock Sahib was ...'

'To be sure, they do not understand anything of us,' said Kirpu. 'We were attacking with some Tommies last night. I did not know what they were doing and they did not know what I was doing. And shells came like stones in the earthquake at Kangra. Why didn't they keep all our companies together? ...'

'We are going to have a reunion today,' said Aslam Khan.

'We are going to be relieved and go to billets.'

'It is all one,' said Lalu. 'Trenches or billets?'

'No, we are going to rest,' said Aslam Khan. 'That will be like paradise.'

A dirty black mist was sucking up the gloom of the night as they lurched along, nerve-racked and worn, towards the billets across a narrow, pitted road, full of puddles and mud. Occasionally they looked back to measure the distance they had covered, or were startled by the shells which burst overhead. But then they adjusted the packs on their backs, lifted their downcast faces and looked ahead.

For it had seemed an interminable time waiting for the relieving battalion to come. And when the 15th Sikhs, which formed part of the Jullundur Brigade, did come, splashing the mud, shouting and rattling, fresh from billets, fooling and enthusiastic like children, they were a long time taking over charge, quarrelling about who should have the trench 'props'.

'You wait, my son, no one has gained immortality in war,' Uncle Kirpu had said to the Sikhs who took over, before emerging into the muddy morass of the fields.

Now that they had been on the road their cold feet seemed to be warming, and, perhaps because they were marching in a column, or because their congealed blood flowed, they hurried forward, full of the urgency and exhilaration of escape.

'Any news of spring?' Lalu asked mockingly.

'After a long day's march,' said Kirpu briefly, 'it will be good weather.'

And for a while they slogged along silently, thump, thump, thump ...

The villages looked strangely grim in the half light with the debris of their shattered bridges, of the naked ruins of houses, with horror-struck windows and charred wood gaping out of roofs and walls, with the gaunt, dismantled churches rearing their shadows across the hundreds of old and new mounds of graves, where the spirits of the dead seemed to crowd together, waiting to possess the living who came that way.

Such was the ghostly dread of the uncanny gloom that Lalu felt comforted to see the wooded slant of the ridge on the left, raked by shell fire. But it was an area of small hillocks and the broken ends of numerous ridges.

On they went across the narrow circuitous road which had now entered the plains, on and on.

Someone began chirping a melody as if at the sight of hills.

'One dies, another sings folk songs!' Kirpu said.

Indeed. Lalu thought, it seemed unholy to sing a sentimental ditty of the hills. And he looked back along the columns to see who it was. The hedges alongside the roads precluded a good view of the troops, they were passing by a cluster of houses outside which a group of children stood, whispering to each other even as they looked at the strange apparitions, and whistled in sympathy with the singer.

'Tish, mish, tish,' Uncle Kirpu aped their accent with a smile that creased his face. And he lovingly smacked his lips to caress them as if they were the young ones of birds or animals.

The children smiled and some of them ran among the fowls to the doors of their houses, while the others began to run with the troops as Kirpu beckoned them.

'Eighty years of age and named Infant!' mocked Lalu.

But Uncle Kirpu was not to be restrained and waved to some dirty, war-worn Tommies who were crowding round a roadside café, their eyes rolling restlessly in their curiosity to see the Indians pass.

Lalu's blank face struggled to smile. But his eyes glowed feverishly and his limbs sagged. He felt he was a different species of man from the Tommies who were cheering the troops, not because they were white soldiers and he was a Hindustani sepoy (for from the way that the Tommies had lived and moved in the trenches under the same conditions as the sepoys that difference had now ceased to exist), but because the men outside the café, like the enthusiastic Sikhs who had relieved the 69th, had already rested and were living to a different rhythm from the sepoys who came from the black hell of trenches.

'I wish they would stop us here somewhere,' Lalu said as they crossed the square.

'That house is yours,' Uncle Kirpu said pointing to a farmhouse at the end of the village. 'Only don't stretch your hands to it.'

Lalu persevered.

Curiously it was, as Uncle Kirpu said by a fluke, the farm-house where they were going to rest.

For Major Peacock Sahib halted the men with a gesture, while Dunlop Sahib went ahead with the other officers.

The Major did not open his mouth to shout orders, but the Ranks made themselves into some kind of array with a grim, weary shuffle. And then, automatically, they began to call their numbers with cracked voices. Out of a total strength of seven hundred and fifty, there were four hundred and fifty left.

All was still for a moment.

Then the word 'Dismiss' came as a long wished for magic.

The ranks walked up in fours, hard and rigid, as if still held together by the invisible chords of discipline. But as they filed away from the road they lurched off, lightfooted, relaxing their muscles and dissolved into the musty lanes behind billeting officers.

That night the No. 2 company slept on beds of straw in a large dusty barn near the farmhouse by the brook. Most of the sepoys did not even take off their uniforms or taste a bite of food.

❦ 9 ❧

THEY WERE SERVED tea early in the morning and they revived, clustered about in groups, smoked, rested and took off their puttees, boots, belts and water bottles.

'There is a brook of clear water running outside,' Uncle Kirpu said as he came back singing hymns from where he had gone in the half-dark to relieve himself. 'I had a dip. Why don't you go, son, and have one?'

Lalu wanted a bath badly, but he shivered at the thought of the cold outside. He leaned back on the uncouth pillow of his equipment and tried to make up his mind.

'Go on, son,' Kirpu coaxed him. 'It is cold but you will feel fresh afterwards.'

The boy only smiled a cowardly smile.

'What a dirty swine you are!' Uncle Kirpu reproached him.

'You haven't bathed all these days, and now when you have a chance, you sit there, frightened like a baby.'

The boy mustered the necessary courage and walked out.

Outside a mild sun was shining and there was a slight breeze, And the world seemed full of light after the dull, monotonous grey skies of the days in trenches.

Behind the barn, the brook moved swiftly by the queer fan of the wind-mill, bubbling like a hill-nullah.

He hastened towards the sepoys who were laughing as they splashed each other or pushed their unwilling comrades into the cold water.

There was a happiness in their antics which was contagious and set

144

him quivering with memories of his early mornings on the village well with his cronies. The simplicity of their behaviour gave them a certain dignity in his eyes, a view which some of the Tommies, who sat on the canal bank admiring them, seemed to share.

Excited by the hilarity of the atmosphere, he wondered at the joyous indifference with which he himself and these others could forget everything, and the light-heartedness to which they could abandon themselves immediately after the endless days, and nights in trenches.

'Come on,' the men shouted. 'Hurry! Throw him into the water!'

He capered aside, out of the reach of the two men who lay in ambush for him, but they leapt at him and caught him, one at the legs, the other at the shoulders.

'Now talk to us!' one of them said. 'Did you want to fly out of our reach?'

'Leave me,' Lalu said. 'I won't run.'

'Promise,' they said.

They let him down tenderly but much to their discomfiture, he ran away.

By the small wooden bridge, where the stream elbowed past another farmhouse, some village women were washing their garments like the Indian women, while they gossiped or cried shrilly to their broods of children, who stood watching the sepoys performing their ablutions to the tune of holy verses, the names of God and the various spiritual conundrums. Apparently these women did not mind the hairy semi-nudity of the sepoys for they went on beating their linen without any embarrassment, cackling like a cluster of hens to each other. The sepoys, too, usually so afraid of the white folk that they could not make the slightest gesture which might be considered disrespectful, were now casual and hearty, almost as if they were at home.

The laughing, rippling eager rush of the water was inviting and he stripped, careful to be modest. But just at that moment a Punjabi Muslim, having no apron to tie round himself, entered the water stark naked and a chuckle arose among the crowd of sepoys and the French women.

Lalu waded into the water gingerly. At first he tried to play with it, then trembling, shivering, smiling, he took a dip and began to rub himself furiously. The dirt and scum of days began to roll off his limbs. He called to some sepoys who were retreating towards the farmhouse for soap. They called to some of their comrades who were soaping themselves by the windmill to throw the soap to Lalu. The chunk was passed from hand to hand. He soaped himself and, after dipping again, ran out of the freezing water and began to towel himself, smiling to the platoon of children who stood watching him.

. 'Savy,' one of the more forward of them said, mimicking the shivering men.

'What are you saying?' he exclaimed in Punjabi and mimicked the boy: 'Savy!'

'What are these kids saying?' asked a sepoy who crouched by the brook, sunning himself.

The children laughed at the incomprehensible speech of the sepoys and the sepoys laughed back and cheered them with a crude bluff of tenderness for the little ones.

'André! André,' a shrill call came from the bridgehead. And a woman who was washing clothes called even as she rolled her sleeves up to her shoulders, dipped her linen in the water, scrubbed it with a soap board and dipped it again.

André, who was one of the boys in the group, looked around, then turned a deaf ear and looked at Lalu with a smile, as much as to say, 'I don't care for their rebukes, I want to talk to you.'

As Lalu was getting into his coat, however, a young girl came rushing out of the farmhouse and, grimly catching hold of André, began to drag him back while the kid attempted to wrest himself from her hand.

'Maman,' shouted the girl, her long dark hair glistening across her flushed red cheeks.

Mama shouted back what seemed like a string of long drawn out curses, imprecations, entreaties and injunctions to André.

André protested with 'something, something, something Marie.'

And a tussle began between the two, André viciously obstinate, beating and kicking, Marie laughing, and weeping as she dragged her brother.

'Don't fight, ohe!' the crouching sepoy said.

But that advice, delivered in Punjabi, was of no avail.

Encouraged by a word from the stranger, André now bit Marie on her hands to secure release from her grasp, till the girl shrieked again hysterically, 'Maman! Maman!'

Lalu lunged forward and picked up André, and carried him towards his mother. At this the boy became docile, and forgot all about his quarrel with Marie, who followed modestly behind.

As they got to the door of the house by the bridge, Lalu laid the boy down.

In triumph André poked his tongue at Marie, a compliment which, as soon as Lalu had turned his back, Marie returned by poking her tongue at André and Lalu both.

Lalu could not help smiling to see the girl twisting her face like a child, even though she seemed grown up from the fullness of her breasts. And there was such light gaiety about her that he looked back and contemplated her again, with intense amusement. She caught him in the act of looking and poked her tongue out with deliberate mischief. He laughed a hearty laugh of embarrassment and sauntered back to the farmhouse.

Having fed to satiety on the feast that the cooks prepared for the day, the sepoys dozed off to make up for the sleeplessness of the nights in trenches or sat aimlessly about, smoking the while. And, the strange thing was that the Sikhs, to whom tobacco is taboo, did not object to the Hindu Dogras puffing away with asthmatic coughings.

Lalu sat smoking, his restless memory keeping him awake, and the awareness of the gap left by Dhanoo and Lachman growing on him through a confused medley of visions and feelings, when Jemadar Subah Singh came into the barn.

'Where is Kirpu,' he asked, in his familiar authoritative manner. It seemed that he had just sauntered down to the barn from a house across the road in which he was staying with two other officers, to see his old cronies. For what else could he want with the company, Lalu thought, on the first day in the billets?

'*Ohe*, Jemadar Subah Singh!' Lalu whispered as he shook Kirpu. 'Jemadar Sahib has come!'

'*Ah*, Jemadar Sahib, come on my head, come on my shoulder,' said the old man with a special emphasis on the Temadar Sahib as he sat up, belching and heavy. '*Ohe*, give the Jemadar Sahib something to sit on.'

'No, no, I just came to tell you something I had done for you,' said Subah, 'though you remain the ungrateful wretches that you have always been ...'

'Sit down, son, have a little tea, sit down,' said Kirpu with an ease which sprung from the strength of his simplicity. 'You can tell me the worst ...' And then the old man turned to Lalu: 'Go and fetch a tumblerful of tea from the cook ...'

Lalu was about to get up from where he sat smoking, but the Jemadar raised his arm officially and protested.

'Don't make a fuss, let the others sleep.'

'Acha, you can stand and be a gentleman,' said Kirpu, 'but my old limbs are a little cramped from the war and it is a holiday — so you will forgive me, won't you, Jemadar Sahib?'

'No, I must go and see Babu Khusi Ram and give him a report of yesterday's action,' began Subah. 'The Commanderin-Chief Sahib Bahadur is coming to inspect the troops and arrangements have to be made.'

'Really, Jemadar Sahib?' Dhayan Singh queried.

'Where is the parade, then?' Rikhi Ram asked.

'The *Jangi Lat* himself, did you say, *Huzoor*?' said a Sikh sepoy.

'Whose pride is greatest — that of the soldier or the General?' Kirpu said to rob the news of the element of dramatic surprise which the Jemadar wanted to put into it.

'He is said to have fought on the frontier,' said Lalu.

'*Han*, son, there is a rumour that he was also in Afreeka,' added Kirpu.

'Don't tell lies and spread rumours,' ordered Subah.

'Son, this was before you were born ...' Kirpu began to explain.

'Shut up!' the Jemadar said sternly, flushing a vivid red and turned to go.

Then he suddenly realized that he had not said what he had come to tell Kirpu. But he had brought about a wall between himself and his friends by shouting.

He stood for a moment, hesitating about the best way to retreat from an uncomfortable situation, and sought to assume the hard, cold mask of authority without betraying the slightest emotion.

But by now he had aroused the sepoys in the barn from their siesta. And the unrest, bred by the arrogance of his manner, quivered in the stubborn resistance of his will not to retreat without showing a sign of strength.

Luckily for him Lance-Naik Lok Nath came into the barn at that moment.

'Lance-Naik Lok Nath,' said the Jemadar directly, 'you are to present yourself with Sepoy Kirpa Ram to the officer commanding Sahib Bahadur tomorrow morning for your stripes.'

And he turned on his heels with an attempt at a dramatic abruptness.

'Have I been promoted Havildar?' said Lok Nath, his face lighting up with the only smile with which its thin lips had ever been known to be illuminated.

'*Han*, it is about your promotions that I came,' said Subah, 'but that fool Kirpu will not listen ...' And he walked out showing an excess of energy.

Lance-Naik Lok Nath followed him ingratiatingly.

'Make yourself a sheep and the wolf will eat you,' Kirpu muttered under his breath. And, fetching a cigarette out of his pocket, wetting it with moistened lips, he continued: 'Come, son, give me a match, it takes great wisdom to laugh at one's high rank.'

'Why did you not let him speak?' Lalu rebuked the old man. 'He had come to tell you of your promotion, as he said.'

'Now what could I do with him?' said Kirpu. 'He has grown up in my hands and is the same to me as he was at five. And he shows off so ...'

'But you are in the army and he is your officer.'

Uncle Kirpu sighed as if he were hurt at the conduct of the Jemadar.

'Cheer up, you are yourself an officer now,' said Lalu. 'A Lance-Naik! Uncle, brother-in law! Son of a Lance Naik, ho!'

'That stripe won't give me a permanent cramp in the neck,' Kirpu said. 'Two days of glory! I have no wish to be half Sahib and half man, half partridge and half quail ... after Lachman's death.'

'Come and let us eat the air,' said Lalu, after a little while, and he dragged Uncle Kirpu from where the old man sat brooding.

They emerged from the farmstead where they were billeted and tried to make a short cut through some out-houses by the edge of a field.

But as they proceeded beyond the shadow of a haystack they found themselves in a shed.

Hens ruffled themselves with loud protesting cackles, dropping feathers as they ran with swarms of chicks across the manure heap that lay neatly stacked in a corner; cows mooed defiance from somewhere in the sheds; pigs grunted their forebodings of room.

The sepoys were about to retreat when there was a shrill exchange of opinions in the house and, first, André and Marie, then Babu Khushi Ram and a red-cheeked old Frenchman, with a huge aureole-like beard came rushing into the courtyard.

'Where have you come from, dead ones?' greeted Babu Khushi Ram effusively.

'Our dead are still better than your living, Babuji,' said Kirpu. 'But we are happy to see you.'

'Let me congratulate you on your promotion,' Khushi Ram said to Kirpu, embracing him. And, then turning to Lalu, he said in a voice that sounded curiously new after the few days of their separation: 'Son, I hear you showed great bravery.'

The old man with the beard who had been beaming all this time mimed to Khushi Ram indicating the house.

'Papa says you must come in,' the Babu interpreted.

149

'If he does not drag us through the thorns, we would like to see the farm,' said Kirpu.

Lalu would have been equally keen to go into the house where Marie had withdrawn at the call of her mother, but he willingly followed Papa and the others 'through the thorns' by which Kirpu meant the parcelled allotments of vegetables beyond which lay the stables surrounded by sheds, enclosures and farm tools.

They looked in from the open upper doors of the wonderful cages, first into the warm comfort of a cubicle in which sat pigs, clean and red and fat.

'Almost as well groomed as the Sahibs,' Kirpu said, looking towards Lalu whose predilection for *Vilayat* was notorious.

'To be sure, the stable is not ankle-deep in manure as in our villages,' retorted Lalu, 'and these pigs are not like the lean, shrivelled mice that spread like plague on our countryside ...'

'*Acha Huzoor!*' acknowledged Kirpu and moved on to the neat cowsheds, whose stone floors were spotless. The hefty, small horned, well-polished cows raised their snozzles at them, stared and bowed. 'What are they saying?' Kirpu continued.

'Praying to God that they might be transported to Uncle Kirpu's village,' mocked Lalu, 'so that they can roll about in the mud, eat grain out of their own dung and be under no obligation to give milk.'

'They yield three times as much as one of our own spindly cows,' informed Khushi Ram. 'And what's more you don't have to tie their legs. Papa Labusière has a machine to milk them with.'

'A machine to milk cows with, really?' Lalu asked almost stunned.

'Look at their sheep,' added Babu Khushi Ram.

'Where?' said Kirpu non-plussed.

'There,' indicated Lalu. 'I suppose you expect them to be an agitated, frightened mass, huddled in one corner.'

'But they are diseased, eaten up by the worm,' shouted Kirpu to keep his end up.

The farmer apologized in incomprehensible words and gestures about the shaven, powdered patches on their bodies, and Babu Khushi Ram explained that they were being treated with some medicine which was marvellous. Uncle Kirpu began to suggest some herbs while the Babu interpreted this to the Frenchman in gestures.

Lalu strayed farther ahead and looked at a couple of mettlesome horses with dark, velvety winter coats, snorting at the hay as they stood in an immaculate stable. His eyes bulged as he stared at this wonder farm. If it was typical of *Vilayati* peasant households then all his righteous indignation against his own village folk had been justified and his aspiration to live as European farmers lived, a great ideal. He wished some of the old fogies of his village were here, for then he could show them how true had been his talk about reforming the village. In the absence of any of the elders of Nandpur, he vent his spleen on old Uncle Kirpu, as he suddenly turned round and said:

'Now, tell me, would you prefer us to live the lives of bullocks or would you have your bullocks live like human beings?'

'This peaceful stone-floored, clean world is agreeable enough, son,' said Kirpu, 'but ...'

'But what?' inquired Lalu impatiently. 'I suppose you think there is no God resident here because there is no warm dung and urine mixed up into a dough with the bodies of the cattle?... To the Hindus cow dung is sacred ...'

'No, son, but even the rats in the Sahibs' houses seem shrewd,' said Kirpu lamely. 'They are rich people ... though I wonder why they are killing each other and making a large graveyard of this land ...'

It seemed to the old man that there were as many people in the world as there were stars in the sky, and they all lived according to their own different ways. And life was short and it was no use worrying about it. People were born, grew up and died so rapidly, especially in a war like the one in which they were engaged to fight. And the different parts of the world were so little acquainted with each other. And men so quickly forgot what happened to them that one could not change anything. This war, for instance, would have driven him crazy if he had tried to consider it, to say nothing about stopping it.

'To cry before the blind is to ruin one's eyesight,' said Lalu desperately.

The farmer was still smiling and explaining. His son, André, was all for dragging 'Les Hindus' to the chicken coops.

Babu Khushi Ram thought that the excursion was ending in the unfruitful controversies of yokels with whom his urban mind had no sympathy.

'Come,' he suggested, 'and have a little coffee at the café where I generally go in the evenings.'

After much polite bowing to the old farmer, he led his friends out of the yard towards the main road.

A slow drizzle of rain began almost as they issued out of the farm-house and walked across the bridge, past some small cottages. A cold wind stirred the trees by the brook and leaves fluttered down and mixed with the profusion of autumn rubbish on both sides of the road.

They did not speak to each other for some time. The even tread of their feet showed that they were suppressing their secret thoughts in the stiff-ened muscles of the 'lef-right, lef-right' into which they fell so easily.

After a little while, however, Lalu noticed that Babu Khushi Ram, primarily a quill-driver for all his pride in the uniform of the Colour Havil-dar, and unschooled to parade, was dot keeping step and was glancing furtively this side and that, as if making up his mind to ask a question. He was sure that the Babu wanted to know their experiences and of what had happened to their friends or something to do with the war, the destiny which encompassed them and beyond which there were no thoughts. But he felt tender about his memories of the days in the trenches.

'Strange for a farm to be so close to the line,' he said to avoid Khushi Ram asking any questions.

'The family is very affectionate,' the Babu said, noticing that the sepoys seemed very touchy and did not want to talk of the trenches. 'And the chil-dren are very attached to me.'

And they were all silent again.

For there was a gulf between the soldiers and the Babu: the sepoys being part of the war could not separate themselves from it, much as they wanted to, and the clerk was not only separate from it, because he stayed behind the lines, but a superior in rank and therefore the object of a distant respect which they resented.

There were crowds of soldiers in the market square, Tommies walking briskly along in twos, sepoys standing in little groups watching the twilight, or proceeding tentatively towards the café on the cross-roads. An officer of the 129th Baluchis passed by and they saluted efficiently, eyes straight and heads erect.

Lalu caught sight of a young girl who came from the direction to which they were going and thought of his adventure with Marie and her brother André by the brook in the morning and the coincidence by which the girl who had cheeked him had turned out to be the daughter of the farmer with whom the regimental office and the British officers were billeted. And, beneath the weight of his bent head, he recalled the puzzled, incom-prehensible look of recognition she had given him and the furtive, mean-ingless look which he had given her and then withdrawn to keep up appearances in the presence of his companions. The two looks seemed to become one look, and into this he wanted to put a meaning, so that he could linger and yearn to realize the promise of contact with her budding beauty.

From glimpses of the café behind swinging doors, the place seemed full of French and English soldiers, and smoke, illuminated by the garish light of gas lamps.

They stopped and looked at each other, and knew that they were all thinking the same thought – whether to enter.

'Have you lost your way?' Lalu asked Babu Khushi Ram, since it was he who had brought them here.

The Babu had frequented the place before there were many Tommies in the village, but now felt timid and afraid.

'Why?' asked Kirpu. 'What is the delay?'

'Let's go in, come what may,' said Khushi Ram mustering courage, though he really hoped that Kirpu would decide against it. And he regretted that he had not offered them tea at his billet in the farm.

'This is not Hindustan but France,' said Lalu to assure himself against the fear of the white men that baulked them.

'The boy is trapping us into a strange situation,' the Babu said even as he advanced

'They can't eat us,' said Lalu sharply.

But two British officers with Sam Browne belts stood by the counter.

'I at least am going back,' the Babu said, turning tail.

'I feel afraid to enter,' Kirpu whispered as he stood in the doorway. 'We might be reported.'

Just then, however, a Sikh Subedar of the 69th pushed past them into the café with a Havildar.

'Come on,' Lalu dragged both the Babu and Kirpu.

'The boy's senses have left him,' Uncle Kirpu protested faintly as he entered.

They stood stupefied to find themselves in a crowded, smoky room full of the babble of tongues, and waited uneasily for a moment.

Lalu assumed responsibility and sought to conduct himself and his companions with assurance even as his heart throbbed at his daring. With a grim effort, which exaggerated his demeanour to a show of haughtiness, he walked towards a table where there were four chairs and beckoned to his companions authoritatively. His heart thumped and he looked this side and that to survey the scene, full of French and English officers and men and a sprinkling of Indians.

Hardly had Kirpu and Khushi Ram come up to join him when a French officer marched up towards them, reeled, sat himself down, produced a piece of shrapnel, and began to explain something about it in words and gestures from which they gathered that the shell had fallen somewhere outside.

A dark, sleek little girl with green eyes came for their orders, and was going to ask them by signs what they wanted, when the *Francisi* caught hold of her by the waist, while she shook and wriggled and shrieked even as she smiled provokingly.

As Lalu turned round to look he found that they had become the centre of attraction in the café. He was afraid some officer would come and ask them to quit. Instead there were only catcalls, wild thumping of tables, passionate shrieks of laughter and bursts of desire as if the pent up appetites of the men had suddenly found a target.

The officer let the girl go and, signing towards the Indians, said, 'Cognac.'

Babu Khushi Ram nodded assent and the girl went to fetch the drinks.

The officer now began to discourse in broken English about the piece of shrapnel.

'German shell aah!... German big offensive make in trenches. Lesindu brave, very brave!...'

And he solemnly shook hands with all the three Indians and then continued with appropriate gestures.

'This town! Shell! Horribil! ... *Celagare*! ... Front, machine-guns, shells, shells, shells, no sleep, earthquake! '*Celagare*! ... Pop-pop, pop, fire ... dead! *Celagare*! ...'

Lalu and Kirpu laughed mirthlessly at the mockery which his pantomime made of the war. And they lifted their heads to Babu Khushi Ram, as much as to say, 'Did you hear that; that is war, it is a joke ...'

The drinks came.

The officer began to pay for them, but Khushi Ram wouldn't have it and insisted on paying and there was a war of courtesies, in the midst of which arrived a Lieutenant of the Connaughts who spontaneously stretched his hands to the Indians without any formality and complimented them, '*Bahadur* sepoys!' as he drifted away.

Elated by this high honour, intoxicated by the noise and bustle, the lightheartedness, the *bonhomie* of the café, they were now pleased they had come.

The Frenchman paid, gulped down his drink and began to sing loudly.

The song was taken up by some other French soldiers and soon they were embroiled in the aura of a familiarity which both embarrassed them with the strange impact of the incomprehensible, shouted melody, and delighted them with the broken jolts of its zigzag, like the bellyache of some animal about to be butchered.

And to make the atmosphere more exciting the Tommies now began one of their songs and tore their throats in hearty unison till the faces of all the Indians flushed red hot with incomprehension.

But with a native impetuosity which had not been smothered by the fear of 'Duty', Lalu bravely started to sing the rustic song, 'Toomba'.

'Aha, Toomba, delights himself... Aha ...'

Though Khushi Ram did not join, Kirpu lent his voice to this and the Sikhs in the café not only raised their voices but, with a little more cognac in them than Lalu had had, added the clapping of their hands to the chorus which rose from the polite accents of the first intonation to a height of rowdy hilarity and melted the ice of all those inhibitions in which the sepoys' sense of inferiority and fear of the Sahibs had enslaved them.

Lalu was flushed with his own laughter at the end of the song and drank ostentatiously to keep up the spirit of jollity that was in the air, his eyes scanning the faces of the people in the café, as if he had been familiar with this world for a long time, though in his heart there still lingered the rigid sense of responsibility.

The young officer who had brought the piece of shell got up abruptly, said something, smiled, cordially shook hands with the frightened Khushi Ram, the nervous Kirpu and then with Lalu, who was eagerly seeking to come up to scratch, and left.

'Didn't I tell you that we would be all right if we came in?' bragged Lalu now that the visit had been a success.

'Your own wisdom and another's wealth always seem great,' said Kirpu.

'He is a *Captan*, his mother runs a bakery,' said the Babu superciliously.

'Anyhow, let us have another drink,' Lalu proposed, though his voice lowered to a whisper with fear at the excess of his own enthusiasm.

'Have some sense, son,' said Uncle Kirpu.

The wave of another song which the *Francisis* had taken up smothered Kirpu's words.

The song mounted the rhythm of stamping feet which shook the hundreds of bottles arranged above the counter, where a bald-headed, clean-shaven man stood, vigilant but kind to the boisterous refrain. Now the whole café shook with its deafening noise and ended with exchange of hoarse compliments and mad raucous laughter.

'Tell me about *Holdar* Lachman Singh and Dhanoo,' said Babu Khushi

Ram, after all, thinking that a suitable moment had arrived to ask that question.

'Oh, leave go Babu Khushi Ram! ... Brothers, I feel hungry,' said Kirpu. And he got up, assembled himself carefully and strode forward.

Lalu followed.

At this, Khushi Ram also got up.

Outside, the darkness seemed to have thickened, except where the café lamps were throwing out a few quivers of pale light. There was a sinister whisper of rifle and machine-gun fire, almost like the rattle of a beetle or a cockroach far away.

'How shall we find the way?' said Kirpu.

'Even I can't see whether I am at Lahore or Amritsar,' said Khushi Ram.

'You come with me,' said Lalu, cocksure in his reliance on his instinctive sense of direction, though his heels struck the cobblestones with an uncertain emphasis.

There was a tearing sound and a bright rocket soared across the black night, flowered into a star among the particles of rain, extinguished and fell with a sharp, spluttering sound somewhere in the fields miles away.

Babu Khushi Ram ran a little caper involuntarily.

'No matter, no matter,' whispered Kirpu to put confidence into him.

'Rape-mother! It goes on day and night,' said Babu Khushi Ram. 'I shall go mad.'

The grace of two days rest was all that was to be allowed to the troops by the Sarkar. For, though they were still to remain in billets, they were to be subjected to a succession of fatigues, parades and inspections, as the corps was said to have lost its sense of discipline in the helter-skelter of the trenches.

At least this is how Lalu interpreted what Lance-Naik Kirpa Ram said, when he came back from the office with the stripe on his shoulder. 'The master thinks of hunting when the dogs are tired,' Uncle Kirpu began. 'And orders are that the men will get gout if they don't exercise. So tomorrow, Sunday: Reveille at 5 o'clock in the morning. Troops march to a place called "Fon, phon, phon". Then they unload rail wagons for cement, iron, planks, and barbed wire; load them on mule carts and motor lorries and march back. Day after tomorrow, Monday: Parade for inspection at 8 o'clock in the morning. Show everything you carry. Account for loss of properties to the quartermaster *Holdars*. Then bayonet practice, exercise and drill. Disperse. Have your meal. Get ready to go on a working party at night. Tuesday: Foot parade, bath and rest. Wednesday: Bayonet practice, exercise drill. Thursday: Route march in the morning; go digging trenches at night. Friday ...'

'*Ohe*, stop it,' Lalu protested. 'We will do it. "A dog's tail has to keep wagging even if it is allowed to sit down". We know the fate of the hounds in hell ...!'

'You need not complain, son,' Kirpu assured Lalu. 'You are being taken on to help in the office. They want someone who can write letters home for the illiterates. Babu Khushi Ram wants you to go, and see him about it. The Ajitan Sahib, who was wounded in the arm, is coming back. Lance-Naik Lok Nath has been made *Holdar*. Sepoy Kirpa Ram has been made a LanceNaik. So that when anyone tries to get ahead of you just tell me and I shall ...' And he made a comic gesture with his upraised hand as Lok Nath was wont to do when he was angry, and made a mockery of Lance-Naikism.

The routine of rest announced by Uncle Kirpu persuaded Lalu to choose the paradise of the office, even before it was offered to him. It was better to be a scribe in Heaven rather then a sentinel in Hell. Besides these was the prospect of being near a houri.

He began to get ready to go and see Babu Khushi Ram. But before he had rolled the puttees on his legs the Babu himself arrived and gave him the news.

The Hindu laws of hospitality alone would ordinarily have demanded that the N.C.O.s, the men, and the cooks should run round making tea when so exalted a personage as the Babu deigned to visit the barn, but this morning there was Uncle Kirpu's stripe to be celebrated, and, what was more important from the point of view of the average sepoy, all the subterfuges, the innuendos and the subtle suggestions of flattery, had to be brought to bear on the Babu in order to wheedle out of him advance information about prizes, medals, grants of land and life pensions won for distinguished gallantry in the trenches.

For when they first joined the army, these legionaries did so because, as the second, third or fourth sons of a peasant family, overburdened with debt, they had to go and earn a little ready cash to pay off the interest on the mortgage of the few acres of land, the only thing which stood between the family and its fate. Of course, these second, third and fourth sons 'sprung from the loins of tigresses', as the recruiting sergeant used to call them, living the confined life of small interests in the remote villages of the hills and plains, were sensitive to the elegant cut of the tight white trousers, the double stud tunics, the shapely turbans with red under-turbans and the well-oiled soft shoes which the Sarkar gave as regulation mufti to the sepoys to be paid for, by instalments, when they went home on furlough. And though the five or six rupees they could save out of the eleven rupees standard pay could not feed the insatiable greed of the land-lord or moneylender, it helped to feed the pigeon-bellied grandmother and to make up the gaps in the arrears of rent for five year ago due to the Sarkar. Besides, the soldier pledged to fight the battles of the King-Emperor, brought the necessary prestige to keep the local policeman at bay and to bail out brothers, fathers, or uncles, who were arrested for non-payment of rent or debt. And, of course, always the proud family imag-ined that the second, third, fourth son would win promotion, a sudden prize, a grant of land, or a life-pension for conspicuous bravery in battle, and that would help them to pay off all arrears and start clear of all the misery once again with full possession of the land.

Generally the second, third, or fourth son just returned to a family, which was all dead through a local famine or epidemic or grown old and beggarly out of the bitterness of keeping its end up in a world of rapacity and greed. And the second, third, or fourth son became a scarecrow, a peon, or a caretaker for the shopkeepers. Sometimes a war was on some-where, in a geography of which the family or the son had no conception, and he faded out into thin air, only to confirm his own and the family's prejudice that all who went beyond the mountains or across the black waters were destined for hell.

But, occasionally, one man in a village returned, with a stripe on his arm or a star on his shoulder, or a medal on his chest, and demanded a large dowry before he would wed the daughter of any worthy in his broth-erhood. And the young men of the village looked at him and soon the recruiting offices of the district became busier.

And once now in a while in a district arrived a hero, a man who had earned both a medal and a pension attached to it. And he soon became a legend and people came to see him, the wonder, especially as he had left an arm, a leg or an eye behind, and used a miraculous wooden substitute.

The son of the landlord of a certain village in the district who had been promoted to a direct commission as Jemadar, was known to have returned, not the proverbial prodigal, but a Subedar Major with a breast full of medals and some squares of land to his name. He was sixty, but a hill Rajah sent him not one but two young princesses in marriage, and the countryside rang with stories of how young he had looked when he rode the bridal horse with his beard dyed in henna and, wonder of wonders, the Deputy Commissioner Sahib, the head of the district, had come and put a garland round the neck of the brave Subedar Major Sahib.

Information about rewards was, therefore, the chief preoccupation of the sepoys, talking about it their main consolation in exile, the inspiration of it what spurred them on to battle. How happy would be the dear ones at home if only a ready sum could help to pay even a tenth part of the moneylenders' interest and towards the repair of the roof which had been washed out by the last monsoon before the drought!

'Babuji, what is the news then?' a Sikh sepoy asked after he had spread a special blanket for Khushi Ram, and given him some tea.

'The generals at the headquarters are very busy,' the Babu said evasively. 'And, of course, it is difficult to tell what will happen. Only God knows!'

'Still, what is the news, Babuji?' the Sikh persisted with a smile. 'Our *Paltan* fought with great valour ... And what may we tell you, conditions were very difficult ...'

'What happened to Holdar Lachman Singh?' Khushi Ram asked, deliberately evading the Sikh.

It was obvious that he was just trying to be discreet about rewards.

'Next you will ask where Daddy Dhanoo is and Kharku,' said Uncle Kirpu bitterly. 'In the judge's house even rats are shrewd. And I hear that they have become thin because of their anxiety for their friends, the mice! ... Are you such a fool as not to know that Lachman is dead? And he did not die of gout like the Jarnels, of asthma like our *Karnels*, or of piles like our Babus, he died like a lion fighting! ...'

'He has been recommended to the posthumous award of the Indian Order of Merit, which carries a life pension,' said Babu Khushi Ram, gulping his tea.

'Encouragement is a great thing,' said Kirpu with a breaking voice and a flaming tongue. 'Promotion is still better and a life pension addressed to *Holdar* Lachman Singh, Village Pool of Blood, Tehsil Purgatory, District Hell — *Wah*, don't speak of it! ...' Anger had no eyes such as this old soldier's as he flared up at Khushi Ram.

'The Sarkar is very anxious to bestow well-earned awards on Indian troops,' said Khushi Ram in a cold voice, ignoring all the indignation and the resentment that was in Kirpu's utterance. 'The *Karnel* Sahib told me that our Jarnel has told the Commander-in-Chief that the Sarkar must not commit the mistake of being niggardly in the bestowal of honours on Indian troops. Also, he is generally recommending Indian ranks who have shown gallantry in action for the Indian Order of Merit, because there is a life pension with it. It is likely that almost all those who have been recommended will get the awards, though the Commander-in-Chief is anxious to curtail this generosity. And, you may not know, that the Victoria Cross, the highest medal, was opened to Indian troops at the Delhi Durbar in 1911 and can be won. There is a recommendation now for a sepoy … You can rest assured …'

'Boys, it is my duty as a Lance-Naik to tell you that there are some gold medals being given by the women in the Red Lamp shops,' said Kirpu, getting up and breaking the party. 'And now, get ready for work. As some one of blessed memory used to say: "Men are tested when set to work".'

'Is there no land being given, Babuji?' asked Lalu inadvertently as if the echo of the voice of some one at home was knocking at his brain. He had so far sat still, but had apparently yielded to his hereditary love for land.

'The son of land!' abused Kirpu. 'Thank your luck that you are still alive after the shelling of those trenches. Lund! he says, the brother-in-law!'

The regimental office was housed in the ground floor of the dwelling house attached to the farm, and looked out towards a stretch of ground by the brook, about fifty yards from the main road and the bridge.

When Lalu reported to Khushi Ram in the morning, the Babu gave him a table by the window of the front room, on which lay regimental files, and asked him to clear it and procure himself a stool or dispatch box from somewhere to sit on.

As almost the whole battalion was on fatigue duty that day, no one came in to have a letter written, so Khushi Ram gave him the job of tidying up the room because, he said, Owen Sahib was coming back and the two company clerks, Thanoo Singh and Muhammad Din, who were in the parlour, were too busy to dust the place.

Lalu realized that he was to be a kind of orderly-cum-scribe in the office and was well-pleased that he would have to be moving about, since there was no fire, except in the holy of holies, the C.O.'s room which was also the head clerk's.

He set about the business of dusting and arranging things, tarrying for long whiles surreptitiously to contemplate with wonder and amazement a large picture of a naked woman with a pitcher of water overflowing across her shoulder under which he read the title 'Ingres — La Source'. The name did not mean anything to him. He was excited by the open exhibition of a woman's nakedness in a painting, a thing which he had never come across among the lithographs which were pasted on the doors of Seth Chaman

Lal, the moneylender of his village, nor anywhere in the picture shops of Sherkot or Manabad.

'What a shameless fool is this who has been thrust upon us!' said Muhammad Din, the Muslim clerk, a sharp-beaked old bird with the long crest of a turban on his head, irritated by the fact that Lalu was mechanically brushing the leg of a table while his passionate stares sought to explore the beauty of the innocent, sylph-like maiden who stood spilling water from the pitcher on her shoulder. Apparently Muhammad Din had already been staring at this picture.

'When you people dive into the brook naked that is not shameless,' said Babu Thanoo Singh, a perky sparrow of a hillman, easing off from the strain of work, 'but women must remain shrouded in white veils like ghosts ... But when the day that must come, that shall come, when Gabriel shall announce your approach to Allah, *wah* — then what to say! the Prophet will give you a seat on couches adorned with gold and precious stones, and youths who continue to bloom forever shall go round to attend you with goblets and ewers and cups of flowing wine — and there shall come to you *houris*, with large dark eyes like pearls hidden in their shells, as a reward for your past labours.'

'But you shall not hear any vain discourse,' said the Muslim, straight-faced.

'No, you will be too busy love-making,' said Thanoo Singh rolling his eyes impishly.

'And no one will accuse you of Sin,' added Lalu on whose mind the word had preyed ever since those lessons by Padre Anandale and the other Christian masters in the Mission School at Sherkot.

'Don't bark!' Muhammad Din pecked at him, 'or I shall report you to Babu Khushi Ram.' And he settled back to his files, for there was no bigger insult to a Muslim than for two Hindus to mock at the Prophet's idea of Heaven. 'Debauchees, what goes on in your temples at home? Hardly any of you is the son of his own father! ...'

That put an end to the protracted thrill that Lalu was having through the contemplation of the nude, but instead he turned with equal pleasure to the knick-knacks and the bric-à-brac on the mantelpiece, the clock, the statuettes, the books in an almara with glass doors and particularly, the shiny splendour of the phonogram, and he felt a secret exaltation at being in the strange and rich exuberance of a home in *Vilayat*, where Sahibs were billeted and which was replete with the aroma of their cigars and liquor.

But he heard vague stirrings in the inner sanctuaries of the office; beyond which was the officers' mess and he felt the pressure of the strong will of the Sarkar which dictated complete silence in the execution of duties, the special form which discipline takes in a regimental office.

While he was still pottering about with the duster and zealously cultivating what he imagined to be European skill and efficiency in the re-arrangements of the objects d'art in the room, there was a shuffling of forms outside the hall and the orderly was presenting arms to someone who seemed, from the easy, soft Hindustani of his Salaam, to be Owen Sahib.

With an impetuosity that burst the bounds of discipline, Lalu went to the door and saluted the Sahib.

'Ah, Lal Singh,' said the Adjutant with that smile with which he had greeted him when the boy had come as a recruit in charge of the recruiting Havildar. 'So you have come through unscathed, eh?' And, with a familiarity that hadn't the slightest trace of discipline, but was more akin to tenderness, Owen Sahib pulled Lalu's cheek and laughed.

'And *Huzoor* — *Huzoor's* arm?' Lalu said, seeing the Sahib's left arm in a sling.

Babu Khushi Ram, Thanoo Singh and Muhammad Din came into the hall and, trying to put as much efficiency as they could into their limbs used to soldering on paper, saluted.

'Hallo, Khushi Ram, still alive? Thanoo Singh, no more flesh on your bones yet? ... Muhammad Din, how many mistakes in figures?' Owen Sahib greeted each according to his deserts and putting his hat on a stand, went towards the head clerk.

'Where is my office?'

'Here, *Huzoor*. The C.O. and you are together in this room,' said Khushi Ram, nervous and panicky, walking and running as he led their way. '*Ohe*, Lal Singh, come and dust the Sahib's chair,' he called as an afterthought.

'All right, Khushi Ram, don't fuss,' said the Sahib. 'Where is Major Peacock?'

'*Huzoor*, gone to headquarters,' answered Khushi Ram, standing to attention while the Sahib stood by the fire and began to take a cigarette out of his case.

Khushi Ram was too obsequious to see the difficulties of the Sahib with the cigarette, because of his sling, and still stood rigid. But Lalu advanced, in spite of the stare of the Head Clerk, took the match box from the mantelpiece and gave Owen Sahib light. Then he began to dust the furniture.'

Huzoor, are you quite recovered?' Babu Khushi Ram asked. The Sahib flushed a little, waved his head and evaded the question by asking:

'Well, what do you think of the war, Khushi Ram?'

Perhaps, because the Adjutant of a regiment combines the function of a kind of Deputy C.O. with clerical work of all kinds, he invariably establishes a familiarity with the office staff, which leads to an abeyance of the military virtues deriving from the shooting range, the parade ground and 'quarter guard' and makes for humanity. At the best of times, however, the position of the Babus is somewhat invidious, as they are spicy pickles of military and civilian behaviour. How the Sahibs respond to this depends on the state of their palate. And the Babus, completely insensitive to military values, try to find out how jaded is their appetite at any particular time.

'War, sir,' the Babu said standing on the fence as it were, 'war has its drawbacks! Men get killed. And women and children starve. But it has its advantages also. It seems to clear our minds, making us able to see straightforward. It makes things simpler even at the cost of bloodshed. We are able to do things in war time which we seem unable to do in peace. War brings out the bravery of people like *Huzoor*.'

This was flattery with a vengeance. The Sahib wondered what Khushi Ram really felt behind these words.

'And what do you think of war, Lal Singh?' the Sahib said ficking the ash of his cigarette and scraping his boots on the fender, perhaps in order to give a natural and unofficial air to his inquiry.

Nevertheless, Lalu was startled by so direct a question from the Sahib and could hardly think of an answer, or dare to give an opinion out of respect and fear. And yet for these very reasons he had to say something.

'*Huzoor*, Havildar Lachman Singh is dead,' he blurted out, since he knew of the special friendship which had always existed between Owen Sahib and Lachman, Gymnastic instructor, saint, hockey player and the most popular N.C.O. in regiment.

'Yes, I know,' said the Ajitan Sahib, and bent his head.

'*Huzoor*,' continued Lal Singh to cover the tension that seemed imminent. 'The air and the water of this place is different. And because we were separated and put with English and French regiments, most of the sepoys felt that no one knew anything about us, and, some of the sepoys not knowing the language, lost their way ... and it was ... like hell! ...'

The Sahib sauntered slowly over to where he stood and patted the boy, hesitated and patted him again, as if consoling him for some loss, and then said, 'Bravo!'

'There are heavy casualty lists, *Huzoor*,' said Khushi Ram, now swinging over to another line of approach as he perceived that this Sahib was, unlike other Sahibs, rather eccentric and not quite so enthusiastic about the war. 'And the shelling must have been very terrible because some shrapnel even fell here in this village ... I hear the ground over which the battle raged was difficult ...'

'There was little or no cover,' said the Sahib, and the ground was water-logged ...' He winced as he said this and then, after a puff at his cigarette, continued: 'Rain fell all the time and the trenches were deep in mud and water ... Terrible!'

'It seemed a gunnery duel from here, sir,' ventured Khushi Ram.

'Rather one-sided,' said Owen Sahib, 'because we hadn't many guns ...'

'Uncle Kirpu said so,' Lalu mumbled to repress himself when he found that the Sahib had confirmed his friend's prognostications about the absence of artillery to back the German lines.

'Who is that?' the Sahib asked.

'Kirpu, *Huzoor*, Sepoy Kirpa Ram,' answered Lal Singh.

'Lance-Naik Kirpa Ram,' Babu Khushi Ram corrected.

'Oh Uncle Kirpu, um, give him my salaams and congratulations!' said Owen Sahib with a smile. 'He fought well! All the sepoys fought well ...'

'They may help to save the cause of civilization,' said Khushi Ram pandering to what he imagined was every Sahib's idea in this war.

'You mean, they may become victims of civilization,' said the adjutant suppressing his annoyance. And then, excusing the Babu for a phrase to which the Sarkar had given currency, and which he knew Khushi Ram was only repeating to flatter him, he said, more impersonally: 'All rules, theorems, all ideas - everything has been shattered in this war, buried in mud ...'

Babu Khushi Ram stood guilty and apologetic and silent, his head bent, and felt he had made the Sahib angry.

The tension communicated itself to Lalu who wished he had never come into this office, for the Babu might take it out of him for being a witness to his discomfiture.

'Oh well, buck up, Khushi Ram,' said Captain Owen, coming over and patting the Babu with a deliberately happy air. 'Civilization also means a sense of humour, you know. Don't let us fall victims to the mere solemnity of civilization ...'

'I am your servant, *Huzoor*,' said Khushi Ram a little relieved.

'Come along, then, and help me to get some work done,' said the Sahib. 'Is Lal Singh orderly here?'

'Yes, *Huzoor*, and, as he is literate, he is going to write the sepoys' letters for them,' answered Khushi Ram respectfully. And, turning to the boy with the efficiency of a frightened superior, he said: 'Lal Singh, Sahib is going to work.'

As Lalu withdrew he knew he had Owen Sahib's sympathy.

Almost every time Lalu came back from the office into the barn or emerged from the barn to go to office, there was a whole platoon of children under the command of André, standing by Santu and the other cooks, who were preparing meals in the improvised kitchen in the farmyard. Whether it was the genius of the Hindus for improvisation that attracted them, or the Sepoys' strange methods of cooking, or the kind of food cooked, no one could tell. But they stood, fascinated by the picturesque vision of little marked off squares in which were fire-places, built of parallel mud-plastered bricks in the middle of which crackled branches of fuel, wood and logs, throwing out volleys of sparks across the black-bottomed cauldrons in which lentils and vegetables were being cooked. Indeed, the spicy smells which steamed out from under the half-open lids of these cauldrons spread far into the village and brought even Tommies and French soldiers to the barns.

And the taboos of religion, against the beef and pig-eating Sahibs, having broken down long ago, the *Goras* were provided with a feast, not only for their eyes, but for their superior 'double-roti eating' bellies, as they were treated to the hard, crisp chapatees of white flour that were being baked on huge griddles, with helpings of ladlefuls of lentils or vegetables.

André had by now come to recognize Lalu and generally ran up to him whenever he saw him.

'Shoo them away,' an N.C.O. shouted to the sentry. 'A Sahib might come and see them here.'

But with a latent fatherliness, they just turned a deaf ear to such orders. And the kids had the most wonderful treat of their lives. The Sikhs, whose unusual appearance made them the favourites of the children, would lift them on their shoulders, and play camels or elephants under them. And so taken were they with them, that they even unrolled their turbans and showed them the buns of long sacred hair on their heads and uncoiled the knots of their beards and showed them how uncannily they held the plaits by means of little black strings under their chins. The children asked questions which, of course, the Sepoys could not understand. But André persisted in his inquiries on one point, and even brought a Sahib as interpreter. It turned out the question he was so concerned to ask the Sikhs was:

'If you have to roll that beard and the long hair on your head in funny knots, why don't you have it cut off?'

'You are my twin brother,' Lalu said to him in the ensuing laughter.

And he sat him and his cronies down in a row by the kitchen and got Santu to give them some sweet semolina.

The sweetness of the dish won them over to Lalu with an affection such as no camel rides or elephant rides could ensure. And, henceforth, André became his boon companion.

André insisted on his mother asking him to a meal. Mama was too busy attending to the officers billeted on her and couldn't entertain an extra. But André was importunate. Not knowing that there was a rigid caste system among the Sahibs and the Sepoys, that no Indian soldier could ever dare to aspire to such heights of dignity as to sit down to table with British officers, Mama Labusiére conceded so far as to let him fetch his friend to coffee after lunch.

Lalu was ushered into a low-ceilinged kitchen-dining-room, warmed by a copper. But fortunately, apart from Papa, Mama, Marie and André, there was only Owen Sahib at table.

The Sepoy was taken aback, and saluted, remaining respectfully aloof even as his face flushed with embarrassment. But the Sahib put him at his ease.

'Salaam, Lal Singh,' he said. 'So your friend won't even eat without you. Sit down. Other Sahibs have lunch in the dining room and I am late, so I have been eating with the family ... And let me introduce you.' He pointed at each individual as he mentioned their names. 'That is Monsieur Labusiére, Madame, Mademoiselle Marie, and here is your clown friend, André ...'

Lalu bowed, his eyes bent down, his face still flushed with a shame that seemed to press the life out of him, and stood rigidly at attention. For a moment he glanced surreptitiously at Marie's face. But then he withdrew his eyes and stood more confused than ever, his blood swirling through him in waves of warmth that seemed to rise like smoke of frustration to his head and blind him.

And André began to drag him roughly to a chair.

Lalu sought to balance himself and stood like a tree, bending to André's pressure but not moving. And he could see Marie as he had seen her by the brook for the first time: she had seemed like a young animal, a playful doe, teased by that lion cub of an André, and teasing him, her budding youth bursting in her cries and shrieks with a turbulence that had confounded his senses and made him stare at her for recognition ... And now she sat demure, but clear and still, remote and near, her challenging eyes bent over her full pouting mouth, altogether not beautiful, but full of a light that seemed to stream through her dark head.

With a comprehension that was unique, Captain Owen decided to leave the room and put the boy at ease.

'Come and sit here, Lal Singh,' he said as he gulped his coffee with a deliberate shake of the head and got up to go.

Lalu made sheepishly for a chair to which André was dragging him.

At that moment Mama began to chatter away to the Sahib over Lal Singh's head, some long-winded explanation, and the boy was unnerved again, looking up to them flustered and red with guilt.

But Owen Sahib interpreted in Hindustani:

'She says you are at home. And she says the Indians are very nice. Not so the Germans. She says, that this village was captured by Germans twice and she has cooked for German officers. No good ...'

Mama said another mouthful just then.

'Oh, she says,' continued the Adjutant, 'Hindus are tall and handsome, cultured, gentle and *sympatique* ... *kas-kase*, — ah kind. She likes your bronze faces, especially when you smile ... So, smile! ...'

And having interpreted he laughed his nervous shy chuckle. Lalu smiled too.

Mama was pouring out another effusion, but now, unhappily, with a voice which suddenly seemed to break, till she averted her face and began to wipe her tears, while the Sahib patted her and made her sit down. Papa got up and went to her.

'Her eldest son died in the war,' Owen Sahib interpreted.

Lalu was now more embarrassed than ever. He did not know where to hide his face. He knew that the Sahib would not mind his being there. He had seen a Mem cry at a station on the way. But he did not know until this moment that Sahibs and Mems were also human. They had always seemed like gods, distant and self-assured ... But from the sorrow of this mother with tears trickling down her cheeks at the memory of her dead son, he knew that these people were also susceptible to sorrow as well as to joy, and to every other kind of inward tumult, that they also broke down when they were struck ...

Not wishing to intrude on her grief the Sahib left.

Papa took charge of Mama and she recovered, got up, and made a brave effort to smile.

Before long Lalu found himself talking to the whole family in the language of gestures and he was completely at home, helping to clear the table, playing snakes and ladders with André and Marie. And he arranged to go shopping with them all on Market day.

The Market day was held in the square of the town on Wednesdays.

And to Market they did go on the next Wednesday, Papa and Mama, André and Marie and 'Lulu', as they began to call him.

Of course, before Mama had finished the washing up, or Marie had dressed for the occasion and done her hair, and while Papa was still examining the gates of the pen folds in the courtyard beyond the kitchen garden, André insisted on 'Lulu' tying a turban on his head like his own. And since everyone was busy, getting ready, the child tore round the place, shrieked and shouted to be given a length of cloth which could do for a turban. Lalu indicated to him the length of the cloth. André rushed to Papa in the pen fold. Papa sent him to Mama, the custodian of all rags, which could be washed and worn and the varieties which were used to polish different things with. Mama gave him a bit of old towel, but he was completely dissatisfied with it, having been ostensibly struck with the neat and regular folds of the Dogra's turbans. Mama asked him to choose one of the dirtier dishcloths. André, however, was meticulous in his taste if he was anything. Besides hadn't Mama herself taught him cleanliness. Mama, full of resource and vitality, took a bandage out of the official first-aid box and handed it to him with an exhortation which showed that she had reached the very limit of her concessions to André's idle conceit. The child submitted to the bandage roll being tied round his head and, hurrying to look at himself in a glass upstairs, and showing himself round to Papa, Mama and Marie, even seemed well pleased. Unfortunately, however, as Marie came down in a black dress, which showed her vivid face to advantage, and a red silk scarf on her head which heightened the intensity of her even black hair, Lalu pointed to the scarf, nervous and admiring. Forthwith, André demanded the red scarf, and he must have the scarf and nothing but the scarf. And he barged like a bull at his sister when she protested that it was hers. In order to save herself from the ritual of another, more protracted toilet, if her brother tore her dress, she yielded the scarf and got herself a pale green one instead. Meanwhile, André demolished the bandage which had made him look like a wounded soldier, and had the few folds of a light little princely pugree tied on his head.

'Rajah', Lalu remarked as he turned him about.

And the resemblance was so unmistakable that Mama agreed and said frowningly, '*Le roi*! *Le roi*!' and Papa laughed a cynical old laugh, and Marie came and brushed his clothes, willing and affectionate, in spite of her sacrifice to her brother's vanity.

By this time the animals in their folds had been examined, instructions left with a farm labourer, the valuables locked, and the family trailed out.

They hadn't far to go to get to the market place. But the journey across the bridge through the streets became an ordeal for Lalu.

For as they walked along, Papa and Mama arm in arm behind, and Lalu, with André holding the forefinger of his right hand, and Marie digni-fied and demure on his left, the sepoys, who were drilling, left their bayonet practice for a moment and shot pop-eyed glances at the entourage with Lalu as the centre piece. And the Tommies in the street whistled or twittered and stared and made him feel what a lucky black bastard they thought he was.

As the family threaded their way towards the centre of the town, a herd of strong, spotted cows arrived from up a side street with a gaiter-legged cowherd who was struggling to keep them together, to avoid a collision with pigs from the right. With a remarkable genius for ventriloquism, which André seemed to possess, from the exact imitation he gave first of the bovine voice and then of the hog grunt, he ran and offered his unso-licited services for the maintenance of order among the two species. The cows as well as the pigs seemed appreciative and brawled loudly as if in greeting to André as well as his family, but their masters warned him off.

The boy was undaunted. From now on he seemed to become the leader of the party. He shot through the collection of booths and stalls, replete with the conversation of all the species, then came back and led them first to the cattle pens, making straight for the sheep and rousing the herd from their timid, sleepy clusters to some sign of life, even though it was in one direction. As his family tarried, he called to them to hurry as if they were also sheep. But Papa objected, Mama complained, Marie seemed to have had enough of it and the human qualities, even in a creature so sheepish as Lalu, asserted themselves. And one of the owners in the cattle pen did not seem at all graceful about André's turban.

The sepoy was struck with the urbane, almost polished utterance of the auctioneer of cattle who was straining to sell cows to a crowd, among whom the most vocal were a Sikh, a havildar, and some sepoys who were examining the cattle as if they were going to select the best of them and teach them bayonet fighting and musketry. Lalu noticed that here, as in the fairs in the Punjab, the owners brought their cows unmilked, so that the udders might look overstocked and the buyers may not be able to guess the normal yield of an animal. He tried to ask Papa about this, but the old man was looking for Mama who had gone to the vegetable stall and the language of gesture failed because it was difficult to touch the cow short of being suspected as a possible buyer. But his hand itched to milk one of them and to treat André to a drop as he used to treat his little cousin, Jitu, sometimes, when he milked Suchi at home.

At that instant, however, Marie came persuading Papa with the tenderest appeal in her eyes to come to the booth where hundreds of chicks were being sold, took the place of Mama on the old man's arm and led him further into the whirlpool of men, women, razors, knives, shoelaces, eggs and cabbages.

Papa stopped to see some ducklings, while Lalu helped to interpret a deal between some Muslim sepoys on fatigue duty, who were buying mutton for their cooks and the red-faced, hefty butcher Sahib with a clean white apron on his paunch. It seemed to be a deal which had gone on for hours like the bargains of the sepoys on other stalls. The stall-keeper wrote down the number of 'frongs' on the board or the earth with his fingers, and pronounced it, the sepoys lifted their fingers and counted, and when the right number was arrived at they shook their heads and offered less. This was difficult for the Frenchman to understand, as he was used to one price. And, as they could not agree, they laughed, the shopkeeper indulgently explaining to them the qualities of his wares by showing the points. So a stray Tommy came forward and helped. But the *Goras* did not know much French either. And they waited until someone more knowing arrived. When Lalu thrust himself forward and asked the congregation at the butcher's stall what it was all about, Lance-Naik Aslam greeted him and said:

'These rape-daughters, won't understand that a bargain is the only way of finding out the real price of an object: the shopkeeper asks the highest price and you offer the least, and as he goes on lowering the price and you go on raising it, you come to a price when he gets a little profit and you get a reasonable object, because while the bargain is going on you have been inspecting it.'

Lalu was helpless in the face of this homespun logic.

A British officer arrived and interpreted. The sale was negotiated and

Aslam Khan began to advise the butcher to cut the meat nicely for curry. And there were genial smiles and a goodwill which enabled the sepoys to get a piece of liver or kidney thrown in as a free gift even as they were used to receiving hucksters' profit in the markets of Indian cantonments.

Papa still hung about watching the bidding for live poultry and waited for Mama who had harnessed young André, with a loud remonstrance, to lift the basket of shopping, seemingly with the promise of a carrot, while Marie was still bringing all the blandishments in the armoury of youthful persuasion to move her father to come and have a look at the chicks. But it seemed from the grave manner in which Papa talked to her that he was not game. And as Mama had still a long list of things to buy, Papa moved off to support her. Marie called André to come, and André dragged 'Lulu' and, when the sepoy hesitated for a moment, Marie pulled him away behind her by the mere force of her nascent femininity.

The tension melted somewhat by the time they came to the chicks. For the man by the chick-stall was urging the cluster of men around him to go on bidding. It seemed strange to Lalu how casual and resigned these people were. They not only sowed and reaped the harvest, but bred live-stock, reared poultry, tended sheep, bought and sold within a bomb's range of the front. But he knew from instinct that men got used to anything. For instance, at home the peasants had long given up worrying about rains and droughts till famine showed its parched tongue to their faces and they had to move off elsewhere. These people too had come to regard the war as a nuisance, but so long as they did not actually die they seemed to be content to go on living in shattered homes and spoiled fields.

And here was Marie so concerned with these chicks that she had put her hand into the cage and begun fondling the little squeaky, velvety things, dozens of them not more than a week old. '*Poulette, Poulette,*' she murmured the most tender caresses, and tried to catch them in her hands even as they playfully slipped out of her grasp and went in rows, picking, pecking and shrieking shrill, discordant squeaks of pleasure and displea-sure, while the auctioneer's voice struck infrequent hammer blows as there did not seem to be a ready sale for these newly-hatched little ones. André was bored with his sister's sentiments, but she seemed to have wrought some magic on Lalu.

'How beautiful she is,' he said to himself, as she uttered little cries of happiness and despair at the chicks rustling in and out of her hands. 'How innocent!' For nothing seemed to exist to her, neither the war, nor the soldiers, only the chicks. He recalled that when the soldiers had whispered and twittered and called as they issued out of the house, she had ignored them utterly, and had walked along, demure and grown up, but simple as a child. And now she was lost in her little game.

He thrust his hand into the cage and began to play with her. She would catch the chicks and let them go while he picked them up and handed them to her. One of the chicks made as if to bite her hand, and, nervous and timid like a doe, she fell back. But then she came to them again, her face, her eyes, her voice, her hands all charged with a miraculous glow that seemed to make him desperate for some supreme happiness or sudden disaster. If she did not have the chicks he felt she would break her heart, and his into the bargain. He got up, and surveyed the auction stall for a moment. There was a basket round which there were one, or two unenthusiastic buyers making tentative bids which went no farther than the last. It seemed no one was very interested in little chicks. Lalu raised his hand without a 'combien', and the auctioneer pushed the basket towards him. André snatched at the chicks and shouted in French: 'Marie, Marie, sometiing, something, "Lulu",' and he ran to show Papa, and Mama what 'Lulu' had bought them.

Papa came, protesting, but grateful, and helped to settle the account by counting francs for him. Mama was touched and rushed up shouting a thousand 'Merci beaucoups', Marie took a chick and hugged it and kissed it and spoke to it.

Lalu lifted the basket and walked through the noisy, busy market, his tear-stained eyes averted from Marie, his head surcharged with madness.

André began to imitate a pig's reflections on mortality and then a duck's appeal to heaven for a little rain. It was drizzling anyhow and Lalu could not restrain himself from laughing at the boy and said: 'Chal ohe, Sab!'

After a brief lull Lal Singh was kept fairly busy writing letters at the dictation of the sepoys. Probably because they were hard-pressed for time between the various fatigues, inspections and exercises, or perhaps because they had come to accept the war, they generally asked Lalu to put down a short message of 'razi-khushi' well-being on a post card, character-ized by a kind of uncomplaining loyalty to the Sarkar, a philosophic endurance and a fatalistic view of the privations and sufferings of war, with a special redundant phrase or two about the necessity of paying the interest on the mortgage or an injunction not to sell the land on any account, or a suggestion for an application to the Sarkar for relief from land revenue through the Depot.

As if the sentiments of the sepoys for their kith and kin had stirred the depths of his nature, Lalu took advantage of the spells of leisure and

himself wrote a letter to his mother in Punjabi, on a signaller's pad he had
rifled from the office:

'To Shrimati Gujar Kaur (Mata Gujri), the widow of Sardar Nihal
Singh, Haveli Walla, in the village of Nandpur, Tehsil Sherkot,
District Manabad, Punjab, Hindustan, this letter is sent by Sepoy
Lal Singh, number 1112, 2 platoon, 2 company, 69th Rifles, stationed
in a village near Ypres, Tehsil Ypres, District Ypres, Subah Flanders,
near Franceville.

'Mother! After respects to you, my sister-in-law Kesari and aunt
Uttam Kaur, to my brother Dayal Singh and Uncle Harnam Singh
and love to my cousin Jitu, I have to say that I have not written to
you nor have I received a letter from you since I came across the
seas. The wire about father's death reached me at Karachi, but I was
too sad as I crossed the Kalapani, and too sad about having left you
all behind, to write. I was not seasick, have no fear about my health,
I have been well. Specially did the air and water do me good as we
came past Arab country side through Misr to Marsel. Only I
worried about you folk, because I knew that you would be
mourning for Bapu and my eldest brother Sharm Singh, and would
beat your heads and breasts and I would not be there to prevent
you. My loving mother, have patience. For as Uncle Kirpu, who is
my companion here, always says: "God, who has soaked you will
dry you again."

'They give us good food, specially chocolates, which is a sweet. And
they give us good rum. But even if one could put one's mouth to a
pump and drink rum to the heart's content it would not keep
anyone warm. Cold! Oh, mother, don't mention the name of it. It is
like the frozen hell which the followers of the *Budh mat* believe in.
But, mother, have the wax taken out of your ears and listen.

'Tell Dayal Singh that here one cow gives a pitcher full of thick milk.
Tell my saintly brother to forget God for a little while and do as
these people do, feed the cattle properly on straw and greens and
oil seeds. I know our elders will say "There is lack of money to pay
for the sowing and he talks of reaping". But cattle must not be fed
on grain sifted out of its dung. We must put a stop to that.

'Mother, the land of France is wide and fair, even as the Punjab, and
the people are like us too, open and free and loving, and I am happy
I came here. Ask Uncle Harnam Singh and my brother Dayal Singh
to strengthen their hearts and listen to this: This country is full of

precious things, such as machine ploughs, steel implements, sheep, pigs, cows, chickens, beetroot, potatoes and apple wine. The *Francisis* of Franceville and the Flamands of Flanders are wonderful cultivators. They plough five times as much land in a day with tractor machines as we do in ten days with a wooden landscratcher. And they use manures full of medicines such as the Sarkar ought to invent in Hind.

'What a country! What a country!

'The house in which I live is like a palace and yet it belongs to a farmer. Only he does not think it below his dignity to keep poultry and sell eggs or to rear pigs. Oh, how clean is the farm! The floors of the stables shine like mirrors! And smell — you never hear the name of it!

'The reason why these people are happier is because they do not borrow money from moneylenders, but from the Bank at very low interest. When I come back, I shall ask the *Karnel* Sahib to order the bania to give back our mortgages, and to get the landlord to return the lands he has seized from us as a reward for fighting in this war. Saying is one thing, you will say, doing another; but have faith, mother, trust in me.

'Pat Jitu on the head for me, and tell him that the children here all read and write. Every child is put to school, and boys and girls study together. So tell Jitu to put his heart into studies and he will be like *Francisi* children. My *Francisi* mother at whose house I live, has a small son, André by name. He sends his greetings to Jitu, whom he calls his "brother in India."

'My French mother is just like you. She is very kind to me. She never sits still. She had another son who was killed in the war some months ago. So she says I am her son now in the place of the one killed. During the few days that I have been in the house she has ministered to me as if I were an orphan.

'The women here walk in public without purdah and look straight into the eyes of men. They read, write, play, ride on horses and play cards, but no one dares to call them immoral for these things. The daughter of my *Francisi* mother is a young girl, whom I like. But, mother, rest assured that it is not considered wrong for men and women to like each other and there is nothing bad in it. I remember that you told me to regard every woman as a mother or sister, but, mother that would be a lie because men do not look at all women as sisters even if they say they do. For love, fire and itch are not concealed!

'When we go back to the trenches life is a burden which one cannot carry lightly. We dig into the earth and then shoot at the enemy with guns. It is said in Sarkari newspapers that the enemy is savage Hun, that the nature of the Hun is to commit shame upon women, to kill children, to defile the shrines of his own faith with his own dung. They may be a caste apart from other Sahibs, though they look the same and sometimes greet us across the trenches. Tell the villagers that it is true that there are birds with iron wings which fly in the sky — that machines cannot only conquer the earth but heaven.

'And, mother, do not be afraid on my account. I have been in trenches, and, somehow, now I am here in billets, I shall probably come through unscathed, because I don't want to die, though who can tell in this war, for who has seen tomorrow? Anyhow, if I don't return, think that I have gone to the cattle fair at Amritsar, mother, or that I have gone to a marriage party.

'My head is kneeling at your feet, at the feet of my aunt Uttam Kaur and sister-in-law Kesari. My respects to Uncle Harnam Singh, my love to Jitu and a pat on his head, my "fall at your feet" to all the elders of the village who ask after me and my poked tongue to the landlord Harbans Singh, Seth Chaman Lal, Mahant Nandgir and all the burnt up ones, my embraces to Gughi, Ghulam and Churangi.'

I am your loving son.

Lal Singh (Sepoy)
2 Company, 69th Rifles.

On November 11th it was announced in the orders of the day that General Roberts Sahib, who had been Commander-in-Chief of the Indian Army, and who had been appointed Colonel-in-Chief of the Indian Corps in France, was coming to see the sepoy's the next day.

Uncle Kirpu read the orders out from his Hindi script, forcefully and authoritatively, as he stood in the barn, turning round several times with a hunted look in his eyes as if to look at someone who was goading him to action or keeping a watch on him.

The Sepoys were exploring the seams of their clothes for lice and seemed inattentive.

'Am I to be excused from this parade, *Holdara*?' Lalu asked challengingly.

'No, no one, not even Mishter Páte Khan, letter-writer of the regiment, is to be excused from the inspection parade on such an auspicious occasion,' says Lance-Naik Kirpu Ram, impatiently but still with a humorous play on 'Mishter Páte Khan.' He was against all parades, but since, as an N.C.O. he had to give orders and enforce discipline, he was short and tried to bluff like a martinet. Or, perhaps he was afraid of superior officers finding fault with him, as he looked round to make sure no one was listening to him and began with a mockery of his best N.C.O. voice and manner:

'Orders are orders. I tell you this in my capacity as a LanceNaik, when before I said it in my capacity as your Uncle in all matters ...' And he blew an imaginary particle of dust off the stripe on his shoulder and pretended to be so respectful to himself that the sepoys laughed or smiled and grunted 'Han! Han!'

'A soldier must not question an order given by a superior,' he now began to fool with a hyperbolic exposition of the army code. 'He must obey promptly and willingly, if possible by crawling before the officer or by tying the officer's shoelaces. For an officer is like the king, father and mother, though he has no beard like Jari Panjam. But he is appointed by the Shahinshah Salamat Jarj, and privileged to wear the Sham Browne belt. If you are still not convinced of the importance of an officer's position, as issuing from the King's instructions, then you have only to look at me!' And he made a wry face, put on a scowl and began to twist his moustache at the tips with deliberately heroic efforts to make them stand.

'You want a little grease,' someone suggested.

'Discipline!' Uncle Kirpu shouted in a bluff of rage. 'If you laugh too much, and the discipline of the army becomes bad then the army is little better than a mob, and cannot be depended on in an emergency ...'

'What emergency?' Lalu heckled.

'Such an emergency as faces us tomorrow,' shouted Kirpu, 'when we have to make up a contingent out of our depleted ranks sufficiently large to impress our Lat Robert Sahb, the Jangi Lat, that, as our grandfathers remained true to the salt of the Sarkar and fought with him in the mutiny, blowing off hundreds of rebels out of the mouths of the guns, that as our fathers stormed, under his direction, the last entrenched positions outside the fort of Kandhar, so we are fighting loyally and dying nobly for him, for our King-Emperor and the Sarkar ...'

'Oh, *Holdara*!' Lalu said with exaggerated politeness in sudden panic. 'I have not been to a kit inspection, and the sepoy who showed my clothes at parade for me when we came back to rest said that I shall have to have new socks.'

'You will have to be polite to the quarter-master Holdar and call him a Subedar, even as you have called me a Holdar, and go and complete any deficiency that there is in your kit today. If you get nothing, but abuse from the Quarter-Master then that is what you deserve, for kit is meant to be kept in store or to be given to favourites and not to the fighting sepoy. If you are told off at the next inspection parade by myself or another N.C.O. for not having made good the deficiency then don't grumble but regard it as a law of the army that a soldier is the donkey who must bear all the burden of the army on his back! ...'

'Lance-Naik Kirpa Ram!' the voice of Havildar Lok Nath broke upon the barn.

'*Huzoor*,' answered Kirpu.

But hard upon the exchange of calls came the dreaded Havildar himself, solemn and grim as if he were ready to drink the blood of some innocent victim with those tight thin lips of his.

'There is a war on, you know,' he said surveying the men from the doorway and seeing them settled peacefully for a siesta. 'Is there nothing for you to do but to sleep? Lance-Naik Kirpa Ram, is there no parade or fatigue duty today that they are sitting here killing flies?'

'Not flies, *Holdara*, because there are no flies here, but fleas and lice,' said Uncle Kirpu. 'There are lots of fleas about in this barn. The rape-daughters seem to get into one's skin and bite one in the haunches, the armpits, the soles of the feet, the neck and even one's bottom ...'

'Lance-Naik Kirpa Ram, there is no time for idle talk,' said Havildar Lok Nath sensing the ambiguity of Kirpu's description of fleas and lice. 'There is a war on and there is work to do!'

'Oh war! — I have given them the orders!' said Kirpu. And turning to the sepoys, he stiffened himself and bawled: 'Listen, boys, you get ready for the parade tomorrow. Assemble in the market square. Tip top. Boots polished so that the Jangi Lat can see his face in them. If he comes in his motor, alights for a moment, shakes hands with the Afsars, does a little git mit, and goes away without looking at his reflection in the leather, still polish the boots, because the boots are the most important thing, even if you forget obedience, courage, loyalty and the rest.'

'A strange way of giving orders,' Lok Nath said, exasperated, though he could not pick on anything to be wrong.

'And I don't suppose you have forgotten how to present arms just because you have been spending a little time in paradise,' Kirpu continued.

'Come on, Lance-Naik Kirpa Ram,' said Lok Nath sternly.

'Your servant,' Kirpu said, with exaggerated humility and followed Lok Nath out.

'I hope that swine doesn't report Uncle Kirpu,' Lalu said, after they were out of audible distance. 'The old man should watch his words and not play the fool so openly.'

But there seemed to be no ripples on the surface the next day when they fell in by the pillars of the gas lamp in the open market square, under a dull sky, torn by the detonations of artillery some miles away, with a chilly breeze blowing from west to east. The army machine worked as usual with the ponderous efficiency of a force which had, for the time being, ground out all individual considerations, though the air was tense with all the potential battles of wills that would arise out of a false step, an inadequate item in the kit or from the slightest accent on the wrong syllables of a parade which every man was supposed to consider his greatest honour and privilege to have attended.

'Black clouds frighten,' Uncle Kirpu murmured to Lalu, 'grey are the rain-givers.' By which the boy supposed the Lance-Naik meant, this routine of presenting arms to a General is as nothing to the fear of being taken to task for a misdemeanour by the superior, Omnipotent, Omnipresent, Invisible God of Death, the inexorable doom compared to whose judgment everything else seemed a paltry irrelevance.

As they stood on the uneven bricks of the market square, it seemed more a kind of fair, a deliberate piece of showmanship in which the actors were involved only to the extent of their curiosity, without the slightest trace of that loyalty in the name of which they had been called. For, most of them believed that, perhaps, the great Sahib might suddenly announce a rise in pay or even recommend one of them for a reward, and all of them felt honoured to have the opportunity of seeing a General, they seemed to have seen through the pretext of devotion since they had been in the war, and felt they ought to be absolved from parades during rest time, although in the peace of the cantonments they would have regarded this as the red letter day of their lives. They did not know the name of one General from that of another, and though they had heard of General Roberts Sahib's legendary doings from old campaigners, they did not know who he was, and felt impatient at the solemnity that was being forced upon them on the occasion of his visit.

Lalu felt slightly elated at being watched by the civilians, men, women and children, Tommies and the French soldiers who stood round the market square. For the Indian troops looked heroic and important today as a great English General, who had made a reputation in India, was coming to inspect them, whereas ordinarily, much as they were loved by the natives as curiosities, they often felt themselves ignored by the Tommies who had been to India and who were prone to regard them as the inferior 'black men used to relieving themselves on the ground.'

Owen Sahib walked up with the Subedar Major, and N.C.O.s called out 'Eyes front'. Then Major Peacock Sahib came with Major Dunlop Sahib, and the few company commanders who had not taken their places fell in. All was serious and there was not even the flicker of an eyelid for a few moments. And it seemed as if they would crack with the strain of waiting like wooden soldiers. But the engine of a motor car was heard even as the distant guns shook the window panes of the adjacent houses, as if even the enemy were concerned to honour the greatest General of India, who stepped out of his motor, a brisk little old man in Field Marshal's uniform, with the tall General Willcocks Sahib and other staff officers behind him, and took the salute of the mixed British and Indian guard of honour. The vigilance of duty demanded 'eyes front' so strictly that the sepoys could not see what the great General was doing, though Lalu caught a glimpse of him talking to Subedar Major ... But with the quick, impulsive, knowing movements of a man who was at home with the Indians, he moved among the first few lines, said a word here, shook an officer's hand there, and stood to make a speech in the broken Sahib's Hindustani, of which Lalu could only hear meaningless snatches:

'... so many campaigns ... feared that the strange surroundings ... duty to fight ... duty as soldiers ... your commanding office... filled me with pride... suffering much, but... loyalty to Empire and King ... your homes ... shattered villages around us... Law, liberty Europe... in India... long... Do not think... enemy... defeated... Empire not safe. Let every man do his utmost duty until the enemy is defeated... your duty... Empire... the glory of your deed... *Hindustani log bahut acha!*'

He finally gave a salute and entered his car with the alacrity of a doll and drove off, leaving the troops warmer in their hearts, for he had a winning manner about him, but colder in their bodies, for it must have been the coldest day of their lives in this country, with the wind piercing through all their warm clothes, numbing their hands, and freezing their feet.

They broke up ranks at 'Dismiss' and walked *burrburring* down.

'The moon of Id has passed,' said Kirpu sighting his friend Aslam Khan, the Lance-Naik of the Punjabi Mussalman Company.

'A little eclipsed,' Lalu added.

'He did not beam on me with a smile,' said Aslam Khan with a cynicism that Lalu had not suspected in the man who was all for the Sarkar in the Red Sea.

'I have not congratulated you, on your promotion,' said Aslam Khan thumping Kirpu. And the two cronies began to chat, while Lalu looked aside and walked away.

Hardly had he gone two or three steps when he found that Marie had come and slipped her arm into his.

The officers and the men of the battalion were walking along the street and, as Lalu proceeded towards the billets with the girl, he felt embarrassed.

'André?' he asked in order to emphasize the casualness of his relation with the girl.

'*Il est la,*' she said, perfectly unselfconscious and happy to be walking down with him. And she began an exposition of the parade with a fluency to which he listened attentively, without the slightest comprehension of what she was saying; to give the impression that there was nothing 'black in the pulse,' as the sepoys were whistling, hissing and making catcalls.

But she hung on his arm now with a pride and a childish affection that he knew would certainly be construed as a breach of the unwritten law that no sepoy was to be seen on familiar terms with the women in this country. And yet he felt the panic of abandon at the touch of her arm, and the pride of walking along next to her coursed in his veins, blinding him to the military and social prohibitions and weakening the defences which he had built up against the mire that had been stirred in India because he had dared to look at the landlord's daughter fondly.

'*Ohe,* introduce me to her,' came Jemadar Subah Singh's voice from behind.

'Jemadar Subah,' Lalu gasped, half relieved that now the officer too would have to take responsibility for being seen talking to her. And he turned in a fluster to Marie, saying: 'Monsieur Officer.'

'Bonjour,' Subah said readily.

'Bonjour, Monsieur,' the girl replied. But she went on with her explanation to Lalu.

'Is she your friend, *ohe*?' said the Jemadar to Lalu significantly.

'*Qu'est ce qu'il desire votre camarade*?' the girl said, turning to Lalu, noticing a sudden stiffening of her chaperon's arm.

'Monsieur,' Lalu mumbled quickly, agitatedly in his horrible hotch-potch of Punjabi and French. And, pointing to the Jemadar, he struggled to say 'my friend will entertain you,' but unable to find the elaborate *Francisi* necessary for the purpose, blurted out, 'Mon Ami, Mon Ami', and, apologizing with an 'Excuse,' released his arm and ran back towards Kirpu affecting a serious business.

But before he had got very far he met André who embraced his legs, caught hold of his rifle and prevented his escape.

At that instant Marie left Subah and came prancing back to him and André.

'Oh God!' Lalu cried to himself, a sudden apprehension about the consequences of this insult to the Jemadar burning his cheeks and the tips of his ears.

During the next few days the silent fire of jealousy and revenge began to wither the shoots of Love.

Actually there was no love in the lives of these Sepoys. And there was no necessity for revenge. They were men who had been brought up for generations to a law which dictated that every woman was to be looked upon as a mother or sister. This did not mean that they had never gone to bed with their wives, or that they had never felt the need for a woman during all the years of their service in the army. Only the customs of their homes did not allow for the kind of kissing and cuddling which they saw the *Goras* indulging in, but that was only a difference of technique; the husband and wife in their privacy or the lovers trysting in the lentil fields outside the villages, expressed the same human impulses.

But in *Vilayat*, much more than in the cantonments of India, the unwritten laws of the Sarkar prohibited tender impulses, especially for the black and brown men. The natives thought of them first as people who had walked out of the *Arabian Nights*, then they treated them as they treated their own colonials, with that ease and grace which the French bring to their social intercourse. Even better, for to the common Frenchman the Hindus were vaguely an ancient and civilized people with a great past culture behind them. And, in the flesh, these Indians seemed fine men, tall and handsome, and so well proportioned, their warm brown faces radiating gentleness and sympathy that was deeper than their native embarrassed smiles.

The sepoys could not get over their feeling of inferiority to the Sahibs, however, and they could not easily shake off their fear of the Sarkar. Outwardly they began to regard the women in this country as part of the landscape of *Vilayat*, Mem Sahibs who were superior to them in status and beyond their reach and whom they were forbidden to be familiar with, though the French Government seemed to feel differently about the Negroes, Senegalese and Moorish troops, who were allowed to talk to the local women in the cafés. Inwardly they aspired to them with all the suppressed urges of manhood which the sense of their loneliness exaggerated into the sheerest hunger. But, inured at home to rigid orthodoxy and custom, they did not exhibit eroticism so much as they showed extremes of asceticism, obscenity and a mawkish sentimentality which found expression in snatches of maudlin songs or of abuse.

Among young people like Lalu there was, however, a subterranean life of desire, vague and uncertain in the face of woman. But the series of incidents which had led him to fly from his village and join the army after the landlord had seen him playing with his daughter, Maya, had left a shame in the grooves of his heart, which was also the fear of new miracles. 'The hurt of the wounded lover', said the poet Waris Shah, 'is like the meeting of the accuser and the accused.' And the terror of the Sarkar, vigilant in the phantom stares of Sahibs, in the exploding voices of N.C.O.s, in the cavernous eyes of the prying sepoys, shadowed his wandering heart. The one-eyed pony and the stupid servant could not seek the consolations of that spell bound wonder in the light of Marie's grey-green eyes.

The girl had moved him. But 'there were no she-asses in the Emperor's household.' Reclining back to the abandon of a moment, he chased the phantom of her presence in the moonshine of the Sahib's heaven like one of the damned in the netherworlds, who had forfeited the dignity and pride of manhood, who had been dragged through the blood-soaked and murky waters of several hells to rest for a little while before he was sent to taste the air and water of fresher hells. Abjectly grateful for the smaller mercies of life, he sought to crush the luxury of desire and went about like the dehumanized toy of destiny, which was the unknown will of the Sarkar. And yet, in the face of the unknown, in full view of the spectacle of destruction and death, in the muteness of obedience, he yielded to the suggestions of an instinct which was the revenge of his body upon sadness — a strange purblind tenderness for Marie.

Jemadar Subah Singh resented the very suspicion of this tenderness.

At first the Jemadar began to frequent the regimental office on various pretexts just to get a chance to see Marie. But, catering for the British officers, Madame Labusière, her mother, found it necessary to avail herself of any little help that her daughter could give her, and Marie remained closeted in the kitchen. She was only seen when she came into one of the other rooms or when she went out towards the river to call André. And while 'Lulu', whose duties lay in the office and extended from being the letter-writer to a kind of orderly to the Ajitan Sahib, could go into the inner sanctums and was often asked to sit down to a meal with the family after tile officers had finished dining, Jemadar Subah Singh, pretending to come to the office on business, had to hang around in Babu Khushi Ram's room or in the front parlour where Babus Thanoo Singh and Muhammad Din sat, waiting for the chance of catching a glimpse of the girl.

Only once did he see her as she came back with her mother from some shopping expedition. Passing by the window where Lalu sat, she pressed her forehead to the window pane, dilated her green cat's eyes, knocked with her knuckles and shouted 'Lulu'.

'Ooof, my life!' Subah sighed, his face red, and stampeded towards the window.

But seeing a stranger coming towards her, she ran and followed her mother.

Chagrined but persistent, Subah tried other ways of getting into contact with her.

'*Ohe, yar,*' he said to Lalu, 'you know her, why don't you bring her out on some pretext so that I can take her into a field? She excites me with her coquettish face, irritates me with her body ... May I die for her, may I become sacrifice, I could crush her in my arms ...'

'Deception and fraud – that is what a woman is!' said Babu Muhammad Din with a frown on his puritanical forehead which was contradicted by the leer on his lips.

'Deception and fraud? — *Wah! Wah!* Our Maulvi Muhammad Din!' said Babu Thanoo Singh. 'You ought to see him caressing the hips of all those *Francisi* women who come to wash clothes in the brook there. There is no bigger lecher in the regiment than him, except it be our Jemadar Subah …'

'God forbid!', protested Muhammad Din.

'The son of God!' mocked Thanoo Singh. 'He pretends to be a puritan. You Kafir Hindus, why do you eat hog's flesh?' he says to me. And he is not above or below accepting the crumbs of Major Peacock's table if he can thereby work up an intrigue against Khushi Ram. Son! There is no sin in having a woman in heaven, but here you call her Deception and Fraud! …'

'Muhammad Din is right,' said Subah. 'They are cunning, these whores. I went into a Red Lamp place the other day and the girl there who had had fifty others before me began to simulate the hisses and the shrieks of a passionate gipsy even before I had started, till I had to give her a dig in the ribs to quieten her. She was an Arab girl …'

'Are there places like that here, Jemadar Sahib? *Toba*! You don't mean to say so!…' interrupted Muhammad Din, frowning even as he swayed agitatedly in his chair, and he laughed a dry laugh which intensified the atmosphere of salacity which had come to prevail. And then Muhammad Din asked, 'Was she good, Jemadar Subah?'

'Of course, she was wonderful value for the money after I had corrected her with a blow or two. She gave me a good time. I would like to go back again.'

'Where is this place?' asked Thanoo Singh, dropping the pen from his hand …

'Jemadar Sahib, where is this den of iniquity?' asked Muhammad Din.

'In this office,' said Lalu softly, not daring to raise his voice in the presence of his seniors.

'Then Muhammad Din will be smitten with a red hot iron!' said Thanoo Singh.

'But I was only asking for information with a view to reporting to Major Peacock Sahib how the morality of the troops is being spoiled,' protested Muhammand Din.

'To be sure you are a Deception and Fraud!' said Subah. 'Come, Lalu, let us go, before the Maulvi tells upon us.'

'Have no fear of that, Jemadar Sahib,' answered Muhammad Din, 'your revered father was gracious to me. He who recommended and got me my position as quarter-master clerk.'

But Subah wanted to talk confidentially to Lal Singh and left the Babus to smack their lips.

Lalu said that he would have to ask Khushi Rain's permission to leave the office. And since the Head Clerk was closeted with Peacock Sahib and no one could dare to go in there, he told the Jemadar to wait.

But Subah could neither subordinate his passion nor the assurance of his self-will to understand Lalu's position.

'You will pay for this insolence!' he told him angrily before be stamped out of the hall.

Sure enough Lalu received orders to attend parade the next day.

Uncle Kirpu began to beat about the bush before coming to the point.

'Boys,' he said, 'that great *Jarnel*, Lat Roberts Sahib, once Commander-in-Chief of Hindustan, who inspected us the other day, has become a resident of the celestial heavens ...' And he paused deliberately and assumed the solemnity associated with the moments after such an announcement. This made the sepoys solemn.

'I know,' he continued exaggerating this mock seriousness so that every muscle of his face contracted, 'it has been a great shock to you. You and I who stood to attention on that cold day could think of ourselves dying of pneumonia, but that General who inspected us seemed like a God, above common ailments to which flesh is heir ... If only he had lingered in bed with gout we might have sympathized. But to die of a mere cold ... he with top boots and warm coat and medals and ribbons ... he did not set a good example to those who have to go to the trenches and fight and do fatigues ...'

'Who is going to do fatigues now?' Lalu asked amused but apprehensive.

'*Holdar* Lok Nath thinks that some men have got slack because they have not been doing fatigue duty or drill,' Kirpu said.

'Am I on, then?' Lalu queried more directly.

'You — let me see, you have got to attend parade in the morning and do the scribe's work in the evenings, if you are not sent with Ration Parties at night.'

'Oh, I shall live through all that,' muttered Lalu affecting the bravado of chagrin. 'A man does not die from an officer's slap.'

'How did you bring this on yourself, son?' Kirpu said softening.

'Refused to be a go-between for the Jemadar Sahib,' said Lalu.

'Leper, and he has got the itch!' said Uncle Kirpu full of pent up fury of disgust. 'This itch is not only in the loins ... After all we must have an itch to make love to escape from this beastliness ... Seems he has a worm in every grain of his flesh ... This worm give him the itch ...'

'No, it is the worm of malice, because so and so has a grudge against someone who stood in the way of an extra stripe before his death,' said Lalu.

'Also the worm of jealousy because someone has been able to rub up against a woman,' added Kirpu. 'What can one say? We are rotten. Never so happy as when we are up and someone else is down. Never seem to see that soon our number may be up. No fear!... No shame! Especially these two swine! Lok Nath and Subah! Lepers and Impudents!'

'*Acha*, there is no talk, Uncle, let us forget all about them,' said Lalu to cut the canker of resentment.

But they could not forget all about them. For the 'lepers and impudents' made it their business to remind them that they were not only omniscient but omnipresent, particularly as they had the itch rather badly.

'What is the matter in this camp that so many people can be heard talking in their sleep?' said Havildar Lok Nath, coming into the barn from the courtyard where he had been prowling round the kitchen on a zealous tour of inspection.

'If one door be shut a thousand others are open,' said Uncle Kirpu.

'You shut the door of your mouth,' said Havildar Lok Nath, digging his feet into the ground as if he had come to stay and lifting his chin with exasperation. 'I dare you to utter all that about 'lepers and impudents' in my presence! You let me hear you talk about me again and I will teach you the lesson of your life!' For a moment he frothed and worked himself up into a fury and then burst: 'Swine, it is not the first time I have heard you demoralizing the regiment! Come on, boys, run along and fill in! ...' And he swept the barn with a glare, surveying the faces of the men to explore for any traces of defiance there might be.

The men remained silent, doing their beds or arranging their turbans and puttees in readiness to go out on parade, but their silence spoke through uplifted eyes.

'Have you given that man orders to parade?' Lok Nath challenged provocatively.

'No, he is not going on parade,' said Kirpu for sheer cussedness.

'Why not?'

'Because he is going to the office to write my last will and testament,' said Kirpu with grim irony.

'Then he had better scribble his own will too, for he will be presented to the commanding officer with you at the office,' said Lok Nath finally.

No one was more surprised than Lalu at Kirpu's curious defence of him.

'Meanwhile,' continued Lok Nath, 'you can come along with me and see the Jemadar Sahib.'

'Listen Lok Nath, I have got work to do before the parade.'

'Lok Nath me again and I shall have you handcuffed and arrested,' hissed the Haviidar, his tight lips twisting into a snarl.

'*Holdar* Sahib, I have told you I have work to do,' began Kirpu with a sullen humour. 'Orders, to pass on ...'

'Your first duty is to obey the orders of a superior officer,' shouted Lok Nath. And, with a desperate aggressiveness, he leapt at Kirpu and tore the Lance-Naik's stripe from his arm which he had specially hated all these days.

'Oh *Holdara*! *Holdara*!' the sepoys came clamouring up to Lok Nath.

'You know *Holdar* Lok Nath that Uncle Kirpu was joking,' urged Lalu seeing that things had taken a serious turn. 'It is just his sense of humour. Of course he gave me the orders to parade from tomorrow.'

'You keep your mouth shut,' bawled Lok Nath. 'I have had enough of his humour, his snivelling, dirty, demoralizing talk. He thought he had become a Captain just because he had got a stripe. I shall see to it that he is court-martialed. Don't call me by the name of Lok Nath if I don't! And, as for you, you are to go on parade if you've been given the orders. Come on, proud Lance-Naik, to the quarter-guard...'

'Oh *Holdara*, forgive, forgive him,' said Rikhi Ram.

'Oh *Holdara*, I fall at your feet, don't take him to the guard room,' said fatty Dhayan Singh.

'Oh *Holdara*, don't insult his white head!'

'But it is my fault, *Holdarji*,' Lalu protested. 'He did give me orders and he was laughing ...'

'I know who will have the last laugh,' said Lok Nath, brushing them aside and dragging Uncle Kirpu forward with a determination to prosecute the matter to the end.

Almost as soon as Lok Nath went out of the barn with Kirpu ahead of him, it was clear that the Havildar regretted the course that his visit had taken. Lok Nath had come primarily to give orders for the men to get ready to go to the front again, and to bully Lalu in some way so that both he, who had a grudge against this sepoy since the Ferozepur days, and Jemadar Subah Singh, who seemed to be angry with the man now, could knock the swank out of him with a parade and a fatigue. Instead he had provoked old Kirpu who, though stubborn and independent, was harmless enough, or rather against whom it was difficult to take any rigorous measures because of his general popularity in the regiment and his connections with the Subedar Major. But, equally was it clear that, since Lok Nath had pulled the Lance-Naik's stripe off Kirpu's arm, matters had gone too far for the Havildar to retreat without loss of face.

Lalu decided to rush to Jemadar Subah Singh to accept the onus of responsibility for the incident, and to appeal to him for old friendship's sake to drop the matter of the quarrel in the barn. He smoothed his puttees, brushed his turban with the palm of his hand and went.

Jemadar Subah Singh was not in his billets in the peasant's hut across the road, and had presumably gone to the office where he mostly hung round for a sight of Marie.

And Lok Nath had gone to trace him there as Lalu found when he went towards the office and saw the Havildar and Kirpu waiting outside.

The difficulty was to get past Lok Nath and go to see Babu Khushi Ram, explain the whole matter to him or perhaps to see the Ajitan Sahib. For a moment he hesitated by the Guard Room on the corner of the road, talking to the Sentry even as he watched Lok Nath's movements at the office door. The Havildar was apparently talking to an orderly. Lalu decided to brave it and go right past him into the office.

As he came near Kirpu, however, he could not help stopping to have a word with his friend.

'Have you seen anyone, Uncle?' he asked.

'No,' said Uncle Kirpu averting his eyes as he crouched with his chin in his hands, patient and still.

'I am not my father's son if I don't present him to the C.O. himself since the Jemadar Sahib and the Ajitan Sahib are not here,' Lok Nath ground the words in his mouth. 'And now that you have come sneaking round to help him you had better sit down too ... I will present you both.'

'I want to go and see Babu Khushi Ram, *Holdara*, and, give over charge before I go with the Fatigue party tonight,' lied Lalu.

'You will not stir from this place, son of a pig, not till I have settled with you!' said Lok Nath finally.

They waited in the sombre, cold afternoon in the grim silence that radiated from the room where the C.O. sat working overtime. And, for a moment, Lalu regretted that he had put his head in the noose when he had escaped from any liabilities except fatigue. Then he chastised himself for the ignoble thought and affected the dauntless manner of a man who would not even mind dying for his loyal friend Kirpu who had got himself into trouble on his account.

'Go, *ohe*, and call Babu Khushi Ram to me here, for a minute,' Lok Nath said to the Muslim orderly.

'The Babu is in the Major Sahib's room,' said the orderly with the cocksureness of the sepoy on office duty who, because he hears important news and rumours, generally thinks himself superior to everyone in the ranks, even the N.C.O.s.

These obstacles in the way of his ability to execute a summary court-martial seemed to enrage Lok Nath more intensely and to fill him with hatred of the victim, which had tended to cool off with the change of scene and air. Now he was more determined than ever.

At that moment he caught sight of Major Peacock Sahib in the hall, with Babu Khushi Ram behind the C.O.

Immediately he rushed into the hall, clicked his heels, saluted and said:

'*Huzoor*, I have arrested Lance-Naik Kirpa Ram for disobeying orders and for insulting a superior officer.'

'*Kya hain*? What do you want?' said the C.O. frowning and in a forbidding tone.

Major Peacock seemed preoccupied. The forehead of his pug dog face was creased by several lines of thought, his hard grey eyes were tired, his head hung down. He was looking at Havildar Lok Nath from the background of the many matters which were engaging his attention, about which the Head Clerk had been discoursing to him till just then.

'*Huzoor*,' began Lok Nath, pale and rather frightened, but persistent, 'I want to present Lance-Naik Kirpa Ram for insubordination.'

The Major Sahib did not let him finish his sentence.

'Oh take him away, take him to the guard room and present him tomorrow. Havildar Sahib. I have no time to see anyone. Report to the Indian officer of your company and the Company Commander.'

Major Peacock's manner was first impatient, then kindly, then official and detached, looking at the report from the distance from which he regarded almost all such minor domestic complaints in the regiment. Although as a Company Commander of long standing he had known his Indian officers and N.C.O.s if not the men, now as a second-in-command who was well on the way to be Lieutenant Colonel, he was losing touch with even the officers and preferred to leave the smaller and more intimate matters to them.

Lok Nath clicked his heels, saluted and returned, chagrined with what he considered was a rebuke which the Major Sahib had administered him.

Babu Khushi Ram would have put in a word to discount Lok Nath's report, but, noticing the Sahib's irritation, he could not muster the necessary courage. He intended, however, to whisper into the Owen Sahib's ears as soon as he saw him. For he knew that Lok Nath had it for the protégés of the deceased Havildar Lachman Singh. He wanted to know what had happened, but waited till the Major Sahib was out of the way. He followed Lok Nath into the hall and looked out of the door.

'Why, Kirpu, what have you done to *Holdar* Lok Nath?' he asked in a knowing whisper.

'Everything, Babuji,' Kirpu said waving his head with an embarrassed smile. And he couldn't help his sullen humour. 'A leper has got the itch, and when a man has got the itch he wants a companion.'

'I will show you who has got the itch,' said Lok Nath finding the odds against him. 'Come, I will rape your mother, your grandmother and her mothers for ten generations! Come to the quarter-guard, Major Sahib's orders. And I shall see that you get to hell in court-martial, swine!'

'Oh Lalu, is that you?' said Khushi Ram seeing the boy. 'Come, son, I have a file for you to take to the officer of the Gora regiment.'

'He is coming to the quarter-guard with me,' said Lok Nath.

'No, he is not,' answered Khushi Ram gently but firmly. 'He is on duty here.'

'But Babuji, he is the cause of it all,' protested Lok Nath. 'Jemadar Subah Singh has ordered him on fatigue party tonight and he is to go on parade from tomorrow.'

'He is in my charge in this office,' said Khushi Ram, 'and here he is going to stay until you show me orders signed by Ajitan Sahib ... Come, son, I have an urgent job for you to do. The regiment is going to the front tomorrow and all that *Holdar* Lok Nath thinks of is to quarrel with this man or that man, intrigue against this N.C.O. or that ...'

'Control your tongue, Babu Khushi Ram,' flared Lok Nath. 'And you, Lance-Naik, you come to the quarter-guard. You are under arrest.'

'Take him, but don't "buk" to me,' said Khushi Ram. 'I have seen many like you rise from nowhere and become the sons of Lords, so don't try to impress me!'

'We shall see tomorrow,' said Lok Nath and pushed Kirpu violently forward.

'The angry man listens to no counsel, Babu Khushi Ram,' said Uncle Kirpu and went submissively forward.

The men were lying down to sleep when Lalu came into the barn after having seen to Uncle Kirpu's comforts in the guard room where he was imprisoned for the night. Everything augured well. For he had told Khushi Ram the whole story and the Babu had been to see Subedar Major Arbel Singh, who had assured him that though he could not release Kirpu against the C.O.S orders, he would see to it that nothing adverse happened to the Lance-Naik when he was presented the next day to the Adjutant, who was the commander of No. 2 company. What was more he had called his own son, Jemadar Subah Singh, and rebuked him for his behaviour, and he had promised to take Havildar Lok Nath to task. In spite of all this Lalu felt rather tense as he came in soaking wet, for it had been raining heavily all the evening and he had been on his feet several hours and Uncle Kirpu had seemed strangely reticent when the boy had left him.

'Why, what happened?' Dhayan Singh asked him from where he lay reading by candlelight at the other end of the barn.

Lalu told them briefly of the developments, while he took off his clothes and prepared to get to bed.

'A sour apple, that Lok Nath!' Dhayan Singh commented.

'And rotten to the core,' added Rikhi Ram, another Sepoy.

'More like the sucked up stone of a sour mango,' some one else added.

'*Ohe*, keep quiet, he might be listening,' Lalu warned.

'Let him listen,' said Dhayan Singh. 'He can pluck my *lund* if he likes ... And the Major Sahib too! Why did he order Uncle Kirpu to be kept in guard room? — he goes about being the *Karnel* of regiment! ... Couldn't Arbel Singh release him?'

'Rape-mothers, they are all alike, these *afsars*,' said Rikhi Ram.

'Seems a shame, our Uncle Kirpu in disgrace, locked up in the quarter-guard,' said Dhayan Singh, tilting his head high and then subsiding on to his pillow.

And then everyone was silent, as if they were all oblivious of each other, as they lent heavy browed on their elbows or laid open-eyed on their beds, waiting unconcernedly for the hurricane lamp to be blown out or, perhaps, for the reveille to sound the hour of sleep. But beneath their apparent calm was tension which made them turn their silent uncomprehending faces to Lalu, as if they wanted to tell him how sad they were for him and for Uncle Kirpu. For these simple uncouth hillmen from the Himalayas, brutalized by the experiences through which they had been, still had sensitive awareness of each other which was always bursting through the dumb indifference to which they had become hardened. They had no hope or faith in their hearts except the fate to which they had resigned themselves, their *kismet*, which, more and more, had begun to look like the premonition of a horrible death. And yet they instinctively turned to each other with tenderness which was the more poignant because it expressed itself through a clumsy gesture or the classical curse of Hindustan, 'Rape-mother,' the inverted defence of the sacred mother.

Lalu who had contributed nothing to the conversation felt awkward at the kindliness shown by the men and withdrew his eyes to himself even as he was trying to gather his thoughts. But the furious activity of the afternoon had left a despair-heart nothingness in him which the chill of the evening intensified. He smoothed his bed and sat down shivering in seminudity.

'I hear that snow has fallen in the trenches,' said Rikhi Ram. 'Was there any news about the front in the Subedar Major Sahib's quarters?'

'Some of the sepoys of the 41st Dogras have been taken to hospital, because the toes of their feet got frostbitten,' informed Lalu. 'The Subedar Major is going to demand warm vests for us before we go to the trenches.'

'Warm vests, warm coats, warm shirts, warm socks, warm mufflers — everything will come and stay in the quarter-master *Holdar's* store and be given to those who stay 'behind the lines', said Dhayan Singh bitterly.

'They say they are even going to supply braziers with charcoal in the new lines to which we are going,' said Lalu.

'Where are these new lines? Did you hear anything about that?' ventured Rikhi Ram.

'The Subedar Major Sahib talked of a place called Festubert, some miles from here,' said Lalu.

'What? Farishtabad?'

'How many miles?'

'When do we really start?'

'To be sure we go to Farishtabad tomorrow,' said Lalu with a grim smile which showed his teeth in a mockery which threatened to turn to anger: 'To be sure, the abode of angels ...'

But he was not disposed to talk. He looked at the empty bed of Uncle Kirpu by his side with a near tears face, stiffened the muscles of his mouth and lay down like a silhouette of silence, the echoes of the hopeful words of Subedar Major Arbel Singh and Babu Khushi Ram conversing with whispers of the coming doom against the hard walls of his head.

There were all kinds of rumours current in the barn when Lalu got up in the morning.

Sepoy Dhayan Singh, who was habituated to going out to 'jungle-pani' at dawn, said that there had been an enemy raid on the quarter-guard last night.

Someone else said that enemy aeroplanes had come over during the night.

Another Sepoy had it that the regiment was to receive orders to go to the front at once.

The most exact information available was that Sepoy Rikhi Ram, who was the senior man in the platoon after Lance-Naik Kirpa Ram, had been called by the Subedar Major Arbel Singh in the dead of night.

And since Rikhi Ram was absent from the barn Lalu felt vaguely disturbed.

He rolled his puttees on his legs, adjusted his turban hastily and hurried to the guard room.

The guard of the previous night had changed and the Sikh sepoy at sentry-go challenged him as he tried to go into the room where Uncle Kirpu had been kept prisoner.

'Halt!'

'I want to go in and see Lance-Naik Kirpa Ram,' said Lalu. 'I am Sepoy Lal Singh from No. 2 company.'

'Go back to your lines,' said the Sikh sentry, lifting his rifle and coming to a stand at ease. 'No one is allowed to go in there.'

'But he is a friend of mine and I want to give him a message,' said Lalu.

'Go back to your lines,' roared the sentry.

Lalu thought that the Sikh was just being stupid.

'Come, Holdara', he flattered the Sikh sepoy by giving him the status of an N.C.O. 'I only want to give him a message before he sees the Company Commander.'

'Who is he? What is this now going on?' came the voice of Havildar Chanan Singh, a friend of Uncle Kirpu in the Sikh company.

'It's me, Lalu, I want to give a message to Uncle Kirpu in there,' the boy said.

'Come, son,' said Chanan. 'There is a message here from Uncle Kirpu for you.' And he pointed his finger to a small board on which the orders of the day were posted.

Lalu went up eagerly smiling at the victory he had won over the sentry through influence.

'How are you, *Holdarji*' he asked cordially even as he began to read the hand-written notice:

RGIMENTAL ORDERS
69TH RIFLES

Lance-Naik Kirpa Ram of Number 2 company committed suicide last night at 2-30 a.m. while he was detained in the guard room for insubordination to a superior officer on duty.

'Ooof!' Lalu burst involuntarily and stood back staring at Havildar Chanan Singh.

'No matter, son, what had to happen has happened,' consoled the Havildar, 'This was God's will.'

Lalu read the orders again, annoyed at the words 'detained in the guard room for insubordination, etc.' They would have a worse elfect on Kirpu's reputation than the commission of suicide.

'But, *Holdara*, what happened? Why did he do it? He was only kept in custody through a mistake and both Khushi Ram and I got a promise from the Subedar Major Sahib that he would be exonerated from all blame and set free this morning? ... And Uncle Kirpu, so sensible, so wise — committing suicide! And it is my fault because he quarrelled with Lok Nath about me! ...' The words flowed out of Lalu, like half-screams waiting for an explosion of anger and indignation.

'It is the will of *Wah Guru*,' said Chanan Singh, 'I don't know what happened to make him go and kill himself. I was awakened at the dead of night to come on duty. It seems Kirpu got hold of a sentry's loaded rifle in his cell and, adjusting the barrel end into his mouth, let off the trigger, and blew his brains out. The guard was changed. The body has been removed. And the Subedar Major Sahib has issued that order on the notice board.'

Further orders arrived in the morning that billets were to be cleaned up and that the regiment was to be ready to march to the front at midday. They were to go to a new sector, some ten to fifteen miles south through a place called Richebourg to Festubert, where they were to join their old comrades of the 129th Baluchis, a company of the Connaught *Goras*, the 3-4th Pioneers and the 9th Bhopals. The vague rumours of the previous days were therefore confirmed, though vague rumours and precise information were more or less the same to these Indians, for the names of places were confusing to them and they did not know where they were at any time or where they were being taken. They accepted the orders, however, without complaint, even with a certain degree of enthusiasm after someone had said, 'Brothers, first earn and then enjoy rest,' and smothered any fears they had in a collective effort to prove true to the salt of the Sarkar.

Even Lalu resigned himself and began to believe that everything was the reward for one's past deeds, as the elders said. Though obsessed by a sense of guilt about Uncle Kirpu's terrible death, he said to himself reproachfully, 'Why is it that men like Kirpu, Dhanoo and Lachman, who were so good, should have suffered and died when I wretch am alive? Was it because God punished one person for the evil deeds of another? But no God could be so unjust. Except that people said that the righteous suffered because God was testing their saintliness through harder trials. If so God was a fool to do that ...' But he was becoming increasingly afraid both of God and of men and suppressed his naive questionings and hesitations in an imperturbable military calm that betokened efficiency above the shadows of despair.

A bugle call sounded the assembly and they fell in by the brook. Major Peacock, the acting C.O. accompanied by the Adjutant, made a solemn inspection, passing down the ranks. Somehow it turned out to be a mutual inspection, for the sepoys too scrutinized the officers' faces, turning more willingly to Owen Sahib's tired, gentle face than to Major Peacock's clean-shaven visage, which looked sterner than ever, as if he were restraining his personal idiosyncrasies into the attitude required of a C.O. But he had always seemed rather wooden and hard to them during cantonment life in India and he was known to be a very stern officer, a hard disciplinarian on the parade ground though homely and jocular when he played an agile centre forward in the regimental hockey team. One of the few officers who could talk Hindustani well, and who remembered the names of the Sepoys, he was yet somewhat un-understanding of the Sepoy heart. He was an old style officer who lived to a formula, accustomed to thinking of the sepoys as looking for example and guidance to the British officer, treating them with 'justice tempered with kindness', regarding them as a loving, rather distant father regards his children. To the extent to which the contacts between the Sahibs and the Sepoys at work and play, had assumed certain traditional modes, his attitude evoked a workable response and the rest did not matter. But the naive, often illiterate, Sepoys were, through a prolonged heredity, rather more sensitive and human than the army code gave them credit for. Above all they were shrewd judges of character. They called him 'the Mule' and looked at him with the awe that that stubborn animal inspires, because they did not know what he would kick in an awkward situation. On the other hand, they called Captain Owen a gentleman, because he looked upon them with soft-grey eyes and the ever-present hint of a smile on his lips. And in the strange atmosphere of 'Franceville', where these Sahibs were the only link between their native land and *Vilayat*, they, who were supposed to be less than human, turned instinctively to Owen Sahib rather than to the efficient Major Peacock.

'He is hardly a *Karnel* yet but swaggers like a ten foot tall Jarnel,' whispered Rikhi Ram to Lalu when the C.O. had passed by and they relaxed their taut, breathless faces.

But Lalu was exploring surreptitiously among the crowd of men, women and children by the bridge who were watching them, for Marie. In his disgust against himself over the tragedy of Kirpu's death, caused, he felt, through Jemadar Subah Singh's jealousy over the girl, he had not even gone to say farewell to the family which had treated him so well. The regret rankled in his heart, specially as he had persuaded himself to believe that the girl had liked him ... But he was afraid that Jemadar Subah Singh or Havildar Lok Nath might be watching him. And he tried to maintain the erect attention, eyes front and breath held back. Only the fumes in the jungle of his heart seemed to be choking him.

The Colonel gave the words of command and they moved off in silence accentuated by the rustling of their uniforms.

The children on the bridge rushed alongside of the men and before the regiment was on the road, André sought Lalu and caught hold of his coat.

'Marie?' Lalu asked him.

The boy pointed to the door of the farm.

In one swift glance Lalu took in the figures of Papa, Mama. There he saw Marie standing by her parents' side. The family was solemn and grave, as if they knew the Sepoys were going to their doom, as others, including their own son, had gone before them. Lalu wanted to shout a greeting to them but he felt strangled by his equipment and only patted André's head awkwardly, a plaint from the poet Waris Shah screaming on the edge of his thoughts:

'Oh your love, oh Hire, dragged me into the dust of this world ...'

✥ 10 ✥

THE LIGHT WAS FAILING before they had gone two or three miles. They could not keep the combat order as their boots hit each other's heels on the uncertain surface of the road. But they tramped on, as if the spirit had been taken out of them by the prospect of going to the front again. For, in their simplicity, they had believed that they had done their part in the two battles in which they had fought and would now be allowed to rest somewhere or drafted back to Hindustan while they were still whole. And, now, on the way to 'Farishtabad', they felt a resentment which expressed itself in sullen silence.

Lalu had felt the gap by his side, a continual reminder of the friend he had left behind. And the sense of guilt became a cancer and the fear that he was now left alone to face Havildar Lok Nath and Jemadar Subah Singh, both of whom swaggered about as if they bore no responsibility for the ugly incident of Kirpu's suicide, though, for the while, they kept their distance from him, their real victim.

The numbness of fatigue and exasperation had somewhat atoned for his sadness and, after a time, his mind just became a blank, noticing only the automatic movement of the sepoys' feet as they cut across the highway, past sombre woods, bereft of all leafage, their stark trees lifting their gnarled hands to God in a kind of prayer for life. A few stars glistened in the sky and a pallid half moon thrust its head against the rough contour of the wintry heaven.

As they passed by an occasional farmhouse, the natives came out to stare at them, men and women watching with bowed heads and humble

198

mien, as if offering a kind of repressed apology from themselves and the irresponsible Generals of their country for this war in which the stranger had had to be called in to fight.

Lalu was affected by a sight of an old woman who was feeding her chickens and kept up an incessant flow of incomprehensible chatter till the tail of the regiment had vanished on a corner of the road beyond her cottage. She was wrinkled and had a knowing air about her ugly face, like his mother's. And, in spite of himself he felt nostalgic, and began to hum a melancholy Punjabi melody in his throat:

'Only four days to play, Oh mother, only four days to play!

Night has fallen, mother, my Beloved is far away,

Oh mother, four days, only four days to play ...'

'Oh louder, sing louder,' coaxed Rikhi Ram with a weak smile on his energetic, commonsensical face. He had respected Lalu's grief and not intruded on his silence throughout the march, and the boy warmed to him, but, of course, would not sing.

'Let us sing "Lachi", boys,' Rikhi Ram said hilariously. 'Come on.' And he began.

'Aha, in one village two *Lachian*,

Two *Lachian*, two *Lachian*,

The younger *Lachi* started all the trouble ...

'Come on,' Dhayan Singh shouted with a wholehearted laugh which seemed to issue from his tummy.

'Aha, in one village do *Lachian*,

Aha, the older *Lachi* asked the girls,

The girls, the girls, the girls,

Oh, what colour veil suits a fair complexion?

Aha, the girls said truly,

Said truly, said truly, said truly,

A black veil becomes a fair complexion ...'

The simple strain rose beyond the original soft pitch of Rikhi Ram's hard accent to a chorus, broken at first by the voices of those who joined a little later, or stressed a phrase too early, or slurred it and varied a line according to the version current in their locality, but then rising to an uproarious, high-pitched duet which relaxed their grim set faces and melted the congealed blood in their veins.

'Let us sing "Bazar Vakendian", someone ventured.

'No let us have, "Come put your arms round my neck, Oh Puran, I am dying",' suggested Dhayan Singh.

'No, no, no, let us have "Harnam Singh",' said Lalu. This was a duet which they had themselves evolved about the typical sepoy in the war and his sweetheart, Harnami, and her insistence for presents from *Vilayat*:

I want a pair of shoes,
I want a pair of shoes, I want a pair of shoes,
Vay Harnam Singha ...
Oh, I shall fetch for you,
I shall fetch for you, I shall fetch for you
A pair of fine shoes, with high heels,
Ni Hamamiae ...

The frank ribaldry of this set them laughing, and it would have gone on but it released their inventive genius, and too many different versions were forthcoming, and they were afraid of the officers farther ahead, though both the Sahibs and the Indian officers were relieved to hear their voices.

Now they were becoming more and more profane and tended to break ranks, because they were tired. Rikhi Ram cautiously suggested that they should look to their steps before someone should turn on them and rebuke them.

Lalu reverted to another melancholy tune. 'Oh mother, one day one has to go ...' when they began to see the vague contours of wrecked houses looming across the highway and defining themselves into a longish village. Before they had entered its main street, orders rang out, for their officers, had met the billeting authorities. They were drawn up in the shadow of a huge château and waited there in the cold dark for a while. Presently they were shunted off into the outhouses of the château across a magnificent courtyard, into comfortable quarters.

The company cook woke them next morning by respectfully shaking their toes. But even as they came to, they lay in the snuggery of their versatile blankets, involved in those prolonged indecisions about the necessity of getting up to dress to which these inhabitants of warmer climes had become prone in the French winter. But it was raining outside.

'Tea, Sarkar, *chota hazri*!' Santu repeated humbly coaxing them ... They were his superiors in rank, as he was merely listed as a 'follower' though they were inferior to him by caste, because he was a high-caste Brahmin. But his was the kind of transformation everyone had long learnt to take for granted, because it was the prestige of rank and higher pay which was the proper measure of authority created by the Sarkar, the old distinctions between the learned man, the warrior, the shopkeeper and the rest were only subsidiary, applied on suitable occasions, but otherwise only retained in official files. And to Santu, the Brahmin turned cook, every sepoy was a man of higher species. Better by rank and under the Commander-in-Chief was Sarkar. And to him, all the hierarchy of the High Command up to the father of the family of nations, George Vth, Colonel-in-Chief of the Indian army, was Sarkar.

'Go, rape-mother, the son of *chota hazri*!' Rikhi Ram abused him, as he still slept, with his blanket on his head. 'Brother-in law! He fancies himself as the son of a Sahib! *Chota hazri*.'

Lalu sat up at this outburst and accepted the tea instead. He wondered why Santu had gone to serve Rikhi Ram first, except that the cook knew that this senior Sepoy was soon to be promoted to the rank of Lance-Naik in place of Uncle Kirpu, and perhaps he hoped to be recommended for a medal and a reward if he could win the favour of the new N.C.O. Santu had entertained the hope of recognition of his services for months now, struggling hard to give satisfaction. But whatever he did, turning from their own miserable lives in chagrin and disgust, bullied by their superiors, they turned on him like vultures upon their just prey, till he had become a frightened, abject creature in one part of his nature and a stubborn, unmindful ass in another.

'Maharaj, forgive me, but I am frightened of *Holdar* Lok Nath who ordered me to serve *cha-biscoots* at six o'clock,' Santu said, going up to Rikhi Ram again. 'And the *Holdar* asked me to wake you up specially and to give you a message that you were to be ready when he came.'

'Why does that Pelican come nosing into our platoon?' shouted Rikhi Ram sitting up. Then he rubbed his eyes, frowned, looked round, shaking his shoulders for warmth and accepted the tea, shouting: 'Where is *Holdar*?'

'I don't know, *Huzoor*,' Santu answered wincing and stepping back all a tremble.

'Oh, brother, drink up tea,' said Dhayan Singh. 'And here are the *biscoots* which the Sahibs and Mems have sent from *Vilayat* for their loyal Indian Sikhs and Gurkhas.'

Rikhi Ram got up and began to dip the biscuits in the hot liquid before gobbling them up and sipping the tea with loud spattering sips.

'Truly the Sahibs are wonderful, *Huzoor*,' said Santu. "The rations which the Sarkar has sent for the company this time are so plentiful that all of you will have feasts in the trenches: sugar, lentils, ghee, flour, and potatoes. There are dried fruits and *Angrizi* sweetmeats of dark colour in boxes.

And the *Holdar* told me that goats are coming and also *chillums* for hookahs sent by Maharajas, and cigarettes and rum ...'

'It will be feasts for those of you who stay behind the lines,' said Rikhi Ram.

'*Huzoor*, you can count the rations,' protested Santu meekly. 'I may die if I have ever tasted what is meant for you people, Sarkar; *Holdar* Lok Nath is coming to check up ...'

'He — he comes like a watchman and stays like a thief.' Rikhi Ram said, 'Go and do your work and don't talk so much.'

The bluff of Rikhi Ram's dry manner asserted itself. He was at times quite a fearsome person. Having drunk the hot mixture of tea-leaves, condensed milk, boiling water and sugar, he belched profusely in the best Indian style, as if to communicate his gratitude to the Sahibs and Mem Sahibs who had sent him all the luxuries. Then, wiping the ends of his rather thin moustachios, he leaned over to Lalu and said: 'Give me a cigrut, brother, and forget about Lok Nath.'

'But he has joined hands with the son of the Subedar Major Sahib,' said Lalu. 'So God save us.'

'But the Subedar Major Sahib's son is one thing, the Subedar Major Sahib himself another,' said Rikhi Ram, buoying up Lalu deliberately, as, indeed, he had been seeking to do all the time. At that instant an orderly came and told Rikhi Ram that he was wanted by Subedar Major Arbel Singh.

On being pressed for the reason why Rikhi Ram's presence was demanded, the orderly yielded that there was some good news in store for him.

The sepoys had hardly washed and dressed when Rikhi Ram returned and ordered them to fall in on parade: 'Acting Lance-Naik Rikhi Ram's orders, fall in and behave, for *Karnel* Green Sahib is going to address the regiment before we march.'

The men were pleasantly surprised by both announcements.

As they fell in, the *Karnel* Sahib stood talking to Subedar Major Arbel Singh and the other British officers in the courtyard. He looked almost half of himself, having been reduced by his illness to the ghost of his former tall imposing, broad-shouldered self: his small beady eyes had lost that glint with which they used to fix every sepoy, his face had an unhealthy pallor, and his arm was still in a sling. And yet his determined chin seemed to become more pointed.

The N.C.O.s called their companies to attention.

The Colonel took the salute and ordered 'Stand-a-teeze'. And then he began to address them in the casual, conversational manner with which he had endeared himself to the regiment. 'I am glad to be back with you,' he said in his indifferent Hindustani. 'You have all had a good rest, and now you have to do some work so that the Sarkar may not say that you ate and drank at its expense, but only gave a salaam in return.' This homeliness made them all smile. But the Colonel's voice rose from the jocular to the serious pitch as he continued: 'It is going to be hard work — and dangerous. But I know that you will face it with courage. Your bravery has been highly commanded by all your officers, and the *burra* Jarnal Sahib himself told me his high opinion of your conduct at Ypres.' Them he ordered: 'Company commanders forward!'

The British officers, among whom there were some new Sahibs today, attached from other regiments it was said, came out and gave a series of orders, and the regiment swung out of the courtyard and began to stamp across the cobblestones of the village.

Unlike Major Peacock, the Colonel had not spoken of the great things at stake but had talked as man to man. And they Tiked him for that. But he had not told them anything about where exactly they were going. Perhaps, like them, he also obeyed orders and only knew what he saw. And the only persons who knew anything were the Generals, the Commander-in-Chief and the King-Emperor.

The rain had stopped for a while and a pale but welcome sun showed its head above the village houses, redolent of the smell of coffee and newly-baked bread. Some of the Indian sepoys from other brigades, billeted in the village, were hurrying up and down the hilly street, while some were washing their shirts and stockings at a pump and hanging them on the bushes in a garden. Farther up some Tommies were rubbing down their horses, while Indian cavalrymen were polishing their saddles and accoutrements. They hailed each other and there were smiles and laughter, and the atmosphere seemed playful and easy.

'Almost like Ferozepur cantonment,' said Lalu to Dhayan Singh next to him.

But off to the north some cannon boomed.

'*Han*, it has just struck the hour,' said Dhayan Singh pointing to where the sound of the guns came from.

After this they marched solemnly, silently, efficiently, so that the sound of their feet filled the hillside.

———

Towards the afternoon the sky became leaden with the clouds which had been mustering throughout the day, and dusk gathered over the land. But on they went, tramping with heavy feet on an endless road, skirting past deserted houses which dotted the plain, into a dark damp wood.

Suddenly a streak of lightning flickered across the sky illuminating the forest trees in a vivid gold. They shook their shoulders to shift their heavy packs and ducked their heads. But, instead, a storm of rain and hail burst upon them. The wind and water swept across and lashed the bare branches of trees. Their turbans and overcoats and puttees were soaking wet and the heavy packs on their backs seemed to have become heavier. They shivered and broke the company columns.

The storm passed leaving only a drizzle behind and, luckily, they came to the ruins of a château beyond which, from the smoke of burning wood streaming from steep roofs, was a small dreary village. They were hurriedly dismissed and allowed to rest. They limped off into some huts, which were indicated, with floundering feet.

While they lit fires and tried to dry their turbans and puttees and took off their boots to ease the footsores of a long day's march, they were given tea and a ration of rum. And, as rain still fell steadily, they waited, listening to the pit-a-pat and to the persistent crack of rifle and machine gun fire which seemed not far away.

Orders came that the troops were to go into trenches beyond the village, across the main road. As a concession to their persistent inquiries about where they were going, and whether the village they were now in was 'Farishtabad', they were told that the line they were going to occupy was to the east of Festubert. This information, of course, got them no further than they were. But for once there were some definite details: with the 129th Baluchis they were to take over the right flank of the left section of the line next to the Connaughts, the 34th Pioneers and 9th Bhopals. That was reassuring.

The battalion dressed ranks with a brisk clattering of rifles and began to march. The sepoys were almost hysterically joyous about going to the trenches now, a shrill enthusiasm possessing them, a kind of mockery or pretence of bravery which hid all the private doubts and fears that they

had ever had. And they moved forward with sudden cries of their religions: '*Kali Mai Ki Jai!*'... '*Sat Sri Akal!*'... '*Allah ho Akbar!*'

***

As they penetrated farther into the village and passed by the debris of
ruined houses, their enthusiasm died down a little.

'Seems we are in "Farishtabad!" ' a sepoy said.

'Look at those ghosts in the dark?' another added.

'Can you hear the firing?' a third asked.

'Silence,' came Havildar Lok Nath's voice. 'No noise.' Apart from the
shadows of ruined houses and spasmodic bursts of machine gun fire there
was nothing dramatic about it, nothing which could whip up a false sense
of heroism.

The street came to an end by a vast heap of debris, and they were met
by guides and runners from the Connaughts and Baluchis, who told them
that there was a patch of road directly under fire and that they would have
to fall into single file so as not to attract notice.

'Silence! In line at seven paces,' the word was passed from mouth to
mouth.

'But you put that cigrut out!' Dhayan Singh called to Jemadar Subah
Singh at the head of the company.

'Don't know who some of these officers think they are!' Rikhi Ram
grumbled. 'Having us all marked out with that glow!'

'They don't care if you are killed so long as they can enjoy their smoke!'
Lalu whispered.

'Fall in again on the road after you have crossed this patch!' the
Jemadar ordered from ahead. 'And now go.'

There was some desultory machine gun and rifle fire in the distance,
and then a curious lull fell on the scene.

The troops moved slowly, warily, on tiptoe across the dangerous patch,
with their rifles held aloft in their right hands, their heavy boots disturbing
the silence against their wills. They breathed with relief as they got across
the hundred yards. From the intense silence ahead there seemed to be no
danger now that they had crossed the patch.

'Are we far from the line?' Dhayan Singh asked.

'The communication trench is about forty yards away in that field,' a
Baluchi runner informed them, while they stood mopping the sweat off
their faces. Apparently the line was not far from the road and even took in
some houses farther ahead.

'Creep into the trenches, boys, just as you are,' Rikhi Ram said. 'And follow the runner.'

They fell into the field with hunched backs in a zigzag line.

Before them spread a dark, dead plain dotted by clumps of trees, and interspersed with mounds of former habitations over which reigned the ghostly terror of a furtive calm. A light flickered in the distance and then the earth and sky closed their grip, so that the sepoys could barely see the silhouettes of each other's bent backs.

'Where are you, Dhayan Singh?'

'*Ohe*, where are you?'

'Where …?'

They whispered and cried as they thrust their necks like bullocks going uphill with the driver's goad working into their haunches.

But, one by one, they were filing past the guides and their officers, almost at a running pace, into the communication trench, sweating and messy, the brittle points of their fidgety nerves on edge.

The main trenches were almost parallel with the road and protected by thick lines of barbed wire like the hedges around a field.

'Halt!' the word was passed down the ranks before they had travelled far into a communication trench.

For a moment, Lalu stopped to listen and to see if there was anything new in this line. But there was only the now all too familiar sound of machine gun fire, almost as when he had entered the trenches on the Wytschaete-Messines road.

He inhaled a lungful of cold air and felt relieved. The danger was in the anticipation, he thought to himself. He would soon get used to it as at Ypres.

———

But conditions were slightly different here from Ypres. For one thing, it was much colder. The whole sky remained overcast with grey, leaden clouds overnight, and in spite of the fact that they wore two shirts and two pairs of socks each, and heaped overcoats and blankets on themselves as they lay in the clay cavities, they shivered and could not sleep. When they emerged in the morning, rigid with cold, their hands under their armpits, teeth chattering and their faces drawn and red, they found that snow had fallen a foot deep during the night and the land was covered with a thick layer of woolly flakes, except where the barbed-wire entanglements stuck out like grim sentinels on the German outposts and where the depressions of the shell holes showed the soiled clay of the ridges.

'Come and have some biscoots and tea,' said Dhayan Singh who did the manual work eagerly in spite of the layers of fat on his body.

'More than that I should like a fire to warm my hands on!' Lalu said. 'Where are those braziers that brother Rikhi Ram promised us?'

'Here, come by the fire, here,' Dhayan Singh said. 'Boys, make room for him!'

'It is you who are occupying all the space,' Lalu said, as the boys made room for him round a small Huntley and Palmer tin, full of twigs and burning biscuits on which they were warming themselves.

'Charcoal is not heard of in these parts,' Dhayan Singh said. 'But they have promised us some coke, which Rikhi Ram has gone to fetch from the village behind.'

Lalu sat down and accepted the lukewarm tea from the kerosene oil tin which lay by, and began to gulp it in his aluminium can.

Just then there was a great whirring in the air and the Sepoys shouted.

'An airship!'

'Oh, an airship!'

And to be sure, an aeroplane dived down almost grazing the trenches of the Indian corps and leaving a trail of smoke behind.

'Killed!'

'Undone!'

'*Ohe!*'

There was utter pandemonium in the trenches, shrieks of panic, shouts and abuse, as if they expected the wrath of heaven to descend on them through this sudden visitation.

But then they saw some papers come fluttering down into the lines, while a very tornado of rifle and machine gun fire chased the aeroplane higher and higher into the even sky.

The sepoys ran helter skelter to catch the droppings of the steel bird which fluttered in the air, as if they were catching paper kites at the spring festival outside the fields of their villages. But most of the paper drifted away from the trenches.

'Paper, paper, nothing else but paper,' a sepoy shouted from the Afridi company.

'Give us some to brighten this fire with,' said Dhayan Singh. And he ran to fetch some.

'Oh take the name of God, something is written on them?' he said as he returned with a handful. 'Here, Babu, read them and tell us what the Kaiser says.' And he gave them to Lalu.

Lal Singh snatched at the leaflets and tried to read. There was something printed on them, not in the flowing calligraphy in which Hindustani is written but in lettering such as the Sahibs of the Salvation Army used in India for their Hindustani Bibles.

' "True information"!' he read. ' "Salaam-e-lekum"!'

'Ram Ram!' said Dhayan Singh.

'No!' answered Lalu laughing. 'It says "Salaam-e-lekum".' And he read: ' "The Sheikh-Ul-Islam has proclaimed a holy war on the Id festival day at Mecca against the British, Russians and the French. The Sultan of Turkey has started a war against the same oppressive people, and he has been joined by the King of Afghanistan." '

'But we are Hindus,' said Dhayan Singh. 'What is the Sheikh of Mecca to us?' Lalu read further: ' "Brothers, this is a letter from your well-wishers and friends. Why do you fight and die for the unbelieving, against the Kaiser who is an ally of your Khaliph, the Sultan of Turkey ... Do you realize that in fighting for the English you commit irreligion and may die an inglorious death and never reach ..." '

At this instant there was a hubbub of clamouring voices in the Afridi company and a Pathan Havildar came rushing up saying, 'It is a message from the enemy asking us to desert. Give the papers up or you'll be court-martialed. Subedar Sahib's orders!'

Lalu thrust the leaflet into the tin and assumed a pose of nonchalant correctness. He sat with his hands over the tin to take as much warmth from the glow of the fire as he could before he got up to handle the cold butt of his rifle.

Lance-Naik Rikhi Ram came back cold and pinched, the shoulders of his angular body hunched, his ears red with the biting wind that was blowing, his nostrils running till the liquid had formed a crystal on the tip of his nose, his boots striking crunch crunch upon the hard, freezing earth of the trench.

'What's the news, *Holdara*?' Lalu asked him, his impetuosity returning after days of living in the stupor produced by Uncle Kirpu's death.

'News, brothers, what difference does halt or march make to a soldier?' Rikhi Ram said boredly. 'You live in comfort: the sun shines by day, the night is lit as on a feast of lanterns, and you are warm when I go about in the cold. What more do you want?' And he sat down tired, shrinking into himself.

'Have some tea, *yar*,' Dhayan Singh said pouring him remains of a lukewarm dirty liquid in a kerosene oil tin.

'Ooof, the trenches are ankle deep in mud up there!' Rikhi Ram began as he got warmer. 'The wind is sharp. Fierce gale round the corner of the communication trench. Some of the Sikhs in the Pioneers have had to be heaved out of the clayholes by means of ropes, because they were frozen at night. The feet of some *Goras* and sepoys of the Baluchis are stricken with frostbite.'

'So was your mouth a moment ago,' said Dhayan Singh. 'What's the news that boy asked you and you seemed as if you were going to bite him.'

'The first thing is about those leaflets,' said Rikhi Ram. 'The Sahibs say that there are some scoundrels from Hindustan on the German side, agitators who have run away from the clutches of the law at home and prefer to work in the pay of the Kaiser than to go to the scaffold ...'

'Really,' said Dhayan Singh intrigued. 'I would like to embrace them.'

'Who wants to go to the scaffold?' said Lalu. 'I wonder what the Germans are like to talk to?' Since they had arrived in these trenches he had been curious to know where the German positions were, and what the enemy was doing, for the disposition of the lines seemed to him somewhat complex. Perhaps the mantle of snow that enshrouded the place was confusing.

'But one of our sepoys is said to have practised a strange ruse upon them,' Rikhi Ram said. 'The Captain of the platoon on our left told the Subedar Major Sahib that a man called Rustam went out, on patrol in "no-man's-land"! As he was crawling along by a German trench the enemy turned a big light on him. Behold, the brother-in-law thought to take his hand to his head and salaamed the Germans. They beckoned him and, though he nearly had dysentery with fear, he mustered up courage and jumped into their trenches. He thought that his end had come. So pointing to our trenches he abused the *Angrez* Sahibs and made a sign as if he meant to cut the throat of the whole *Angrezi* race. Whereupon the Germans were pleased and gave him sweets and coffee. Then, by using gestures, he told them that there were other traitors like him in the Hindustani Army and got permission to go and bring them back with him. The Germans feasted him, it is said, on meat and wine, and allowed him to creep back ...'

'Has he been given a medal for it?' asked Dhayan Singh.

'He is lucky to escape with his life from what is told about the Germans by the Sahibs!' said Rikhi Ram.

'What else is the news?' asked Dhayan Singh.

'Well, only God knows,' said Rikhi Ram emptying the bowl of tea. 'But the Sahibs say that we are going to win. Only the enemy has built saps ...'

'Only what?' queried Dhayan Singh anxiously. 'Why don't you speak up? Ever since you have become Lance-Naik your talk has become crooked!'

They were feeling rather peevish and short with each other with the intense cold.

'The enemy has built saps,' repeated Rikhi Ram, speaking with an effort, as his utterance was inhibited by the contraction of his mouth through exposure to the wind.

'What are "saps"?' Lalu ventured.

'The talk is,' began Rikhi Ram, 'that the difference between the enemy trenches and our line is some thousand to a hundred yards according to the nature of the ground in no-man's-land at various places.'

'Now you know that no-man's-land can be swept by rifle or machine gun fire everywhere. Also, artillery can play havoc with the opposing trenches. So, in order to give an attack the best chances, it becomes necessary to shorten the distance to be traversed before reaching the hostile trenches.

'And the Germans have thought of the idea of building saps or winding trenches by which they reach almost up to our lines, thus becoming immune to our artillery fire and achieving a position from where they can attack.'

'There is going to be an attack then?' Dhayan Singh said.

'They are lucky, those men with the big guns at the back,' said Lalu all to himself, as he slapped his hands against his sides and jumped to warm his feet. 'While we have to rush into the open jaws of death, the artillery wallahs stay out of the range of rifle and machine-gun fire, of the hand grenades and the trench mortars ...'

'I bet though that aeroplane this morning went looking for them,' said Rikhi Ram.

'But if the Germans have made their trenches like portable ovens which can be taken where the guns can't find them we will be burnt long before the enemy is scorched!' said Lalu.

'Do you mean to say,' asked Dhayan Singh, coughing as he blew a mouthful of breath on the straw to start a flame in the tin, 'Do you mean, then, that the Germans are only forty, fifty yards from our trenches?'

'At certain places they are nearer,' informed Rikhi Ram concernedly. 'They have built winding trenches from their lines for quite up to three to four hundred yards of the lines held by the 34th Pioneers and the Connaughts, but at other points they have yet only come a hundred yards and are busy building a firing line parallel to their original trenches. It must be difficult work for them to cover their diggers. But wherever they have built these "saps" they can collect men within a short distance of us and rush our trenches ...'

'And what are we supposed to do? Sit freezing?' said Lalu his face twisted in a scowl.

'Don't be impatient, brother, some men are to be selected to go out on patrol tonight, to see how far the enemy is from us,' informed Rikhi Ram comfortlessly, in a suppressed tone.

For a moment, they searched each other's faces and then hung down their heads. This was ominous news. The cruel whisper seemed to go through the listeners like the bitter wind on the corner. The men stood or sat stiffly about, uncomprehending and still, ignorant of what awaited them in the murderous devices of the devil who controlled their destinies, speculating vaguely for the reality behind that information which the N.C.O. had given them about the position in which they stood in this phase of the war.

All that day there was considerable activity on their left flank, specially where the 34th Pioneers held the line. The Germans attacked the Sikhs from the sap-heads, which they had constructed almost right up to the lines held by the 34th, with a bayonet charge supported by bombs and hand grenades. And then the enemy used enfilading machine-guns to such effect that the Pioneers were overpowered and fell back into the lap of the Connaughts on their left. A company of the Pioneers tried to take back their trenches; but, immediately as they advanced, they were met with more enfilading machine-gun fire and they hadn't a chance. The Germans kept forcing their way through the communication trench, battering at the Connaughts and driving them back from traverse after traverse as the latter were handicapped for want of ammunition. The Connaughts retreated step by step, till they were able to build a barricade in a trench on the right of the 69th; and, there, they defied all the enemy's efforts to shake them.

The 69th, though vigilant as a supporting unit, was not, therefore, directly involved. But they had to be very alert and make as effective a use of the extra ammunition that they were given, over and above the small quantities which they were usually doled out. The tension of the attack had, however, worn them down. For, from the time that the Germans suddenly burst out of the bitter mornings and surprised the Pioneers with the unprecedented fury of a storm, to the tune of a roaring screeching artillery, exploding hand grenades, they had, in spite of the heaps of dead and wounded they left on the way, forced their way with such terrible effect, in full view of the defenders, that each minute seemed to the supporting units to carry the threat of their extinction. It was perhaps the fear of the 'Huns', 'the wild men of the European jungles', built up in the sepoys' minds by the Sarkar that the sight of the tall, ruddy, grey-uniformed Germans, with queer helmets, dashing forward with the ferocity of bold animals, fascinated them, held them spellbound for long moments, in a curiosity mixed with terror. But the 69th were sufficiently far away from the trenches, where this attack was localized, not to be actually involved. And in the afternoon, with the Connaughts holding out and a thick mist partially obscuring the land, the heavy fire died down and they sought to recuperate for a while.

The Ration Parties had not been able to come up to the trenches because of the intensity of German artillery and the sepoys began to warm up the remains of the tea in their mugs over a fire of rags in the kerosene oil tin, and they tried to thaw their hands and faces numbed with the bitter cold, crowding round the tin and catching hold of smouldering rags.

'Don't smother the fire,' Dhayan Singh shouted. 'Keep away ... We have no more fuel, and your tea will never be warm.'

'I will give you my handkerchief to burn.'

'You can have my puttees.'

'I don't want the tea.'

The sepoys pushed, pulled and grumbled. They would have gone without tea, refreshments, food, anything, for a moment's warmth, for the glow of a little red flame that could brighten their hearts.

'Go to your places,' said Dhayan Singh, greedy and exasperated. 'Some officer or N.C.O. may come. And the attack may still be on up there.'

But they hunched round the tin, dumb and careless, hissing imperceptibly with inner shivers, shaking and trembling. For it was not that they had not faced explosive shells calmly, but the cold, the cold, the cold had got them, paralysed them.

Lalu had been going about with a drooping head. He seemed to be indulging in an orgy of tentative heart-searching. In him the two poles of nature seemed always to have been quarrelling, as if he had not decided whether to burst out of his skin, as it were, and live outside himself, or to recline back, self-exiled, pain-marred, mutilated with the memories of those hindrances which the world had put in his way. The two anti-types had revolved in a furious whirl of the axle tree during his boyhood. He was the contradiction who had cultivated a pride in excess of dignity, even as he had gone carelessly about, playing pranks with the boys of his village and laughing at the greybeards, bent on the consummation of his unrestrained impulses, as if he could cheat nature and take happiness by surprise.

As he sat by Dhayan Singh without saying anything for a long time, he was suddenly overcome by the desire to lift the pall that lay upon him and his companions.

First he gave a shove to Dhayan Singh, which dislocated the ring and sent everyone tumbling. Then he picked up a handful of snow and slush and threw it at Rikhi Ram. The Lance-Naik was taken aback, as he stood by the sandbags, and looked quizzically round, not knowing where it had come from. Dhayan Singh laughed, as he recovered his balance, and got up to revenge himself on Lalu, but seeing Rikhi Ram's solemn face, shot a handful of snow at the Lance-Naik instead. At the instant when this fell upon him, Rikhi Ram ducked his head to remove some of the previous snow. Dhayan Singh scored a bull. Rikhi Ram looked foolishly round. This encouraged the other Sepoys also to have a shot at him. Most of them missed the now wary Lance-Naik, who was laughing at his own discomfiture and abusing them kindly, 'Rape-daughters!' But this only intensified the mock fight, for now the sepoys on Rikhi Ram's left and the Lance-Naik himself took the offensive.

'Ohe, illegally begotten!' came the sharp rasping voice of Jemadar Subah Singh, whose arrival no one had noticed. 'Stop it.'

But the boys were happy with the warmth that this riot had worked up and continued throwing the snow-balls as if they were practising at throwing hand grenades. One of the snow-balls fell on Temadar Subah Singh's face and froze the solemnity of authoritative outlook till he burst:

'Is this the festival of your mother's marriage that you are hinneying like donkeys and throwing all this muck! Swine! Shun! Cockeyed sons of blind bastards! Couldn't you see me? Shun!'

The men checked themselves and went sheepishly to their places.

'What is this *Holdara*? Can't you keep order?' asked Jemadar Subah Singh.

'The boys were just playing, Jemadar Sahib,' said Rikhi Ram with lowered head.

'They will have to do some work for a change,' said the Jemadar shortly. '*Laften* Hobson Sahib and I are going on patrol tonight. I want two men to come with me.'

'*Acha, Huzoor*, I shall detail two men,' said Rikhi Ram.

'Detail yourself as one,' ordered Subah Singh. 'And ...'

'*Huzoor*, who will be responsible for the platoon in my absence?' said Rikhi Ram.

'I shall see to that,' answered the Jemadar. 'You'd better obey in order to learn how to command, and ...' He looked across the trench to trace the face of his second victim.

'Dhayan Singh, *Huzoor*?' said Rikhi Ram. 'He has always been my companion.'

'No, he is too fat for the job,' said the Jemadar. 'Where is he, Lal Singh? You and Lalu.'

'Did you call me, Subah?' Lalu said coming forward.

'Jemadar Sahib, illegally begotten!' said Subah. 'I have told you before not to address me as if I was a sweeper!'

'Forgive me, Jemadar Sahib,' said Lalu cowed.

'I will not do anything of the kind,' said Subah. 'You are to go on patrol with me and Rikhi Ram. Get ready!'

'Meet me by Lok Nath's dugout, Rikhi Ram, and bring that insolent swine!' ordered the Temadar. 'We are to go out on reconnaissance. Get ready, and call at nine sharp.' And, tightening his face muscles, he peered through the dark to survey the faces of the men, then turned about, bent and retraced his way.

───────

Come, *yar*, let us get ready,' said Lance-Naik Rikhi Ram when the Jemadar was out of audible distance. 'I wonder what is the matter with him today?'

'It is cold and he remembers his mother, perhaps,' Dhayan Singh ventured an explanation.

'He has got his father here to look after him,' said a sepoy tentatively.

'The bastard! — he is the son of his mother by some sullen swine!' said Rikhi Ram coming towards Dhayan Singh and the illusion of warmth in the tin where the rags lay smoking. 'At least Subedar Major Sahib has got breeding!'

'He is more likely to be the son of his father by some washer-woman,' said Dhayan Singh. 'He has got Arbel Singh's arrogance.'

'Whatever his ancestry,' said Lalu with the broad sweep of the final arbiter, 'he is afraid of going out on patrol.'

'You are not, are you, son?' said Lance-Naik Rikhi Ram, wiping the soot inside the tin and applying it to his face.

'No,' Lalu said, out of bravado when he really meant to say, '*Han.*'

'*Acha*, then, smear your face with this black as I am doing.' said Rikhi Ram.

'*Holdara*, where have your senses gone!' said Lalu. 'Your blackened face will show like a bull's eye above the white snow to practitioners of musketry in the German trenches.'

'To be sure, that is the right talk,' agreed Rikhi Ram shaking his head. 'Now the difficulty is how shall I get the soot off?' It seemed that he had been dazed by Jemadar Subah Singh's sudden appearance and had not covered from the shock of being asked to go on patrol.

'Wipe your face with your spittle,' suggested Dhayan Singh jocularly. 'Because there are no water carriers here to help you.'

'Oh, leave go, "Death to me, amusement to you," said Rikhi Ram.

'I will give you a rag to wipe your face, *Holdara*,' offered a sepoy in a muffled voice from afar.

'Take this handful of snow, Holdara, and rub it on your face slowly,' said Lalu, who had taken off his equipment and was bandaging his head and face with strips of gauze from his medical supply bag. 'And you will emerge with the complexion of a *Memni.*'

For a few minutes they continued their preparations in silence. It was strange that now, with the prospect of death before them they forgot to grumble, enduring the insidious miseries of the cold without a murmur. But, inwardly, Lalu felt his ego looming larger and larger over the trench face. 'So, after all, I am in for it,' he said to himself. And he thought of his cronies who had already fallen in one way or another, Daddy Dhanoo, Havildar Lachman Singh, and Uncle Kirpu. Because of the complicity of Subah and Lok Nath in the intrigue which had ended in Uncle Kirpu's death, and, because he sensed that the Jemadar had picked him out for the grudge that he nurtured against him since the incidents in the billets, he put the responsibility for the disbandment of the whole group on him. The vague search for imaginary wrongs satisfied him, even though it made him uncertain of himself.

'Come, then, brother,' said Rikhi Ram. 'We have to go to Lok Nath before we meet the Jemadar.'

'So we have to meet that bastard!' said Lalu. 'I shall give him a farewell message ... Here, Dhayan Singh, I am leaving my haversack. There is nothing in it except odds and ends and a letter for my mother ...'

'God bless you,' said Dhayan Singh as he got up suddenly to shake hands.

'*Ohe*, embrace each other; it may be the last time,' said Rikhi Ram with a shy smile.

Dhayan Singh and Lalu put their arms round each other with a laugh.

'Bring me a gift if you kill any Germans,' a sepoy said.

'I will bring you a peg to sit on,' said Rikhi Ram rudely, and he proceeded to embrace Dhayan Singh with real warmth.

'Keep your thick head safe, anyhow,' Dhayan Singh said to the Lance-Naik, 'and don't let fat blind your eyes.'

Tense and rather pale though hard, as if they were stiffening themselves to resist something outside them, they filed out towards the left, greeted by stupid messages, cheerful, encouraging words and inane good wishes.

As they came up to the end of the Dogra company they met Havildar Lok Nath.

'Oh hurry, both of you, and get some bombs for yourself from the Sahib's dugout,' Lok Nath said.

'I thought this was going to be a reconnaissance patrol,' whispered Lalu to Rikhi Ram as they proceeded through the communication trench towards the officer's dugout.

'Brother, what does smoke matter when you are caught in fire?' said Rikhi Ram as he traced his way in the winding trench.

They were just getting to level ground when they met Lieutenant Hobson, almost a young boy of an officer, who had been recently attached to the 69th from an English regiment.

'You two men for party?' he said, seeing them camouflaged.

'*Huzoor*,' they answered coming to attention.

'Where is the Jemadar Sahib?' the Lieutenant asked.

'In the dugout, *Huzoor*,' Lok Nath offered the information. 'I shall go and fetch him.'

'Those bombs, *Huzoor*,' said Rikhi Ram, moving his hands to signify the grenades in the officer's hands, 'they must be heavy.' And he offered to relieve him of the weight.

The Sahib, emptied his right armful into Rikhi Ram's hand.

'How do you shoot them, *Huzoor*?' said Lalu coming forward to take his share of the burden.

Lieutenant Hobson handed him the consignments in his left arm. Then, without more ado, he took a grenade, capered to the trench face and flung the ball across no-man's-land towards the Germans — timing its explosion with a loud, mocking burst from his mouth, 'Pop'.

The two men thought this was dangerous, but they seemed to catch the contagion of the boy's enthusiasm and ran one after another hurling a grenade each towards no-man's-land. The noise of the detonations was followed by a sound which might have been hoarse laughter or weird shrieks.

'Where is the Jemadar Sahib?' said the Sahib now impatiently.

'Here, *Huzoor*, he is coming,' came Lok Nath's answer.

'Salaam *Huzoor*,' said Subah.

'Have the sentries been told that we are going out, Jemadar Sahib?' the Sahib asked.

'Yes, *Huzoor*,' said Subah, but looked for confirmation to Lok Nath.

The Sahib did not notice the prevarication and asked, 'Have the men had instructions?'

'The plan is to crawl out towards the German trenches and see how far are the saps which they have built,' Subah began immediately in a cock-sure manner. 'And then ...' he continued but belched.

'The enemy is improving his position,' said the Sahib with impatience. 'We share out the bombs and keep them ready to throw ... Each of you will fix the bayonet to your rifles ... We have our revolvers ... Don't stray too far from each other — and follow me.'

'Simple and easy,' said Subah trying to steady himself even as he sought to explain the Sahib's words.

Lalu sensed a sharp whiff of brandy coming from the Jemadar's mouth.

Lieutenant Hobson led the way through a lane at the end of which was a sentry post and climbed the parapet. Jemadar Subah Singh and the two men followed, almost falling over each other in their eagerness to hurry into action. Once on even surface, the Sahib waited for a moment, then went towards the opening in the barbed-wire entanglements. Here he seemed to find his way barred by some obstruction, for he lay still.

Lalu crouched tensely, waiting for the firing to burst over his head. But the German attack of the afternoon had been exhausted for the while, and the remnants of the 34th Pioneers and the Connaughts were resting. Still this patrol seemed a hazardous if not a foolhardy venture.

The Sahib at the head turned to the left and began to follow the barbed-wire towards the next opening. Now they were proceeding parallel to their own lines, they were not very far from the sepoy's bullets.

Lalu felt that if Subah had not really told sentries on the observation posts to keep in mind that the party was out Lok Nath might shout. He reproached himself for not pressing the point when the Jemadar had recently given an evasive reply to the Sahib's question. There was a sharp breeze just round the corner of the 69th trench, and it seemed to bite the exposed tips of his ears, while beneath him the snow melted and became slippery so that he could not be sure of his steps. He lay down and began to crawl behind Lieutenant Hobson.

Again, however, the Sahib at the head of the expedition halted.

'Oh, what is the matter?' Jemadar Subah Singh almost shouted.

'Steady,' the Sahib whispered.

'Quiet,' Lalu conveyed the message behind.

Apparently, the opening in the wires here, too, was blocked.

'Oh go ahead!' Subah bawled at the same time as the Sahib ahead whispered something to Lalu.

Unable to hear Lieutenant Hobson's words, and frightened that the panic of the Jemadar behind him might attract the attention of German snipers, Lalu went off on his own initiative to the wire and tried to lift the tangles which blocked the right hand corner of the opening. It seemed as if it could be lifted, with some effort.

He raised himself on his haunches and applied himself to the task. By levering it from below, the tangles eased with a metallic whirr and a clang. Hobson Sahib came to his aid and held the loose wires, while Lalu tried to unhook them. The barbs were stiff. He shook them, impatiently, but gave up force for design, twisting the wires upwards till they rose about a foot and a half from the ground. Some furious kicks of his heavy boots and the sides detached sufficiently.

Without more 'sapping and mining' he lay down and began to crawl through the opening.

'Bravo!' the Sahib encouraged him even as he caught Lalu's coat.

A few wriggles and shakes and he had detached his hind parts from the barbed wires and was crawling headlong into a crater full of snow. He got up and held the wire high up for the Sahib.

'Follow me,' Lieutenant Hobson whispered as he crawled, emerged on the other end and sat up, brushing the snow off his face and hands.

Jemadar Subah Singh went next, laughing, as if this were some wonderful game and, patting Lalu on the head, shouted:

'*Ohe, yar*, you are marvellous!'

'*Chup*,' said Lalu, unable to repress his anger and irritation.

But as soon as he had administered the rebuke he felt afraid, lest Subah might turn on him and thus expose the party.

Lieutenant Hobson and Rikhi Ram ascended the incline, breathing heavily, as they dragged the grenades. And then the Sahib began to crawl away beyond the outer edge of the pit to reconnoitre the position.

'Come on,' Subah said as he got up to his full height, his puffed, young face stretched taut as if in the attitude of a brave leader and started to run.

Rikhi Ram pulled him back by the leg so that the Jemadar fell headlong into the next pit with a groan.

'Wait!' whispered the Lance-Naik following him. 'You will be the death of us.'

'He is drunk, I told you,' Lalu burrburred to Rikhi Ram.

'What is the matter?' Lieutenant Hobson asked, turning back.

'Nothing, *Huzoor*,' Rikhi Ram lied. 'The Jemadar has slipped.'

As Subah lay where he had fallen Rikhi Ram touched Lalu's arm and, pointing to his bayonet, asked:

'Shall we put him out of his pain?'

'Oh no, *Holdara*!' said Lalu, scandalized. He hadn't dared to think of this way of getting rid of an embarrassment. For a moment he was dazed.

Meanwhile, the Sahib had already crawled out ten yards and was making his way slowly with a sinuous, serpentine movement towards a boulder which seemed like the shovelled up earth of the German saps covered with snow.

A shell flew across the sky, somewhere away to the left, instilling an added sense of danger into Lalu's eyes full of the cataract of fear.

After the flare had died down Lalu began to climb out and follow Hobson Sahib, who had made quick progress towards the boulder.

'This bastard!' came Rikhi Ram's voice.

'Leave him,' Lalu answered, 'and come along by yourself.'

And for a moment, he waited for the Lance-Naik, anxious however not to lose sight of Hobson Sahib whose pace was defying danger too abruptly not to seem reckless. While Rikhi Ram was still two yards behind him, Lalu sighted some corpses at the foot of the debris; fantastic hulks which seemed to fill the landscape with grim sense of desolation, covered as they were with snow in patches.

'He is sick,' Rikhi Ram informed Lalu.

'But the Sahib has gone ahead,' said Lalu. 'Let us hurry.'

They began to work their way, veering towards the right, but sufficiently under the shadow of the boulder of the supposed sap-head. For a while they could not see Hobson Sahib and went ahead blindly. Their hands felt frozen at the finger tips and their clothes dripped with the melting snow. The smell of the dead bodies under the boulder was nauseating. It seemed to them that they were going at tortoise speed. They accelerated the pace, rolling the bombs forward instead of dragging them, their rifles getting in the way.

'Can you see the Sahib?' Rikhi Ram asked.

Lalu explored the ground ahead of him and tried to distinguish the Sahib's form from the several corpses of sepoys which were scattered around.

'There he is, by the sap,' said Lalu.

But before the words were out of his mouth he heard Subah's voice:

'*Ohe*, where are you?'

And the Jemadar came running up, crunching the snow, and threw himself down by them.

'God!' Lalu sobbed, frightened out of his wits at this madness.

But Rikhi Ram lifted himself and struck a resounding slap on Subah's head, hissing, 'Lie still, misbegotten! May I rape your mother and sister!' And the Lance-Naik held the Jemadar down from the neck, hard against the ground. 'Just stir, you bastard, and I shall kill you! You don't call me by my name, if I don't.'

Just then there was a resounding detonation and some hoarse shouts and shrieks in the saps twenty yards away. Lieutenant Hobson's arm could be seen completing a semi circle. Another detonation followed, and another one, hard on the last. There was a moment's hustling, a cry of pain and raucous words. Then a German machine-gun began to speak the language of death.

Lalu lay still, pressed hard to the ground, and guessed that Hobson Sahib had disturbed the wasp's nest with his bombs. The machine-gun belt seemed endless, filling the earth with its rat-tat-tat incessantly. Lalu closed his eyes and waited for the bullet in a frenzy of chagrin and fear.

After a minute he opened his eyes and raised his head. Horror! — he saw what appeared to be Lieutenant Hobson lying flat.

He left his ammunition and began to creep up towards the boulder. His heart was in his mouth and his body seemed to be cramped by movement. Sighting a depression on his left he rolled down and struck a corpse. For a second he stopped to breathe. Then he crawled diagonally towards the boulder, abusing Subah for delaying them and for drawing enemy fire. He was sure that the Sahib would not have thrown the grenades if he hadn't heard the Jemadar making a row at the back.

He touched another corpse and pulled himself up unable to bear the stink of the dead heaped in the crater.

He heaved himself forward and touched the Sahib's feet. There was no response. He shook the body. It was inert and heavy. Dead!

He crawled up under the shadow of another corpse till he was parallel with the Sahib. He knew it was madness to do so because the officer lay in full view of the saphead. But his instinct was to blunder through at all costs and rescue the body if only to save himself from censure for this split patrol.

There was a noise as if someone were chopping wood in the 'sap', and then the sound of raucous words.

Lalu sat up into the crouching position which was so natural to him, and put his arm round Hobson Sahib's body. He strained to weigh it in the scale of his arm before lifting it.

He was sweating now, and scales of darkness and light seemed to be ascending and descending over his eyes.

Grimly he heaved the body, still crouching.

'Hokh, ho, hoi!' some rasping German voices shattered the calm.

He dropped the body and laid down suddenly, shaking and terror-stricken.

The resounding gunfire died down after a few seconds.

Lalu moaned like a child in his throat and then began to crawl back hurriedly.

'Why, what happened, is he dead?' Rikhi Ram whispered as Lalu came up to him.

Lalu waved his head up and down, breathless. And, opening his eyes, he saw that he was hanging half way down the tip of the crater.

'*Acha*, son, climb down into the hole,' said Rikhi Ram soothingly, dragging him in even as he still held Subah by the scruff of his neck.

Lalu contracted himself like a porcupine till his body and legs were all assembled in the crater.

The Jemadar was sober by the time they had worked their way back to their trenches, or, at least, not having done a thing on the patrol except be sick, he looked sober, while it was Rikhi Ram and Lal Singh who seemed to be drunk, as they staggered into the ditches streaming with sweat, and dumb with thirst. Subah had not told the sentries to look out for them and they kept up an intermittent fire mistaking the patrol for the enemy. Havildar Lok Nath received them from where he had been crouching by some other sepoys round a brazier.

'Jemadar Sahib, did everything go well?' Lok Nath asked solicitously.

'Holdara, why did you not warn those rape-mother sentries that we were out?' Jemadar Subah Singh returned, swaying.

'Huzoor,' began Lok Nath.

'Huzoor, Huzoor!' repeated Subah standing erect. 'What is the use of asking you to do anything! We were nearly cut off in no-man's-land between two fires!'

Aware of his own default, and guilty in the eyes of his companions, he was seeking to pacify them by a vigorous attack against the man whom they hated.

'Oh, leave this talk, Jemadar Sahib, and let us go and report to the Subedar Major Sahib,' said Rikhi Ram who was not taken in by Subah's tricks.

'You can stand down now and go and rest,' said the Jemadar. 'I shall report tomorrow.'

'Huzoor, the patrol was split, and Hobson Sahib is dead and since you were disabled, I have to do my duty,' insisted Rikhi Ram.

'The Sahib is dead!' said Lok Nath. 'How did he die? What happened?'

'You will know what happened in the regimental orders tomorrow!' said Rikhi Ram menacingly, for he seemed intent on carrying out his duties as an N.C.O. faithfully so far as the Jemadar was concerned.

'Why, Sepoy Lal Singh, what happened?' Lok Nath asked the boy who was standing in the glow of the brazier, head bent and weary.

'The Sahib went too far and some of us stayed too far behind,' said Lalu without coming to attention and forcing his cold mouth to pronounce the words.

'Is the Sahib killed, then?' a Sepoy asked.

'Gone to celestial heavens,' Lalu said.

'Indeed, he is in safe keeping now,' said someone.

'Did you bring a trophy?' another Sepoy asked.

'Han, take this?' said Lalu shortly, pointing to his haunches.

'You can get a trophy yourself,' said Rikhi Ram taking Lalu's side.

'Really?' said the Sepoy.

'Han, a bullet in your own —,' said Rikhi Ram.

'Tomorrow is the big day,' said Lok Nath.

'Why, is there something on tomorrow, *Holdara*?' said Subah, who wanted to while away time so that Rikhi Ram should cool down.

'An attack all along the line', said Lok Nath.

'Is that official?' asked Subah.

'Come, Jemadar Sahib, we will soon find out,' said Rikhi Ram. And he took the initiative and touched Subah's arm, saying to Lalu at the same time: 'You go, brother, and have some food.'

Lalu showed the tips of his hands and his feet to the fire and then lurched away through the slush towards his dugout.

'Why, brother?'

'How was the patrol?'

'Have you returned?'

The sepoys on the way pelted him with questions.

He waved his head but did not answer till he saw Dhayan Singh squatting with some others by a brazier.

'Safe, brother?' Dhayan Singh asked.

'There is a story told of Akbar and Birbal,' Lalu began standing by the fire. 'Birbal said the whole world was blind. The Emperor and his courtiers said "No!" ... "Come outside the palace gate tomorrow and see," said Birbal!'

'Then what happened?' a sepoy asked.

'Well, the next day Birbal sat dressed as a cobbler mending shoes. As the courtiers and the Emperor passed the gate one by one, each one asked: "What are you doing, Birbal?" "Can't you see," said Birbal, "or are you blind".'

The sepoys laughed.

'All right, two eyes, come and eat. I have kept some food for you and Rikhi Ram.'

'Not food, no food for me, but a drink,' Lalu said, and he tottered exhausted at Dhayan Singh's feet.

'I'll go and get some rum from Lok Nath for you,' said Dhayan Singh and hurried away.

As he dragged himself into the dugout and lay wrapping his coat around his body, Lalu felt relieved to find himself still breathing alive. But he could not stop trembling. The shock of that moment, when he had heard noises in German 'sap' as he had been crouching by Hobson Sahib, still gripped him. How lucky that he had escaped being shot when the firing broke out!

He tried to stop the shaking in his limbs, saying to himself that the danger was past. But though the fear of death had passed he was afraid that the death of the Sahib and the splitting of the patrol might lead to difficulties.

There was a boom outside and a large shell roared overhead and fell with a crash somewhere on the fields. He waited breathlessly. Another shell followed. And then ... the monotonous rat-tat-tat of a machine-gun ... And rifle fire increased in intensity. The sepoys were shouting outside. He felt panicky. Perhaps Rikhi Ram was coming in to drag him before the Subedar Major or the Adjutant ... More shouts. He felt the confusion spreading over him, his heart was beating fast. He raised his head and called: 'Dhayan Singh.'

But his voice was smothered by the overtones of lead outside, he waited and listened. Hundreds of rounds of ammunition were being let loose and, from the glow outside the dugout, the sky seemed full of the fireworks of bursting shells. He cursed his luck, afraid that, having escaped being killed in a hazardous patrol, he might be engulfed by the avalanche of fire in the dugout and finished.

As the planets tore across each other outside, thoughts rushed through his head and his body throbbed. He felt sick and wished he could stop the shaking of his limbs. Above all things he wanted to hang on to his life, to hang on to it at all cost. 'Dhayan Singha, *ohe* Dhayan Singha,' he called, afraid like a child in the dark, though he could see his will to live as a somewhat ridiculous wish among the hundreds of astronomical annoyances, any of which might snuff him out.

The tension of his nerves increased through the long wait for someone to come. He felt that he had been cowardly, especially as he had left Hobson Sahib's body where it lay.

For a moment, be rebuked himself for harbouring accusations of cowardice against himself. But as he looked inside, he felt in the honest part of him that he had always been afraid, that he could not understand those like Subah who bragged that they felt no fear — though it was just like that bumptious swaggering fool to get drunk before coming out on patrol and help to undo the whole thing from the start! Hobson Sahib had gone to the other extreme, the recklessness with which he had gone ahead of them all, reached the 'sap', and thrown the grenades! Before the light of his conscience he felt guilty, even though he had gone to rescue the Sahib's body, because he had done this without thinking. He clearly remembered

224

having been frightened from the moment he touched the dead officer. It was extraordinary how the threat to one's own existence affected one, how naked and selfish it made one, stripped of all the sentiments of loyalty and the illusion that one could give one's life for another.

He tried not to think of the episode. He tried to control his shaking limbs and wished that either Rikhi Ram or Dhayan Singh would come and end his suspense. The explosions overhead were diminishing in intensity. But the Sepoys were busy shooting and no one was interested in him. He felt a cramp in his bones where the cold was numbing him and moaned: '*Hai Mother!*' His lips were parched and he hadn't the strength to shout. And his mind was racked as to what Rikhi Ram and Subah would say to superior officers, and whether the Ajitan Sahib would think he was a coward. To be sure at no time had he been whole-hearted in this fight. He had always grumbled and found fault with everyone and everything and himself. And he had been the undoing of Uncle Kirpu, and now he was perhaps responsible for Hobson Sahib's death ... He should have been conscious of his responsibility from the very beginning of the patrol and asked questions and reported that Subah was drunk.

'*Hai!*' he sighed as he turned, gathering his clothes around him against the cold.

'Patience, brother. I am here,' said Dhayan Singh in a caressing voice. 'Come and gulp this.' And he patted the boy's head.

Lalu raised himself on his elbows and took the liquid with a wry expression on his face. It was bitter. He belched and his face contorted as if he had drunk poison. Then he rolled over and lay down.

'Now, tell me what happened,' said Dhayan Singh spreading blankets over him.

'The Omnipotent Judge Yam tried to get ahead of me,' he said, with a smile, 'but I beat him.'

Early next morning Lance-Naik Rikhi Ram woke Lalu and said that Subedar Major Arbel Singh wanted to see him.

'What does he want to see him for?' was Dhayan Singh's automatic reaction. 'Let the boy sleep, he is tired'.

'How should I know what he wants to see him for?' said Rikhi Ram impatiently, though he did know.

Anyhow as Lalu hesitated in the illusion of warmth before shaking the

225

weight of the blankets and fatigue off, he surmised what Arbel Singh wanted to see him for.

'Jemadar Subah Singh has been in the lines this morning,' said Dhayan Singh.

'Has he really?' said Rikhi Ram a little more interested.

'Where did you see him?'

'Up by Lok Nath's dugout going over some papers,' informed Dhayan Singh.

'Orders of the day, I suppose,' said Rikhi Ram.

'Is it true that we are going to attack?' asked Dhayan Singh.

'The wind is blowing that way,' said Rikhi Ram.

'You are always talking a twisted talk,' commented Dhayan Singh. 'What happened to the patrol last night?'

'Come, *ohe yar*, Lalu,' said Rikhi Ram evading the question, his face strained after a sleepless night.

'Neither of you will tell me what happened,' said Dhayan Singh. 'So how can I sympathize with you.'

'The Sahib was beside himself with daring,' said Lalu emerging from the clay hole and ruffling his clothes free of the straw, 'and the Jemadar had eaten hemp'.

'And the Sahib was killed?' said Dhayan Singh.

'Come on,' insisted Rikhi Ram. 'If you give such a report you will also have crossed the oceans of existence before long.'

'I don't care,' said Lalu as he corrected a fold of his turban and followed Rikhi Ram.

'The cure of one is two, boys,' advised Dhayan Singh. 'Stand by each other.'

They stood by each other for a long time in the void of the traverse leading to the Subedar Major's dugout, but nothing happened. Only Arbel Singh's orderly, Din Dayal, who used to be a friend of Uncle Kirpu, gave them tumblerfuls of tea and the hope that the Subedar Major Sahib would see them soon. Apparently the Indian head of the regiment was busy with some private business, so that even the most privileged people, officers like Subedar Adam Khan of the Afridi company and Havildar Chanan Singh of the Sikh company, were turned away.

At length, however, they were called in.

They both entered and saluted correctly, as far as the low ceiling of the dugout allowed correctness.

'Come, sons, come, this rape-daughter cold gets me,' said Subedar Arbel Singh, smiling cordially from where he sat in a chair, a bandage round his beard.

'Subedar Sahib — I hope all is well, that bandage!' exclaimed Rikhi Ram although he knew that the old man had merely been dyeing his beard black.

'Brother-in-law!' said Subedar Arbel Singh with a glint in his big brown eyes. 'You are mocking at one old enough to be your father!'

'*Nahin*, Subedar Sahib…' began Rikhi Ram tamely.

'The son of negation!' said Arbel Singh. 'If you boys took your responsibilities seriously and kept yourselves in trim you could all seduce the *Francisi* girls and rise to be Subedar Majors. The trouble is you go about with glum faces as if your mothers have died …' And he lifted his voice towards the doorway and called, 'Din Dayala, come and undo this puttee on my face, I can't jaw so easily…'

'Coming, *Huzoor*,' the orderly answered running in with a circular movement.

As the orderly removed the bandage and disclosed the finely blacked goatee on the Subedar Major's face, Lalu could not help warming to this rake who had time enough even on the eve of battle to look after his appearance as if he were in a cantonment. And whether he knew his son was wrong and wanted to win them over or because his tyranny could afford to be light-hearted, he certainly eased the strain of this presentation.

'Go and call that rascal, my son,' he said to Din Dayal after the orderly had finished with the beard. And then be turned to Lalu and said: 'Why, son of Lalu, you are a mischievous bastard, aren't you? Always making trouble for yourself or someone else! Now tell me confidently to one who is like your father, did you have that Memni in billets? Handsome swine, aren't you?'

'But Subedar Sahib …!' Lalu protested righteously.

'Fool, there is nothing to be ashamed of,' said Arbel Singh.

'You two boys quarrel about a woman and my old favourite orderly shoots himself by taking your side and you try to deceive me. You fondled her then, if you didn't …'

'I stroked her hand,' said Lalu blushing red hot.

At that instant Jemadar Subah Singh came in and stood bent head before his father.

'Why rape-mother, you two used to be such friends in the cantonment,'

Arbel Singh said to his son. 'Now you take advantage of the position I have secured you and bully everyone! At least keep some friends. At first you go quarrelling with this Lalu about the love of that girl ... well, if she preferred him to you why didn't you go and find another one? But for me you would have been court-martialed for causing the death of Kirpu. And now, what happened last night?'

'Subedar Sahib ...' began Subah but was overawed by his wolf of a father.

'The main trouble is that illegally begotten Lok Nath,' said Arbel Singh. 'You have joined hands with him like a fool. It is not my blood in you which makes you such an inept creature. I begin to doubt the honour of your mother ...'

'Perhaps my stepmother suggested that ...' said Subah inflamed.

'Don't buk, and take a joke as a joke,' said the Subedar Major... 'Lalu, what happened on patrol last night?'

'*Huzoor*, Jemadar Subah Singh was drunk and ...'

'I won't have it!' shouted Subah.

'I have no doubt you were drunk,' said Subedar Major Arbel Singh lightly. 'You should have shared out the bottle with your comrades, swine, and not been so greedy. As it is you made a nuisance of yourself. Go on Lalu.'

Lal Singh told the story

'That is the tale which Rikhi Ram told me,' said Arbel Singh. 'Are you sure you two didn't cook it up between you?' And he laughed.

'I have written the report!' flamed Subah in a rage. 'I charge these men with disobeying my orders: Not following me when I commanded them to run forward to Laften Hobson's aid, which is mutiny. Lance Naik Rikhi Ram threatened to kill me with a blow on the head, which is again mutiny. He kept me forcibly down in the crater, which is mutiny a third time. They both insulted me, their superior officer, alleging that I had lied about warning sentries, which is enough for a court-martial.'

'To be sure there is plenty of evidence for a court-martial, *Huzoor*,' said Rikhi Ram calmly, seeing that the Jemadar had already given the game away. 'Splitting patrol through drunkenness. Reckless leadership in charging forward. Complete breakdown in face of danger.'

'All right,' said Subedar Major Arbel Singh with a laugh. 'You can hardly mention the vomiting fit before a court-martial ... but, tell me did you really threaten to kill my prince?'

'Yes, Subedar Sahib, I did,' said Rikhi Ram.

'There, he admits his guilt,' shouted the Jemadar.

'That is very serious,' said Arbel Singh with a quizzical look in his eye. 'But what are the charges against sepoy Lal Singh?'

'Insubordination,' said Subah.

'Mutiny, to be more exact,' added Lalu.

'I will recommend you for a medal,' said the Subedar Major addressing Lalu. 'As for you, Rikhi Ram,' he continued, turning to the Lance-Naik, 'forgive me if I was hard on you last night. A Sahib's death is a difficult matter to explain. But it seems you could not control his enthusiasm as you controlled the Jemadar's recklessness.'

'But father!'

'Jemadar Sahib,' said Arbel Singh in a mock heroic manner, 'I will advise you to bear in mind that to be a Captan, because your father happens to be a judge, implies responsibilities. And the biggest is not to bring shame on me by forcing me to degrade you for being drunk on duty.'

The Subedar Major was silent for a moment as if swallowing a bitter pill. And then he growled like a wolf:

'I tell you I will not shield you any more. Dismiss. Go to your places.'

All the three men saluted and crept out of the dugout.

The 'air and water' had become terrible. For though the temperature had lowered somewhat, the snow had begun to thaw; the fields behind the lines, pitted with shell holes and pillboxes, had almost become impossible with mud and slush, and all traces of paths were lost in the cesspool. The trenches were slowly turning into water channels; the soil of the dugouts was water logged; and a foul, nauseous smell began to ooze from each corner as if the thousands of sepoys and the Tommies who lived and moved and had their being in these ditches had suddenly got dysentery. The N.C.O.s ordered the men to clear the slush and snow, but, as there were not enough big spades to go round, some of the sepoys sat hugging themselves into knots while the others heaped up the snow into communication trenches. For, though it was snugger and warmer for the natives, used to these cold climes, than it was to these men from the scorching plains, some of whom had only seen snow from the distance of a hundred miles when one of the peaks of the Himalayas showed up on a rare clear day, and most of whom had never known ice except at the shop of a sherbet seller, to these men who remembered the last hailstorm seven years ago, to these men for whom even the summers of Europe were like winters, it was the intensest misery which assuredly God had sent to the warring world as a just retribution for their evil deeds in the Iron age. For, was it not said that as the end of the Iron age drew nearer the winters would become colder and the summers hotter, till all mankind was either frozen or just scorched to death. Who could tell that they were not nearing the eve of Judgment Day when everyone would be tried before the throne of God!

As Lalu worked his way from the communication trench, where Rikhi Ram left him to fetch the orders of the day, to his post towards the end of No. 2 company, through the press of all the men who sat or stood, talked or merely brooded on the utter hopelessness of their lot, he felt a vague exhilaration creeping into him at the thought of his easy release from what might have been an awkward situation. But the Subedar Major had been extraordinarily just and kind. He warmed to think of the old rogue. The man had wonderful qualities and hadn't risen to his rank for nothing, thought his son had not inherited the best in his character.

'Why, what happened?' Dhayan Singh greeted him from where he was shovelling the slush into a traverse.

'Old Arbel Singh was in a good mood; he let us of,' said Lalu. 'Even reprimanded his son.'

'Your *kismet*,' Dhayan Singh said, wiping the profuse sweat that covered him.

'*Ohe*, leave *kismet*, it was the Jemadar's folly,' said Lalu.

'Don't say that, you are courting bad luck,' said Dhayan Singh.

'Oh forget about bad luck?' Lalu exclaimed.

And yet, as he said so, he wondered if there was any thing in what Dhayan Singh said. These men were so superstitious, always attributing things to fate, repeating the magic word '*kismet*', even as they did in the villages, cultivating the land; losing the produce in payment of their loads of debt and unpaid rent, living frugally on unbuttered bread and a ladleful of lentils. like animals living on roots. Throughout he had disbelieved in the talk of the elders and sought to mould his life according to his own desires, cocksure about the practicability of his own ideas of getting his family out of debt and of increasing the yield of their land ... And yet here he was thousands of miles away from home, just escaped from the threat of a court-martial and not knowing what was going to happen next. As on several occasions before, in spite of his disbelief, he asked himself what was in his *kismet*, what was his destiny? ... More pain? Sorrow! Death? Return home safe?

'*Acha*, what is the matter now?' said Dhayan Singh. 'You ought to be happy! What's the news?'

'Rikhi Ram has gone to fetch the orders of the day,' he answered.

And he reflected his destiny. The upsurge of wave in his blood led him to forget everything. But then he recalled how he had upset his dough lamps by falling in love with Maya. For, apart from flouting the customs of the village and his irritation at the trust deeds on behalf of his father's creditors, which were piling up, it was Maya, the love of whom had been his ruination. But it was the horror that Ramji Das, the matchmaker, would bring the match of a girl for him as he had brought one for his brother, that had made him dream of choosing a bride, some fair complexioned redolent girl whom he could hug to his heart. And then the landlord and the police, had come up with a warrant for his arrest on a trumped up charge and he had run away...

The only escape from prison was to join the army.

'Oh wake up,' reproached Dhayan Singh. 'What has come over you all today? If you sit like that you will melt like the snow, and I shall have to shovel you away with the mud.'

'I am thinking what would have happened to me if I had not joined the army,' Lalu said with a smile.

'You would have gone to jail from what you told me,' Dhayan Singh said. 'Because, there are not many men in the world like Ajitan Sahib.'

'A sentence of three to six months,' said Lalu. 'But surely nothing worse. I should have gone back to look after my family. My eldest brother would not have murdered the landlord's son in revenge and been hanged, and my father would not have collapsed with the weight of misfortunes and died. And I would never have come here.'

'If my father had not gone to bed with my mother,' said Dhayan Singh, 'I should never been born, nor been so fat...'

'I have been happy enough to come here,' Lalu said naively. 'It had been the dream of my life to see *Vilayat*. And it was a great adventure ...'

'But now after having tasted some of the fruits of *Vilayat*!' began Dhayan Singh. 'Oh, brother, it's all in God's hands. Come and take a hand with this shovel and don't sit weaving a web like a spider.'

Lalu got up and took the shovel. Dhayan Singh was resigned more than the others. All of them had joined the army of their own accord, but, as one in every three of a peasant family had to go and earn a little extra money to tide through the droughts, they really had no choice. They had little hope and less desire. But had anyone any control over his destiny, if one's life was not one's own to live? Could anyone possess himself?

He swept the slush from the observation post. The snow sticking to the walls fell at his feet. He began to throw shovelsuls towards the barbed-wire entanglements. For a moment he stopped to breathe. It was just a flat expanse on all sides with not one big hill or valley in its lap, except the small mounds of no-man's-land and the artificial barriers of sandbags over the saps from which issued occasional sniper's bullets.

'There is Rikhi Ram,' Dhayan Singh said still stewing in the juices of his body, phewing and blowing hard.

'General offensive tonight,' Rikhi Ram proceeded to read the orders of the day as if in answer to fatty's upturned eyes. 'We are to attack all along the line and advance. The Connaughts and Pioneers' trenches must be restored before dawn and held at all costs ...'

'The dressing station behind the lines was shelled last night and the doctors of the 69th and 129th were killed when the building caught fire.'

'Lieutenant Hobson Sahib was killed on a reconnaissance patrol last night. The men secured valuable information, though their movements were greatly hampered by the snow-covered ground which showed them up distinctly and made them easy targets, etc.'

Lalu shrugged his shoulders and began to shovel the slush up into the communication trench again.

'*Ohe* look! *Ohe* look! Dhayan Singh interrupted him. 'There's a truly strange phenomenon.'

'What is it?' Lalu asked panting.

'Look there, in no-man's-land,' Dhayan Singh said.

Lalu turned his head.

'To be sure, it is a strange phenomenon!' he said and, shading his eyes against the glare of the snow, peered deeper, into no-man's-land. There were two English *Goras* and three German soldiers, shaking hands and talking to each other with gestures, even as they laughed little nervous chuckles which could be heard ... And now ... they were offering each other cigarettes ... what had happened? ... There had been no shelling this morning and he had heard the sound of singing in the Connaught's trenches while he had been talking to Dhayan Singh.

'What is the matter?' Dhayan Singh asked him.

More groups of Tommies and German soldiers were scrambling up from their respective trenches and running, hesitatingly, towards each other.

'There, they are eating sweets out of each others' hands!' said Lalu, 'Strange!'

And he blinked his eyes at Dhayan Singh and a few of the sepoys who now stood with their heads erect to watch this bonhomie between the two enemy sides, completely unmindful of their N.C.O.s' constant advice not to expose themselves. But there were no snipers' bullets about. Instead there were ripples of laughter going across no-man's-land in spasmodic bursts making a mockery of war, then jubilant shouts from various trenches.

'I saw much coming and going between the trenches yesterday also,' said a sepoy cocksurely.

Lalu scratched his head, smiled and wished Rikhi Ram were near so that he could ask him the reasons of this startling behaviour. But presently he heard a loud exchange between a German and an English soldier and then saw the German rush out of the opposite saps, with a cake in his hand as if he were taking an offering to the temple.

'That is the crown of the German Badshah being brought to the *Angrezi* army,' said the all-knowing Sepoy. 'This means the end of hostilities ...'

'Oh, it is a cake,' said Lalu laughing at this naivety. 'A Christmas cake! ... It is the Christmas festival today and both the enemies being Christians by religion they are wishing each other happy Christmas ...'

He had tumbled to it from all the associations of the Christmas holidays, the feasts and the ceremonial at the Church Mission School at Sherkot.

'I am going to get some sweets from the enemy,' said Dhayan Singh struggling to scramble over the parapet with terrific alacrity.

'*Ohe ohe*, look out,' the sepoys called after him.

'Go ahead, go ahead!' Lalu spurred him on and even gave a shove to his heavy buttocks so that Dhayan Singh was on top.

After months of shells and grenades, rifle and machine gun fire, this simple antic of fat Dhayan Singh made them laugh. It was their contribution towards the festivities. And they hoped he would bring some cakes back.

'Run, fatty, run to it,' they now called with loud happy yells. And for a moment they seemed to have caught the contagion of innocent humanity in the air.

'The Germans are tall and strong like us North Indians,' a Sepoy said who suddenly saw the Germans as human beings for the first time.

'And they can smile,' another added.

'Of course they can smile,' said Lalu a little impatiently. 'They are men like us, not hinneying donkeys.'

'They are said to be the cousins of the *Angrez Goras*,' the first sepoy said.

'Their uniforms are good, neat and coloured, but look at our small *Goras*, besmattered with mud! Look at that Tommy with his woollen muffler! …'

Lalu wondered if these sudden happenings had anything to do with a peace move. It would be wonderful, he thought, if suddenly, out of the blue, they were ordered to withdraw from the trenches and taken on a trip to *Vilayat*.

But he saw three English Sergeants and Lance-Corporals jumping across the parapets and calling to the *Goras* to come back, with vague, angry gestures. And Dhayan Singh and another sepoy who had gone over were running back with chunks of that Christmas cake in their hands.

One of the Lance-Corporals growled at them and it seemed that he would come and wring the necks of the two sepoys who had gone over. The cowed Indians came back with nervous smiles, hanging on to their portion of the cake, however, and were helped down.

For a moment there was a tense lull over the lengths of the trenches as in a school room where an angry master has been shouting at some naughty pupils. Apparently the officers didn't like this fraternization. Even the pieces of cake the two sepoys had brought lay uneaten in their hands. Then the LanceCorporal seemed to have disappeared and the sepoys distributed equal shares of the offering as if they were in a temple.

By the time they had swallowed their mouthfuls, the silence of peace had crumpled up into the silence of hate: a couple of bullets rang out from the Connaughts just to confirm that the war had not ended.

———

Soon after the incident a rumour ran through the trenches that a Padre Sahib, no less a person than the Bishop of Chetpur, who had been 'home' on leave, had come over to see his flock from India.

The sepoys were fascinated by him as he came through the communication trench, a strong, gaunt, be-spectacled, red-faced Sahib, with a well-trimmed grey beard, dressed in a long black cloak with knotted white cords round his waist, a felt hat on his head and gloves on his hands. He was attended by the tall, shy Owen Sahib, the adjutant of the 69th Rifles, N.C.O.s of the Connaughts, a Subedar of the Baluchis and some Tommies.

Owen Sahib had sent a message down the trench for Sepoy Lal Singh to be fetched. And Lalu hurried towards the junction of the two traverses, where Havildar Lok Nath was stationed as the guardian of the marches, thinking that some other quite unforeseen catastrophe was going to befall him. The whispers of the sepoys that a queer phenomenon had arrived from Hindustan did not allay his fears and he rushed down the slope of the trench towards the shelter by the cross roads where a veritable multitude of Tommies, Sikhs, Baluchis, Gurkhas and Dogras had now gathered.

'There is Sepoy Lal Singh,' someone announced.

'Oh, here, sir,' said Owen Sahib extending his hand towards Lalu, 'is a lad who was educated in a mission school, he can speak English.'

The Padre Sahib beamed from behind the bush of his great beard, which spread like the aureole of the sun around his face, got up from the precarious camp chair in which he was seated as the guest of honour and shook hands with Lal Singh. The physical beauty of his shapely presence somehow contradicted his spiritual eminence in Lalu's mind because the boy associated faith in God with ascetic, emaciated bodies.

'What mission school were you at?' the Padre Sahib inquired in bad Hindustani, still beaming.

'I was at the Church Mission Middle School in Sherkot, *Huzoor*,' said Lalu.

For a moment, the Padre Sahib twisted his fingers as if in a sudden effort to recall the name of someone he knew there, as if it should have been on the tips of his nails.

'Padre Anandale Sahib was my headmaster,' Lalu offered the clue which he thought the Sahib was seeking.

'And did you read the Bible?' the Padre asked.

'Yes, *Huzoor*,' said Lalu tentatively.

'He speaks English, My Lord,' emphasized Owen Sahib with a twinkle in his blue eyes as if he were enjoying himself immensely in taking the Padre around. 'Come on,' he said to Lalu, 'tell the Bishop what you learnt of Christianity.'

Lalu crossed himself and smiled.

'A good boy,' the Bishop said nodding his head.

'Oh look, oh look,' a sepoy whispered, 'he can do what the Padre did!'

'He is a Sikh, but he must be a Christian!' another sepoy ventured.

'I learnt to pray there, *Huzoor*.' Lalu said, unable to resist a smile at his own histrionics. And then he began to recite like a parrot in English.

'Behold, O good and most sweet Jesus, I cast myself upon my knees in Thy sight, and, with all the fervour of my soul, I pray and beseech Thee to vouchsafe to Thy humble servant, Faith, Hope and Charity. With true sorrow for my sins with bowed head I kneel before and contemplate Thy wounds before my eyes and remembering Thy words, oh good Jesus by the Prophet David: 'They have pierced My hands and My feet; they have numbed all my bones.'

'Oh, *wah wah*, son, you have kept our honour!

'*Wah*! *Wah*!'

'Oh, where has he learnt to talk git-mit, git-mit so well?'

The sepoys yelled at Lalu.

'Bravo!' said the Adjutant Sahib.

'Most apt, most apt,' said the Padre Sahib. And turning to the Tommies, he explained: 'A plenary indulgence may be gained by reciting this prayer.'

'It is also applicable to souls in Purgatory,' said Lalu in English.

The Tommies who had been marvelling at this sepoy with unbelieving, humorous faces spluttered into a laugh. Owen Sahib, the Padre and everyone joined in this.

The sepoys could not understand what the joke was about, but they began to discuss the merits of Christianity from their respective points of view.

'We be cousins — Muslim, the Christians!' said the Baluchi.

'*Han*,' chimed another Muslim, 'our Prophet recognized Yessuh Messih as Prophet.'

'The only thing is that they eat beef,' said a pious Gurkha Hindu.

Reflecting on the boy's remark, the Padre Sahib assumed a more serious expression. After all he had carne here to cheer the troops up and not to be flippant. And soon he must go because it was time for tiffin and the General would not like his guest to be late.

'I have been very heartened to come here,' he began in English addressing the Tommies mainly and giving up the heathen for lost. 'The country through which I came is splendidly cultivated; only this part is flat and monotonous. But our Allies are fine people. They have fine churches, one still standing in St. Omer, which is your headquarters, and another at Ains, though in many villages they have been damaged by shell fire ...

'I held a service for an Indian Brigade in a village, and a good number

of German prisoners and Gurkhas, Jats and other ranks forned congregation ...'

At the mention of Gurkhas and Jats the sepoys began to whisper among each other, wondering what the Padre Sahib had said about them.

'There were some Generals and officers.' he continued.

'I bet they were in the front row,' said a humorous Tommy.

And there was laughter, the sepoys looking at each other, perplexed.

'Never were hymns more beautifully sung, or prayers more earnestly offered,' said the Bishop firmly, assuming an expression of deadly seriousness.

'His cheeks look like the testicles of a monkey,' said a sepoy and walked away.

'Attention,' said Owen Sahib sternly and the N.C.O.s hushed all comment

They all became ready and solemn listeners for a while and the Padre Sahib took for the subJect of his address what he called "Our Saviour's first recorded utterance: 'Wist ye not that I must be about my father's business.'

And he tried to show in an eloquent, rather feminine voice how the great principle of obedience to his father's will underlay all the Saviour's life, illustrating his talk with apt quotations: 'My wish is to do the will of him that sent me and to finish his work'... 'Father, not my will but thine be done'.

Then using the question which St. Bernard was wont to put to himself, 'What dost thou here?' he asked the congregation to put that question to themselves. And he proceeded to answer it for them, saying: 'No British soldier in France but has seen the horrors of an invaded country. So you can all answer the question. You know that you are here for the defence of civilization, to succour the weak and to resist evil.'

He reiterated that it was a holy war and the general principles for which they were contending were above all, justice, righteousness and truth.

He further delivered homilies on the need for attending Divine Parade, 'the absolute certainty of victory of our righteous cause in God's good time,' on the conviction which each man ought to cherish the blessed hope of everlasting life.

As the congregation broke up, the sepoys took the earliest opportunity to scatter away, because, delivered in English, the sermon had bored them.

The Padre Sahib began to talk informally to the Tommies while Owen Sahib chatted with the Indian N.C.O.s.

'How is life behind the lines, sir?' a Tommy asked the Bishop.

'Oh,' he said, dropping the sermonizing accent and quite chatty again. 'A strange contrast! a strange contrast! At one moment one may be moving in places where the ángel of death is brooding, in less than half an hour, five or six miles away at the rear, one may be at lunch or dinner at head-quarters where it seems as if there was no war on, as if one were back in India or smoking in one's club ...'

An English Corporal who had evidently been a member of the Padre's congregation in Chetpur came and shook hands with him. But the Padre continued in answer to the Tommy's question.

'I only wish everyone could see what great care the chaplains of the Indian Army Corps are bestowing upon the little cemeteries in every part of France: each grave has its wooden cross with the name of the fallen soldier or officer inscribed on a tiny metal plate ... And, of course, the graves of many Indian officers and men, too, are being cared for ...'

But tiffin time was approaching perilously near. He fished out his huge watch from somewhere behind his cloak and turned vigorously to each of the men around him, shook hands with them, irrespective of caste, creed or rank, gave a pat to Lalu, telling him that he would remind Padre Anandale Sahib of his pupil and proceeded on his way back.

Owen Sahib and the Indian officers and the N.C.O.s followed him.

When Dhayan Singh asked him what the Padre had said to him, Lalu laughed and said that the Sahib had given them an inspiring sermon. And, affecting a pious face, he began mockingly to mime a prayer:

'Oh Lord Yessuh Messih, we pray you teach us to hate the enemy and help us to tear out his guts! We join our hands to you and pray to you, son of God, intercede on our behalf to God who is your Father, to allot us nice graves with little brass plates with our names inscribed on them; we kneel before you and pray you to destroy the enemy, to help us to annihilate him ...'

'Oh, have you gone mad!' shouted Dhayan Singh. 'Rikhi Ram, this boy is going crazy.'

All day preparations for the offensive were going on. But they were so conducted as not to obtrude on the notice of the enemy or even on the men in the trenches, except those who were detailed off to fetch hand grenades, ammunition and other requisites for the attack. Of course, the N.C.O.s were going up and down like busy bees. Most of the Sepoys, however, slept, dozed, smoked or talked and relaxed in a way which was not quite

ordinary and which suggested they were resting before going on a journey or something. There was an insidious fear spreading over the battalions which, mixed with the oppression of the hard sky overhead, became the unknown fate incarnate, the question mark of death, which no one had been able to answer and yet everyone was conscious of, and which, therefore, made their actions and words, incalculable, tense, hysterical. Above all they wanted to know what was going to happen, particularly what was going to happen to them...

'Why, *Holdara*, what's the news?' Dhayan Singh pestered Rikhi Ram with the question every time his friend came back from up the line. 'Why, *Holdara*, how?' he inquired when Rikhi Ram came back towards evening.

But the Lance-Naik was apparently tired after having supplied him an almost hourly bulletin.

He sat down to have a smoke, his eyes red from a night of sleeplessness.

'Still, tell us what is going to happen!' said Dhayan Singh screwing his fat face in abject beggary.

'You will know soon enough, fatty,' said Lalu coming out of the dugout where he had been trying to sleep off the fatigue of the previous night's patrol. 'The angel of Death will himself deliver the message.'

'Don't talk like that, it's bad luck,' husked Dhayan Singh.

'Rape the mother of bad luck, I tell you!' Lalu said. 'Give us some tea.'

'There is no talk,' said Dhayan Singh. 'You can have tea and some biscuits.'

There was no questioning his generosity in regard to food, both to himself and others. Of course, he maintained that he had to support a big belly. But he was not sparing to others, as he sat with his full girth over the newly arrived brazier, doling out little tinfuls of the warm tea mixture, a perfect master of ceremonies.

'Take this, *Holdara*, you have some too,' he said to Rikhi Ram.

'I have to supervise the fatigue party which is coming to put more sandbags over the parapet,' said Rikhi Ram. 'But, hurry, I shall have a sip.'

'Sandbags! Why, we have plenty?' said Dhayan Singh.

'Oh, brother the enemy knocked out whole perapets last night,' said Rikhi Ram. 'If only you would lift your paunch and make a tour of inspection.'

'I don't know how we shall take him with us during the attack?' said Lalu with a smile.

'The exits in the barbed wires are not going to be too wide,' said Rikhi Ram.

'But there were no exits last night at all,' said Lalu, 'if you remember, we had to creep through a narrow space by lifting wires for each other.'

'The Generals are seeing to that,' informed Rikhi Ram.

'Working parties are going to cut lanes through the entanglements tonight before the attack.'

'Why didn't you tell us this before?' protested Dhayan Singh. 'It is things like this I wanted to know. What is the use of your being our friend, *Holdara*?'

'The advantage of my being your mate is that I can warn you.' said Rikhi Ram grimly.

'What about?' said Dhayan Singh eagerly. 'I am not being detailed to go and cut the wire, am I?'

'How do you think you are going to escape the penalty of being my friend, then?' said Rikhi Ram.

'Why it isn't Lok Nath at our throat again, is it?' said Lalu.

'If it isn't Lok Nath, brother, it is the Jemadar, and if it isn't him it is some Jarnel,' said Rikhi Ram resignedly.

'I don't know why they are launching this attack at all,' grumbled Dhayan Singh.

'That is understandable, but what I want to know is why they are fighting at all?' said Rikhi Ram.

'I can understand a little about that, but what I can't understand is how they will settle this war,' said Lalu naively. 'Will a victory be achieved by killing all the soldiers of the enemy or will they just frighten them into surrender?'

'At the moment all that they want to do is to take back the trenches they have lost and more,' said Rikhi Ram, with the common sense of the practical N.C.O.

'But even if they take several trenches,' said Lalu, 'it will only mean going fifty yards and then stopping there, having pot shots at the enemy and receiving the same, with compound interest, for they have guns and can decimate us!'

'Oh, don't talk like that,' said Dhayan Singh. 'It is bad luck, I tell you.'

'Oh, do people only die when the crow caws?' said Lalu. 'Death is coming to us, anyhow.'

'It is the surest way of courting it, to say it is coming,' said Dhayan Singh.

'*Holdar* Sahib, what is the truth in those rumours that the Toorks are with the Germans?' queried a Punjabi Muslim, who was shovelling earth into sandbags with some other sepoys and sappers. 'Our *Holdars* will not let us talk about these things, because one or two men have deserted to the Germans.'

'Someone has been reading those leaflets which the Germans threw into the trenches,' said Rikhi Ram noncommittally and walked away so as not to be drawn into the conversation.

'To be sure, it is true that the Sarkar is fighting against the Germans and the Toorks,' said Lalu.

'*Lahol*!' protested the Punjabi Muslim, throwing his spade away and taking hands to his ears. '*Toba*! Then we have been fighting against the Khalif of Islam!'

'But the Hazrat Sherif of Mecca and the Arabs are on the side of the *Angrezi Sarkar*,' said a Baluchi N.C.O. 'And what matters to us is that we should be able to go on pilgrimage to holy Kaaba and nothing else.'

'That is good, I would fight for Kaaba against the infidels in a holy war,' said the Punjabi Muslim, satisfied that Mecca was on the side of the English.

'But it has been told all along that our king and the Kaiser are cousins,' put in Dhayan Singh, naive but awkward.

'Brothers,' said Lalu, 'blood relations have fought each other before in this world. People of the same religion against their brothers of other religions. So it is told in big book *Mahabharat*.'

Dhayan Singh heartily agreed. 'My brother-in-law's uncle's son sued a cousin for two acres of land and fought him in the courts for five years.'

'In our Hindu religion,' said a Jat Sapper with a black face, there is told the story of how the hundred sons of the king of Hastinapura fought their cousins, the five Pandus, in the great war of *Mahabharat* to ensure their right to the throne.'

'Actually,' interposed Lalu, choosing the words he had read in the paper issued from General Headquarters at Simla, 'the spark was lit with the assassination in Serajevo, but Daddy Dhanoo of blessed memory used to say we have eaten the salt of the Sarkar.'

The bit about Serajevo confused the Sepoys who thought in legends.

'*Ohe* don't talk of people who are dead! It is unlucky!' said Dhayan Singh.

'*Han*, brother, ghosts are about, specially at dark,' said the Punjabi Muslim, rapt.

'To be sure, brother, greed is the cause of hatred,' said the black Sapper slowly, thoughtfully. 'But, say the Holy books, no one has ever won anything through envy.'

'Not even wealth?' interrupted Lalu.

'No, not even that,' said the Sapper. 'Only man is dazzled and made blind. It is the curse of our Rajahs and Maharajas that they love display, loading their necks, their heads, their feet, their ears and their turbans with jewels. And if they hear another has more money, more jewels and is getting more powerful, they burn with envy. All is vain ...'

'Uncle Kirpu, who had been to China, to Burma, to the frontier and has now returned to the celestial heavens, used to say ...' began Lalu.

'I am going if you must talk of those who have gone to the celestial heavens,' threatened Dhayan Singh.

'Did your friend get a medal for going to Chin?' asked the Punjabi Muslim.

'And two clasps for other campaigns and — a final clout on the head from an N.C.O. of our regiment,' said Lalu bitterly.

'Our landlord in Campbelpur district, Captan Khizir Hayat Khan, won the D.S.O. in the Afghan War,' said the Punjabi Muslim hopefully. 'And Captan Umar Hayat Khan Tiwana, who is in France with Sarkar, said at a Durbar when I was home on leave, that there will be grants of land for bravery and prizes besides medals ...'

'Why, a sepoy, Khudadad Khan, of our regiment,' said the Baluchi, 'has got the highest medal, Victoria Cross!'

'But when we asked Babu Khushi Ram in the billets whether there will be grants of land,' said Dhayan Singh, 'he said that the Sarkar had so far been lenient to the Sepoys but would be much stricter in recommending men for medals from now onwards.'

'Medals! medals! medals!' said Rikhi Ram coming up. 'You have been detailed off to cut the wires. You are sure to get a medal tonight.'

'Oh *Holdara*, don't talk like that, it will bring us bad luck!' appealed tubby Dhayan Singh. 'Tell me what is going to happen?'

'I don't know, I tell you that you are on duty cutting entanglements,' said Rikhi Ram impatient out of fear for his friend.

'God knows, brother, God only knows,' said the Sapper, brushing the ends of his moustache and getting to work.

'Allah knows, brother: Allah knows,' said the Punjabi Muslim. 'He is the caretaker of all.'

'The true talk is that no one knows,' said Lalu.

And they dispersed.

However soft-footed the Sepoys who brought hand grenades to the trenches, however careful the fatigue party which repaired the parapets, and however unostentatious the party detailed off to cut lanes through barbed-wire entanglements, the Germans had not remained completely unaware of the impending attack. The enemy scoured the area behind the lines continuously, their snipers knocked holes through three spades which happened to rise above the shoulders, and they machine gunned the barbed-wire party. Dhayan Singh and six others failed to return. And with the gloom of the night, the oppression of the doom, the unknown fate, was intensified. No one dared to think of it, lest it might bring bad luck as the very mention of death had brought death to Dhayan Singh. The God of Death was about with his hosts. And there seemed no way to exorcize the ghosts, jinns, bhuts, howbattes and hobgoblins.

The elemental upheaval of an artillery barrage shattered the calm of the trenches before dawn. It had an element of surprise about it, a strange, inexplicable newness, as if life were again going to fight a duel against death. The Sepoys had spent so many hours in solitude and silence without hearing a shot or catching a glimpse of anything, only listening to the intermittent rattle of a machine-gun or some snipers' bullets, that a big barrage seemed startling. Apparently some new guns had arrived.

They got up from where they had been dozing, smoking, coughing and whispering even as they crouched or squatted on the steps in full battle dress, or from where they had slept a fitful sleep, and clustered together in the trenches. It was drizzling and a sharp wind was blowing, though the temperature was appreciably warmer, because the snow was melting in little rills and rivulets of water all over the trenches and kneading the dough of soft earth and slush into mud. The damp didn't disturb them much, however, for they were absorbed in the solution of much bigger problems. 'What are the exact orders?' was on everyone's lips and 'what is my destiny?' in everyone's thoughts. And they crowded round the N.C.O.s to see if they could catch these mercurial and important beings.

'Wake up! wake up! all of you! up on the steps! Stand to! Stand to!' Havildar Lok Nath ordered as he came right through the trench.

'But, *Holdara*, what are we to do?' the Sepoys grumbled. 'What time is the attack hour?'

'Now, don't whine you swine,' Lok Nath said, patting them on their backs for once. 'Trench warfare is the supreme test of discipline: it calls for courage, patience and resource. You have had nothing much to do for days and have eaten the bread of illegality. Now when you are called upon to do a little work you get into panic.'

'We are not going for a walk on the Mall road exactly!' someone whispered.

'What?' Lok Nath shouted, and now he seemed to lose his temper. 'Where has your manhood gone, talking as you do, weaklings! What has happened to you? What more glorious opportunity could you wish for if you are Rajputs and not begotten by your mothers from the seed of sweepers! What other occasion could you hope for than this to show yourselves as the true sons of your race and win decorations! You are lucky to be given the chance of fighting side by side with the Sahibs! Bastards, your fathers and your grandfathers died fighting! Why have you suddenly become cowards? ... Anyone would think your mothers had died! Stand up and come laughing to fray!' And he towered over the men after this relentless lashing with the whip of his tongue, lean and lanky, made taller by the bayonet fixed to his rifle.

'Oh, *Holdara*, talk straight!' challenged a daring spirit. 'What are the orders?'

'The straight thing is that I want to make you straight,' said Lok Nath inflamed. 'I want to break your cramped bones and make you march straight! — I was a drill instructor and my job was to make people straight. You have become bloated eating the Sarkar's food and you can't see straight, think straight, or act straight! ...'

But the din of artillery was increasing and he was nearly hoarse with rage.

'Stand to! stand to!' he roared. 'All of you to your posts! Alert! Up on the step! ...'

'All right, *Holdara*, spare them so that they can listen to me for a change,' said Rikhi Ram coming up from the communication trench. 'These are the orders, boys. At zero hour all ranks are to rush forward over the parapet and support the left flank of the Connaughts and the 34th Pioneers. You are to occupy trenches in front of you. Now all of you to your posts ...'

'Come on, brothers, stand to,' said Rikhi Ram. Lalu stood to his position, waiting patiently and staring at everyone, curiously unaffected by the fury of Havildar Lok Nath's shouts or by the artillery barrage. His blood seemed to have congealed and he seemed to be looking at all the men standing by him emptily, as if he had no sympathy left either for himself or for them. He speculated about how many of them would be alive after an hour. He saw that they stood solid and strong along the line, rugged mounds of clothes, as if they were waiting to catch a train for Pathankot from Amritsar junction, and eager not to be left behind, lest they should lose a day of their furlough ... Perhaps they knew that they were going on the last journey. Of course, they did, he said to himself, from the way they had sulked before Lok Nath forced them into action. He wondered what they were thinking ... They were burrburring, perhaps saying their last prayers ... A wave of warmth seemed to go through the cold hysteria of his being and he hesitated on the edge of the question whether his own number was up. He had escaped so far ... He wanted to live and he tried to buoy himself up by refusing to contemplate his own doom. But the thought of the possibility that he might be finished returned. His eyes caught the gleam of the bayonet on his rifle and he shrank at the thought of being degutted. Now that he had looked one possibility in the face, another stared at him: he might be shot in some limb which might disable him or disfigure him. Still that would be better than utter extinction. But no woman would even look at him. He could not bear the humiliation. He had rather go clean out of life. But he might be saved. He wanted to believe that he would be ... So, he censored his thoughts and listened to the barrage.

The Germans seemed to be aware of confrontation. The boom and crash was deafening. A shell rose illuminating the fantastic bodies of the dead in no-man's-land. Their ghosts seemed to be shrieking, mingling with the hosts of the God of Death, demanding the spirits of those whom they had left behind. Perhaps Dhayan Singh's spirit was there by the barbed wire, beckoning him. The uproar rose higher and higher. What a noise! They could hardly feel their breath come and go. And yet they were pale, still and determined as they waited for the fatal hour ... The crest of an uprise along the German trenches had been ranged by the British artillery: the German barrage returned the compliment with a cordiality that was embarrassing, shelling the whole area from the Allied front line to the village behind, sending up rockets and bursts of fire so sustained that Lalu thought the Sahibs would call off the attack against Germany's superior strategy in the situation. For gale upon gale of sound swept across the air, spreading the pungent smoke of hell over the landscape and sending splinters of steel mixed with eruptions of mud in all directions.

The orders of the N.C.O.s were squashed by the deafening sounds. There was a momentary stillness, when the guns at the back were charging, during which shrieks of wounded could be heard among the 129th Baluchis on the left flank and calls for stretcher bearers. But presently every voice was smothered. The men cowered under the barrage, shook their heads and scowled, as if by shrinking into themselves they would escape the wrath of the storm.

But the whistle rang through, indicating the order to jump off.

Lalu could see Peacock Sahib climbing up the parapet and beckoning the men to follow. Then the Sahib came running across the whole length of the company with open mouth exhorting the men to follow. Havildar Lok Nath raged and abused the men with the fury of the Martinet, goading them to mount the parapet. The men began to scramble up, clumsily gripping at the soft mounds of muddy earth to get a handhold or a foothold, slipping and falling.

Revolver in hand Peacock Sahib was leading the men towards a lane in the barbed wire ...

Rikhi Ram jumped up.

Lalu followed him.

Just then the Sahib fell back wounded by the wire, while some of the men ran forward.

The German machine guns sprayed the entire sector with deadly ferocity and sepoys fell headlong, or back over the parapet into their own trenchs.

'Crouch low,' Rikhi Ram screamed.

And as three men fell wounded into a depression Lalu recognized Rikhi Ram gasping, a bullet right through his temple. Lalu could not look at him.

Some of the wounded were weeping, whimpering and shrieking.

Lalu crawled forward and craned his neck to look. Turmoil and confusion.

The Connaughts and the Pioneers, seeing the centre decimated and fearing to be outflanked, were retiring and trying to take cover.

'Our machine-guns will cover us,' exhorted a voice very much like Lok Nath's. 'Rush and take over the crest. It is only thirty yards away ...'

Lalu waited just below the edge of the depression to take a deep breath. It was suicide to advance against the withering fire. But the martinet was prodding them.

The men were over.

They were racing along splendidly for fifteen yards.

Lalu felt intoxicated by the urge to get to the crest and ran forward blindly.

But they were being mown down and fell in surges splashing the mud by the German saps.

He felt a warmth go through his left thigh and he stumbled and fell.

As he looked up he saw himself staring into the barrel of a rifle.

Instinctively a moanlike sob rose from his throat and with a face contorted by terror, he began to sit up, his eyes half closed, his hands lifted in the air.

A bullet went through the calf of his left leg and he fell face forwards.

He hoped he was not dead. Lifting his eyes, shivering, hissing and sobbing, 'Hai Mother,' he saw a lion-moustached German dragging him and two other sepoys into the trench.

So he was not dead.

The attack had petered out.

He resigned himself to the mercy of his captors ...